The Wild Roses

The Wild Roses

Third Road Press

Cover design by Dawn Austin

ISBN-13: 978-0615841199

ISBN-10: 0615841198

To my grandmother Rose

Liberté, Egalité, Sororité

v

TABLE OF CONTENTS

Book One

CHAPTER ONE

Heavy hooves crashed along the ground, kicking up deep chunks of sod in their wake, as the determined animal and rider tore across the field, unconcerned with their avoiding the ease and comfort of traveling by road. Speed, speed alone, was all that mattered. Nearby farmers heard the relentlessly pounding noise, and at first some swore it was like the sound of thunder from the force and swiftness.

Crashing across a field, a young Musketeer's tunic whipped and glistened in the sun. Man and beast raced across the countryside, flew through a creek and forest, and over farmland.

The guardsman's face was drawn, almost oblivious to the world speeding by him, his eyes focused tightly ahead, only occasionally glancing around for a better path, and deeply anxious that he would be too late to deliver his message. He had his horse to near-breaking point, its heavy breathing and snorts filling his ears, but he had no choice, the journey had taken longer, much longer than it had in times past, even just a year past.

Once the vibrant heart of France, national roads had been blocked in recent months from passing through feudal lands, cutting off the livelihoods of farmers and tradesmen whose needs relied on those routes the most. Routes that brought crops to market for the rest of the nation. But bridges, too, had been blown up by aristocratic interests to protect access to

4

private baronial property.

Throughout the country, the powerful and troubled cries everywhere were the same.

"The crown won't stand for this. I know the law."

Yet it all fell with an unfeeling deafness in the air. "On his estate, the Marquis is the law," came the cold response of private toll collectors.

"And can the Marquis tell me, I am to survive how? I am to get my crops *how*? If I take the river route, I will lose two days' work! Each week."

Yet there was no answer to this desperation. There was no judge and jury to hear their place. They faced the judge and jury in the single person before them.

"I believe you will find most other estates have reclaimed their roads," came the hard verdict. "Eight francs."

And most tragically of all, too often the deadly results are the same, as well. Driven to rashness, having no recourse in their drive to survive, the cries escalated, the confrontations escalated, and peasants were shot to death for the mere act of challenging these outrages. For with the growing strength of the aristocracy, protecting their property and rights they claimed, military response had been drawn thin across France to meet fires as they erupted.

Unrest had risen across the land.

And amid all these hurdles now in his path, the tense Musketeer pressed on. Pressed more urgently than ever, because his mission, he knew, was more urgent than ever. More urgent than anyone could imagine.

He had ridden through the night, ridden across detours, ridden in the face of rifles, forgone meals, ignored pain, and raced on, knowing a life was at risk.

Riding, riding, riding, pounding his horse on. It was his duty. It was his training with his horse. They were as one.

And finally, he had entered Paris. With the sun low in the sky, the young man galloped down the narrow street to the Musketeer headquarters at the majestic *Palais Royale*. Before even stopping to dismount, slowing only, the Musketeer leaped off and hit the ground running, rushing out, and called the alarm for all to hear.

Though out of breath, the young man reported the grievous dispatch that had been passed to him in great secret to carry. The threat it foretold was so clear and the danger even more imminent that his words flew inside headquarters to those in charge as if they had been delivered there on the spot. Before stopping with the luxury to think, acting on meticulous, well-ordered training, a unit of his fellow King's Guards organized at once and raced on instinct to the palace.

Making their way inside, a battalion of Musketeers bound up the grand staircase with overwhelming urgency.

Across the third-floor landing, the men spread quickly across a marbled floor. A Major barked orders.

"The king is in his chambers! Defend him! *Allez!*"

Half a dozen men raced off. Major Delacroix spun to those remaining with him.

"Save the Regent and the Cardinal! <u>Now</u>."

Without a breath of hesitation, they rushed off.

Outside the king's doorway, the first group had by now reached the closed door to the bedroom chamber.

"Your Highness," a Musketeer shouted, "come at once with…"

They didn't even wait for him to finish, but crashed into the king's chambers – and stopped in their tracks. The room was empty!

By now, the Musketeers had hurriedly regrouped along the landing, as a winded Lieutenant returned and reported in.

"Cardinal Mazarin and the Queen Mother are safe. Their quarters are secure."

But that wasn't good enough by half for the Major, who whirled and spotted a startled butler.

"You!! The king. Where is the king??!" When the poor man was made speechless by his bewilderment, and only a mere second passed in silenced, Major Delacroix didn't wait on politeness. "Where is his highness?!!" he demanded.

"He – *Mademoiselle* – he and his cousin are in the gard…"

The Major raced off, his men following close behind. Across the landing, down the hallway, crashing through the palace with the intensity of a single-minded mission.

The doors to the palace garden smashed open, as the Musketeers charged into the walled grounds.

A group of kidnappers were climbing the back wall on a rope. Several dragged a struggling 10-year-old boy, the king himself, King Louis, over the top. And then, to the Musketeers' horror, he was gone. The king of France had vanished.

But the others, many others remained. And in the center of the madness, a young woman, Anne, the Duchess of Montpensier, pulled at her captor. There was struggling everywhere.

A musket blast killed one intruder. Several others dashed to flee over the wall; fighting for their lives, the grasp on Anne was released; a few more invaders escaped.

Amid the hell crumbling around him, Major Delacroix barked more orders.

"You! Outside! Find the king!" Several Musketeers raced away. "Alive. Take anyone alive." They were needed alive. They needed a way to track down where the king had been taken. But they needed, as well, to defend themselves against an attack that was ruthless and growing more so.

It was a fierce combat. Swords flashed. Three intruders were killed, and one Musketeer fell. A single kidnapper was all that remained inside, and he writhed free.

"Seize him!"

Before they could reach him, though, the kidnapper jumped on a tree, climbed a window to the palace – and broke inside. The Musketeer blasted after him.

On the second-floor landing, a young guard who had remained there on duty head the shouts from outside and spotted the elusive kidnapper. He took off after, and the two men engaged in a duel of swords, steel blades clanging.

The Major led his men up the grand staircase to the landing. They could see the fight going on above.

The kidnapper caught the guard in a moment of distraction, and wounded the young man, whose sword dropped and echoed on the marble floor, as he fell to his knees. The Musketeers had made their way up on the landing now. Spotting them closing in on him, the intruder saw that he had just one way out – he jumped off the balustrade down to the first floor!

The Musketeers were helpless. Alone on the landing above, they could only watch as the kidnapper raced towards the door and escaped. Major Delacroix had no choice. His musket blast felled their last witness.

CHAPTER TWO

The magnificent country estate of the Chateau de Longueville sparkled under the night stars. The land dominated the countryside, looming in the truest sense of the word over the lives of all who surrounded and were touched by it. And dominating the land itself was its majestic structure, with wings and spires and a tower of the most exquisite architecture. Together, edifice and grounds, they didn't merely express importance, they said they were more important than you will ever dream of being. And stay away unless you are asked. And don't expect to be asked. Indeed, if you hope to be asked, know that you won't be. Those who enter, belong. They belong either by *droit du noblesse*, or by command.

Seated in the graceful study, and holding a cigar like his personal royal scepter, Marquis Eduard de Longueville was an elegant stiletto of a man in his late-30s, a gentleman among gentlemen who owned every room he entered.

"But we were able to get the king, m'lord. The *king*," one of the conspirators said imploring, hoping beyond hope he'd been convincing.

Eduard puffed his cigar at length before quietly replying.

"You captured a 10-year-old boy. You must be especially proud."

He almost winked, while the others in the room added ridiculing laughter, in part because they agreed, but mostly because they thought it wise to agree.

Central to his circle, Count de Beaufort, 31, stood by, a bit apart from the others. The Count was nouveau riche, which in his circle of society meant his wealth and land only went back a few generations rather than centuries, but he was eager to learn all that Marquis had to offer. More circumspect was General Henri Turenne, a quiet man when he had nothing to add, and someone not as willing as others in the room to kowtow when it wasn't earned – and earning respect from the highly-decorated soldier in his early 50s was honor indeed.

"You were supposed to get all three!" the Count de Beaufort snapped.

"But – yes, but we have the person most important," the intruder amongst them replied anxiously, believing it in his heart, but praying the others would agree, the Marquis most of all. "He is the king, and…"

Eduard held up a single finger which silenced the room.

He strolled to the brigand and gave him a small, polite nod which said, "sit." Then he knelt beside the bewildered man and motioned him close. No, no, his fingers said, closer.

Speaking as if to a child, Eduard patiently explained, "The Queen Mother rules as Regent. Cardinal Mazarin is Chief Minister. If the beloved Child King were to perish, royal succession would remain stable in France. There still would be royalty."

Eduard motioned him even closer still, and now

nearly whispered.

"That – cannot – be – allowed."

"M'lord, they found out the plan somehow," the dusty vagabond entreated.

Eduard suddenly grabbed the man by the throat, lifted and dragged him forcefully across the room, his legs flailing, and slammed him into a glass cabinet, shattering it, the shards cutting into his skin. It was a controlled, but violent frenzy.

Ice was in Eduard's voice. His words cut through the man as sharply as the broken glass. "Perhaps I may not have been clear. You <u>failed</u>. This is not a second chance endeavor! The Royal Family must all abdicate by nightfall of the *Gala National*."

*

Along the palace hallway, candles illuminated the night, as Cardinal Jules Mazarin and the regent, Queen Mother Anne, walked briskly past guards.

The Cardinal was 46 years old, officious; he was always officious; he couldn't help it, even if he had wanted to, which he didn't. Yet he was courtly and full of a grace, with curled hair and sharp eyes that stood out to anyone near.

"To be blunt, Your Highness, I don't believe your son dead. I apologize if I trespass on your feelings. The Musketeers are combing the countryside. It is much too early to know more."

The Queen Mother was only three years his junior but not one to fade into the background. Regal in the fullest sense, she was a vibrant presence, even to Mazarin, who intimidated most in the court and out, through his manner and leadership.

"To be blunt, Cardinal Mazarin, right now I do not have the luxury of feelings. For France, I must hide what is hell."

Their words were kept low from those who followed them, but even still, those aides marveled at something so clearly important could be handled so dispassionately, as most of their talks were, the public ones they saw, at least. "We are under attack to be sure," Mazarin replied with polite but pointed restraint, "but our strength remains that the People have confidence in your regency."

The two regarded one another from an intriguing, and complex, relationship, ever since he rose to Chief Minister six years earlier. There was admiration at the very least, it seemed, and he was a talented diplomat and executive to be sure, yet no matter how skilled an adviser may be, and no matter how strong, any ruler wants to be seen as the wisest of all. And strongest. For so they must be if they wish to keep ruling.

"The People know war with Europe is at our doors," she said. "Their sense of security is already threatened. If the king's disappearance makes men believe their government is unable to protect even itself – God. Help. France."

*

Lying in her palace bed chamber, Duchess Anne,

known in France as simply "*La Grande Mademoiselle*," had her arm bandaged in a sling, attended by a physician. Major Delacroix by her beside snapped to attention as the Regent and Mazarin arrived.

"*Mademoiselle*," the Cardinal asked, "how are you, brave one?"

The girl shifted up in her bed. Tall with delicate features, she had an admirable resolution that belied her 21 years.

"I would feel better if I could only tell the Major here more of what happened."

"My dear niece," the Queen Mother comforted her, "don't tax yourself."

She sat at the bed's edge, as Mazarin focused his attention on the Major, who now felt he had been granted permission to speak. Delacroix had spent almost 12 years directly in the crown's service, and by now had understood all the intricacies that entailed.

"*Mademoiselle* says when the king heard his cousin arrive, he joined her down in the garden. The Musketeers were never informed."

The Cardinal scowled. "It is their duty to be informed."

"He just wanted to play," the girl defended her young cousin.

"I understand. But he should have known better," Mazarin replied without feeling.

"He is just a 10-year-old boy."

"He is the king." The Queen Mother at last spoke and commanded the room's attention. "And we must find him."

CHAPTER THREE

A wide-brimmed hat filled with coins rested on the grass. A hand dropped some francs in. And then, another hand dropped even more.

Half a dozen young men stood laconically in the open field, each of them grasping swords, but none wanting to show how eager they were as teams were chosen.

"...and I pick Gerard," the first team captain selected.

That left just one. "Okay, I get whatever your name, the new kid," said the other captain.

A smaller, new kid in a floppy cap had been lingering shyly at the hat. In this time of uncertainty, even a franc was to be cherished and protected. Was it worth it for a game, for the risk? The kid stared, and finally the last coins got dropped in. The two sides were now chosen, the game was now set.

"Everyone is in. Winning team gets the hat," the first captain called out, the oldest among them, a swaggering youth just barely 20, but who liked the others to think he was more worldly, named Alain.

The teams separated. Spreading out, they each took their positions, eying their opponents for weaknesses, considering their own first moves. For a brief moment, they waited, anticipated strategy, passed hidden signals to teammates. And then...

"*En garde!*" the other captain called out.

The game began. The two teams challenged one

another, tentatively at first, feeling out the opposite side. It was like the first school dance where no one was quite sure if they should make the first move, or if they even wanted to.

But suddenly, the new kid attacked with a grand flurry, knocked the other's sword out – grabbed it mid-air and tripped the man, who found the point of a sword at his neck. He immediately yielded, acceding defeat. One down – already!

A nearby foe watched, stunned at the unexpected challenge and its inconceivable swiftness. And that was his mistake, for the pause was enough: the new kid attacked him now – a swing with one sword, and then the other from the left hand, and with the young man's defenses down, a forearm to his head flattened him. Not just down, but momentarily unconscious.

That was enough for the newcomer's teammates, as they circled the remaining adversary. He dropped his sword and knelt in submission.

As quickly as it began, remarkably it was over! The winners cheered! They couldn't believe it, dancing around in gaudy enthusiasm, slapping one another, ridiculing their vanquished enemies, and then chiding them some more. You really can't make fun of a defeated opponent enough, after all.

"*Victoire*. You lose! Amazing!!!" a young man yelled.

"Kid, you were *incroyable*," the winning captain acknowledged with actual admiration. He'd never seen something so impressive. "Absolu…" He looked around. "Kid? Where's the new kid?"

The kid was walking off.

At first, Alain didn't know what to make of this, but then realized to his great pleasure it was a good thing. "Ha! Let him go, more money for us to…" but he stopped and noticed something. "Where's the hat?! The money??"

The two winners realized it was gone, and raced off after. The other team, defeated, bruised and humiliated, started to run after, as well – until they remembered that they'd lost, and it wasn't their money. What did they care? They just laughed and chided the swindled victors.

The kid, though, walked faster as the two neared, shouting to stop, and then this would-be thief broke into a trot.

With the pursuers racing hard, they split off and circled their adversary and caught up. The swaggering and now red-faced Alain spun the kid around.

"What the hell do you think you're doing?" he sputtered. "Where's our money?"

The other young man ripped the kid's cap off. As he did, however, hair dropped out, a bit longer than they expected. The two men were taken aback. Words failed them.

"You're a girl??" the young man at last stumbled.

The new kid glared back. "You have my cap."

She snatched it back.

"Wait, I know you," Alain peered at her. "You're the gypsy girl. – It's the gypsy girl."

Racine Tarascon may have been around 28 years old, but – well, she wasn't quite sure. Thin, with

17

piercing coal eyes and short raven hair, she was a striking figure. She was absolutely impassive. She had taken taunts before – often, in fact. Most of her life, in fact. Actually, all of her life. Being used to it, though, didn't take any of the sting from it.

"You stole our money," Alain Simone continued. "Where is it?"

He frisked her – lingering more than needed. She knocked his hand away. She was used to that, as well. Finally, he found the money hat in Racine's hidden jacket pocket.

"You made a big mistake, gypsy girl," he spit out and called to the others. "The gypsy girl tried to steal our money! How about that, gypsy g…"

"My name – is Racine Tarascon. Remember it."

With a grin spread across his face, Simone replied, "Remember this." He grabbed and kissed her. And then strutted away and swaggered. He was very good at swaggering.

As his teammate laughed with him and slapped him on the back, Racine snorted pointedly. "Who do you practice kissing on? Your sister??"

He suddenly reddened, now the object of his friend's laughter – and strode back, grabbing her arm that now held a sword when she saw him coming. Quickly, though, she flipped the blade to her left hand and swung. He released his grip just in time.

"I'd say 'Go home to your family,' but you don't have one," he laughed bitingly.

The two taunted her, jeering. Racine held her calm, something that wasn't particularly in her nature.

18

But these young snits were far more stupid than cruel, and she could deal more easily with idiocy. After all, that was pretty much the way of the world, she felt.

"I won that money for you," she said. "Give me my share."

"Share?! You forfeited it," young M. Simone said.

His confederate stabbed at her with thrusts, but she stopped them all.

"You owe me," she repeated.

The angry fellow had had enough challenge to his leadership for one day. He strutted close, but Racine just ignored the popinjay. However, he pressed his sword to her neck, and it drew blood. "I owe you *this*."

In our life, we are called upon to make decisions. Some are good. Some are bad. This was a bad decision on the young man's part. Racine held a moment. And then – she spun away, parried his jabs, kicked him in the groin and he crumpled instantly, writhing in pain.

She turned to the other, who realized quite immediately he shouldn't have waited.

"You have my other hat," she said

He dropped the money-filled hat. Then, tore off running. With sword on her shoulder, she sauntered off across the field.

*

A mighty crash filled the room!

With a spark of clashing steel, a stunningly beautiful woman with flowing blonde hair as breathtaking as she was, intensely battled a wiry man

19

who had a look of anguish in his eyes, their swords clanging relentlessly against the metal of the other. Though in a quaint parlor, the feud was far from dainty. The man was skillful, aggressive, unrelenting, but with her it was near-ballet, spinning, leaping over a divan to safety.

"If justice can't convict you of ruining my life," the man spat out, "I will needs be do it myself."

"Never. Not whilst I have left a breath."

Emotion in the room ran high. The 25-year old Gabrielle Parnasse escaped one time with a backflip, and then evaded the swipe of his sword even with a cartwheel.

"Tonight, that breath will be your last."

Suddenly, she was caught off-guard. The man, Pierre Lavec, 40-ish, drove his sword into her. With a look of shock, she collapsed. Gasping for air, she reached out for help, for anything, but she heaved her last breath, and expired.

And then…there was a burst of applause!!

The audience in the small theatre sat cheering the melodrama before them on stage.

Gabrielle lay motionless, as Lavec continued to hold his pose. But surreptitiously she opened an eye to check the crowd…and then leapt to her feet! She headed downstage and began bowing.

"What are you doing???" Lavec hissed through his teeth.

"They love me."

"Get back. You're supposed to be dead."

Still bowing, she backed up – then dramatically,

oh-so-dramatically dropped to the floor, dead.

So, too, was any chance of any success of the play.

After the performance, backstage in her theatre dressing room, Gabrielle was out of her costume – and in the arms of a young man, Armande. Though he kissed her with great, impassioned ardor, she kept turning her head to avoid him.

"No, Armande, you shouldn't have come, we had our affair but it's long over, and just the other day I was telling Clarisse, did you meet Clarisse?, she and I worked in the bakery, and one time, well, this was of course before I was fired – "

"Gabrielle. Stop talking. Use your lips for something more productive."

He softly ran his fingers across their red fullness and then moved his mouth in closer.

"Armande, no…Armande. You know I'm getting married tomorrow."

"We're all French. I'm very happy for you."

He drew the voluptuous young actress closer.

Gabrielle sighed. Not out loud. No, men didn't like it when they had you in their arms and you sighed. It broke the moment, they would say. Well, yes, she thought, that was sort of the point. Even if the sigh happened naturally. She couldn't help it if she sighed. It's just what she felt. That was sort of how she lived her whole life. Couldn't they see that? Apparently not. Besides, it wasn't like she asked them to hold her. Usually. So, she learned to sigh inside. And much as she did like Armande, and his arms and his lips, this, alas, was not one of the times for it. It was like that time when she and her friend Marie had gone to Rouen for an adventure one weekend, and to eat at a fine bistro and see a play, and even though everyone was so upset that they wanted to travel, they went anyway, just because, and when they were there walking around one day...

"You really *have* to stop...," Gabrielle said to Armande, focusing her attention back on him. She knew what she had to say. That wasn't a problem, ever, but she knew Armande would be difficult. "Here, wait," she had a thought, "there's something I need to show you."

She led him to the window, and with a nod, referred outside.

"I don't see anything."

"No, no. Down. Down there."

He leaned far over the open sill, into the night. All he could see though were bushes covering the ground, a floor below. He leaned even further to see – and Gabrielle pushed him out. She calmly crossed the room, with a confident air.

"One down."

And she opened her cabinet, and Pierre, the actor from her play, stood hunched inside.

"Now the other. Out," she said. "You were not invited here."

She grabbed him by the collar and dragged him to the door.

"Gabrielle, wait, I want to rekindle our former passion."

"You courted me. Once."

"Do you think I hired you six months ago because you could act?" he said incredulously. "You can't even play a death scene!"

Anything he could have said she might have accepted. Not this. "Don't ever say that. I can."

"My God, it's 'dead.' All you have to do is lay there."

"Jealousy," she said petulantly. "You hate that they cheer me."

"They like watching you bounce across the stage."

She pushed him into the hall.

"If you close this door, Gabby, you're fired."

"I won't be fired. I'll be married."

Slam! The door shuddered. Then, she opened it again.

"And I'll find another acting troupe!"

Slam!!!

*

The grand foyer of *Chateau Le Renaud* was as lavish as a museum. Into this sunny hall Charlotte Le Renaud entered, lost in admiring a bouquet of lilies. She was a delicate flower herself. Silken auburn hair fell upon the shoulders of this porcelain young lady who had just turned 18 only two months earlier.

As she passed along the hallway, she noticed that the jade and emerald carvings on the étagère had been shifted and looked a frightful mess. Charlotte was never insistent on order, but she always noticed such things. She had a good eye and knew what looked right and where things should properly be. Order gave comfort – not just the placement of things, but when people knew who they were and what was expected of them, it gave their life meaning, the young girl felt. She shifted the antiques and…definitely, they looked better. When people entered the estate, she thought, at the very least they should have something pleasant to the eye greet them. Of course, kind though her thought was, it was difficult for anyone to enter the grounds anywhere and not have something pleasant to the eye greet them. Though to Charlotte, that was all second nature to her. Still, it was a kindness.

People said that she reminded them of her mother, and Charlotte loved hearing that. Even though Charlotte had had a governess to always attend her – two of them, in fact, funny old ladies one of whom always seemed cross, though Charlotte never thought she really was – her mother was always there. It was her responsibility to raise her daughter, teach her, support her, love her. And Charlotte had always felt loved, and still did even though now it was just her and her dear father. The governesses and butlers and valets had been there when she was so little, yes, but only to tend to the child when her mother had her own social responsibilities, as one of position simply had and simply accepted. (*That* Charlotte learned from her dear father, who knew more about the responsibilities of the world than any man alive. Responsibility, duty, support and fairness, and for all that and much more, Charlotte adored him. Of course, it helped too that he was so funny and always made her laugh, like the time when she had lost her cherished floppy doll, *M. Vagabond*, and couldn't be consoled – until her father walked in dressed just the same in baggy clothes and torn hat and asked, "Will I do instead?")

Charlotte didn't remember much about her mother, but she did remember how kind she always was to everyone, not just her equals, but the vassals who lived on the estate, people in the town, and even the servants. That's what Charlotte tried to live up to. The lessons one learns at the age of four, when her mother passed, are often the ones that stick longest with us. And in the end, when you try hard enough to emulate something, that is what you become, even without trying. Sweet and kind and warm.

Happy with her flowers, with the display of antiques, with the day, Charlotte hummed a little tune. All was right with the world. Outside this enclosed world others might have a different thought about that, but Charlotte simply knew nothing of it.

Far down the hall by the study, Gilles St. Chapelle heard the music and spotted her.

"And there is the missing sparrow," he said, crossing back across the marble tiles.

"Gilles! *Bonjour.* I was only in the garden. So, you've come to see me?"

He shrugged. "It's just my luck where my horse takes me."

Charlotte pretended to pout. Or maybe not precisely pretend. "Oh, well," she tossed off. "I suspect that is to be expected when one has a horse that is the more thoughtful of the two."

"Or well-trained to have a mind of his own. Perhaps you would like him to give you lessons!"

Before Charlotte could respond, Gilles took her hand and gallantly kissed the finger tips. Disarmed, Charlotte offered a slight blush. Whatever she was planning to respond, that was now a thing of the past.

Gilles was a *chevalier*, the middle son of nouveau aristocrats whose estate bordered the Le Renaud's. On the edge of dashing, he had a determined way about himself, which Charlotte much admired. Older by eight years, Gilles had always treated her as the naïve, privileged child she was, but he liked that about the girl, her innocence. And he liked teasing her; she pouted so well. The thing was, he always knew how to handle her when she pouted. In truth, she was such a sweet girl. And he had to admit, she had really grown quite lovely, as well, which didn't hurt.

As they spoke, a muffled commotion could be heard nearby. It kept growing louder.

"I certainly hope that if you – " Charlotte tried her best to block out the disturbance, but was too distracted by it. " – if – that – " She listened briefly, and then became concerned. "One moment."

She headed towards the noise.

That noise, increasing by the sentence, was coming from inside the oak-lined study, where gray-haired Baron Le Renaud was arguing heatedly with the impassioned Count Philippe Gascogne.

"You speak far out of place for your youth, Philippe. Watch yourself, boy."

"And you are a damn fool, Baron. I heard your ill-advised words in *Parlement*. I nearly leapt and put hands on you."

The Baron, good-natured though he was in his life, was also not one was used to being spoken to so bluntly, least of all by one so young.

"What is ill-advised, sir, are those who wish to return France to feudal law, where only the wealthy, the few, the noble born rule their fiefdoms. With private laws and private armies, it will be the death of the common man."

"You enjoy being called a traitor to your class??!" The young lord's voice rose.

Le Renaud held his glare, as tempers grew. "Traitors are those who seek secret treaties with outside empires."

"I have warned you, Baron. Heed my words. You act rash and foolhardy. And if I...

"Papa."

Charlotte had entered the room and overheard the exchange. She politely stood her ground, knowing that she was an unwelcome intrusion, but concern for her adored father overcame convention, and she took steps towards him.

"All this talk of civil war, conspiracies. You know I don't like your fighting. It works you up so. Leave that to...*others*."

Though her words were spoken to her father, no one in the room could mistake that they were directed at the haughty, impassioned young man.

"Your daughter shows proper concern, Baron," he said, with his high-toned bearing.

Finally, though barely, Charlotte turned, but ever-so-slightly to acknowledge him.

"M'lord," she coolly nodded. "Though with respect, my concern is none of yours."

The Baron smiled with a private pleasure. He loved this side of his child. He knew that most people saw her as fragile – and indeed he believed that Charlotte thought herself that way – but he was well-aware that she had a spirit underneath it all. It was one of his greatest pleasures about her. And he appreciated the well-deserved discomfort she was giving Philippe Gascogne. A count, no less. He was not yet 30 and could stand being taken down a peg.

"My daughter has long heard me rail, sir, that when you have more than others, you have more responsibility," he replied in a steely voice and pointed glare. And then started in once more. "I will not be deterred from confronting Eduard de Longueville, whose every action…"

"*Papa*," she interrupted protectively, recognizing her father's anger again start to get the best of him. "Please. Be kind."

Le Renaud held eyes with Gascogne, wanting as was his nature to finish his high-minded harangue – and then continue saying so much more. But what he knew he must say was far more important. And so he sighed, a beaten but happy for it man. "I can refuse you nothing, my angel."

An angel she may be, but even angels have their limits. Charlotte kissed her father on the check, and then came storming out of the study, still angered by the encounter, so upset that she didn't even see Gilles, who had been waiting there by the door. He had to run to just keep up with her, muttering under her breath. Angered as much for simply being angry, for in Charlotte's well-ordered life, all should be at peace.

"I can see this is not the best time to be here," he said.

"I hate such unpleasantness when it concerns my father. Would that more nobles saw him as I do," she said.

"It is difficult days," Gilles comfortingly replied, agreeing with her. And while his words were true, what was also true was that he probably would have agreed with her about most anything. "Attend to him. And hence, Charlotte, I must take my leave."

He took her hand and affectionately kissed it. For the briefest moment, she wasn't certain how to react. It was such a bold thing to have done. But though bold, his actions were also not unwelcome in the least.

"I am sorry for being so distracted," she said. And then added coquettishly, "See, you *can* be charming if you try."

"Let me try further at dinner tonight. Meet me at 8 o'clock."

"Oh, no, I really shouldn't."

"If I said I would die?"

There was a silence between them. The wait was short, but interminable for Gilles. "M'lord," she said at last, with the smallest, but most noticeable of smiles, "if it is a case of life and death."

CHAPTER FOUR

In a small country village, a couple was eating lunch inside a café. Outside, Racine Tarascon watched as the wife washed down a mouthful of cold chicken with some red wine. Her husband swallowed half a croissant. It all looked good to the hungry gypsy. A bite of the roll would have looked good.

She strolled down the street past an épicerie, the groceries inside lining the shelves almost seemed to be laughing at her. An apple cart stood out front, piled high. As she passed by, it was short one apple.

Racine was quick with her hands. She'd been on her own for too many years, and ever since that day – she only cared to think of it as "that day" – it was live by her wits and quick hands. A lot of apples had given themselves to a greater duty, she laughed. So had a lot of things that hadn't protected themselves well-enough.

Walking on, she bumped in a wealthy man. "Watch it, *mon frère!*" she snapped at him aggressively.

The man took one look at the ragged clothes of the ragged young woman and scoffed. "You have no right to speak to me like that."

"And you have no right to think you own the street." She would take no affront from anyone. It didn't matter who they were, how fancy they were.

"You walked into me!" the man challenged right back, saying he had half a mind to call the *gendarme* for assault.

Racine threw her hands up in disgust, and said something about being absolutely sure he had half a mind, and walked on. And turning the corner, she pocketed the wallet she had just picked.

Continuing her prowl through the village, the young woman later spotted a nicely-dressed gentleman on a park bench, reading a book. She pulled her bandanna out from a pocket and wrapped it around her head, knowing it made her appear mystical to most people. Sidling over, she joined him on the bench, and before he even looked up, grabbed his palm to read.

"May I?" she asked, not remotely concerned whether she may or may not, immediately continuing without giving the startled man even a breath to respond, "Ahhh. Great news will come from a lost uncle. And you will get a fortune. And find love. And…"

"I'm <u>married</u>," the gentleman cried.

"I was right!!"

She held out her hand, waiting to get paid – but nothing was forthcoming, except a blank stare. She immediately grabbed his palm again and peered back into it.

"Hmmm, I can't tell. It looks like you might also die a slow, very painful death, covered with boils…"

Quickly, he gave her a franc.

"Ah, no boils," she now replied. "Definitely no boils."

She bit the coin to make sure it was real. She figured it was, but sometimes that made the mark embarrassed enough to give her another as proof. As she pocketed the money, "That's her," she heard a voice that sounded vaguely familiar. The wealthy man who she had bumped into earlier that morning had arrived with a police officer and pointed.

"She's the one. She stole my wallet."

Without waiting to challenge the charge, Racine jumped up and raced away for all she's worth. At first she was pursued by just the one policeman, but then two more joined him, like always, it was like they lived in packs, she thought, but then worse, other people followed after, and it had it become a citizen posse.

She dashed down the street, turned corners, ran through alleys, and barreled through the town. Just as she eluded one person, more showed up. It was exhausting – and it was also nothing new to her. Her people had been despised and usually run out of wherever they'd set stakes. It was a vagabond life, but bad as it was when she had people, even if there wasn't safety in numbers, there was at least comfort. Now, on her own, she was always looking over her shoulder, far too often on the run.

And on the run she was. She blasted past houses, down roads, and as she hit the outskirts of the village, when she should have been getting away, the chase posse just kept growing. And so, she ran more, and ran and ran. Gulping for breath, her legs burning. But she was in good shape; this wasn't her first chase. It wasn't like she had a choice. It was life.

By dusk, Racine was hidden in a ditch in the countryside, carefully hunkered down far out of sight, branches covering her. She'd certainly had enough practice at hiding. When you're lying there, all you can do is stay quiet and think. It was the one part she liked least of all this, but the devil does like a mind at rest. And far too often Racine couldn't help return to that that day, and remember it, the most wrenching of her life. It wasn't that she wanted to forget – no, she wanted to always remember. But that didn't make it easy. But she liked remembering her family. Not just her parents, but the village; to a gypsy they were all her family. She gave a quick shudder, but finally under the branches she felt safe.

And then three muskets appeared. And they were pointed right at her head. A voice shouted out triumphantly.

"We found the gypsy witch!"

Soon, she was surrounded. Soon, the *gendarmes* appeared. Soon, she was taken and carried through town. And soon, no longer hidden, no longer safe, Racine sat huddled in a jail cell, very alone. The darkness enveloped her.

*

The young man stood patiently at the altar, immaculately dressed in a morning coat, as any respectable, immaculate, prospective groom should be. Sunlight streamed in the stone church denoting the brightness of the occasion. The room was full. The priest ready. It was perfect. The only thing missing was the bride.

Monsieur Parnasse, Esq., sat impatiently. He was

the picture of business propriety, though with his jaw set, it was not possible for others to see his teeth being ground. His good lady wife waited anxiously with him, refusing to look behind to the door, as if waiting for the bride was the most natural thing at a wedding. Their three sons were less proper, having no pretense to put on a front for their sister. The rest of the room, middle-class bourgeoisie all of them, muttered amongst themselves what one would have thought was beneath the middle-class bourgeoisie, but apparently not. Business associates, family and friends and more business associates had spent the past hour dressed up and had long-since passed being uncomfortable for it.

Awkwardness itself long-since passed, and unease filled the church as the absence of Gabrielle became impossible to avoid. Murmurings began to become less circumspect. The priest looked at the mortified parents of the bride. He motioned, again, "Where is she??" Their silence was deafening.

The stained-glass window high on the wall was gorgeous. The tiny church was most proud of it, designed by an almost-famous glazier, telling the story of the Crusades. Where earlier in the day, though, when guests had once arrived and the sun had shone through that beloved window, reflecting magnificent beams of light off the glass throughout the church, now there were only the beginning of shadows as the hope of the mid-day wedding had turned into afternoon.

All there were left in the church were the seething groom, her sullen parents, and a very bored priest.

Suddenly, a harried Gabrielle burst in. She was dressed in a French maid costume, and struggling mightily to attach a veil.

"I'm so, so sorry," she gasped for air, trying to catch her breath. "I hate a late entrance. I'm sorry. It's just that, well, the audition ran late, and I could have left, should have, but this was for the play, *The Winter Snow*, and it would be such a major role, and actresses rarely get — well, I know you all understand, again I'm so sorry, I am really so very sorry, please forgive me, but I kept waiting and…"

"Gabrielle." The seething groom finally interrupted her, finding a spot to jump in. "I won't have this. I've told you. If you are to be my wife, there will be standards. I've told you. I don't care that you are late — I care where you were. Yet another audition?? Another play? *Play*?? My wife does not 'play.' My wife does not 'act.' I've told you. And I've told you repeatedly. My wife…

"Excuse me," Gabrielle said, though she wasn't addressing her fiancé. Instead, she had turned to the priest and spoke to him. "Sorry. I'm terribly sorry. Did you already get to the 'Do you take this man' part?

"No," the startled priest replied.

"Ah. Good," Gabrielle answered with a look of relief. "Because I don't."

It was not long after she had made this proudly defiant pronouncement that Gabrielle found herself in a familiar room back home. The two plush sofas, carved chairs of cherry wood, well-appointed china plates and etchings on the wall were all familiar. But though familiar, there was nothing comfortable about it. She sat expectantly on one side of the stylish room, while her parents sat, still in shock on the other, a great distance between them.

For a long while, there was nothing but silence. It was her parents' place to speak, such was the order and decorum of what was right and proper, but they couldn't find the words. Finding the words, though, was never a failing of Gabrielle's, so at last, unable to bear the tension, she burst.

"He doesn't love me. He wanted to become business partners with father. You know that, you arranged this. You keep arranging matches for me. And I so want to please you, I so hoped that this time, finally. I wanted to please you. But it's like when I did the play, *Empty Mansions*, and the child…

"Gabrielle, please!" her mother cried. "This is too much, always too much. This is a respectable family, and you've never thought of doing anything but embarrassing it."

"Mother, I've never wanted to…"

"Look at you. Dressed in a costume. Always showing off. Prancing on stage. Always the men around. Always the attention. He told you to stop. *We* told you to stop."

Gabrielle knew her parents were unhappy, and had been unhappy for many years. They hadn't even mentioned the last play she'd been in. They didn't speak to her for weeks when she went to Rouen. And Marseilles. They had only been to two of her plays, and even walked out of the second. But this – this was different –

"I did nothing wrong, mama. People come to me. They like me. *They* come to me."

Until that moment, one voice had been mute. Not just in this room, at this moment, but through much of the day. Observing all around him, feeling more, but saying nothing. Yet simmering. And then, the dam that was her father – stoic, silent, holding his thoughts inside, as a good and stolid man should do – broke open.

"'They come to me, they like me.' Always 'me.' Always blame someone else. But we are who suffer. Even your brothers."

"It doesn't concern them, it is my life."

"And today this final humiliation," the patriarch continued, oblivious to her words, so wound up was he in his outrage that had become almost a kind of grief. "Repeatedly. Three proposals I have set for you. And you turn your back to my face. And now *this*. You shame us, you shame my business that supports us all. The pretending, the selfish preening. Enough! This is not *your* life. This is *my* family. And you show you do not want to be a part of it. Which is as it should be. Because I no longer wish you a part of it."

Suddenly, the room grew shatteringly still.

"I have warned you," he said in sharp, crisp tones, "and from this day forth, you are disinherited. Shame us no more."

And the world for Gabrielle just totally stopped.

*

A world away, Charlotte Le Renaud rode peacefully and slowly along a country road in a fancy carriage. The moonlight shone down on the land around her. Her family's land. The coachman and valet added to the sense of comfort that made her life so grand.

Dinner with Gilles had been quite the windswept carpet ride. And she blushed thinking about how he had touched her cheek. He was always impetuous and so irresponsible. But she always knew how to handle Gilles. When he got too spirited, as always, during their tête-à-tête; when he tried too hard to impress her, as always; when he showed up late even tonight, as always; when he got ridiculously haughty with the staff, she knew how to coyly, yet politely put him in his place. Gabrielle was not adept at courtship, but she was French, after all. Some things you just knew.

Someday she'd like to get married. She remembered how it was with her mother and father. She'd like that, very much. Was Gilles that kind of man? Thinking about it, her hand drifted to her cheek. She really had no idea. But she had a long time to decide. A year, at least.

Sitting in the dark of night, her carriage turned down a lane. The landscape ahead was lit up by an odd, diffused glow. Suddenly, her body tensed.

In the distance, her father's estate was in flames!

"Quickly!!"

The carriage rambled down the road. The dirt path curved around a grove of trees, and Charlotte leaned her head out as far as she could, her heart racing faster than the horses.

As the carriage pulled up, the magnificent Le Renaud edifice was a lost cause. Staff was carrying out as much property as possible. Paintings were strewn across the ground. There was the magnificent, mahogany banquet table. The harpsichord. Chairs. Things, just things. They were so valuable and meant nothing.

Gilles was in their midst helping them all. The inferno of the flames had been so intense in the sky that their light had illuminated the countryside and reached his family's estate. His clothes in tatters, he saw Charlotte arrive and ran to the shaken girl, holding her tight.

"When did this happen, Gilles?? How?!!"

"Don't look. Don't."

She was numb. But then, a more terrifying thought slammed her.

"Papa! How is papa?!!"

And then she saw it. A covered body on the ground.

Charlotte screamed. But no sound escaped. Her body was in shock, and Gilles led her away, out of range, into a clearing, where the poor girl's life was ashen. She could only react, without thought.

"He's all I have, Gilles. No one. How could such an accident happen?"

It was very hard for Gilles to answer. Finally he had to.

"They say the fire was no accident. Your father

was shot."

"Nobody would ever – Because he wanted to protect France? Why are you saying this?"

It was all surreal to her. Just images they were, one blurring into the next. People had come from all over, a crowd, faces. The grocer bumping into the blacksmith. The seamstress carrying out a large Delft vase. Philippe Gascogne who had argued with her father, moving among the staff, helping to install some sense of order.

They caught each other's eyes. It was all mad, too much…and she had other, greater concerns and turned away to Gilles.

"I want to see my father."

And off in the distances, flames shot high from the chateau.

CHAPTER FIVE

As the sun broke through the early morning haze, the open field was still wet from dew. Gnats skipped across the grass top. Off by the road, a herd of horses lingered idly, peacefully pawing at the dirt and chewing straw along the ground.

Racine was no longer in prison. She was, however, far from free, being led across the range by eleven men. Not coincidentally, it was just one short of a jury. Her hands were tied behind her back.

"This is so unjust," she spat out.

They reached a tree, where a rope hung down from a heavy branch. Their twelfth compatriot held a waiting horse.

Now, there was a jury.

"There are laws. You've heard of them?"

"Yes, gypsy, there are laws," the leader noted with indifference. "And his Lordship makes them. His Lordship oversees a decent village."

Something about his words deeply affected Racine. She sneered.

"Decent village. I know all about decent villages. My people were mistrusted, chased, always hiding. And then one day a great lord invited us to live on his estate. His 'decent village' threw a celebration for us all."

A noose was dropped around her neck.

"And that night, separated from one another, all of my people were dragged out of their beds, beaten, put in cages like animals and sent across Europe. So the town could keep its lands decent. I've never seen my family since."

The rope was secured to the tree.

"It took eight years for me to get back. But my people, my village, all I knew were gone, taken from me."

There was so much more that Racine wanted to say about "that day." It was seared so deeply into her memory, the pain of the cries, the helplessness of wanting someone, just a single good person to speak up to help, but it never came. But as the loop pulled against her neck, there were far more appropriate words that came to mind.

She glared daggers at them all. She wriggled her wrists, but to no avail. The twine of the ropes only cut tighter. The leader spat into the grass.

"And now it's time for you to go," he said.

"You little pissant. Tell your Lordship he will answer for this."

"His Lordship answers to no one, save the Marquis de Longueville."

"Then, I demand you take me in protest to the Marquis, at risk of *your* heads," Racine said defiantly. "Take me to the Marquis de Longueville. Now."

She spoke with such command that one of the men took a step back in fear, until he realized that this young woman was in no position to do anything, least of all make demands of them.

"Ha!! Protest to the Marquis? Who do you think gives this estate its protection?!!" The leader laughed with disdain. "Better luck in hell, gypsy witch."

There was derisive laughter among all the men. The noose was tightened.

"Listen well. I don't know where my family is – but I'll find them. Understand that. *I will find my family.* And then you'll see hell. This I swear."

Her words fell on deaf ears. The men formed an orderly semi-circle around her, sitting atop the horse, as one of them waited for the signal to send the animal racing off and leave their victim dangling.

"By the laws of this estate," said the man in charge solemnly, though not *too* solemnly, "you are sentenced to hang until you are dead. Go with God."

Racine watched all this with growing fury. And then finally –

"Oh, the hell with this."

Suddenly, in a blur, she lifted herself up from her seated position, pulled her hands underneath her, ripped off the noose and galloped away, gnawing at the knot feverishly with her teeth, and undoing it.

The men were in shock. When they finally recovered and ran for their horses, Racine had already scattered the skittish animals. The vigilantes rushed around, desperately doing their best to track any of them down.

But Racine was history – and had galloped far off into her next life.

*

In an empty village square in the early morning,

before much of the town had even stirred, Gabrielle sat in the bed of a farm wagon, grasping a satchel. A priest had come by to offer comfort, but there was little to console her with. Some warm words, a few platitudes, but the reality of the moment transcended all. Up front, the driver waited.

"This is so unfair," Gabrielle finally let out.

"Much is, I'm afraid. Go with God."

There was another painful silence. Then, at last –

"I will. But I will come back to Mont Vert. And it will be in triumph. If my family – if the people of this town – if my family... – People will be proud of me. Mark my words. This – I – swear."

The wagon started to pull away. They exchanged wistful looks.

As it reached the outskirts of town, the sound of the wheels churning up the dirt road were all that was heard. Gabrielle felt at a loss for words. And she never was at a loss for words. She always told stories. Her father used to laugh at them all the time. Her mother encouraged her on when she was little, because people liked the stories, liked her, thought it was so cute. She was the little one, with all the big brothers. People adored it when she put on shows. It always got attention. When she grew, yes, her father expected her to be different, but that's who she was. And now...this?

After a bit, the driver looked behind him into the rear of his rig. He thought a moment.

"You look familiar," he said quizzically. "You in the theatre?"

Gabrielle didn't even appear to hear him. There was only silence. Finally, she climbed to the front of the bed, near as she could to the driver, looking out forward – out down the road towards whatever lay ahead. Then,

"Perhaps you saw me in a comedy? I've had quite good notices in them. Most recently, I was the second lead in a big...

*

Though it was still early morning, there was already activity at the Le Renaud estate, as valets carried a large trunk from the charred remains of the once-majestic structure. The remainder of the staff had gathered, as well, and stood out front, sullen for the occasion.

A distraught young girl was in black – dainty, well-mannered, and thoroughly unprepared for the life ahead – walking silently with the housekeeper.

"Is there anything you need?" the old woman asked as solicitously and heartfelt as the heartbreaking situation allowed.

Charlotte didn't utter a word. But her expression said, "*Everything.*"

But all she had was nothing. Her father had given her so much. He gave her parties, clothes, comforts, admonitions to be kind to everyone. To be good and fair. He was always protecting her. He was so silly that way, he even gave her sword lessons so she could protect herself. But she was no good at that, she couldn't protect herself – or now, even protect her father, when he most needed it. All that he'd given her, did for her, trying to give her all he could without a mother – it meant nothing, because all she had was a hole in her heart. And it was so deep inside. The best she could do was fill it for him. For herself. That, she knew, would be what he would want. But first she had to get out of the hole. And how could she possibly do that? The only thing she was able to do or see ever doing, was remember the love of her father.

"Your cousins in Paris will I'm sure give you much comfort." Her thoughts were interrupted by the matron. But they were just sounds. They didn't seem to have any meaning.

Gilles was waiting at the carriage for Charlotte. He kissed her hand. When he finally spoke, his words came hard.

"I look to when we do meet again. You deserve a gentle life. Go with God."

Charlotte was about to get inside the coach, but turned and just looked out for a moment.

"This is so wrong," her voice broke, as she searched not just for the right words, but any words. "My father was the most decent man, a great man. What he showed me about fairness – if his life is gone, so would be mine. Whoever did this horrible act will pay for it. He must." And then with a guttural resolve, she added, "I will find him. This I swear."

As she stepped in the carriage, the door closed on her life here…and the vehicle headed down the lane to her new one.

CHAPTER SIX

To a distant eye, the expansive military base was in a swirl of pitched activity, preparing for imminent maneuvers. Armed men were drill training. A group of infantry practiced sword thrusts at makeshift figures. Battalions of soldiers marched. Sharpshooters took aim at targets with long-iron muskets. Yet this was no army headquarters, but the magnificent grounds of a chateau, spreading to the horizon.

Two scraggly enlistees headed through the crowd towards a waiting queue.

"They say Count de Valvere pays even better at his chateau in Le Havre," the first young man said.

"Yes, but who wants to live in Le Havre?"

The pair shared a laugh, and then elbowed their way past others, eventually finding a place in line among the hopeful throng.

Soon there was a commotion, as the officers became aware of a presence coming their way. The training came to a halt. Even the would-be inductees stood back in awe. For astride his horse, overlooking his distant realm, rode a stoic, resolute Eduard, the Marquis de Longueville. A cheer reigned through the air.

"To the Marquis! The Marquis!"

Throughout other realms of France, the mood was not filled with nearly the same high spirits. Yet those very spirits present here had a long reach, for what was taking place at the Chateau de Longueville could be felt across the land, even if most in France didn't know it. What looked elsewhere like nothing more than small, private exercises by chateaux to protect their own land were, in fact, tributaries of what the Marquis was organizing on this grand scale.

These private exercises, maneuvers, operations, and actions may have been small wherever they took place, but their impact was felt just as powerfully as the most elaborate.

So it was when a four-man posse brigade marched determinedly towards a chapel. The curé met them at the door. With a calm, but resolute voice the gentle man warned them.

"Sanctuary has been made claim with…"

But the brigade continued to march right past him, into the chapel. The protection of sanctuary held no sway with them. They trooped through the holy temple, eyes searching, until they came upon what they had sought, a frightened man who sat huddled in a nook.

The curé raced back after them.

"Stop! You may not touch this penitent."

The bridge leader put out an arm to stop the priest. "By law of the estate, his fields are in default to the lord of the land."

The terrified farmer shot his eyes to his defender. "Father, the tariff for my crops was raised four-fold. I'll lose my property. I'll be returned to serfdom. Our whole village is becoming like slaves."

The curé turned sternly to the officer. "There is only one Lord here," he insisted, "and He protects all in this chapel."

"This chapel, mon Père," the commander returned dripping with polite dismissiveness, "sits on the land of Count Vernoux and exists by his leave. If you wish, we could tear it down now."

They waited for the priest to answer, but only for a moment, and no reply came. They grabbed the man, and dragged him past the helpless curate.

It was not only in the countryside and small parishes like this where such outrages of power and self-imposed estate law took place. And everywhere it occurred, its growing impact was felt over France. In the country, in villages, in the city. Even in the greatest city of all.

For as law in France continued to break down, a small riot was taking place on a cobbled street of Paris. People were shouting, pushing. And no *gendarmes* were in sight. They had far too much to attend in other parts of the city.

Such was the reality that everyday life was becoming in the nation.

At a charming country boulangerie in Limoges, a nervous clerk was ringing up an order for a customer waiting for her sack of baguettes. An anxious line stretched long outside the door, for food shortages of even the most basic commodities were being felt everywhere. And a shortage of bread would try the patience of even the most patient and understanding of Frenchman. And those in the line were not the most understanding of Frenchmen. An angry woman was next.

"Bread," she snapped. "I want bread."

"*Oui, madame*," the clerk tried awkwardly to explain. "This is of course…"

She quickly interrupted, "At a price that I can afford!"

The poor clerk knew his explanation would not satisfy her. He had satisfied no one all day. It had not satisfied even himself. "With the roads closed, and so much cut off, all I can do…

"Bread!!" she shouted.

She grabbed a loaf from the man's hands and ran out. Seeing the precious staple disappearing with rapidity before their eyes without recompense or compunction, several others quickly broke line and snatched up rolls, croissants, muffins, whatever was in sight.

At other boulangeries, it was the same, just as with the boucheries that had to convince their customers that horse meat was as fine as lamb. Worse, perhaps, to a Frenchman, the shortage of sugar meant that patisseries prepared confections without the sweetness that made the harshness of life tolerable. Their whole lives, pêcheurs struggled with the seas to bring in their daily catch, but now they had to also fight more turbulent conditions on the land so that the people would have something to eat. Each day, whoever it touched, the challenge of life was pushed to the edge.

It is one of the insurmountable truths of life that so often the actions of a few affect so many. And the more powerful they are, the fewer are needed. Such was the case when the Marquis de Longueville had come to Cardinal Mazarin's study. Yet with so much at stake for the two great rivals, a visitor walking in would have been surprised to see nothing more than the best of friends engaged in just a genteel game of chess. Such is the way of grace and manners, where only the most skilled can master the language for which words and smiles are never what they seem.

Eduard intently watched his opponent pondering his move, not missing a breath, or twitch of the Cardinal's face, hoping to glean even the slightest advantage of intent, not just of what his next move would be, but what he was thinking it might be, could be, yet then dismissed. Every point was important. Mazarin took his time to give nothing away, before shifting a knight.

"I can only assume Your Worship's play is afflicted by distress over the disorder throughout the nation," the Marquis said offhandedly.

"His Lordship confuses distress with responsibility."

The two men circled the board, and each other.

"I am never confused," Eduard replied with a nod and then moved a pawn. "Thinking so is why you are losing."

Mazarin politely returned his nod. "His Lordship presumes to know my moves, which is a fool's game. Some of us attempt to protect one's entire board."

"And that hubris of yours is what leaves one at risk. One cannot handle the details." Eduard hovered his hand over the bishop on the table and watched his opponent's reaction. But Mazarin was implacable.

"And with so many details to maintain, you get overwhelmed. And that is why you will get crushed. In this game." He smiled at the Cardinal. "Perhaps you will do better in the next, if we make the rules easier for you."

"I am comfortable playing the king's rules."

De Longueville took out a cigar and offered one to the Cardinal, who politely waved it off.

"Speaking of Louis, the fifth anniversary of his crown is upon us. He is well?" Eduard asked pointedly, with the greatest-sounding wishes of sincerity.

"He is better even than you."

"I rest certain that the people of France await seeing him at the *Gala National*," Eduard took a long puff. "I can only imagine their pain in these difficult times should he not appear."

"Yes, the People do love he who leads them."

"That is my very hope. You have no idea." The Marquis looked at the chess board. His face lit up. "Ah! It appears your king is taken. Check."

CHAPTER SEVEN

Along a row of elegant apartments in the most fashionable section of Paris, a shy Charlotte Le Renaud repeatedly knocked on the ornate door. And then knocked yet again. She spotted a servant girl out front of the home next door, dumping out her sweepings.

"I beg your pardon," Charlotte forced herself to ask. "I'm sorry to disturb you, but I am looking for my cousins."

"Oh, my, they moved to the south months since, m'lady," the girl quickly replied. "It's not been safe here, you know."

She scooted into her building. The stranger may have appeared a fine gentlewoman, but the girl had no interest to speak with anyone without an introduction these days. Standing there alone, Charlotte called to her.

"Where am I to go?"

But it was as good as calling to no one. She heard a latch click from within. It was a sound from this side of a door Charlotte was unaccustomed to hearing. But then, most of her life now was unaccustomed. Perhaps she should take a room, she'd heard that phrase before. But what she hadn't heard was how one took a room. It was all so bewildering, so very different. Yet she would persevere. She had sworn herself. But...how?? How?

Three young men were walking by. Charlotte headed to them.

"Excuse me but could you please help move my trunk to storage? I'm told four francs is a fair price. I'll give you six."

The three swaggered over. It was the city, Charlotte thought, not just the city, this was Paris, and she didn't know what decorum called for in such transactions, perhaps she was expected to pay for services before the work was completed, as a show of faith. They eyeballed Charlotte up and down. Though she understood they were deciding, it made her a bit uncomfortable.

"Ten. Each."

"And the necklace," his buddy snapped. And then he ripped it from her neck. The other grabbed her purse. And they ran off.

Charlotte was terrified , but couldn't move.

*

Along a quiet, tree-lined Paris neighborhood, Racine Tarascon was on a calm, morning stroll, peacefully taking in the pleasures of the town. It was really far less nonchalant than a careful observer might recognize, though, for in truth her eyes weren't taking in the oh-so charming sights, as her smiling face appeared, but carefully searching. It was a skill of misdirection, which for Racine was survival, that she had long-since honed. And at last, she spotted a man putting away a thick wallet.

A mark! The gypsy unobtrusively took the lay of the grounds. From the corner of her eye, she determined the best path of attack. Another glance showed the best escape route. As she moved in, she kept a careful ear for any unwelcome sounds. There wasn't much. Muffled voices nearby broke the quiet. Then a whistle.

"Please, no," a man cried out clearly now. "I must care for my baby."

"I beg you. My husband, let him go."

The dispute distracted Racine. Only a little at first, but as it grew, the words bore into her, and she ignored her mark completely. She stopped and stared cross the street.

Two landlords had the young husband in their grip, dragging him and tooting a whistle. His young wife was holding a baby.

"Please," the man repeated. "Don't leave my family here alone."

"How can we pay if you take my husband? Mercy. I beg mercy."

Mercy was in short supply these days.

A police wagon with barred windows pulled up, carried along by horses. The couple tried to hold onto one another. Their baby wailed. The wife cried, as well. The police shouted for order. The husband continued to struggle.

Racine's emotions grew. And gnawed deeper. It was a scene she understood far too well. And though she had lived a life learning to survive on her own, letting others fend for themselves, there were some things that strike us where we reside inside. And such things have nothing to do with survival, but who we are. And as much as Racine's most ingrained instincts were to walk away, to run away, to escape from the police, to go after the money to survive, to not be there, she couldn't take her eyes off the misfortune in front of her. And her emotions grew. And her eyes tightened. Her teeth clenched. Her body tensed. The cries continued, the pleading, the pulling. Her emotions grew more than even she ever believed they could grow. And finally –

Racine raced across the street, howling, and threw herself into the landlords, like a bowling bowl knocking down pins.

*

The *Boeuf et Bière* Tavern was bustling. In a frilly barmaid outfit, which was required but whenever she passed the long mirror she had to admit she looked quite good in it, Gabrielle Parnasse skillfully managed to balance a heavy tray, overloaded with mugs and plates.

She spun through the crowded maze of rowdy lunch customers, piling more mugs on her tray, wiping tables, getting pelted with food, grabbing pitchers…yet all with a gracious smile.

"Excuse me, pardon me, coming through, serving my gents, excuse me, pardon me."

A drunk tried to kiss her, yet exhausted as she was she pirouetted away, gracefully missing another patron, but a third smashed into her, and she went sprawling, everything on her tray landing with a crash.

Amid the laughter filling the room, the tavern owner looked over and grimaced.

"That's coming out of your pay."

*

The doors flew open at the headquarters of the Musketeers, and two of their men dragged a petulant and struggling Racine across the oak-paneled room. That it took two men surprised both the Musketeers. It surprised Racine, as well, though she was surprised that it only had taken two. She must have been very hungry, she thought.

They brought her to a low, mahogany table, where Captain André Mersenne looked up. At the age of 33, he was a bit rough-edged perhaps, but a leader. He was used to taking charge, but before he could get a word out –

"The devil bastard pig-scum of a landlord was having the father thrown in prison!" Racine spat out.

"Disturbing the peace," the arresting Musketeer noted to his superior.

André gave the man a sardonic look that said, "No kidding…" And with a motion from him, they released their hold of the struggling young woman.

"I have a pardon from Cardinal Mazarin!" she instantly snapped and slammed a parchment down on the table.

Mersenne quickly skimmed it. "I'm very impressed," he nodded, and then glancing again at the paper to double-check what was written there, he added, "…'Lady Racine.'"

And then tore it up.

Racine churned inside to his dismissive action, but rather than showing her hurt — and concern that her surefire ploy had failed — instead took the offensive. For if Racine had learned anything in her life, when you take the lead it throws other off their guard and often, if you're lucky, makes them think you actually *are* in charge of the situation. Or at least they see that you believe you should be.

"Are you calling me a liar?!" she snapped with as much outraged, feigned umbrage as one could possibly muster.

"No, no," Mersenne replied with the most decorous and considerate calm. "A very talent forger."

For just a smallest moment, it was Racine's turn to be taken aback. But Racine was rarely ever taken aback by anything longer than the smallest moment. Immediately, she charged back. "I'd like to speak to your superior! Which I assume is anyone here."

"Miss Racine," the Musketeer warmly smiled, "if we arrested everyone in France these days for disturbing the peace, there would be no one left to defend it. We'd just like you to spend an hour as our guest, to calm yourself."

Though he may have expected his words to be taking as defusing the situation, what the officer didn't realize was that, unlike most rational humans, it was the very wrong thing to say to Racine, and had the most opposite effect.

"Calm myself?" she said, taking a step towards

him. "If my family hadn't been destroyed while your big, fat, Musketeer asses sat, looked the other way and let it happen, I wouldn't need to calm myself. But here's what you *can* do. You can set up an audience for me with the king. He has said he wants to protect his people. All of them. *All*. So, maybe he can help get my family back. Because as sure as hell the Musketeers can't. I don't need the Musketeers, what I need is to talk to the king. Now!"

And with that, meaning every word she said, and building in anger as she said it, she slammed her fist and glared the most penetrating glare at the officer and held her ground, almost daring him to arrest her.

So, it was the last thing in the world that Racine expected when Captain Mersenne leaned forward and replied, warmly. "Between you and me, I don't think anyone needs the Musketeers either," he smiled with almost a sense of friendly confidentiality. "Unfortunately, the law is written that way. I am very sorry."

Racine stood there, not knowing what to say. He came over to lead her courteously to the bench. But as soon as he yanked her arm, she then knew exactly the words.

"No, what you are…" and she pulled her arm away, "is a pigheaded, frightened little moron."

André stopped, and stepped close to her. He was so very polite, but even more steely. "If you want to be belligerent, I can play that game far better than you can imagine. You *must* trust me on this."

Racine had never dealt with an officer like this.

Again, she struggled to regain the offensive. But she found it. "What's your name?! I want to remember it."

He paused for just the briefest moment.

"My name is André Mersenne. Captain of the Musketeers. Please. I implore you. Remember it."

CHAPTER EIGHT

Along the boulevards of Paris, business went on, but not as usual. Little in this grand city was as usual these days. Shops were open for business, but their doors were not kept invitingly ajar for all to enter. Most were shut, allowing for the owner to have a few extra, valuable moments to decide if the visitor entering was there to buy or steal. Some shops even now kept their doors locked during business hours, requiring permission to enter.

The parks and gardens, long the soul of Paris, still stood lush and green, for even in a time of suspicion and mistrust no Parisian would let beauty lapse. But though picturesque as ever, they seemed like a lonely beauty who men avoided, sure they had no place with her. After all, with their woodlands and ponds, parks provided far too many places for toughs to hide, and offered places where bodies could be more easily disposed of. Where there *were* visitors, it was almost always in pairs or more. Lovers still walked hand-in-hand, that would never change in Paris, though they no longer sought out furtive spots to slip away to. It was a rare brave man or woman who strolled alone.

Life did go on in Paris, as it must, for the city not only served as the heart of France but, as many French believed, of the world, as well. Others looked to Paris for direction, and it was the city's pleasure, duty and honor to lead, even if it was done with a sense of superiority. Yet even the most special feel wary when conditions demand it. Pickpockets and outright street thugs had their way. Beatings and even daylight murders were more common than ever before. And the dangers outside at night were not to be considered behind locked doors. But life most go on, most especially in Paris. Even if it meant that the grace of life was not quite as graceful as it should be.

But the highest refinement did remain. For some, it gave life meaning. And through the crowded streets of the busy, hungry, mistrustful, amiable, hard-working, corrupt, and poor, an elegant carriage sluggishly clomped along through the streets of Paris. Beautifully appointed with swirling ridges and gold-leaf edges, the white horses wore bridles that cost more than some families they passed earned in months.

Seated inside was the Count de Beaufort, aide-de-camp to the Marquis. As he passed by the bustling activity along the street for block after long block, he couldn't be bothered by the ungainly sights. Indeed, he disdained it and purposefully avoided eye contact.

The voice of a town crier broke through.

"*Oyez, Oyez!* By order of the king!"

But *that* got the Count's riveted attention. He instantly tapped his pearl-handled cane on the front of the cab, and called out to his driver to slow.

A curious assembly had gathered around the crier, whose associate was nailing a flier upon a wall. To waiting ears, anxious to find the important news of the day, he called out for all to hear.

"His Royal Highness Louis Quatorze proclaims that from this day forth, all roads closed by private decree are now open to all, free of tariff, for the transport of food and the national good!"

In his carriage, a look of strained concern crossed the Count de Beaufort. He ordered his driver on faster, and when the coach didn't move fast enough, he banged on the panel hard as he could and cursed the man out.

The carriage sped through the boulevard, knocking several pedestrians down, but no matter, this was important. It made its way down streets and across squares, though avoiding nasty alleys, until finally reaching to the magnificent townhouse of the Marquis de Longueville. Within moments, de Beaufort – a man not given to leaping or fast movement of any sort, that sort of thing was for rabble – had leaped from the carriage and clacked his way through the hallways, stepping past shocked servants who had never seen the man move as swiftly.

Behind closed doors with the Marquis, Eduard – who liked being shocked by anything less than almost anything in the world – was shocked.

CHAPTER NINE

The *Boeuf et Bière* was at the end of its luncheon, and once again beef had been of much less interest to patrons than was the beer. Gabrielle had only just been able to start catching her breath. The tavern had been quite busy that day, but then it was always busier than most bars, given its prime location for lost victims of Paris. Just down the block from where the Musketeers were stationed, they came in shaken, unsatisfied, and in need of something to calm their spirits. Or at the very least, simply a place to sit and commiserate with themselves.

It was hectic, but at least the work paid good tips. A harried, but always smiling Gabrielle carried a tray of food and mugs, though mostly mugs, the food seemed there almost for decoration, to eight beer-drinking men, who would be best and most politely described as louts.

As she handed one his beer, another slapped her on the rear. She held in a sigh. After all, it was part of the job.

"Hey, nice ass," he smirked.

She put on a big smile for the audience. "You have fine taste." And then continued right on serving the meal. A veal chop was placed on the table, just as she received another slap on the rear.

"He's right," the second loud said. "You do have one nice ass."

"We've been together many years," she said.

His friend next to him chimed in, "I hope that chop is as nice as your..."

He raised his hand to swat, but she politely grabbed it. She smiled warmly, but added pointedly, "Two is my limit per table."

The door swung open, and a gypsy girl entered, still muttering to herself about some pig-scum bastard who didn't know his ass from his ass. But no one paid her any attention, which was just fine with her, because she didn't pay them any, either.

Racine headed over to the bar. Biding her time as she waited for someone to serve her, she spotted some loose tip coins laying on the counter. She looked around – trying to find their rightful owner, no doubt – but seeing that no one claimed the money, or saw her, she pocketed it.

Eventually, Gabrielle returned to the bar to drop off her empty tray, and passed next to this new customer.

Service at last, Racine thought tartly, sure she was being avoided. "How you doing?"

"Just fine," Gabrielle replied, "as long as you don't tell me I have a nice ass." She took out a rag and wiped off the counter, looking for the tip she had thought would be left for her, but it was so like these drunks to stiff her. "What's your pleasure? Lunch is over, but you look like you could use an ale."

"Anything to get rid of the stench of that damn Musketeer headquarters."

Gabrielle gave her a look that said you're not the first. "We get a lot of customers who've been there, reporting some crime. Hey, what's bad for Paris is good for business. *C'est la vie.* That's <u>her</u> story."

She nodded towards the front of the tavern where a young, well-dressed girl was huddled alone by the window, protectively holding on to a cup of coffee as if it was her only friend. Which it might well have been.

The girl, a child almost in this den of harsh wayfarers, stood out as seeming not one of their usual patrons. But of course not only did Charlotte not seem one of their usual patrons, she had never been in a tavern in her life.

It would have been apparent to anyone, as it was to one of the tipsy louts at his mug-laden table, where his buddies were busy carousing. He noticed Charlotte by herself and nudged a friend. They all turned, winking among one another. Two of the men stumbled over.

Back at the bar, Gabrielle was serving Racine an ale.

"Actually, this is just a temporary job," she was telling the gypsy, who wasn't listening all that closely, nor making much of an effort to appear as if she was, though that didn't especially matter to the waitress, as long as she was interested enough to follow the theme of what was being said and not leave, yet. "I'm really an actress. I have an audition next week – wish me luck. I guess you could say it's sort of my calling. Okay, true, I've done a lot of other jobs but, well, that's part of the training an actress needs. It's like I told my friend Jacqueline, she's an actress, too, I said you have to have experiences. You have to be a great student of human behavior."

"Not to mention have a nice ass," Racine added sarcastically. "Sorry, d'you mind —"

She noted her ale, that she was busily focused on finishing it, looking for any excuse to end this conversation. Or monologue. And finally, she just turned away. Across the room, a spat got her attention.

Two drunken punks were looming over a young girl who was quietly shaking her head, "no." Not taking the hint, or taking it but not caring that she didn't want to join them, the men simply took things into their own hands, literally. They lifted her chair, and carried the frightened girl over to the table.

Racine tensed, furious at this. How dare they push themselves on someone? How dare they not leave that girl alone? How dare they grab a poor, defenseless — she leapt up.

"Hey!!!"

Her voice cut through the room. One of the drunks couldn't help but turn at the sound coming in his direction. What he saw glaring at him was another pretty young thing. With an aggressive smile, that was more a leer, he said, "You have a problem, *mamzell*?"

"I have a big problem, you little…"

As she stood, Gabrielle quickly reached out to stop Racine and pulled her back.

"No. Please," the waitress quietly said, so as not to antagonize anything further. She'd had enough trouble already that day. "I know how to handle this. I've seen what men are like when they drink <u>much</u> too much."

She pointedly pled with Racine, "*Not now.*"

Racine's instinct was to ignore this person holding her back – actually, her first instinct was to punch someone holding her – but if that annoying waitress had had a bad day and this would make it worse, fine, whatever, she didn't want to keep listening to her, and besides the girl knew her own job, and so Racine sat and grudgingly nursed her ale.

Instead, Gabrielle grabbed a pitcher of beer. Then, ever the professional, and knowing her customers – and herself – stopped and unbuttoned the top buttons on her blouse, and put on a smile.

"It's on the house, gentlemen," she said, as she arrived at the table.

As Racine watched, she had to battle all her anger and keep from screaming, not just at that pathetic, beer-filled scum, but that idiot excuse of a waitress, as well.

And that waitress plopped the pitcher on the table, the foam splashing over the rim.

For the next hour, foam continued to splash over the rims and down the gullets of the eight men. Gabrielle continued delivering beer to them, all on the house, though it was mostly out of her own pocket. Anything, she would tell Racine each time she got a new refill, to keep the men happy. As long as poor Charlotte was wedged in between them, she didn't want to risk even the slightest bit of trouble. She knew what she was doing, she kept telling Racine, trust her. Given that Racine hadn't trusted anyone in eight years, it wasn't an admonition that stood much of a chance of being followed. But as long as Gabrielle saw that Racine was still peering at the drunks slobbering over the poor girl, jostling her in their revelry, and that this hellion would take any excuse to go after them and, therefore, she kept feeding the gypsy free sandwiches, Racine was more than happy to stay in her seat, biding her time, and having her first real and continuous meal in a very long time.

As the afternoon ran into the early evening, Gabrielle kept the flow of ale, and the smiles and the winks and the stories, and the slaps on the backside going, making sure the eight men were happy and comfortable and contentedly drunk as could be. She would slip a bite of food to that young girl, and make sure she was all right, and so the girl would nod that she was fine, though her eyes said please get her out of there. But this was no place to fight against the current. No one in the room was about to help out, not even the owner, and it had to be tolerated. Crushingly tolerated. And so the men yelled and sang and shoved each other, offered Charlotte drinks, laughed at her refusals, and the table was one boisterous, laughter-filled party.

A dozen empty pitchers now covered the table. Charlotte was largely acceptant of her present fate, understanding that it was no worse than horribly uncomfortable and had become almost insensitive to it, unhappily resigned to her evening. Gabrielle patted her comfortingly, and dropped off another pitcher.

All the while, Racine sat at the bar, seething, as dusk filled the room. She had had her fill of sustenance

69

and of waiting, and none of it any longer met her needs. Only one thing would do that. As Gabrielle brought back more pitchers, she grabbed the waitress.

"You're an embarrassment."

"Not now." She busily picked up a new tray from the counter. Hearing the drunken voices, though, louder than ever, she quickly turned back to look at the louts.

"Give us a kiss," one of them slobbered at Charlotte. The young girl shrank back, getting a wet lip on the cheek.

"You know what I think?" His buddy slurred incoherently, as he guzzled his beer incoherently. "The best of here you men to France and you. All you."

Very calmly, as her eyes tightened almost imperceptibly, Gabrielle stopped what she was doing, put down her tray, looked at Racine and then, she said just one simple word –

"_Now._"

It finally hit Racine what Gabrielle had been up to all along: getting these men stone-cold drunk. Her eyes lit up.

The eight drunken louts were swaying around their table. None even noticed when Racine arrived. Her body was tingling.

"It's time all you children apologize to the young lady," she said, catching some of their attention. "Real Frenchmen know how to satisfy women. I'm guessing you'd have a hard time knowing how to satisfy yourself."

Gabrielle came by with a tray to clean up.

The man closest to Racine had heard her little speech and through bleary eyes twisted a pompous, slushed smile at her.

"Bet I you'd like to find out. Want to join us, little lady?"

"Pour us a *beer* a beer beer, wench," his friend bumbled.

"I'm very happy to pour you a beer," Racine replied.

And with that, she took a pitcher, poured it over the head of the utterly-surprised oaf – and punched his lights out.

Gabrielle suddenly whacked a second drunk in the head with her tray, and he went down, as well.

Two other of the inebriated men tried to stand – but they passed out halfway up.

That was four down. And hardly a moment had passed.

The drunk with his arm around Charlotte struggled to his feet to help his friends in trouble. The young girl suddenly realized what was going on with the other two women – and she cold-cocked the man with a pitcher.

One of the remaining three men stood and had the presence of mind to pull out his sword. Gabrielle quickly grabbed a rapier from one of the unconscious men. Not quite certain at first what to do, she started to brandish the sword every which way and dance around him, spinning almost like stage choreography. As he tried to follow her, twirling and turning, he got wobbly. Unfocused. Dizzy keeping her in sight.

71

Wobbling a bit as – and then he dropped like a rock.

Two men were left.

Both were fighting Racine at the same time. Steadier than their friends, they were nonetheless drunk, and she was impressive, holding them off as they thrashed angrily at her. She parried and blocked them, time and again, and even made an advance or two. However, they were two, she was one, and they were strong and fought like bulls. Worse, like drunken, crazed bulls.

And then, with a crash from behind, Gabrielle smashed a chair on one of the men.

The other spun to look. It was a big mistake, because he then whipped back to Racine. And she immediately belted him, and he dropped like a shot.

All eight were vanquished. The three women met up, exhausted, amazed and absolutely, unabashedly thrilled.

Amid the ruins of drunken, beaten men covering the floor, the tavern owner tripped through the rubble of broken chairs and shattered glass to Gabrielle. He looked at her a moment, trying to gather himself and find the right words. In the end, the words were very easy to discover.

"You are so very fired."

Out in the street, the three women were on a high, as they rambled through the night, waving their swords liked captured spoils of war.

"That was *incroyable*. Unbelievable." Racine swashed her sword enthusiastically around her.

"It was quite wonderful," Charlotte stated quietly

in agreement, allowing herself a warm smile, though inside she was so overwhelmed, almost bewildered by what had taken place, unlike anything she had ever experienced. Yet still she found herself bursting deep inside with joy.

"*Magnifique*," Gabrielle shouted. And then with a sort of shrug acknowledged, "I did just lose my room, they let me sleep in the back, but – *C'est la guerre…*!"

"Indeed, we are in quite the same position," Charlotte thoughtfully ventured. "I was hoping to stay with my cousin, the Count de Vieuville, but it's not possible."

Racine threw her arm and tattered sleeve around the young girl. "Ohhh, Princess, yes, we're all exactly the same."

Before Charlotte could react, a brick was thrown by a nearby looter, and it went crashing past. The women quickly headed around the corner.

They found a quiet spot and took their bearings. None of which at that moment were very good.

"I have a trunk in storage of value," Charlotte offered hesitantly. "Perhaps that could be of assistance?"

"You know," Racine nodded with dripping sarcasm, "I'll just bet there is a big market for petticoats and lace hankies."

A pistol shot rang out nearby. There was a clamor of feet across the cobbles and much shouting and the sound of pushed bodies. A small crowd suddenly came running by, which the others deftly avoided, but Charlotte was knocked down. She rolled in the dirt, where her cloak got torn, and only missed being stomped on.

Gabrielle kept herself plastered against a wall for protection. "Ah, Paris. City of Joy."

On the ground, Charlotte pushed to right herself, and pricked her thumb on something small, crying out. But when she looked, a warm, almost comforting smile slowly crossed her face.

"A wild rose." A tear crossed her eye, as it brought back a dear memory to her, at the very moment she needed one more than anything. "My father and I would look for these. It is so beautiful, and rare. It grows alone and has tougher thorns to sustain itself on its own."

"Wonderful. Maybe it's edible." Racine just shook her head and rolled her eyes to the skies. "Come on. Let's go liberate your 'resources.'"

Worlds changed slowly. The continents took eons to shift, mountain ranges needed ages to rise. Yet a future that touches us all can turn in the fastest instant, and be unknown to those at its center. And so it was that the three women, whose lives at any other time should not have ever imaginably crossed, headed off, together.

Book Two

CHAPTER TEN

A sumptuous bounty was laid out across the table, covered with an exquisitely embroidered lace cloth. Minted lamb, roasted pheasant, truffles and yams, a bouillabaisse, two suckling pigs no less, delicacies imported from the South Seas, buttery croissants so flakey they might fall apart just by being looked at, and so much more, the food kept arriving in timely waves, shavings of fruit ice for the palate between each course, and wines, so much wine, the very best vintages overflowing from the very best vineyards of the very best districts of Bordeaux, Burgundy and Champagne. The table was headed by the Marquis and surrounded by his closest associates, along with men and women co-conspirators. Though the finest meal was being served, outrage was the main course.

"It's insolence," the Count de Beaufort snarled. "The Cardinal and Regent continue to block our way. They flaunt their actions to our face. The gall."

It was indeed gall, they all agreed, and far worse. Indeed, one nobleman who had been pontificating all evening had finally begun to have enough. His impatience had grown, so much that he dared even to challenge his host. Politely, of course. For there was a limit to how far one dared go up against the Marquis, and that line was uncertain. But these were all men and women used to getting their own way on their own terms, and Marquis or not, they would be heard. "Eduard," he said politely, yes, so politely, yet far more pointedly, that his challenge was quite clear, so clear that several guests tensed, "some may not be so willing as you to wait. Some may desire change *now*."

Eduard dabbed his mouth, sipped his wine – and a simple look sent the servants out. They knew their master well, down to the raise of an eyebrow. Reading one's master was a language unto itself, and almost more important than a servant's native tongue. The room emptied of all but those conspiratorial souls, and their leader gracefully walked through the room. All eyes were upon him.

Eduard spoke calmly, and carefully. His words direct, knowing the importance that everyone there understood, though making sure to himself that they didn't understand everything. He knew well what he was doing and why. That was all they needed to know.

"All my plans come with assistance from *within* the palace. I have taken great care to bring down our enemy with aid *from inside*. I trust you each understand this simple, yet profound truth – far better to take time and force abdication than face the blood of fighting a Civil War." With a smile, he continued his path around the room, making sure that each person there knew to keep the confidences he was telling them. But most of all, he pointedly fixed his gaze at his challenger. "You know less than you think.

He bolted the door locked.

"What I know is the Royals may _never_ abdicate," came the polite, but sharp reply.

Eduard offered a graceful nod, but inside he gnashed at the smallness of such thinking. Did they not believe he was thinking many steps ahead of them? Did any of them dare challenge his leadership? The mere thought of such insolence was itself beyond acceptable. Yet, his voice simply grew quieter, calmer, it seemed, so that all present were forced to listen closer.

"And if so, *then* we would strike. But in warfare, one strikes only when the enemy is least prepared. And the crown will be least prepared on the <u>day</u> of the *Gala National*. For that is when the crown's forces are pre-occupied for the festival."

He swiped his sword at a candle three times. And then tapped off the still-standing pieces, each dropping to the table. One. Two. Three.

And suddenly, he whirled and stabbed the noble to death.

The room became silent. Frozen faces peered in a combination of disbelief, horror and fear, and for a bold few, even admiration. Eduard watched them all. And made sure they watched him. When he had every last ounce of attention –

"You are with us. Or you fall."

*

So different was the room of those against whom the Marquis was arming his most intricate plans. In the Queen Mother's chambers, there was no grand party, no overflow of nobles, no swords and most definitely no blood. But all was as coldly focused as was the Marquis.

The early morning dusk had only just begun to break. Here, with only the Major standing his guard, the Regent paced by her desk, as Cardinal Mazarin sat studying the latest report that intelligence had gathered, thin though that intelligence was. However, every small word was critical, since it was impossible to know not only where the kidnapped monarch was, but from whom the attack came. And so the two leaders there struggled to hone their response. And the response of each of them was a cause of disagreement.

"We are certain *now*, however," the Queen Mother stated brusquely, "that this was not an attack by an enemy nation. We know, sir, *know* the king is held by aristocrats."

"But the problem is greater." The Cardinal put down this parchment. He was tired, having worked through the night, but they both were tired. He had to make his point understood. "From what I am also informed, we believe a foreign envoy is here inside our borders to build an alliance with them. We may soon be fighting an adversary without, *as well as* within."

"And yet," she shot back, for she needed to make her point understood, "you still refuse to say the traitor is Eduard do Longueville."

"There is no doubt that the Marquis benefits from our distress. Yes. But whether he is the cause of it, or laughing at our expense, it is impossible as yet to swear. This is no time, Your Highness, for a wrong guess."

"Then I strongly suggest we use *all* our resources to determine who."

There was a brief silence between the two. Mazarin offered the slightest sigh.

"With *Parlement* now holding up funds, it has added further burden to our efforts."

"I don't want to hear what can't be done. That is their goal, this is Civil War. Someone has kidnapped…" she paused a moment, unable perhaps to say who was kidnapped, or perhaps it was to find the right word, "…France. If we must use my personal assets, use them! What benefit are they if France falls??"

At that moment, the door burst open, and Gaston, Duke of Orléans bustled in. The Duke was a powerful presence, though with an air of puffery. As his daughter was known throughout the nation as but "*La Grande Mademoiselle*," he was recognized as simply "*Monsieur*."

"Have we solved the world's problems yet?"

"Good morning, Duke," his sister-in-law, the Regent, returned.

Cardinal Mazarin warmly acknowledged the Duke, though with a hidden wariness. "Monsieur Gaston. Your daughter continues to recover from her wounds?"

"*Mademoiselle* is made of strong stock. It comes from her father," he spouted, with a laugh, though he wasn't joking. Turning pointedly from the Cardinal, he addressed instead the soldier who had remained stoic throughout, "But to the point, have you any news, Major, of my nephew?"

"There is a squad of men who may be close to an answer. I cannot say more."

"Cannot, or will not?"

Mazarin regained the conversation. "The Major advises that some things must remain in quiet. I concur."

"Hold, sir," *Monsieur* Gaston spun back. "You take the word of a Major over the demand of a Duke?? No, sir."

"It is how we must proceed." The Cardinal and Duke held each other's glare.

No love was lost between the two men. This interloper, the Duke thought quietly to himself – and said often out loud to others, who agreed – a foreigner from Italy, overseeing France? It was not seemly. Mazarin was much too close with the Queen Mother, *far* too close with her, for his liking, and the liking of others. She was quite a beautiful woman. Where was this Cardinal's loyalty? With Italy? With the Regent alone? With the church? Or with France?

This pompous pretender, Mazarin had long thought to himself, and kept the thought there. The Duke had no skills, no leadership, no accomplishments, yet had always yearned to be king. Jealous of his brother, and far more jealous of his child nephew. Never showing the loyalty he should by his birth. Often siding with the aristocrats against the crown, only returning to favor the crown when it suited him, and then back again, and forth. It was clear where the man's loyalty lay. It was with himself.

"When my brother was king," the Duke said with command and force, drawing himself tall as he could, and taking a step towards the Cardinal, "when my brother was king, things proceeded as they should."

"Alas, *Monsieur*," the Queen Mother interposed, "your brother is no longer king. My son is."

CHAPTER ELEVEN

Shafts of light streamed through the wide cracks in an old barn. Charlotte was sleeping like an angel, laying in a hay stack. Racine came over, watched a moment and then put her face right up to the girl.

"On, Princess. Have to get up. It's morning."

The young, sweet girl lay there with her eyes still closed. She scrunched her nose and rolled her body, wiping away strands of hair that tickled her nose. Her voice was rasped and could barely be heard.

"I'll have toast and jam."

The barn was quite empty, but equipment hung on the wall, and barrels of hay were spread around. A high-hanging rafter stored a lonely sack of grain. Charlotte's trunk, which had been rescued the night before, rested in a corner.

"And me, I'll have poached eggs and tea cake," Racine replied.

And with her foot, the gypsy pushed Charlotte off the hay, and she thudded onto the ground.

The girl's eyes shot open, and though she was now fully awake, she was also totally disoriented.

"What…? Where…?"

Gabrielle was off by a water-filled trough, drying off. She called back.

"Time to face the day."

"I don't want to. I want to stay here." The heiress cowered up in a ball. "I don't like Paris, it scares me."

"Just because no police are around?" Gabrielle asked sarcastically. "Not a *flic* in sight, no Musketeer to be found in the world?"

"This is not the world, it's the world gone mad."

Not bothering to pay much attention to these two, Racine was gathering up her belongings, and while she was at it also grabbed some clothes from out of Charlotte's trunk.

"And I wish you well with it. *Au revoir, mes deux amis.* Good luck to you."

"Where are you going???" a surprised Gabrielle asked.

It was hardly the gypsy's first time sleeping in a barn, and she understood the game all too well. In some ways, such establishments were her abode away from home. And home for her almost never existed.

"Checkout time for trespassing is sun up. You have to believe me on this."

Charlotte quickly sat up, trying to keep a look of concern from crossing her face. "I thought we could all be...we could perhaps talk, get to know one another," she said almost too cheerfully. "I love to read," she added right away. "And dance! What do you enjoy??"

"Well, one time I had a noose around my neck," Racine answered.

"No!" an alarmed Charlotte cried. "Certainly if you stayed here it would be safer."

"I learned long ago that you survive by trusting your own back. And you would be heavy loads to carry." She turned to Charlotte, "And you, Princess, would be a boulder."

At the young girl's reaction, withdrawing a bit, protectively at the insult, but also the truth, Gabrielle came over and comfortingly laid a hand on her shoulder. "Don't worry, Charlotte, we'll find you some place. It's important to have someone you can rely on."

"Oh, God," Racine shook her head, "I just had this image of the blind leading the pathetically blind."

Charlotte had no ready response, but stared petulantly at her. And staring on, she suddenly noticed something, it was clear as day. Though she had no answer to Racine's charges, she most certainly had a thing to say about *this*. And she would. "You took my scarf!" she challenged, straightening up, as close to aggressive as Charlotte could get. "I want it back."

Racine looked at her wearily. Then, almost sweetly – or as close to sweetly as Racine could get –

"I think you are the most precious, little wild rose I have ever met in my life."

"No one should take what isn't theirs," Charlotte said defiantly, not giving an inch. Though a bit wary doing so.

"So, now you're a crusader for justice?" Racine smiled and turned to Gabrielle. "And you? Together you're going off alone? Into this mad world?"

"How is being on your own working out for you?" Gabrielle asked, with more than a hint of sarcasm. This certainly wasn't her fight, but she didn't care one bit for the gypsy dragging her into a snit with the rich girl.

"You have no idea how I fear for you both," Racine shot back sharply. "Really. You can't take care of yourselves."

"I'm *very* good with a sword," Gabrielle said quickly, explaining her experience, less to defend her honor and training than to perhaps make sure her stage credentials were *quite* well-known, thank you very much.

"And my father made sure I could always protect myself. I've taken lessons," Charlotte returned with great pride.

Racine ignored Gabrielle, but stared incredulously at Charlotte. And then suddenly she whipped a sword at her.

Charlotte dropped it.

"God help you both."

"I said I knew how to sword fight," Charlotte insisted, more strongly than before. She glared at Racine.

But the gypsy just scoffed and walked away. With Racine's back to her face and disappearing from view, Charlotte felt deeply insulted, a feeling she was not used to at all. And her spirit showed. She grabbed a sword.

"*En garde!*"

The young girl waited, poised, her sword held upright, taught. Charlotte's positioning was immaculate, and her balance perfect. She peered out with a challenge in her eyes. The sword shook only a little.

Racine turned, and chuckled. But she couldn't help admire the sweet young thing's response. She grabbed a sword and…clink. The two swords lightly touched.

A slight shiver of excitement and uncertainty ran through Charlotte. But then Racine tested the very-overmatched girl and began backing her around the room, with a short jab here and a quick joust there. And another, and more.

"No," Racine offered. "Use two hands if you have to."

She jabbed again. Charlotte hung on, and even did try two-handed, as she backed around the dusty floor.

"Not fair leaving me out," Gabrielle cried, and jumped in with a sword, two now against Racine. The actress, in fact, wasn't bad at all, as she'd showed on stage. Racine easily outclassed them both, smoothly parrying every thrust they made and forcing them awkwardly on the defensive, but what began as a chiding attack now took on a vibrant life of its own.

"Watch your weak side," Racine instructed, as she attacked Gabrielle who tried to spin away but got caught in the charge.

The gypsy then quickly turned her attention and with careful, swift moves guided Charlotte around the floor, and backed her way toward a ladder hanging down from the rafter. The girl awkwardly fended Racine off until backed against the rungs, and as the gypsy kept pressing her, had no choice but to climb the steps – Racine following, with Gabrielle coming after, hoping to find an opening of attack against the talented swordswoman, but still getting rebuffed as Racine would turn and quickly swipe.

Up the ladder they went, higher, until Racine thwacked at Charlotte's sword – which was knocked from her hand…and fell towards Gabrielle, as Racine quickly ducked out of the way.

"Oh, my God…" Gabrielle cried, just barely avoiding the blade, but losing her grip of the ladder. She hung on with one hand, dangling there, but her fingers began to slip. Racine grabbed and pulled her back until Gabrielle was able to regain her footing.

Scrabbling their way up, at last they reached the rafter, jubilant. Overflowing with energy. Laughter filled the barn, with shouts of exhilaration. Gabrielle did a little dance, spinning around as space permitted. Charlotte made victorious circles with her sword, delicate they were, but the mark of surviving this test, no matter how small, for it was not part of her normal day. Even Racine permitted herself a smile, and when Gabrielle gave her a little push, she accepted it with rare good nature, and gave an even rarer salute with her steel. And with so much exuberance, and so little room, there was only one outlet for it.

"Yes!"

Racine leapt off the platform and floated joyfully through the air, far down below, at last landing in the hay pile.

Gabrielle followed.

"Pour la France!!!"

Jumping down, she flew with her arms spread like a bird, tumbling through the air, trusting in faith and the protection of hay, and flopped in the stack, as well.

They waited for Charlotte.

But the young girl stood frozen on the rafter.

"Come on!" Racine called.

"Jump! It's easy."

Still, though, Charlotte didn't move. Not a single muscle. She stood at the edge, peering into what she saw was an abyss. Forty feet into the dark pit of hell. Everything turned blurry and dark before her. She couldn't even move a step back to safer territory.

"You can do it," Racine again shouted, with more urgency, and perhaps a bit of ridicule to press the girl on. "Jump."

"If she doesn't want to jump," a disembodied voice suddenly called out, echoing through the barn, "she shouldn't jump."

A small gray-haired man stood in the doorway. Auguste Fleury may have been in his 70s, and moved more slowly than he wished, with a twinkle about his eye, but he also had a determined way. And right now, with the sunlight streaming in behind him, he was very determined.

The three women's boisterous enthusiasm came to a sudden halt. Not a sound was heard in the barn, as their attention was riveted on the doorway, halfway angry between their private party being intruded upon and half desperately-concerned over being found out.

The silence was thick and palpable. It was left to Racine, of course, to break it.

"What the hell are you doing in here?!!"

When you spend your entire life on the defensive, after all, you learn that not only the best defense, but most often the *only* defense is to take the offensive. And Racine knew she could be as offensive as anyone.

The old man, though, simply looked back. "You mean in my barn?"

"Yes!" she shot back as quickly and aggressively as she could. "How long have you been standing in 'your barn' spying on us?!"

"Long enough to know you're damn fools."

Gabrielle was now far more curious by this odd response than she was fearful. "And how would you know that?"

"Because you're too busy arguing to realize you all want the same thing." And then, he added as a pointed afterthought, "And I trained a swordfighting champion. And I'm guessing *you* haven't."

And with that, the gray-haired *M*. Fleury, turned and waddled off.

Leaving three young women standing in an empty barn with nothing but wide-open eyes covering their faces. And open mouths unable to speak.

CHAPTER TWELVE

Thunderbolts last only an instant and then life goes on. Eventually, the women regained the power of speech, thought and movement. Clearly the old man had not called for the *gendarmes*, nor had he even thrown them off his property. They had no idea where that left them, however, and felt utterly disoriented. Even Racine, who had a well-developed first instinct (and second) at a hint of danger wasn't sure if this was a threat – or A Good Thing. The little fellow had shown a brusqueness, yet also a warmth, and even, it almost sounded, like an offer of assistance. But assistance of what?

The other two couldn't help answer. They were as befuddled. They only thing they did know was that the one person who could answer was walking away. And they went racing out after him.

He couldn't be bothered, he said, he had things to do, though when pressed he had a hard time explaining what those things were. His days seemed pretty slow and empty, but there were chores. Oh, my yes, there were chores, and if he didn't get them done, his dear one would never let him hear the end of it. So, if you'll please excuse him, he had things to do.

As he padded away, the women went with him. There was comfort in his kindness, and they also still wanted to know what in the world he meant.

"Oh, please," he said, "I can tell you're smart young women. You know." And they nodded knowingly. Yes, it was clear. But the truth was they didn't know. So, they did what smart young women do, they kept following him.

When the laundry had to be hung, he tossed it from the

basket over the line, but Gabrielle stepped in and smoothed everything out neatly and clipped on the pins. And they all asked him questions.

When the chickens had to be fed, he struggled with the heavy bucket, and Charlotte took it from him and continued to spread the seed. What a strange world it was, she marveled. This little man, hidden off in a corner of the world. "You trained a swordfighting champion?" she wanted to ask, how wondrous, but a lady didn't intrude into such personal matters.

None of this seemed like it had anything to do with what they'd been arguing about, but the more he talked he made so much sense. He seemed quite wise. Was that simply because he had lived so long? Was that what wisdom was? Experience and remembering it? Or had he lived so long *because* he was so wise?

When a wheelbarrow had to be repaired, he put the new slat in place and took out some nails, but before he could reach the hammer, Racine picked it up – and handed it to Charlotte, who pounded at the board, though she kept missing the nail. Eventually, Racine took it back – and handed it to Gabrielle, who pounded the board in place. Auguste didn't say much about himself, he was shy that way, but not shy about much else. He had opinions about pretty much how to solve the problems of the world. Starting with the three girls in front of him.

There were some vegetables in the garden to pick, and he got half a sack filled before Gabrielle took over.

"You don't have to do this, you know," he said. "I'm quite capable of grabbing a tomato. I'm not dead yet, you know."

"It's nothing," she replied, and it really was. But what Gabrielle wanted to shout was, "You trained a swordfighting champion! Tell us about it!" but left it at "It's nothing." Well, that and, "Once, you know, I played a farmer's wife in a charming little play, *La Petite Jardin*. My friend Louise said she could almost taste my vegetables sitting in the tenth row." She then went on to explain how she practiced for the role with a local gardener which wasn't the same as a farmer, but an actress had to make do with what they have… – to which Racine interrupted to say it was impressive that Gabrielle must have struggled a great deal for her art, and then returned the conversation to Auguste, from whom she still was deeply curious by what he had said, and hadn't said.

As the morning heated up and neared noon, Charlotte labored with the pump to get Auguste a cup of water. She was only able to manage a few drips, but the old man said that even those drop were precisely the refreshment he needed, and the young girl smiled at her accomplishment. Though it was a good thing she didn't see Racine rolling her eyes.

M. Fleury had a basket that was filled with a hearty loaf of bread, plenty of creamy brie cheese, some apples, a bottle of wine and a tart, which his dear missus had made herself. "She's the finest cook, I say, it's why I'm so plump, you know," though Charlotte politely said he wasn't so plump as he thought.

Gabrielle spread the cloth out, Charlotte carefully decanted the wine, Gabrielle made sandwiches for everyone and wouldn't hear a word from Auguste, for he had been too kind already. They all sat around and ate, though Racine sat a little ways off from the others, happy to join in the meal, just happier to join it from afar.

The old man told them of how he met his dear wife, and that their family had a dear daughter, but he was far more

91

interested in the three. What brought them to Paris, how came they to of all places in the world his barn?

The yard became a bit quieter then. Gabrielle and Charlotte told about their homes and villages, of course – and Gabrielle added a few stage credentials – but they each had a difficult time explaining further, leaving their tales that sometimes it was…well, it was simply time you had to leave home, and sometimes one must know the greater world. Racine said little, just that she traveled so much it wasn't a surprise she was in Paris or anywhere, at any time. Yet the old man never pressed any of them more than they wished to speak and understood all too well, he said, about the road of life takes us all where we don't expect it, and that's what makes the journey so exciting. "Am I right?" he said to Racine, as he offered to pour her some more wine. She moved closer with her cup.

"That's what I was telling you," he said, as he leaned back. "I couldn't help listening to you argue with one another about the same thing – the same thing," he repeated, "that brought you here. Trust, you wanted, reliance, protection." He shook his head and laughed. "And there you were, under the same roof. Sometimes it takes an old man with a lot more experience to see." He winked at them. "I may be a small man, and have small family, and live in a very small world, but I know a thing or two. Or three. You shouldn't have been fighting one another, you should have been fighting *for* each other. Helping one another. *N'est ce que pas*?!"

He started to get up, but wavered a bit and began to totter. Racine reached out and steadied him.

"You trained a swordfighting champion??" she asked. "Tell us about it."

92

*

He did more than tell them about it.

Late into the afternoon, the three women were lined up, a little out of breath (well, at least Charlotte was), practicing jabs and thrusts in the air, as Auguste watched them carefully, with the meticulous eye of one unwilling to take less than the best.

"*Eh bien.* Quick moves. But patience. Keep your balance. Parry. Now, thrust!" He kept calling out directions and encouragement.

An excited, flamboyant Gabrielle spun away with a particularly impressive flourish, landing with a theatrical twist.

"You know," she said, with a surprised thoughtfulness, "I should try that twirl at my next audition. Even if you don't get the part," she noted to Racine, "make sure they remember you."

The gypsy didn't respond immediately. Then, she turned to Charlotte.

"You, I get. *She* scares the living hell out of me."

Racine tossed over her sword to Charlotte – who, after just having done seemingly well…of course, dropped it. With a feeling of deep embarrassment, she had difficulty looking at Auguste.

"I just wish you to know I will continue striving to be my best."

"Oh, my dear," he said so comfortingly, and placed a warm hand on her shoulder, "remember, you don't have to be the best – it's that you are better, safer together. *Hélas.* Watch."

He held up his sword and waved it at Charlotte, who parried his move. Then, he waved at Racine.

"Come over here. Rush at her." A look of confusion crossed Charlotte's face as she saw Racine bearing down on her. She was like a deer frozen. Auguste focused her attention, "No, keep fighting me alone. Don't worry about her coming at you." And as Racine closed in on the young girl, he quickly called to Gabrielle, "Protect her. See! *Come ça. Vite!*"

Racine now had to push briefly to contend with Gabrielle who had come over to help, and Charlotte was left to more-comfortably battle Auguste's jabs alone.

With everything balanced, they at last stopped.

"When you trust one another," the old man drilled in the point they had all just observed, "you can walk these streets safely. Protecting yourselves."

An understanding was beginning to creep in. The three young women each stood nodding to themselves, but also daring little looks at one another.

"Your confidence only makes ours grow," Gabrielle said with heartfelt warmth.

"Oh, *mon Dieu*," the little man fumbled and scratched his head awkwardly. "I...You give an old man a way to fill up his days. Too many years ago, my dear daughter became a sword expert, and traveled across Europe. You, here, let me relive many smiles. What I can do to help three ladies, ahhh, you bring me joy."

CHAPTER THIRTEEN

The Marquis de Longueville crossed his library with a relaxed, but intent presence. He calmly placed a book back on the shelf, as candlelight illuminated the dark night.

"It's quite simple," he said to another in the room, not deigning to address the person directly, his back to him as someone of little matter. "All I require of you is to use your own hand to write a letter."

That other person was a child, a 10-year-old Louis. It was a challenging situation for anyone under such conditions. More so for one that young. Yet he was trying his best to be regal.

"I am King Louis XIV, your sovereign. I do not take commands."

Eduard smiled with much warmth, as one would to a spirited tike trying to seem precocious. He sat in his high-back leather chair. The ornate carving was imposing, just as much in the room was meant to be imposing.

"Let's just play a game and say that today you do. And today, you shall write the palace ordering the royal family to abdicate and end the monarchy." Eduard paused here to take out a cigar and light it. And to give time to let his words hang in the air and hold their point.

"Governing will return to the aristocracy," he finally continued. "This will be done before the *Gala National.* I want no celebration of your reign. The monarchy is over. It is a deadline." He took a puff, and lowered his voice even more, to almost complete calm, which made the coldness of the words even more pronounced.

"And let me make clear," he leaned ever-so-slightly

forward, "I chose that word carefully. I offer abdication to avoid bloodshed. But if these *commands*," he lingered for the briefest moment so that the word would be emphasized, "are ignored – you will be dead. Your mother will be dead. And the entire royal line will be…dead."

The child was frightened, but he had the bravado of a king.

"Never. And I will see you hanged as the traitor to France that you are. I am King Louis XIV, your sovereign," his said with all the firmness he had, as even his voice rose and he believed himself of the words. "And I command *you* to surrender. To me."

Eduard sat silently, taking the meaning of all this in. Then, he smiled. And he warmly walked over to Louis.

"I must tell you that I admire courage. And when I see it in one so young, I can only appreciate it more. Nonetheless…"

He stood now by the young boy. And then, with a quickness, his entire demeanor blackened.

There was a loud whack!! He backhanded Louis who fell to the floor. Eduard towered over him menacingly. The little boy struggled back up, but was shaken. If he had convinced himself of his authority before, all pretense now took a back seat to the reality above him, glaring down.

"*Write the damn letter. Now.*"

CHAPTER FOURTEEN

A farmer was doing the best he could under the conditions. He had his children to help, but the two eldest he most relied on were sick, and his wife needed to care for them, so that was another pair of hands he was without. He certainly couldn't afford to hire any journeyman laborers, not for the past several months at least. And though he and his neighbors would often help one another whenever they could, which wasn't often since farming was hard enough without seeking out extra hours, they were struggling as much as he.

As he slowly drove his ox through the field, a troop of Musketeers galloped past along the dusty road. The farmer took a look up from his back-wearying work, for it was a rare occurrence to see the King's Men in these parts. "About time," he thought to himself. "We could use protection here much as city folk do. More. After all, we don't have every man snooping on his neighbor living so close they should rent space up their arse, and telling the world about whatever private thing they see." Here in the country, a man keeps to himself. Minds his business. Well, no matter, better to have Musket Men patrolling late than never. And he went back to plowing and minding his own business, thinking about thin crops, low prices, and how his wife had told him just that morning she'd seen the dairyman spending a little bit too much time with *Madame* Vernais on his delivery yesterday.

Of course, the Musketeers weren't on a patrol to keep the countryside safe, but to protect the entire country. They'd been crossing France the past days and trying to be discreet about it, something difficult for even a single Musketeer showing up where he rarely was seen, and near impossible for a troop of them. But every trail had to be followed, every tale of suspicious activity and gatherings and rumor needed to be checked into.

It was fortunate that wherever any unit stopped, people believed it was routine, or as routine as a patrol during social unrest could be. A tavern owner and blacksmith might be wary of unburdening himself at other times to an officer asking questions – snooping eyes could always come back to haunt a person – but in these day you never knew who might be telling stories about *you*, so best to protect yourself first.

It helped, too, that the Musketeers weren't asking much about villagers, but the nobles, and that was all right then. The aristocrats, they had their own ways and never did the town folk much good. They were secretive enough, and if those secrets might come back to haunt *them*, well, it served them right. It was the gentry as had caused the problems people were facing, so to hell with them. And it was the royalty that hadn't stopped things, so to hell with them, too. At least the crown though had the country in its heart, the aristocracy only had itself. Its own land, its own authority, its own grip on the throat. Their blood might be blue, but we're the ones who get beaten down until *our* blood runs red.

"Yes, his Lordship had several visitors twice last week, come to think of it," an innkeeper told his questioner. "It seemed unexpected."

"In fact," a hat maker explained, "the Duchess threw a party three weeks ago, but wouldn't say who attended, and she *always* brags. About everything. Always."

"I saw a strange coach pull into the *chateau* just yesterday. Very fancy. The blinds drawn, and it was night."

"You know, the Baron seems to keep much more to himself these days than usual," a fish monger said.

"His Lordship didn't pay his bill last week. You should talk to him. It might mean something, you never know. Maybe you could get my money. That's your job, isn't it?"

"It didn't seem suspicious at the time, but I heard the Duke say…"

"My wife said she overheard the *épicier* say that he was told the Baroness had said…"

"It probably means nothing, but…"

And on and on the stories came from whatever corner was stopped. It came in great detail and empty opinion. It was all so helpful and conspiratorial and meaningless and informative, leaving twisting trails that offered hints but nothing that made the Musketeers feel they had uncovered anything of use to their mission – all the more so since they weren't especially certain what their mission was. Their orders were as secretive and merely suggestive as were the bits and pieces they were receiving.

*

In the War Room of the palace, the trails of the search twisted in a very different direction that night, and became far more secretive than before. Those at the top with information are always the most circumspect, having more to protect, but especially with this new turn. And at the top above all, the Queen Regent surveyed the activity with a steely look.

The room was full of advisors who had been summoned late. The evenings of the court with fine dinners, elegant parties and flashing wit were a thing of the past for those with far greater responsibilities at the moment.

Cardinal Mazarin stood alone reading a letter written in the scrawl of a 10-year-old child.

"I agree, Your Highness," he said without looking up, "it is the King's hand. But dire though the words are, we know from this he is alive. And why."

He passed the letter to Major Delacroix, who glanced at it and without notice quietly put it safely in his tunic.

"The crown will never abdicate," the Queen Mother made clear, as bluntly as she could, to leave no doubt with anyone in the room. "Know this well. What must be saved is France, not this family." She moved to the large command table around which the advisors sat, and began to shoot off questions rapidly. "Do we know from where that was sent? Has it been examined? Does it provide any evidence?"

"We have the Marquis's estate under watch," Mazarin replied. "We can place him with those we believe conspirators, but no more. He is far too well-guarded."

For a moment, the Queen Mother thought quietly. Then she turned to the officer in charge, and her demeanor clouded. "Major, we are displeased with the progress."

"Musketeer search efforts remain intense." His bearing was sturdy, and few words were ever wasted.

"We have moved past the point of mere search," she responded tartly. "You do not appear acting with full gravity. I order mobilized all army, *gendarmes*, and Musketeers."

"Efforts will be coordinated through my office," the Cardinal jumped in quickly. Waiting for the nods of agreement from everyone, he made sure he had the attention of the room before continuing. "I admonish you all to continue keeping the King's disappearance silent. We are on the heels of war. This nation must not collapse under fear that its leader is missing.

The King <u>will</u> appear at the *Gala National.* Is that understood?"

There were nods and assents throughout the room. And then silence. The silence grew, for the men all understood as well that for all the action they could plan, they were still much in the dark. Finally, the voice of the Regent cut through the deafening quiet.

"Save France. Stop these blackguards. *And will someone find my son.*"

*

Charlotte's head popped up from a door in the floor that opened up into an attic. Her eyes were open wide in wonderment as she looked around.

Shafts of light brightened a charming, small room with three beds and quaint furnishing. The old man Auguste stood by a small night stand, awaiting her as she stepped onto the floor.

"I hope it fits your needs," he fluttered. "I know it's small, but my dear wife did her best to prepare it for you."

Charlotte ran her hand lovingly over the beds, as the other two women joined her, climbing up after. The duvet was rustic, and roughly sewn, but with a lively color and filled with pigeon feathers. The room was small, yes, but it was sweetly appointed with touches made for people to comfortably live in.

"Oh, sir, your thoughtfulness is beyond words. And the joy," she sighed, her body relaxing, not even realizing that she had involuntarily heaved a small happy breath, "oh, to not sleep on hay."

The old man seemed anxious to make sure everything was just right, just so, fussing about as if his guests had been

101

cherished family members come for visit after years away. He wanted them to appreciate every detail, pointing out a throw rug – so unnecessary, yet its very presence showed there was concern. The chifferobe was small, barely space to hang several blouses, and drawers for less, but that there wasn't a spot of dust inside meant someone knew it was needed, no matter how dusty the clothes that would be put in. His words fell over one another.

"There are the candles, Marguerite thought flowers would make it a little homier, here is a pitcher of water, and the sheets are clean."

It all looked charming. From the fat stub of the candle to the ceramic vase which, if one looked closely enough and had a good eye for such things, were filled with wild flowers, roses, in fact. But charming as it might be to some, to those who are tired and lonely, the smallest details take on another view entirely. Gabrielle leaped and flopped down into a bed that seemed a lap of luxury.

"It's like a palace here to me."

"Finer," Charlotte enthused politely and turned excitedly from it all to Auguste. "Is there a valet we could call upon to bring up our possessions?"

"There is," Racine replied. "But he's busy at the moment giving pony rides."

The old man continued to fuss about the room, straightening things, though really making them a bit more crooked.

"My dear wife regrets it took several days. It's just that you were all strangers to her, and with the danger in the street, it's just – " he paused, suddenly feeling terribly awkward about what he realized now had to be said to explain things, having backed himself into a corner. "— well, she was wary, you see, about taking in," he was so flummoxed that the only way left was to just be out with it, as politely as possible, "...about taking in...I'm sorry, an 'undesirable.'"

A knowing half-smile crossed Racine's face. She had heard it before, her whole life. "Undesirable" was the least of what she'd been called. And she knew that this man and his wife had kindly offered their hand. She let him off the hook. "I understand."

"Oh! No, my dear." Auguste said, so mortified by the confusion. "She meant an actress."

CHAPTER FIFTEEN

There still were places within Paris where grace ruled the day. And so it was in *La Maison*, the gentleman's club that those who were anybody aspired to get into. The House, that was all it needed to be called, and people knew what was being referred to. Business was done there, politics was done there, the intricate dance and maneuverings of society was done there, which in many ways was the most important of all its activities, and so too was there card gambling, getting away from one's *other* home, romantic rendezvouses behind the most private of doors, and much else. It was a hub and haven and desert island of exclusion and the most powerful men in France.

Outsiders were regularly trying to become insiders. And so members comfortably knew that the staff of *La Maison* protected them from the intrusions of life. There, they saw, was the venerable doorman doing his best to chase away the ragtags who didn't belong there. And no one belonged there, except those who were already members.

"I do understand," the imposing figure said with firm politeness and a touch of intentionally clear disdain to the young girl who was still there on the steps, unwilling to grasp the finality of his words, "but once again, as I have said, it is against club policy."

Policy or not, Charlotte would not give up. She was used to getting her way, but this was more than that. Surely she was *right* in what she was asking. And surely he could see that. And surely it was clear she *had* to get in.

She was supported in her efforts by Gabrielle and Racine,

who waited for her on the walkway by the street. They had come together that morning at Madame Fleury's insistence. Charlotte had said she was going alone, it was her business alone and important to her alone, but the good old lady would hear nothing of it. "A young girl like *that* out on the street alone," she puffed, "don't you even dare, or you won't get back in my house." And so the other two women were recruited, with some resistance on Racine's part, until the old lady stared her down, the first time that had happened to Racine since her own mother put her in her place years ago. But then, it made sense to all go, she realized, as the old man took them aside and quietly pointed out how even his dear wife was suggesting that what they did together could benefit them all.

"What nonsense are you filling the lovely girls with?" Marguerite called from the kitchen. "I can't hear you, old man, though that might be a good thing."

And so, together the three went off. Charlotte insisting the others didn't really need to spend their time on her business, but so grateful that they were. Gabrielle happy to go on any adventure through the magnificent boulevards of Paris where there were more beautiful things to buy than you could find anywhere in the world, which was just, she said, as she had told her friend Annette when they were in the play, *The Poor Ones*, an interesting little production in which she had a small but important role as a young maiden who… And Racine found she was actually happy feeling superior to a couple of people for the first time in a long time. She always felt superior, but that was usually when she was being pushed. Here, the others seemed to actually agree with her. It was a new and amusingly enjoyable diversion.

But diversions soon pass and get less enjoyable. And after listening to the Princess going on petulantly to that pretentious coat standing in the doorway about not getting her way, Racine was ready to move on.

"All right," she fidgeted to Gabrielle, feeling her teeth aching, "this is enough already. Just go up and get her, and let's take off."

Gabrielle laughed. "You have somewhere else to go? Enjoy it. Just watching them talk, you can learn things. Studying people. You can understand why they do what they do."

"I know why people do what they do. Trust me. And it's not to study people."

But Gabrielle turned back to practice her craft, as she put it, and Racine stood her ground. All the while, Charlotte kept trying to make her case.

"But since my father had belonged here," she pleaded to the doorman, her voice rising with each moment that she saw her chances slipping away, "I had hope there might by chance be someone to whom I could ask questions."

"Then you know, m'lady, visitor restrictions are most severe. *I'm sorry*," he said politely with the most firm intensity, and louder than before to make the point. "Might a porter escort you home?"

By this point, Gabrielle's attention had been drawn closer, and she had moved up the steps to her friend's side. "The matter, <u>sir</u>," she joined in far more dramatically and obstreperously than Charlotte would ever have dared, "is of importance. <u>Sir</u>."

She smiled at the doorman but held his gaze. He appreciated this beautiful woman before him, but was not moved. "The rule is inviolate. I must insis – "

Suddenly, the door widened, and standing there was the Marquis.

"Is there a problem?" he asked the doorman in a voice that answered his own question. "If you can't handle commotions, perhaps another laborer can."

Charlotte's face brightened at seeing the last thing she had expected, a familiar face.

"Monsieur le Marquis. It is Charlotte Le Renaud. Perhaps, sir, you can help us."

For a moment, Eduard just stared at her, as surprised as she.

"Dear young Charlotte," he finally responded. "I would say it is good to see you, but for your father's passing. I can only imagine your sorrow. What possibly brings you here??"

"We are trying to find who killed her father and hope to find some answers," Gabrielle jumped in for support, seeing how reticent Charlotte was in the shadow of the imposing man.

Eduard continued to look only at Charlotte, ignoring Gabrielle as if she didn't exist. This was not lost on Racine who bristled, and moved closer instinctively. At last, Charlotte was able to summon the words to respond.

"My father often spoke of a conspiracy, but it made no sense. I thought his compatriots here mayhaps help."

"You father was one of France's great dreamers. Bless him. Trying always to save The People. Even those beneath help." He added drippingly, "How grand to see you are following in his footsteps. It's precious. We'll have to watch out for you."

Even Charlotte recognized that his words may not have

been as sympathetic as they might sound, and she bristled the tiniest bit. It gave her the slight courage to take the even-slighter initiative.

"I thank Your Lordship. May we then enter?"

"Alas, I'm afraid not. I only follow the rules of the establishment. Best of luck." And still without taking his eyes from her, as they condescendingly refused to acknowledge the others. "And good day."

He closed the door – but Racine jammed her foot in.

"I'm so sure you could reconsider. She's asking for your help."

For the first time, Eduard deigned to glance at her.

"Deliveries are in the back."

And with that, he kicked out her foot and shut the door. Racine stewed, but for only an instant, and then moved quickly to rush the door, but Gabrielle held her. She struggled to keep the gypsy from causing a much greater and pointless commotion that would only succeed in bringing the police.

All the while, Charlotte stood there alone, feeling lost. Worse, helpless. Worse still, letting down her father.

Finally, Racine recognized the futility and stormed down the steps. Gabrielle put an arm around the young heiress, who had seemed to withdraw into herself. "Don't worry, we'll think of some other way. I'm full of ideas. Let's go."

"I do thank you, but right now, I just – " she moved off to the pathway, "I wish prefer to be by myself."

"Are you sure?"

"She needs to be alone," Racine interrupted. "This I understand. Trust me."

Gabrielle started to argue, but again Racine added, "Trust me. Come on."

Accepting such rare and wildly unexpected insight and thoughtfulness from her, Gabrielle gave a tender hug to Charlotte, and the two of them left her. Still, as they headed down the road, Gabrielle looked back, wondering if listening to Racine on matters of the heart was the wisest course of action – but Racine was insistent that on this she knew best here and pulled her away.

Leaving Charlotte alone.

And alone, the young girl sat on a nearby bench, sullen. Her mind was a whirl of thoughts. Sadness, concern, loneliness, anger. The anger surprised her, yet the more she sat there, the more it grew. This was her father's club. These were her father's peers. These were her father's friends. Such people stood together. They owed it to one another. They owed it to him. Him! They owed it to her dear father. And owing it to him, they owed it to her. Shutting the door on her, that was just wrong. It was not acceptable. How dare they? How dare they??! And as much as Charlotte bristled when thinking of the Marquis de Longueville call her father a dreamer, something she couldn't help feeling was not meant totally as a compliment, she believed it was a good dream. She sat, and thought, and grew more upset, and angrier. And at last, she glared at the club door, very pointedly stood and strode back to it.

Two porters from the club lingered nearby as was their job. They followed her along – and then blocked her way.

"Going somewhere?" the tallest man asked.

"Sorry that the club is closed," his companion-in-arms added, a burly fellow with cold eyes.

"Perhaps we can help?"

"Nothing there for you today."

Charlotte took small steps to avoid them, and headed towards the steps, but they kept easy pace and continued in her way.

"I'm happy to help," the tall man half-smiled meaninglessly. "Truly."

Using wise judgment, Charlotte understand that this was as far as she would be getting and quickly moved off, strolling past a couple of Parisians – but to her distress, the two men followed and taunted her.

"Don't you like us?" the burly porter chided with mock hurt, drawing himself closer to the girl.

"We're here to escort our fine guests. And you are most definitely fine."

"I'm a nice gent," his associate cooed, "very…"

Charlotte shrank with each word. What had she gotten herself into? This was not the way of the world. She never knew such insolence. Such…

"Please, sirs. I just wish you good day."

Her voice held, but barely. She looked at the ground, then held their eyes in hope, and checked around for a way past.

"That's not so friendly."

"I'll you what *I* wish…" the tall fellow offered suggestively.

"This is Paris, y'know," the other offered even more suggestively, and snapped his face in front of hers with a leer.

There was a corner up ahead, and Charlotte felt certain that that would at least lead her to safety, for surely they would not leave their post unguarded. She held her breath and quickly passed around the building.

But as she did, her body stiffened as she could hear that they followed her around the corner. And then they were all out of sight. The area was now empty. Not a soul could be seen.

Nothing.

But a moment later, the two porters were backing their way into the street. Two swords were held at their chests. And at the other end of those swords were Racine and Gabrielle, holding them at bay. A thoroughly confused, yet equally relieved Charlotte followed behind.

The men continued backing their way up the road, not knowing how much danger they were in, but well-aware that they didn't want to make a wrong move to find out. Their attackers were just women, but the swords were as sharp as any man's. The beauty, she certainly looked fine, but with that toss of her flowing blonde mane, you could never trust someone who looked that good and probably always got her way. But that dark-haired one, no, better not test her, she seemed like she could carve them without a thought. The men didn't know, just didn't know, but they knew enough to be very concerned, as the points of the swords jabbed into them enough to bite.

"What? Not a word of greeting to a lady?" Racine asked with what could have passed for malice, if you weren't sure. She jabbed them again. "Where are your French manners?"

"My name is 'You're in trouble.' What's yours?" Gabrielle asked without a smile.

Several passersby had been strolling near, but paused, not sure what to make of all this. Were they about to see a one-sided duel and yet more blood in the streets?

"Please, a moment. Let us explain…" the tallest porter croaked. The men's awkward steps caused them to stumble and almost lose their balance. They had to stop.

And then suddenly – swish, swish – two quick swipes from

the women cut the men's belts. Their pants dropped around their ankles.

The passersby immediately laughed in great amusement and even applauded their approval.

Racine kept glaring at the two porters, not leaving their gaze for a moment, nor did they move. Gabrielle turned slightly to those watching and gave a little curtsey.

Charlotte finally found it in her to speak. She believed she could never feel as grateful as she did at that moment. Her heart had only just slowed to normal. "What possibly made you both decide to come back?

"Come back??" Racine asked, turning to look at the young, ever-helpless girl. "What in the world makes you think we actually left??"

CHAPTER SIXTEEN

It is one of the great truths that advice, no matter how much sense it might make later – or even at the time – is seldom accepted in its fullness when given. We know better than our elders, and so it has been since the beginning of time. Even if what they teach us from experience sounds wise, *our* life is different, we know better, that was then, this is now.

And so it was when Auguste spent his time with the three young women. It was exciting to learn, but he was an old man after all. Life was very changed today. What he taught them about protecting one another made sense, and had been exciting at first, but putting it into practice, ah, that was another matter. Charlotte liked the comfort of others, though she was used to others doing for her, not with her. Gabrielle liked the involvement of others, but she enjoyed their attention and less her following. And Racine, well, no, honestly she didn't have much place for relying on others nor accepting their assistance, and she was certainly not willing to give up even a *soupçon* of her independence, although having others watch your back did have its charms, she had to admit in one of those rare moments when she allowed such thoughts.

They all understood what the old man had told them, they liked what the old man told them, but in the end, it wasn't a way of life that they understood.

Yet that day out front of the gentlemen's club, that was when some of what they had been taught…they began to understand, if only a little. Ah, they each thought themselves, in their own ways, so that's what he meant, that's how it works, protecting one another. Charlotte loved the safety, Gabrielle loved the appreciation, and Racine loved putting in their places those who deserved it. And if truth be told, Charlotte found to her surprise she liked that, too. As did Gabrielle like the safety of it all. And Racine even grudgingly admitted to herself – and only herself – that she found being appreciated interesting. If just a little, perhaps.

And so in the days that passed, the three slowly began to find themselves going through the city together. Not always – no one was quite sure where Racine would head off at times, or how she returned with more money than she had left with. And as Gabrielle noted, an audition was a solitary undertaking, and she continued her quest for the role that would bring France to her feet, even if she always returned with less success than she had imagined when she left. "It's all good experience," she explained, adding that Paris seemed to have a different view of theater than she. Charlotte however was still reticent to go out alone after her experience that awful day. Yet more often than they would have expected, they did wander out together, and without Madame Fleury's prodding usually, just because they had finally begun to see the advantages of the support of the others, if not the companionship, though perhaps that was finding a place, as well.

It was interesting first steps of this new life, Gabrielle thought one morning, as she strolled through the marketplace, pausing at one of the many stalls and purchasing a shawl. She paid the merchant and put her blue, cotton clutch in the basket.

Charlotte and Racine themselves wandered leisurely among the crowd, Charlotte admiring the adorable trinketry, Racine admiring the adorable money being passed around, and she headed off.

114

A quiet man who had been doing his best all morning to blend in with the others shopping had paid much more attention to people than they were aware, his eyes darting around him with purpose. At last, very intently, they came to rest on a blue, cotton clutch resting on top a basket. He stealthily moved in on Gabrielle. And then, in the imperceptible move of a professional pickpocket, he snatched her purse, and just as smoothly passed it off unseen to his partner, who hid it quickly before making a smooth getaway after bumping into a very disoriented shopper.

"I'm so sorry," the embarrassed shopper politely nodded, though the two thieves were long gone with their prize.

What they didn't know was how disappointed they would soon be, for that shopper was Racine, who had been keeping a protective eye on Gabrielle and picked the pickpocket. She waved Gabrielle's wallet high in the air and handed it back, proudly.

"Not bad?" she nodded to Charlotte with a smile that said, see, sometimes what I do *can* come in useful in a world that you think is oh-so very good and noble and decent.

The young girl smiled back. And then attentively, she reached into Racine's coat, and took out several unpaid for scarves. And returned them unseen to a vendor.

Annoyed though she was, Racine had to give the Princess credit. "Not bad," she shrugged.

*

To be the victim of a pickpocket those days was almost a comfort, for it meant no risk of injury and no blood was spilt. But that was rarely the case throughout the rest of Paris in the days ahead. For nothing had changed, and the dangers of the city continued to get worse. It didn't matter the area, it didn't matter the time.

In the broad daylight of an otherwise normal afternoon, a small man was getting robbed by an armed thief. And though several witnesses stood nearby – although not too near – they felt much too threatened to act, as he waved his pistol at them and snarled them off.

That was what was common in Paris these days. That was what those watching understood, how they were the lucky ones not being beaten. Or worse.

"Check again," the thief snapped, as he pocketed a handful of francs. "I'm sure you have more."

He hit the whimpering man with his pistol, drawing blood, and grabbed him by the throat.

"You might want to give that back," came a gruff, but high-pitched voice.

Racine stood at the ready. Alone. And furious. Her face was intense. Thievery was one thing, she could accept that, that's life, but beating an innocent, defenseless man bloody was something else entirely. The robber stopped suddenly, utterly taken aback. For a moment, he was almost baffled, unused to being challenged. But then, just as suddenly –

"Go to hell," he spat out. "What's it to you?"

"Oh, that's a box you really don't want to open," Racine shook her head. "You must trust me on this."

As those huddled nearby watched in a mixture of a fear for the health of this reckless young woman, admiration for her bravery, and excitement that they might see a one-sided gunfight, Racine only had eyes on the poor, abused soul crumpled on the ground, robbed and bleeding from a deep gash in his head. As her anger grew, she not only stood her ground, she took a determined step towards the ruffian, her fingers tightening on the hilt of her sword.

"Stick around, I have an extra bullet." He made clear it was no empty threat. And he hoped she would take him up on his challenge, for he was anxious to prove it.

All of a sudden, though, even to Racine's surprise, she noticed that Gabrielle and Charlotte had joined her, having followed their friend after she'd riskily wandered off alone.

"It would be so smart to reconsider." Gabrielle planted her feet firmly and patted the grip of her blade.

"Just think of us as dreamers," Charlotte added, pointedly.

The brazen robber didn't know what in the world to make of this – but three beautiful women watching him wasn't a bad thing to see.

"I know," he twisted a half-smile that revealed a couple of missing teeth, "you're here for a *ménage-à-trois*."

He grinned happily at Racine. She smiled sweetly back at him.

"A *ménage-à-trois*? You want a *ménage-à-trois*? Fine, we'll give you a *ménage-à-trois*."

She lashed out a foot and kicked him in the groin. When he fell forward, Gabrielle smashed him in the face. And as he spun away from the force, Charlotte kicked him in the ass, sending the man flying into a water trough.

All to the shock of the men and women who had been hiding at a safe distance.

*

Along a busy boulevard, a merchant stepped quickly on his

117

route, and even more warily with a sack of his wares. He knew that such an act was risky, to the point of foolhardy, but it was the only way he could manage business. Try as he might to be inconspicuous, that simply wasn't possible, having overloaded his pack so he'd only need make a single trip. Suddenly, as was all too expected, a robber sprinted by and grabbed it.

His arms full of the newly-acquired swag, the thief kept running, causing a commotion as passersby rushed to avoid him. Certain he had made his way safely, he came to a halt and allowed himself to relax – as he saw a beautiful blonde woman eye him and stop, as well. Though he couldn't understand why, a look came to her eyes as if she didn't mean to let him pass. Gabrielle indeed drew her sword and headed for him. Having watched Racine over time put those in their place who deeply deserved it, whoever they harmed, she had begun to recognize that such a thing had its charms – most especially here when this man was not only safely without a weapon, but his arms were loaded down with merchandise. Seeing his path blocked by someone with a sword, the thief had no need to test this woman's resolve, so he simply turned and headed off in another direction – but stopped again, as Racine herself happened by and walked towards him, having spotted Gabrielle at the ready and drawing her own sword, as well.

And so he just ran – yet there was Charlotte, waiting, directly in his face. She unsheathed her sword. Surrounded in three directions, the man knew he was beat. And with the young girl's sword wavering at him, which he took as an anxious challenge, rather than the nerves it was, he hung the satchel on her blade, and darted past the marveling crowd.

*

118

A morning rain was muddying the city square. It was largely empty, as most people had wisely taken cover. Yet there remained a small crowd because a sword fight had been building before their eyes between three swaggering thugs who had just knocked down several push carts and audaciously terrorized the owners of all their money, almost taunting the citizens around to stop them – and three women. The crowd was in awe as it watched something it had not seen before.

"I'm behind you," Racine called out to Gabrielle.

The women had learned their lesson well from Auguste.

"To your left," Charlotte shouted to her, standing a bit off to the side more safely, swishing her sword when an attacker came her way.

Racine though was at her finest, parrying her sword against her rival, who slashed at her but made little headway and found himself awkwardly sliding in the slick mud. Finally, she flipped his sword away and held her rapier tight against his throat. He stopped struggling.

Gabrielle was doing quite well, too, albeit in her own way against a thoroughly confused opponent. Her foe was backing up, bewildered as he tried to get a handle on the odd leaps around him of the woman, and in attempting to catch her strange moves, he slipped and slipped again and fell. She knelt over him, holding her sword to his chest.

"I hope you don't prefer to be on top," she said.

Amid all this, Charlotte herself was – well, doing her best. Her actions were spirited and in their own way admirable, but painfully flawed. She was able to delay her adversary's advance, swiping her sword at him, and making occasional contact with his, a clink ringing out as metal hit metal. But it was a fruitless and small effort, and soon with a blow he was able to take aim and knock her sword from her grasp. It lay there in the mud. Sensing victory, he lunged at the girl.

However, by force of personal habit, Charlotte did what was completely unexpected – not just for this fight, but for any fight. The dutiful, proper girl she was, she leaned over to get her sword, like she always did whenever her sword got knocked out of her hand, like it always did. The thoroughly surprised man was already in mid-leap and had no chance to change course, and with Charlotte bent low, he flew over her and crashed to the ground.

Charlotte picked up her sword, and calmly walked over and held the man in the mud with the blade.

She looked down at him. *"Touché."*

*

The coach rumbled along through the late dusk with an armed guard seated beside the driver who kept the horses going at an even clip. That the carriage moved smoothly would usually have been of primary concern to the passengers, but these days it was of small comfort. Traveling through open countryside was a risk. Only those who could afford such conveyance did so, and that made them targets. And as the transport was far slower than challenging horsemen, and would never be able to outrun them, it made the journey all the more a worry.

An elderly couple sat on their side of the cabin keeping one another occupied, as he largely was solving all the problems of the world. Sitting across from them were a nicely-dressed gentleman and his daughter, although she could be his very young wife, the old woman thought knowingly, since the two didn't seem to have much to say to one another, and she just kept peering intently out the window. The matron doubted a great deal they weren't together, for someone that young would never be foolish enough to travel alone.

"Not to worry, dear," the white-haired man across from her said with a comforting smile. "I've have friends take this road many a time, and they're all still here."

The girl sat up straight and smoothed her lovely dress. "Oh. Thank you much. One just hears so many stories, you know. But I am fine, truly."

One other passenger was traveling, though it was on the roof. The compartment was crowded, but it was assumed that the overhead traveler had paid much less for the trip, "or preferred fresh air a great deal," the well-dressed gentleman chuckled. The girl thought it must be quite uncomfortable up there, though she did ask when they set out if it would be better for them all to sit inside, but this was the way it was to be, she was told. In the end, she was grateful that there were not too many squeezed inside. That would have been uncomfortable, as well.

Suddenly, shots rang out, and the whinny of the horses cut through the air. The elderly couple had a look of concern and held on to one another. They had left Paris specifically to spend time where they'd hope there was less danger, but the sad truth was that traveling along a country road might have been the most dangerous place to be in France.

Four highwaymen blocked their route, as the driver fought to reign in the horses.

"Stand and deliver," the leader called out, sitting high in the saddle, a cloth wrapped around his face. With muskets pointed, the driver, guard and passenger on the roof were all held helpless. "Out!" he ordered the wealthy travelers inside. "*Maintenant.*"

They stepped slowly onto the cold ground, the couple, the gentleman and Charlotte – for she was the young girl, traveling in the cabin by herself. With a look of wariness, she lugged her small handbag beside her and held it tight. One by one, the head of these hijackers collected his plunder and passed it along to his men. Money, jewelry, broaches, whatever could have value. Reaching Charlotte, he took the full measure of the girl.

"I'll have something for you later," he smirked.

She stood her ground bravely. But so too did the man. Before anything else, he noticed something sparkling in her hair. It stood out immediately, and with a gleam in his eye he made a quick motion to Charlotte. "*Vite, vite,*" he impatiently snapped.

Reluctantly, she removed a large diamond hairpin. Her reddish-brown coiffure, luxurious and stylish, now cascaded down to her shoulders. She shook it sensually.

As she did, the other three highwaymen on their horses leered happily, and winked to one another.

This was the distraction that the "guard" and "passenger" on the roof were waiting for – and Racine and Gabrielle leaped off.

Racine dove into two of the men and took them out with a punch and her sword, knocking them to the ground. And Gabrielle took the third.

The leader was stunned by this, completely caught off guard, and his attention spun to his men lying unconscious.

"And I have something for you, *now!*" Charlotte said.

And she hauled off and landed a roundhouse with her fist to his chin, as he turned back.

"Ow!! Ow!!" she cried, shaking her hand.

Of course, a blow from Charlotte, no matter how much force it was thrown with, had little effect and just glanced off his jaw. Angered, the man shook it off, lifted his pistol and began to take aim, pointing it directly at –

Whack! Charlotte swung her handbag, of all things, and knocked him silly. With a momentary look of shock, he went down like a shot and lay flat on the ground.

Pleased beyond words at her success, the girl beamed brighter than the moon which was just beginning to appear. Then, she opened her small bag and took out a large brick.

Gabrielle raced over to her. "You got the hair flip *magnifique!*" she glowed, and tossed her own hair just like she had taught Charlotte, and threw her arms around the girl with an excited hug.

Racine stepped over the fallen highwaymen. She looked at Charlotte for a moment without saying anything, before finally given a little nod. "You did all right for a Princess."

And through it all, the passengers could only gawk, not believing what they'd seen, nor their good luck. Apparently, the old woman thought, that girl was not with that gentleman after all.

The three women gathered the stolen property, and with a simple nonchalance returned it all to the rightful owners, who were barely able to eke out a "*merci.*" Charlotte calmly took her seat back inside the coach without a word, and Racine, who started to climb back in with her, decided she preferred to lord over everything again from the roof. As Gabrielle climbed up beside the driver, she twirled and faced the others.

123

"If you enjoyed traveling with us today," she chirped, "please be sure to tell your friends."

*

It was a bright and shining morning, and shining most of all were three women, well aware of the glances paid them by so many of the people they passed, several pointing and whispering. "It's them." "Those are the ones." The three didn't quite know how it had come to this, but so it had.

Racine walked with a swagger of clear joy.

Gabrielle, loving each step, strode along majestically. She most especially reveled in the attention, appreciating every eye upon her – thought a moment, and then undid the highest button on her blouse. And then…oh, all right, she undid the next, as well.

Even Charlotte, who had not forgotten the deep sadness of profound loss she'd been feeling for the past months, even she allowed herself to feel happy. What a different life she was living now. Her dear father would be so proud, but then he would be proud of her whatever she did. She caught herself, checking a deep breath, but with a small smile she knew this was what it felt like to try to fill that hole. Looking around at the sights and people, she felt the touch of a purpose to her walk. When suddenly, something caught her view –

It was Philippe Gascogne. The aristocrat from her father's study rode by. Did he glance at her?? She couldn't tell, she strained to see, but he was gone. Why was he here, she thought? It can't be a chance passing. And the bright day all around her now had a shadow cross it.

CHAPTER SEVENTEEN

Across a wide expanse of meadow sitting high upon a ridge, a magnificent carriage covered in gold-trim, with intricately-designed molding and with a coat of arms to match came to a stop. If any passersby were to have seen this, they would have found it most deeply out of place in the middle of great emptiness. Even more out of place would have been the two lordly men who stepped onto the long grass.

Eduard de Longueville strode across the marshy field, but his companion easily kept up. In fact, General Turenne even slowed a bit which forced the Marquis to lessen his own pace, something he would do for few other men. But the general was few other men.

Henri de la Tour d'Auvergne was the Vicomte de Turenne. And he was more, as well, the Duc de Bouillon and Prince of Sedan. All these were mere titles, though. In the practicalities of the very real and harsh world he lived in, General Turenne was the most famous military officer in France.

He had received his first, important promotion to colonel by none other than Cardinal Richelieu himself. Exceeding even his benefactor's high estimation, he won remarkable battles in France, Holland and along the Rhine, and Turenne swiftly was promoted to major-general when a mere 24 years old. So great was his renown – his assaults on Flanders were shockingly brilliant and played critical roles in ending the Eighty Years War – that he often fought under several flags. Nations competed with one another for his leadership and courage, yet his former armies would beg to have him, and his movable loyalties, back.

But it was France to whom at heart he fought. He lived for France, and if need be would die for it. But he had no immediate intention to die. There were too many battles ahead where he was needed. And when Richelieu had promoted him higher still to lieutenant general, he repaid the honor by breaking the impenetrable Seige of Turin, which helped turn that war in Italy for France just four years earlier.

However, France to General Turenne was different from the France of others.

He had been royally-born in Sedan. But though that was a part of France, it was a separate principality on the Belgian border, and so he often found himself torn between his own territory which he led and that of his parent nation. At times he fought for the French crown, and at times was opposed.

Now was one of those times he was opposed. And so, whatever armies the Marquis de Longueville would be able to amass among his coterie of nobles, the greatest general in all of France would lead them.

And so, it is small wonder that Eduard made certain that his pace was quite in step with General Turenne.

As they passed along the ridge towards its edge, a colonel rushed over. He made sure to salute the General first, but reported to the Marquis.

"M'lord. These are the prisoners we caught, spying near your home."

Few things could divert the Marquis, and this was one of them. He came over and stared at five Musketeers being held under heavy guard.

"And what did your wasted efforts discover?"

There was no answer, as Eduard knew there would not be.

126

Yet he let the silence linger. At last, with a disdainful scoff, he headed on past the line of his enemies. And with as little caring as he could muster, added, "Shoot them."

He headed back to the waiting Turenne, as if it had all been just an annoying, wasteful digression of his time.

"This all begs the question, General. Are you ready?"

At last they reached the overlook, rising high above a field far below, stretching far off into the distance.

The field was covered by a massive military build-up of Eduard's troops. The coterie of nobles had done its job well.

The most feared and respected general in the land, if not all of Europe surveyed his command. "Very ready."

CHAPTER EIGHTEEN

The Fleurys lived in a very simple home, but rather than feeling bare and empty, sometimes the simplest places speak loudly for what is important there. The kitchen was that of a poor family, but the room was laid out as the soul of comfort. Pots and pans were everywhere, yet they were all neatly stacked and well-ordered, and an understanding eye would see that this all befit a home where the service of food and the serving of others was its centerpiece. The aromas of bread breaking and pies cooling well-supported that. A square wooden table had a small, colorful cloth on top that added to the cheeriness of the room.

Seated at her place, next to the old man in his regular throne of honor, Charlotte was gracefully eating her first course of dinner, her manners impeccable, as she made sure to dab her lips if even the slightest drop of sauce was misplaced. Auguste was not nearly so careful.

Ignoring it all, Gabrielle's attention was riveted on Racine showing her what was proper, as well, though it was the proper way to break open a lock. The meticulous, detailed twisting of her fingers was an impressive bit of dexterity. Done. The bolt snapped open.

"There, 20 seconds." The gypsy nonchalantly tipped the chamber for the inquisitive Gabrielle to see, though it was like trying to explain a foreign language. "The trick is you have to find the tumblers." Gabrielle nodded thoughtfully, eager to learn a craft, and did her best to remember for certain which things the tumblers were.

A short, kindly, gray-haired woman was at the pantry, busy

at work. Marguerite Fleury had spent much of her married life at the pantry, but it was her pleasure. She loved cooking, but then much was her pleasure. And it radiated from her in most whatever she did. She was one of those people who had warm eyes that simply made you feel welcome. But she could be stern, as well, and hearing the clink of lock's metal on the ceramic plates, called over her shoulder, "Now, girls, no playing at the table. Put that away, or no dessert."

"Tomorrow I'm learning how to pick pockets!" Gabrielle excitedly called back.

Racine proudly wiggled her fingers, looking like a passcode between master pickpockets. It was something she did often, almost without thinking, to keep her fingers limber and in shape. "It's all deception." She prompted Gabrielle, who returned the finger wiggling, with the look of a serious student.

"And just think," Marguerite sighed with a slight roll of her eyes. "Only yesterday they were playing with dolls."

"I think we should go by the *Rue Madeleine* today," Gabrielle said before breaking off a chunk of bread.

Racine wiped her mouth with her sleeve, and then looked back to see if Madame Fleury had noticed. She picked up the napkin that the lady had placed there, but after considering its use for a moment, shrugged and put it back. "I keep thinking we should go back to that gentleman's club. I really would like to return."

"I'm most certain the Marquis will continue to keep us out," Charlotte replied quietly.

"I know. I just thought we could burn the place down." Racine had not been able to get that man out of her memory. She had met few people of rank, unless they were arresting her, but she lived on instinct, and she knew a man like that was always worth remembering. Racine was someone who kept long grudges, after all. In many ways, it was her driving force. The details and minutiae of past wrongs were like the dishes of a great banquet to her. She may not even know who that man was, but for all she didn't know in this life, there was a lot more she understood. And what she understood most about that brief encounter was enough to gnaw away at her. "Is every Marquis in France an asshole?"

"He and my father were at odds for years. They even served in *Parlement* as aristocrats. The Marquis de Longueville was the one man who I knew could get my father so angry. They had so many disagreements of the most bitter..."

Racine had been shoveling in a spoonful of the ragout, paying only some attention to Charlotte, as she usually did, letting the more interesting-sounding comments filter through. But suddenly she stopped eating, almost choking on the beef and let go her utensil.

"Wait, *that* was the Marquis de Longueville??"

"Yes. Do you know of him??"

It was now Charlotte's turn to be shocked. Perhaps the last two people on the face of the globe that she ever expected to cross paths were Eduard de Longueville and Racine Tarascon.

"He gave me a necklace once."

Gabrielle looked up with a joyous smile and clapped. "So, our little Racine has a gentleman friend in her pas..." then she stopped in realization. "Ohhhhhh. You mean – "

She mimed having a noose around her neck and being hung. "That was the Marquis you told us about??!"

"Maybe not him directly, but he let it happen." Racine's eyes tightened. "And having seen the bastard now, I can tell you that's someone who's let it happen for many."

The old woman had returned to the table and dished out vegetables. She was even-tempered as always, but spoke with a concern from all she had been hearing of fires and hangings and pickpockets and worse. She knew well of what the young ladies had been up to the past many weeks, but there were limits in this world. "You girls take care now. I mean it. Helping others is a godsend, but I worry about you so. It's dangerous."

Charlotte turned to her primly, yet spoke emphatically. "We can do more than others, so we have more responsibility." She controlled herself a moment. "You should see their faces, Marguerite."

"Some of them actually *gave* me money," an act that Racine's expression showed she still had a hard time grasping. "On their own. Out of…thanks."

"That's lovely, dear," Madame Fleury replied, soundly unconvinced. "But going 'round all day, rushing about doing whatever it is you do, hardly taking time for yourselves – I worry, you know. You're none even getting enough to eat. You girls are looking so thin."

Gabrielle quickly sat up and spun towards her, a look of joy covering her face. "You think so?!!!"

"She didn't mean it as a compliment, dear," Auguste chimed in.

Marguerite headed back into the pantry to refill a bowl. If these dear ones were going to starve, it wouldn't be in *her* home.

Charlotte called out to her. "And daily we become so much better at our – what shall I call it? – our craft. The support that Auguste has selflessly given to us has tru…."

He waved his hands to hush her. Then, quietly he almost

131

whispered. "The Old Woman doesn't like me exerting myself. She fusses too much. She'd rather I nap. But we'll practice more later. * Yes?" And then stopped a moment and smiled at them with much warmth. "I think you are all quite wonderful."

He kissed Racine tenderly on the forehead. She didn't react, nor really know how to, to such a thing. But inside, it did seem pleasant.

CHAPTER NINETEEN

Even in Paris, where children are raised on wine, taverns are not usually overflowing in the middle of the afternoon. But on this day there was a larger gathering than usual, as a patrol of Musketeers relaxed in the taphouse after their grueling shift had ended. Their captain, André Mersenne, knew well that with the hours his men had been keeping amid all the outbreaks in the city, they needed a release, or else they too might have their own outbreaks. So, some of the King's Guards had trooped down from headquarters and hoisted their ales.

He kept a close watch to make sure the relaxation didn't get too relaxing, but more than anything his men simply wanted a place to forget the growing turmoil they faced, if only for a short while. There was comfort in their numbers and in the closeness of shared confrontation. Few words were needed to understand a fellow's thoughts, which is just as well, since most of them were men of few words.

As the shouts and bantering and songs and spilled drinks went on, three women sauntered in. It was not the most expected of occurrences, and there were good-natured hoots as Racine, Gabrielle, and Charlotte passed by, looking for an open table.

Captain Mersenne turned to see what the reaction was about, and was as surprised as the others, but mostly to recognize his former spirited detainee.

"Miss Tarascon, I believe," as he raised his mug in salute, and then acknowledged the other two with a smile. "Ladies. *Bonjour.* How are you this afternoon?"

Gabrielle and Charlotte politely nodded at the stranger, though glad to have a friendly officer in their midst. Racine, however, ignored him and walked past.

As it was, the women were not all strangers to the Musketeers, since word of their efforts intervening on behalf of citizens in distress had passed to headquarters, and a few of the men had even crossed their paths in the aftermaths. Among the rest of the men, several could be heard asking, "Oh, are *those* the ones?" and laughing, and derisive calls were added to the cacophony.

"Not out strutting today? Saving Paris," one of the Musketeers shouted. "How could the city manage?"

As the women squeezed through a gauntlet of bodies, his friend chortled, "They're probably looking for someone to put a 'long sword' in their sheath."

He suggestively pulled his sword in-and-out, in-and-out, much to the delight of lewd laughter.

Racine stopped in front of him. "You can only dream of having a long sword. You've just got a little dagger."

The room filled with oooohs and shouts of "she got you" from the raucous Musketeers. Charlotte pulled Gabrielle close and shyly whispered.

"I don't get it."

"I'll explain later." And she patted the young innocent on the arm.

Finding seats, Racine and Gabrielle flopped down, while Charlotte went to the bar to place their order.

"Now, there's a good serving wench," a Musketeer laughed, lifting his near-empty tankard at her. "Come by and take my order if you can handle it. If any of you can." He turned towards the other two women, which brought about others knocking their mugs on the table in ridiculing rhythm.

"Come on, now, give them a break. They're here to relax, just like the rest of you under-worked and over-paid wastrels," André chided.

Racine shot back at him and caught his eye. "We don't need your patronizing help."

Charlotte ever-so-slowly returned to the table, carefully doing her best to balance the tray. The steins slid around it as the tray tilted this way and that. Most of the beer remained inside, a bit of foam slopping over, as the girl kept her eye riveted on her charge, determined to make it all the way back, biting her lower lip in single-minded focus. Noticing her close attention, one of the men quickly stuck his leg out in front of her, and Charlotte went tumbling to the ground. The tray spilling over the floor in a crash.

Gabrielle spun in their direction, her normally cheerful eyes were still bright, but they closed a little tighter. "Oh, such big men. So impressive. If only you were as impressive as you think." A wonderful thought came to her at that very instant, and a sparkle shined behind her look. "Hey, I'll bet your best can't even beat our _worst_."

Charlotte was on the floor, cleaning up what she considered her mess, and looked up. Hunnhh?? Me?? She peered over at Gabrielle in confusion with a bewildered expression that asked why in the world would you challenge a Musketeer to fight…me?

"One on one," Gabrielle continued, not even checking in Charlotte's direction. She had something else in mind. "A simple challenge. Your captain against…her."

She pointed, not to Charlotte, but at Racine.

"If your big captain can't take our worst, how could any of

you possibly hope to fair with someone actually *good*?!"

The three women exchanged knowing looks. And the roomful of Musketeers began goading their captain. Pushing him, chiding him, laughingly calling into question his leadership and doubting his skills, but it held no interest for the man. "You're the one who stuck your foot out," he joked to the other, "and now you've got it stuck in your mouth. Or other orifices of your body." And with that, he walked to the bar, turning his back on his men to make a show of total disinterest.

Racine purposefully marched over to him, and all eyes were on her as she neared their boss, step-by-clomping step. It was impossible to miss the sound of each well-intentioned clack, and the captain turned and watched as she neared. At last, she stood challengingly face to face.

"Man enough? First one to quit."

André politely took out his sword. Not threateningly, but held down by his side, to make clear, "Don't test me. I do have a sword, you understand."

But Racine smiled to herself, knowing full-well what was coming next, knowing the first move she had planned had absolutely nothing to do with some silly sword that that egotistical fool was holding. She held his eyes – and then, all of a sudden, she kicked her leg out straight at his groin and –

André snapped out his hand and deftly blocked it. He winked back warmly at her.

"Professional skill. It's a good thing."

"You can take your hand off my leg now. Much as I'm sure you'd like to keep it there."

She spun away from him, freeing herself, and then quickly drew her sword and swiped it at Mersenne. Caught unready that she was taking this bagatelle seriously – the kick had been just a kick, after all, and he'd easily put a stop to that and made his point – he just barely parried her. She thrust her sword again, and he blocked it, pushing back. It was a game, but even games have winners, and there was a reputation at stake. The battle was on.

As Racine turned to get a better position and leverage, she bumped into two soldiers who pushed her away. Feeling unfairly challenged, she swung her sword to keep them off. Being attacked themselves, they challenged back. And so she fought them, as well.

Seeing Racine fighting three Musketeers to one, Gabrielle and Charlotte jumped in to help the best they could. Pushing their way through the crowd, clanging their blades off the steel being held up at them, Gabrielle spinning and sliding away, Charlotte perhaps more ducking and slipping away to safety. They were admirably fearless. And also vastly unnumbered – and outnumbered by trained, accomplished experts.

Still, they tried, if only to show support for their friend. But to the Musketeers it was as much an amusement as anything, watching these attractive and woefully outmatched young women showing hopeless pluck and hopeful loyalty. Holding up her sword with two hands as threateningly as she could manage, with a glare that was just as threatening she hoped (though in reality, quite a bit less so) to the few smiling Musketeers, Charlotte made noble swipes – and retreats. Soon enough though she had her sword knocked out of her grasp, as seemed to be the custom, and it clanged to the floor. As she bent to pick it, a sword tip was held to her back, and she was done. Gabrielle held on longer, in part for her greater experience at swordplay (for ultimately, play this was), but also in part because the men found particular enjoyment watching this flamboyant beauty whirling her way about. Musketeers they may have been, but men are men, after all. Eventually though all fun-and-games must come to an end, and when another of these King's Guards stepped in to join the battle, Gabrielle was lost, as well. With a great sense of drama, she acknowledged defeat with a small nod and a great sweep of her arm.

Racine, however, remained impressive, and the men around her had few smiles in their frustrating effort to win and win quickly, although André stood aside in somewhat-bemused admiration, if not wonderment. Jumping from one man to the next, she eluded their best efforts, knocking swords away before leaping onto a chair and then up to a table, gaining her strategic advantage of the high ground. She evaded an attempt to trip her, and slid across the beer-spilled surface, jumping onto the back of one opponent and sliding safely down while taking his legs out from under him. And then turning to catch another guard off-guard. But in the end, even Racine couldn't defeat a regiment, and she was surrounded. A half-dozen swords pointed at her, along with an equal number of relieved, albeit gritting faces.

André stepped through the gauntlet of men, pushing the blades out of the way. He looked at her kindly, though with a firmness.

"You are extremely good. But we're done."

Racine, though, was in no mood for acquiescence and letting bygones be. She never really was, of course – Racine could hold resentment in her sleep – but as far as she was concerned, the challenge had only been made and far from the end, it was only the beginning. Always believing her credo that the best defense was a good offense, she kept up her fight, despite the reality of the situation.

"You're scared," she snapped at him. "You can't take me alone. And you know it. You're a little *boy*, hiding behind your regiment, that's all, just playing at being a soldier."

Even for Racine, she went too far. With all the Musketeers surrounding him in earshot, moving closer to see how their captain would react to this upstart, who barely came up to his shoulders, challenging his honor. The honor of a French officer in front of the soldiers he commanded. André took a single step closer and stood tall before his men. His face was still friendly, but the eyes were steeled and serious.

"Playing? This isn't a game. We are protecting the head of France. Do you understand? You think you three are Faith, Hope and Charity. Be glad you haven't been arrested for obstruction. It's over."

And with that, he took Racine's sword and broke it over his knee. In humiliation, as worse a feeling as she could feel, Racine wanted to leap at him, but she was still surrounded. She might be hard-headed, but she understood lost causes and the reality of fighting another day.

Two other Musketeers took the swords from Gabrielle and Charlotte, and following the lead, broke the blades in half. A few chuckles and humphs could be heard, but mostly it was a roomful of faces who knew best. It was a moment of embarrassment that couldn't be avoided, and lingered in the air.

"What are you even doing here??" one of the men asked in dripping ridicule.

"Get the hell out of our way," another spat out, pointedly.

And then, several of the Musketeers picked up the three

139

women and carried them to the door. If they had felt demeaned before, it was nothing compared to this simple act. The humiliation was complete. Racine twisted, but it was only for effect and her own well-being. It accomplished nothing else. Outside the tavern, the men dropped them unceremoniously on the street.

Racine was back on her feet immediately, little could keep her down, as confrontational as ever.

"You're sons of an ass, you know that? If it was left to the mighty Musketeers, there would be no France left to save. You fight us, and leave the privileged alone to put a noose around France, with your corrupt eyes closed."

A few of the men ignored her completely and returned into the tavern. Several though were amused, or fascinated, or not quite sure to make of this young women, and stayed. Eventually, they turned to join their compatriots, as laughter and shouts could be heard drifting out amid back-slapping and reverie.

Captain Mersenne impassively listened from the doorway. Then – with great politeness, but with very clear, hard resolve – he finally replied, his words well-considered, experienced, pointed, and full of absolute serious meaning.

"This is a world with death. I like you. I *admire* you. But you are going to get killed. And Racine – I would hate that. Wandering the streets with swords, helping people is not your job. Any of your jobs. It is for Musketeers. And you are not Musketeers. It's over. Stop. Now."

As the women silently looked, he turned and went inside. The door was slammed in their faces.

It would be an understatement that Racine Tarascon didn't take ridicule, condescension or humiliation well, but most especially in combination. She looked at the door, anxious to race at it, but her body knotted up with anger, more than enough to cover the other two women – more than enough, in fact, to cover any other woman or man or beast who might have walked past at that moment. It wasn't that her teeth were clenched, but her ears were clenched, her hair was clenched, and her fingers were clenched.

Which wasn't to say that the other two young women didn't feel put upon, as they shook the dust from their hair and soothed their bruises, which were mostly to their pride. Maybe it wasn't much, Gabrielle thought with a harrumph, maybe it wasn't saving the world, but assisting anyone who needed it, that was real, thank you very much, it was appreciated and therefore had value. But then, happily, she did have experience of bouncing back from public rebuke. It was a gift, she felt. Sometimes you just had to accept the wrong opinions or jealousy of others.

Of course, the truth is that pride always has a way of rejuvenating itself for those who are the most resilient, and often returns stronger than before to protect itself from future onslaughts.

Not that Racine herself needed any outside or even internal assistance to protect her pride. It was there in abundance, with plenty to spare. And so it was that the gypsy paced in a circle, fuming, turning back on her path.

"If I could wipe the smirks off their faces." She stopped, and if a glare could have ever pierced through those tavern doors, it would have been Racine's.

"I know exactly," Gabrielle said earnestly and nodded with emphasis, as she continued to dust herself off. "Oh, you have no idea." She smoothed her blouse. "My friend Marie and I

141

were once in this play, and a critic gave me the worst review, but I know he just …"

If Racine's attention had been riveted on the tavern before, that fixation was now broken. She spun back and could only stare disbelieving at Gabrielle in front of her, going on about – something. She quickly threw her hands over her ears. Kindly, Gabrielle stopped. Her friend, after all, was clearly under distress, and needed time no doubt to comport herself. So, she could wait. At last, Racine flung her hands in the air and stormed off.

Gabrielle followed after, finally able to finish, "…wanted to date Marie and hoped I'd quit, that was the only reason, but that was *never* going to happen because if I knew one thing, it was…"

And so they went, down the street and around the corner, Gabrielle two steps behind Racine, continuing her tale that somehow seemed to blend into another, blissfully content in having an audience, no matter how much the gypsy would speed her pace. Gabrielle was able to keep up. While it was known that some people could not eat and walk at the same time, Gabrielle could talk and do pretty much anything at the same time. A casual observer might even presume that this was some sort of a game: a raggedly-dressed young woman weaving from one side of the street to the other, as a flamboyant girl did her best to Follow-the-Leader, gesticulating with enthusiastic hands and with long, blonde hair flowing in the wind behind her. A more perceptive observer might wonder why the lass in front had a perpetual grimace across her face and didn't stop to throttle the one behind her, but then that was a question Racine was asking herself. Yet, for some reason, she didn't. And down they continued together.

142

Left alone back at the tavern, a wistful Charlotte wandered through the town, not the safest venture, but her mind was on others things. The words of the King's Guard had struck a chord with her. She knew there was good what they were doing, but what *was* she doing there? It was a question she thought she knew the answer to, but so much in her life had changed and so fast, that sometimes she felt overwhelmed by it all.

She walked a bit aimlessly, stopping to look at her sad reflection in a shop window. And it was made all the more pointed amid gorgeous dresses, fine hats, and exquisite accessories. *That* was a world she at least understood. And did so love. She would look grand, she thought, in that gown hanging before her. She was growing up, she knew, looking more mature, and it would fit her in all the right places she wished it to. It was the latest style, too, she smiled. When was the last time she thought about *that*? She used to all the time. And others would ask her about what she thought was fashionable, because her taste mattered. She smiled, thinking how she would glide around at a *belle danse* in it, the soft fabric flowing, feeling luxurious against her skin. She adored the *loure*, it was slow, much better for dancing than the *gigue*. Gilles preferred that, she knew, but then he liked things fast. She recalled his arm around her waist when last they met, and she closed her eyes and could feel it still. Would she ever feel it, feel such a thing again? She looked once more at everything in the shop window and imagined her reflection wearing it all.

Suddenly, another reflection appeared beside hers, though smaller, as if from across the street. It seemed familiar, but that seemed unlikely. And more unlikely, it seemed to be the face she had seen before...Philippe Gascogne. Was he looking at

143

her?? Watching her even? Again? Still? She couldn't tell, for the body was on a horse, and appeared to be half behind a cart. Was he hiding? She looked closer in the glass, not wanting to give herself away, but she was certain it was he. She quickly spun around, but the man had ridden off.

Charlotte took off down the street, rushing through the mid-day crowd after him. It might be futile race, but a horse on a busy thoroughfare had to slow for the people around. Charlotte though ducked in and out between pedestrians and did her best to keep the man in sight.

She turned yet another corner, and rushed through the business district. She was baffled – which way did he go? There were three side streets, he could have taken any. The young girl ran up to a woman.

"A man on a horse," she caught her breath. "Light brown. Please, did you see where he went? Well-dressed. A tall hat."

The lady was flustered by this young girl's energetic insistence, but at last pointed, and Charlotte took off again, running as far as she could. Down a street, around a circle, and there, off in the distance, stood an opulent hotel. And leaving his horse with a groomsman – it was indeed Count Gascogne. Here in Paris. Spying on her, she was sure of it. He swiftly entered the hotel and was gone.

A breathless Charlotte stood watching. And fast as her heart was beating, it now beat even faster.

CHAPTER TWENTY

The jousts between Cardinal Jules Mazarin and Gaston Jean-Baptiste de France, Duc d'Orléans, were legendary. Polite on the surface, but few knew how deep that surface went. Skin deep, most probably.

Today, though, they walked together, in momentary truce. The Duke's daughter, *La Grande Mademoiselle* Anne, had long-since recuperated in the great care of her father's estate from her bout with the king's kidnapper, but she now returned to the *Palais Royale* for the first time, escorted through the courtyard between her father and the Cardinal. They were on their best behavior, though that wasn't saying much.

The rivalry between the two men even preceded their knowing one another. *Monsieur* Gaston had taken part in several conspiracies against his brother, Louis XIII, and had been banished from the court from time to time. He thought little of it, conspiracies were the way of a court, he felt, so what was one more – or a few? And as heir to the throne, at least before Louis XIV had been born, the Duc d'Orléans thought it almost his patriotic duty to conspire.

Not surprisingly, others felt differently, most notably Cardinal Richelieu. The powerful chief advisor had his own enemies, but more authority. And his mistrust of *Monsieur* never wavered.

When very young, *Mademoiselle* Anne knew little of all the politics between the great men, but only thought it all funny, and in the way of little children would often sing comic songs about Richelieu in front of him. As her godfather, he would reprove her politely, though firmly. She just thought the songs were funny and didn't know why he had no sense of humor. But then, being mistrusted, unpopular, threatened, manipulative, and massively powerful often blunts the humor of those in authority.

And being the protégé of Cardinal Richelieu, Mazarin inherited many of those traits, and most of his wariness of those around him. And at the top of that list, *Monsieur* Gaston stood. To most others, the Duke was a harmless fool. All blustering talk. To Cardinal Mazarin, though, he knew better. *Monsieur* was someone his mentor had taught him much about. And little of it was good.

It was of no matter to the Duke what Mazarin thought, since *Monsieur* believed him duplicitous. Many of his decisions seemed to the man's own benefit, and that led down a dark path. How had he become so wealthy, a mere public servant? Was he robbing the kingdom, or worse, selling France's soul? His wheedling influence on the Queen Mother had been growing unreasonable these past many weeks, spending far more time together than regent and advisor seemed prudent. No doubt he would insist it was because of the crisis over the king, but there were always crises. That's what came with the crown. *Monseiur* wouldn't be surprised to find France a vassal beholden to Mazarin's Italy one day soon. Or worse. And he knew he wasn't alone in these beliefs.

Which left *Mademoiselle* keeping the peace between them. Fortunately, she was of a bright, spirited temperament for the responsibility.

She was an attractive young woman, taking after her mother, Marie de Bourbon, everyone said. Though *Mademoiselle* Anne didn't know, since her mother died five days after her birth. Being raised by governesses, she grew up strong and vibrant. But always the Duchess. Always proud of her place in France. Always proud to be granddaughter of Louis XIII. She was highly sought after by suitors through Europe, and matches were regularly rumored. But the young girl was in no hurry to marry. She knew she would one day find the right man. For she deserved well. And so it was that she relished being a lady of the court, with all the airs and honors and fineries and wealth and influence it brought. And so she relished playing diplomat between two such notable men.

As she traipsed along between them, an aide followed behind her with a parasol keeping off the sun. She sweetly slipped her arms between the two men on either side.

"I'm glad you've come to see us again, *Mademoiselle*," the Cardinal noted with great charm and warmth, though avoiding the look of the Duke. "It's good to have our circle strong once more."

"Careful, daughter, when the Cardinal talks of strength. He would rather wage a losing war than wisely meet the nobles halfway." The Duke didn't even try to fake a polite smile, though he did give his dear child a knowing pat.

"Dangerous thinking, *Monsieur*," Mazarin quickly replied. "What you call 'moderation' to our enemies borders on treason."

Seeing the conversation going far off the graceful path she wished, *Mademoiselle* gave their arms both a friendly squeeze and smiled. "I have no doubt that one of you is right."

CHAPTER TWENTY-ONE

The quaint parlor where Auguste and Marguerite Fleury lived was a quiet, simple room. Several hard-back chairs, an oak table that had a few chips and cracks that come from experience and a lace-style doily that the lady of the house had made years ago. A functional sofa faced a fire place that was burning, though not so much for any great chill in the late afternoon, but more for the light it threw on the room, as the sun was dipping. Candles added some to the brightness.

But though the room was always a place of simplicity – madame sat off to the side sewing – tonight it was unfamiliar. There was an air of excitement. The three women were huddled together, as Auguste sat beside them in his comfortable chair, a solid piece of furniture which had never been all that comfortable by itself but was enhanced by cushions his dear wife had made.

"And you say you've actually seen this man following?!" Gabrielle faced Charlotte, as did the others. She leaned in close, not wanting to miss a word.

The young girl was trying to be composed, but her manners were no match tonight for the tumbling of emotions she had roiling inside.

"Count Philippe Gascogne. Yes. I cannot swear to the law that he killed my father. Yet he must certain be involved.

"Of course he's involved!" Racine was almost more incensed by this news than even Charlotte. Her mind was already looking down the road. And seeing how so many pieces fit, she had difficulty staying seated. "Nobody travels that far to follow someone, see them – see them twice! – and then *not* say 'hello.' And those jackals live in packs. *You* know something, you saw something, heard something, and they're terrified." Racine made sure the naïve young girl held her gaze. This was important. "What do you know?? That's the conspiracy we have to prove. Which the Musketeers have ignored. Like the Musketeers always ignore. I just want to be there to rub it in their faces when an arrest is made!"

"If we were the ones to bring him in –" it had finally dawned on Gabrielle the full extent of what Racine was so excited about. And visions of glory now filled her head. "Can you imagine??!"

"I just wish to see justice done," Charlotte stated softly, but with an cold intensity that belied a simple desire to have the law followed merely for the good of society.

Racine had by now given up any pretense of controlling herself, and was pacing sharply around the room.

"We can do this because no one else is looking for him. With Auguste's expertise as a sword expert, we can make plans to –"

From the back of the room, the old woman gave off a little laugh, almost surprising herself. "Auguste isn't a sword expert. He can hardly use a knife and fork properly." She chided her husband, "You told our dear girls a story like that?"

There was an air of confusion, as the three women looked at one another. No doubt Marguerite was having a joke at her husband's expense. She did that often, after all.

"He *was* squire to a fine, fine baron when a young man," Marguerrite added charitably, barely looking up from her work. "Lord Delveaux. Oh, Auguste was quite attached to him." She held the cloth up to get a better look at the pattern.

"Well...how – " Charlotte was at a complete loss what to

ask. This made no sense now. And the others were of no help, as bewildered as she. She tried again, but uncertain. Perhaps madame had heard them wrong. "Is that how he trained your daughter, to become a champion?"

The old woman had no idea what all this was about. "Our daughter? We don't have a daughter. She died when she was six."

There was a silence so deep and cavernous that it pounded in the heads of the young women. Their faces, stunned and blank, were uncomprehending. Bit by bit, the reality of what they'd been told began to sink in. Marguerite sought out an answer from the others, but all she saw in return was the first stages of shock.

"We risked our live, plans – everything…over a lie?" Gabrielle managed to get out.

A look of comprehension came to his wife. She had lived with the man for 52 years after all. She turned to him softly. "My dear Auguste."

He was mortified, more even than the women, and they were sitting there unmoving, not able to say a word. If anyone could peer inside him, they would have seen a heart sinking. He withdrew into himself. He couldn't imagine what they must feel. Worse, he didn't want to imagine it. He couldn't bear the risk he caused them, the danger, the lost trust. All he could do was feel – and feel it over and over – that he was a foolish old man.

He too could not speak. But at last, hesitatingly, the emptiness of the room was broken.

"I am so sorry. I never – Seeing you three girls there. Alone. It seemed you wanted someone to tell you everything was okay. And I got to do that. Do something. And by the time…Watching you grow up so – " he corrected himself, "*Grow* so happy, and passionate. I was so proud. Look at you. You brought such life to this empty home. And I did the one thing I would never want. I hurt you all."

He grew silent. There was nothing more he could say. No words could even think of saying. He affected these dear women and humbled himself.

And no one moved. The faces in the room avoided one another, everyone far too busy thinking their own thoughts, and trying to understand what they were.

And then, Racine stood and walked pointedly up to Auguste. She waited until he looked at her, but he couldn't. At last though, he had no choice. The eyes of everyone now had a place to focus. But not one of them could possibly have looked elsewhere. Every eye was riveted on the gypsy. With breaths held, they all waited. Uncertain how bad this would be.

"We are about to dive into hell to try and bring to justice the people who murdered this girl's father. Based solely on what *you* told us." She stopped and collected her thoughts. The silence was piercing. "Something we never, ever would have done or been able to do without you."

And she leaned in and hugged the old man tightly. Not for a second letting go.

CHAPTER TWENTY-TWO

There was a world within Paris that was very private. It was not secret – indeed, the very opposite. That's because anyone who was anyone, or who aspired to be anyone wanted to be in a salon. And wanted others to know that he or she was in a salon. And in the best salon possible. But even if the salon you were invited to wasn't one of the very best, there still was great value in letting others know you were part of it, provided that they weren't.

At the very best salons, only the very best, the very smartest, the most talented, the wittiest, the most important were invited. It not only gave their lives a credibility (and credibility could often count as much as accomplishment in some circles), but the best of the salons actually did matter. At the lower end, it was true that pretension and the need to impress tended to rule the day. But at the top, the salons drove Paris society, which drove France, which drove Europe by bringing art and literature and music and science and philosophy and medicine and politics all together. And so the very best mingled, and in mingling strengthened one another. The words could be soaring and majestic, they could be biting and hurtful, they could be clear, brilliantly obscure, or empty as a blank page. But even the most foolish words were remarkable. Because they could raise a man or ruin one's reputation.

And the very best salon of them all was *La Belle Vie*. Here, an invitation was admittance to a society others only dreamed of. A place was so sought after it was enough for others to simply know that you *could* be here if you wished. That you were wanted, and it was your choice whether or not you would deign to attend. For at the very top, the exclusive privacy was the *La Belle Vie's* most important feature of all. With an emphasis on the privacy, where secrecy could be at its most hidden, if that was your desire. Such was this beautiful life.

And so it was here that the beautiful people of Paris filled the most *en vogue* establishment of them all. Wine flowed, banquet tables of the finest food abounded, a string quartet played, servants tended your every need without you needing to ask, and wafts of smoke permeated the night air.

Madame Suzanne Lebec d'Avignon, former mistress of the Duc de Montresse, ran the salon, and she maintained it with the grandiosity it demanded and which she commanded in her every movement, from the pointing of her hand to the turn of her bright, red-painted lips, and the glance of her ever-watchful eye. The exquisitely-dressed doyenne led a gentlemen guest, flowing their way through the crowd.

"It was a scandal when he was left off the list. He is yet to show himself *en public*. There was no suicide, though, which was highly thoughtless to the rest of us."

She tossed her head knowingly with a laugh, as they weaved past the guests, around a corner and down a dim hallway. Coming at last to the most private of rooms, she opened the door.

There in intense conversation were two serious men, who quickly looked up at the unexpected disturbance. They had moved their chairs to within arm's reach of each other, less it seemed so that they could be heard than they would not be overheard.

"Oh!" she cried, almost as surprised and pleased by her discovery as she was embarrassed at her mistaken intrusion.

"Cardinal Mazarin. Monsieur le Marquis. I didn't realize you gentlemen were speaking again."

Eduard was stoic, but Mazarin smiled benignly at her. Then, he reached over – and shut the door bluntly in her face.

CHAPTER TWENTY-THREE

The public square was quiet at this time of the day. Most citizens had by now gone home for the evening and locked themselves in. Those who had other plans for the night – for good or ill – were in the midst of preparation. And so only a few people wandered past the shops, cafés, and the grand hotel at the far end. And those who did could barely be made out in the falling dusk.

Under the protective gloaming, three women huddled together, hidden around a corner, but able to make out the entrance to the hotel. Their location was a bit inconvenient, unaccustomed as they were to holding such a secret vigil. Or at least two of them were. Charlotte and Gabrielle kept shifting positions to gain a better vantage point.

"I can't...It's...Can you see anything?"

"Come over here," Gabrielle called out, having moved closer. "There's a better view."

The young girl stepped nearer to join her. "Oh, yes. I believe you're right." She called out, back to her other friend. "You should join us."

"You do understand," Racine noted sardonically, in a low voice, "that the goal here is to avoid being spotted and remain silent. So as to not draw attention to..." and then she spit out, "...ourselves."

The other two scurried back to their hiding spot. In a quieter voice now, Gabrielle covered her mouth. "I would feel more comfortable if we watched the rear. In my experience, men like to sneak around like that, and surprise you."

"You must needs believe me, Count Gascogne would

never depart by any back entrance. I believe him a popinjay. Even if he had something to hide, which I am certain he does, he would stride out the front. Above the world. He strides everywhere. I know him. And I know that he travels in close company with all the aristocrats. I am *certain* he can lead us to information."

Racine maneuvered herself lower to the ground and squinted to get a better look. Gabrielle plastered herself dramatically against the wall, and then peered intently over the gypsy. As she kept looking, though, a thought slowly occurred to her. "How do we even know he's going to be leaving??"

Racine held back a sigh. "We don't," she finally said, without looking up. "That's why we will come back tomorrow. And the next day. And the day after, if need be. It takes patience. Great patience. You do understand the idea of patience, don't y…" – and then she looked up, considered who she was talking to, shrugged and went back to her surveillance.

Charlotte was not only excited, but nervous beyond expectations. She wrapped her cloak around her to cover her appearance from being recognized, should she be spotted by the Count. Anxiously, she ran her fingers through her hair and carefully smoothed it.

"Am I ready?" she whispered, catching herself to stay quiet. "I've never trailed a villain within his sight like this."

Gabrielle looked her over, and then began to nod with an approving eye. "I have to tell you," she said admiringly, "that color is really good for you."

For the moment, Charlotte brightened, her nerves forgotten. "You think? Because I was considering wearing the brown one for night time."

"Oh, no, this brings out your eyes so well. It was a

wonderful choice, and the way your hair – "

"Uh, girls. I really do hate to interrupt this tea party. But, well, the thing is…" Racine noticed that Philippe had just left the hotel.

Charlotte saw, too, and in her excitement jumped to take off racing down the avenue in full view. Racine was barely able to reach her by the scruff of her wrap and dragged her back.

"Hidden, Princess. Hidden."

She dropped to the ground, understanding, mortified, yet shaking with worry. "But if he should get his horse, we'd have no way…"

"If the Count is doing something secretive, he will not go riding out in the open for everyone to see. And if he's not doing anything suspicious – there's no need for us to follow."

As she spoke, Gabrielle's eyes were peeled on Philippe, moving off into the dark. "But he's walking away."

"And so, we follow." Racine turned and looked pointedly at Charlotte. "From behind."

Down the cobbled street Philippe Gascogne went, striding purposefully but with care, his eyes taking in the neighborhood around him. Checking out those passing him by. There was the clack of footsteps all around him, none drawing any more meaning to him than others, just footsteps in the night, several of them off in the distance trailing behind him.

He turned corner after corner, looking around for directions and darkened nooks and untrustworthy faces, and what had started out as a stroll in one of the more fashionable districts of the city had by the block become less well-kept and far dingier.

Yet it was here, of all places, that the elegant Count Philippe Gascogne, he of grand chateaux, summer villas, and a

157

world of the heights of society, turned and entered what can only best be described as a murky restaurant. On a murky street. In one of the murkier neighborhoods of Paris.

And all was once again quiet, without a soul around, for it was a district where few came at night, at least without friends or a purpose. The only muffled noise came from the boisterous activity inside.

The shadows of the disappearing dusk were almost all gone now, blended into the covering darkness of the evening. At the far end of the alley, however, a young girl's head popped around the edge of a building at the corner. Then, Racine's head popped above Charlotte's. And Gabrielle appeared below.

Though the other two women peered so intently at the bistro down the cobbled alley, a quizzical expression crossed Racine's face. "This is hardly a place where the elite meet to dine. He shouldn't be here. He shouldn't. Something is not right."

But that only served to please the youngest of them. For the first time in her life, she was actually hoping for the worst. "That's a good sign, yes?" If Philippe Gascogne was not here in this loathsome brasserie simply to dine – and why in heaven's name would he be? – then this might have been the first piece of luck she'd had since her good fortune had ended.

After being certain that they would not be spotted, the three women carefully made their way over and peeked inside. Their faces pressed up against the glass to get a better look.

It was a seedy establishment. Crowded with an equally seedy clientele. If Philippe had seemed out-of-place arriving there, he looked all the more so seated with a little, shabby man who was leaning across the table, speaking in confidence.

Philippe disinterestedly sipped from a bowl of soup, and a waitress placed salads beside the two conspirators.

Out in the dark night, the anxious women could only stare inside.

"This is not good," Racine muttered and stepped back, as Charlotte turned to her. "We can't hear what they're saying. There's no way we can possibly get close enough."

Gabrielle, however, kept looking in through the window. As the other two stood lost in uncertainty, her gaze grew more and more focused, and her eyes tightened. Then, with a determined look of success, she quickly spun to them. "I know how."

It would be difficult to imagine how anyone could get close enough to hear anybody in the place. The room was noisy and most of the customers seemed the type to distrust strangers. The rest kept to themselves. Philippe fit in because he and his confidante kept to themselves.

As the evening moved on, the two men pushed aside their now-empty bowls and plates so that they could speak closer. The bustle of the evening swirled around them, unconcerned by the two secretive men, since so many of the others were as secretive in their own way. But shouts and songs occasionally cut through the air, regardless.

And then, out of the kitchen, came a striking waitress with flowing blonde hair and a flamboyant way about her. Gabrielle paused to moment to adjust the skimpy wench outfit. It didn't fit perfectly, but it was close enough, and beggars can't be choosers. Well, she wasn't a beggar precisely, in fact the very opposite – she had paid a good two francs to the waitress just to borrow her clothes for a short while. It had taken much less bargaining than she figured, but then that was more than the other women had expected to make for the whole night. Gabrielle was just glad that the fit was close enough. And if it showed a bit more skin than the wardrobe was meant to, well, all right, the clothes never had it so lucky, she thought to herself.

Through a corner of the window outside, Charlotte and Racine almost couldn't bear to watch. Charlotte thought she might shatter her teeth from clenching them so hard and finally had to turn away. Even Racine, who had nerves stronger than many wild animals, had a difficult time keeping her eyes attentive, and then even she couldn't bear watching that girl in the pit of the lion's den, tightrope walking without a net. She joined Charlotte, and neither said a word, instead just standing back in safety and holding their breaths. They had no idea what Gabrielle would be doing, she hadn't told them her plan, just asked to give her two francs. That she was actually there – it was too much for them.

Gabrielle though was oblivious to all of that. The show must go on, after all. And for goodness sake, she knew how to waitress. What's the worst that could happen? Well, okay, she knew the worst, there was always a worst, but her friends were outside, so other than that? She simply picked up a tray, took a deep breath and crossed through the room, sashaying her way between tables.

"Hey, mamzelle, hey, could we get a couple of ales for…"

"Yes, of course, fine…" she responded without paying the slightest attention to the customer and passed right by with determination. All she had in mind was her quarry up ahead, Philippe and his compatriot. As she neared, however, Gabrielle slowed down and altered her walk ever-so-imperceptibly. Even her expression changed, to those who noticed such things.

160

Finally, she stood at the elbow of Philippe Gascogne. A beaming smile cross her face. He didn't bother to look up, still in heavy conversation.

"Hi, I'm…uh," she paused, trying to think quickly, and then added in a slightly bubble-headed way, "I'm Julianne. I'll be your waitress."

"We have a waitress," Philippe said curtly and returned dismissively to his conversation.

"Oh, yes, right, but she…uh, died. Or something. Her mother died, it's okay. Well, not for her mother, but well, I'm just filling in for her. She's fine, thank you for asking." Not that anyone asked. "I'll tell her."

She straightened the table, pleased with how well she had done at improvisation, and seemingly went on with her business, straining all the while to listen as the men confided with one another.

"Like I said," Philippe repeated in a low voice to the snitch, "I don't like surprises."

"You worry too much," the other snapped, "everything seems in order."

"In order? The Marquis's private party is one day before the gala. I don't have the luxury of anything going wrong."

The scruffy little man, whose name sounded like "Maurice," did his best to put the aristocrat at his ease, something he found increasingly difficult, but that's the way all those nobles were, he thought. "My friends say much will be told there."

Gabrielle moved in closer to hear better. Philippe pointedly looked up at her.

"Could we have some wine? Or bread?" Gabrielle didn't budge and just smiled sweetly at him. "Or privacy."

161

She nodded repeatedly, hoping a delay would allow him to change his mind and go back to talking, but he just waited for her to go. "Of course, sir, it's my pleasure, sir, I'll just keep checking back to make sure you always have everything you need."

"No, we're perfectly fi..."

"No, no, sir, it's my pleasure. That why I'm here, I live but to serve, to make sure your dining experience in our fine establishment," she indicated around the musty dive, "is a happy and memorable experience. I'll see you momentarily, you enjoy your fish, or whatever that is," and she scooted off.

Gabrielle did the best she could to return to the table and glide nearby and overhear whatever she possibly could. At last, having gathered as much information as she felt likely and when the gentlemen were picking at the cheese plate and sipping their beer to finish their meal, she most carefully slipped outside – hesitating first only briefly, out of habit to collect the tip for service, though she figured it would be small, knowing the type of men they were, so never mind.

Outside at last, Charlotte leaped to hug Gabrielle seeing her safe, while Racine kept repeating "You fool," "You idiot," and "You're going to get yourself killed," which showed far more concern than she intended. As Gabrielle earnestly delivered her account, she did her best to stay focused and get all the details right with the precision her clandestine effort deserved, though her words fell over one another in a bit of a jumble. Racine and a deeply-shivering Charlotte paid rapt attention, while keeping a close watch on the entrance.

"The other man," Gabrielle used her hands emphatically and even her full body to get across the importance of the whole story, "he seems an informant of some kind. But I couldn't tell why this party of the Marquis is so important."

"If evidence exists, *th-that's* where it will be, at the p-party." Charlotte wrapped her cloak tighter and squeezed her fingers to get the circulation going.

Through all this, Racine was almost bouncing with excitement, the rush and thrill of the chase growing and getting to her. She was so good at chases, she knew. It's just that usually she was on the receiving end.

"They're conspiring. They're always conspiring. I told you! The bastards can't help themselves. And we know it. <u>Us</u>. And de Longueville is involved up to *his* neck in it! This is wonderful. Get one of these two, and they both fall. They all fall. The Marquis, the Count, their whole conspiracy. Everyone. Like a house of cards."

"Honey, are you cold?"

Clearly-freezing and shuddering, Charlotte was determined not to complain, and stoically shook her head, "n-n-no" to Gabrielle. And then shot two "thumbs up."

Behind them and across the alley, Philippe and his fellow conspirator were leaving the café. The three woman stepped back out of the light, and shrank against the wall to watch Gascogne hand a coin to a boy, who ran off on some mission. All the while, Racine and Charlotte concentrated their attention on the aristocrat, and when a carriage rolled up, the gypsy tensed.

Gabrielle pulled them back and in her lowest voice whispered. "No, don't worry, it's fine if he leaves. It's the *other* man we have to follow. The little one. Stay close wherever he walks to. Don't lose him."

But there was much reason to worry. Because when the carriage door opened – it was the raggedy snitch who got it.

And the coach began to pull away. Not just a reason to worry – but a huge problem.

Racine watched in dismay, her mind racing. It was almost out of sight. "OhGodOhGodOhGodOh – See you!" And without allowing a moment to consider her actions, her instincts took over and she tore off after.

The carriage rumbled down the cobblestoned street, and turned a corner. Racine chased it furiously, exploding in pursuit. The horses clomped along, pulling their charge at a comfortable pace, being in no hurry, as long as their driver wasn't, slowing to let a couple pass in front, and then picking up speed again.

Racine closed on the vehicle, but it was still out of reach. Her arms and legs pumped as fast as she could make them, but there were limits. The chilled air cut into her lungs. Yet still she ran and made headway. Closer she got as the coach leisurely moved along, past lampposts, storefronts, and utterly bewildered pedestrians at the sight of a lovely young woman racing exhaustedly after a coach down a Paris street. One man laughed to his wife, "Perhaps it would be easier if she just waited for the next one."

And on Racine chased. Nearing her target. It was within reach. Faster she ran. Almost out of breath, there it was and – she grabbed at – no, she missed, just barely too far away, and yet again she grabbed at – once more, so close, her fingers could almost touch it, but not, could not – and she reached one more time and then – she grabbed onto a ridge at the back, as the carriage trundled away, dragging her legs behind.

Racine strained to hold on, as her feet bumped continuously along the road…and…finally, she pulled herself around to the side. Just barely, she balanced herself on the narrow footboard and, gasping for air, crouched low.

The two men inside the carriage were oblivious to the outside world, with the heavy wooden wheels crushing underneath and overlapping their sound with the clopping of hooves. The little conspirator sat opposite an imperious gentleman who was very much his opposite in almost every way, having an overbearing nature that disregarded his traveling companion except for the momentary need he had for his use. The Count de Beaufort, after all, cared little for anyone but himself and (perhaps more) the Marquis, as his right-hand man. For it was from the Marquis that all future greatness to him would come.

"The coach will leave you off in private," he said dismissively. But then the lord added pointedly, so as not to risk even the slightest chance of being mistaken, "This meeting did not take place."

His eyes were glued on the ragged fellow, who in turn paid close attention. Unnoticed by the men, the top of Racine's head slowly crept up over the window ledge. In a moment, her eyes just barely peaked over, her dark hair blending into the night.

"No, uh, worry," the snitch Maurice awkwardly muttered, and then lied, because lying was his way, even when there was no reason, "I've been alone all night."

"The Marquis tolerates no flaws."

The Count de Beaufort turned towards the window to watch the passing city. Racine quickly popped her head back down. When the conversation began once more, and it seemed safe, she carefully came back up, though only enough so that she could hear.

"I thought you were protected by a spy inside the palace."

"Small comfort if anything goes wrong," de Beaufort sniffed. "At least we have the perfect hostage. Thank heavens that little waste of a king is good for something."

Racine's eyes bugged out in shock! She couldn't believe the words she'd just heard. But the moment it sank in, there was a thud as the carriage hit a deep hole in the road, and she plummeted like an anchor, out of sight. From outside the window came a simple sound –

"Ow."

Count de Beaufort looked around at the cry. All he saw though was the snitch in front of him. With a look of disdain, he sneered, "Oh, be a man."

And the carriage rolled on through the night.

At last, pulling alongside an extinguished lamp in a deserted square, the horses slowed and then came to a halt. The door opened, and a little, ragged man scurried off into the darkness, unseen from a meeting that had never taken place. But what was unseen, as well, that neither that man saw, nor did the high-toned gentleman inside, was that a small body quietly rolled off the footboard and ducked swiftly out of sight.

Later that night, that same small body blessedly perched on the edge of a soft bed in her attic bedroom, having just finished a remarkable tale. Around her, Gabrielle and Charlotte excitedly paced, keyed up beyond belief from this new information they'd just been given, too fevered to sit. Racine herself was fevered, although for a different reason, of course, and was just fine sitting for the time being, thank you very much, still disheveled, jostled, and a bit worse for wear from her adventure.

"This is too…I can't…The King?? They have the King??? He said that?!!" Gabrielle, who was never lost for words,

166

almost was. Almost.

"That must be why they killed my father. If we are certain they have His Royal Highness, should we not tell the authorities?"

Racine had a thought on the subject, though not the energy yet to offer it. Gabrielle, though, was quite able to fill in the void.

"What do we tell them? What can we prove? They won't listen to a word we say. You heard them. It's like 'The Boy Who Cried Wolf.' I know. I did it once in children's theatre. I played 'Suzette,' a local girl. It was quite good for a pastiche. I only had a small part, but the story…"

"Gabrielle, please." For this, Racine found her energy.

Charlotte was deeply stirred up by all she had heard, yet something seemed out of place, and she became a little distracted. "It's so strange," she said, her sweet face twisting in a confusion she couldn't explain, for though she was quite lost in so much of this, if there was one thing she did know it was how a grand *chateau* should run properly. "It is just so strange for a king to have been taken amid all his palace guards and the Musketeers. There surely must have been assistance, from somewhere."

"The King!" Racine seized on that one word, important beyond all measure. Important not just for what it meant to the others, what it would mean to any Frenchman, but the very personal meaning it held for her. Unique, so that it kindled a fire and a thought within her, that had escaped her until that very moment. And her enthusiasm grew deeper and built higher in an instant. "We have to do this. When we catch the bastard killer. When we expose the conspiracy. When we find the – " and she had to catch herself, barely daring to believe what she was thinking. But she *was* thinking it, and of her family. "I'll be able to speak to the <u>King</u>. I'll be able...We must do this. The King."

"If this doesn't make me famous," Gabrielle laughed, though she wasn't really making a joke, "nothing will."

Racine was all intense now, her mind rushing thoughts over one another.

"We need a way to break into the Marquis' estate," her voice snarling at the mention of that hated name, the cause she was sure was behind many pains, but especially so much of hers. "Find out what's there, look for any written plans they have, get whatever evidence we can that he's kidnapped the King. And put an end to this goddamned terror once and for all."

"No doubt it will be barricaded," Gabrielle offered. "Heavily."

Racine had a sharp look in her eyes. And then a very odd, little smile curled across her lips. "That's why we'll go during this party."

"What??!" Gabrielle stopped cold. "No, that's just wrong in so many ways. Listen to me, I know about making an entrance. And I know about *not* making an entrance."

"*We have to go then.*" Racine was steely, but calm. She saw it all clearly. "It will be crowded, but that always is the best diversion. Once you're inside, surrounded by countless people who are strangers from one another, you blend in. And that's our only chance."

"Except for one problem." Gabrielle said bluntly, and then waited dramatically, holding off until Racine gave her an annoyed look to go ahead already. "We have no way of getting <u>in</u> to the party."

168

And silence deadened the room. It was the simplest, most obvious reality of all. And there was no answer. They were stumped. Completely, unalterably stumped.

But then, Charlotte brightened. Sweet, innocent, naïve Charlotte.

"Yes. We do."

Book Three

CHAPTER TWENTY-FOUR

Charlotte was going home. In many ways, she felt a different person from who she was so long ago. But it wasn't really that long ago, her departure could be counted in the months, not years. And in truth, she wasn't really different. This home, that is who she was and would always be. It was where she was born, where she was raised, where she learned what she loved and wanted and stood for, where she was taught manners and to understand beauty and know what mattered. This was her village and her people. They worked her land, and all of their lives together intertwined. It was her foundation and always would be, wherever this new life took her.

And what a new life it was. Even Charlotte didn't quite understand it. But what she understood was that when her father was killed and her home destroyed, she had no life, and now she did have one, even if she felt overwhelmed by so much of it, and out of her depth. But after feeling lost, it was so wonderful to have a depth to be out of.

Yet now she was going back to that home. Even if that home no longer existed as a structure for her, it was never gone from her. She looked out of the coach window and could tell she was getting close. Everything looked familiar, but even more – even better – everything felt familiar. The woods and streams and fields and hills were hers. The small huts and their thatched roofs were ones she had ridden past her whole life. That *chateau* there, she knew it, and its sprawling garden and tall hedges. A warmth filled Charlotte's heart. She remembered a picnic just she and her father took when she was 10, the two of them alone. It was home. Places, birthdays, friends – Charlotte smiled, imagine what Gilles St. Chapelle would think about all this. He'd laugh at her, like Gilles always did since she was little, knowing just how to make fun of her   And she would make fun of him, so proud, so sure of himself, thinking himself so dashing and handsome and so certain.

"Are you all right, dear?" a dark-haired woman across from her asked. "You just got flush in the face."

Charlotte touched her cheek, embarrassed. "Oh. No, I am fine, thank you much. It is just the excitement of the journey."

Charlotte quickly returned to thoughts of the road she was on. What a different life she was leading now.

And soon, that road led her back to her village.

Charlotte felt at ease in the room, it was a solace she hadn't felt for far too long, comfortable to be with her good friend Gilles. She belonged here. She understood the oak bookshelves rising up around her, the plush chairs in the corner, the ornate desk he stood by, the paintings on the wall, the very study they were in.

"I know this is such a favor I am asking, Gilles."

He stopped searching through a drawer to give the beautiful young girl an appreciative look. "It's but a mere invitation. And it is my pleasure, you know that. Whatever I can do for you. I'll simply give you mine and get another."

"I am more grateful than you can be aware."

The young gentleman had a difficult time removing his eyes from Charlotte. "It is so wonderful having you home."

"I wish I could stay." Before arriving, she'd had no idea how deeply she'd feel that. "Alas, I must get back. The coach back is soon."

Finding the invitation, Gilles crossed the room to her.

"You will permit me to say that it's good to have you ready to rejoin society. We've all missed you." He hesitated. "Some perhaps more than others."

Charlotte was not able to hide a coquettish blush. Gilles moved closer.

"Oh, and who might they be?" she asked shyly, though not as shyly she knew as she might once have asked.

"Of course, it's just a rumor."

"And one can rarely believe rumors."

"I will at least see you at the party?" he asked pointedly, and hopefully. Her eyes answered the question most affirmatively. "You look wonderful."

"And…you. As well."

He handed the invitation to her. Their fingers touched, and lingered a moment, before she put it away.

"Being on your own suits you."

"It's been a long time."

Standing close to her now, Gilles laid a palm on Charlotte's breast. She reacted with a quick breath, as much from surprise as pleasure. It was such a bold move, she thought and had difficulty holding his gaze. But then she looked away.

"Would you like me to remove my hand?"

"Yes."

That's what she said, but her hand fondled his and stayed. So many little thoughts she couldn't focus on were filling her head, conflicting with one another, though here she was with Gilles, and most above all felt excited that he wanted to be there with her, and at last she was able again to catch his eyes. Gilles took a step closer, and Charlotte felt her heart pound and didn't breath, though wasn't sure if she could. She didn't

173

know what Giles would do next, or what she wanted him to do. She couldn't stay, shouldn't, she knew that, she would have to leave soon, she knew that. And in those fast seconds that seemed forever and longer, she waited and wondered and bit her teeth together. But he let the moment linger, looking down on her, Charlotte, little Charlotte, sweet and very beautiful Charlotte, here with him, at last. He ran his palm along her bodice and felt her move. He took in every part of her face. A drop of sweat appeared above her lip, and then he kissed her. And Charlotte responded fully – it had indeed been a long time. Their kissing became tender, as she held him tightly in her arms.

Slowly, Gilles's hand moved along the curve of Charlotte's back, and he unlaced the strings of her blouse. She pulled away slightly, though, so he stopped. But again, she held him close. To just hold him, Charlotte thought, to feel his body against her for a moment, or two moments. She knew she had to go, she knew this could go no further, but what was just a moment? And as she leaned her cheek on his chest, feeling its warmth, and let her hair fall against his shoulders, Gilles's hand once more began to...

A knock sounded at the door. The hard tapping cut through the pure silence with a jolt.

Like all good valets, the gentleman's gentleman at *Chateau St. Chappelle* was unflappable to the scene before him. He had been with the family for years, after all, and had known Gilles since a boy. He had but one duty. His eyes went only to his lordship, as Charlotte, her cheeks growing flushed, stepped aside, turning demurely so that the straps of her untied blouse were concealed.

"M'lady wished to know the very moment the afternoon

coach arrived to take her back."

Gilles took a few seconds to compose himself. He smoothed the front of his shirt and ran his hand through his hair. "Oh. Thank you. And may I add, 'Damn.'"

CHAPTER TWENTY-FIVE

The small, scraggly man was feeling good this morning. He liked having friends in high places, something that hadn't usually been the way of his life. Usually he lived in the shadows. He reclined on the park bench and tore off a chunk of a baguette, washing it down with a swig of wine. It was a better vintage than he was used to, but then he was into a bit more coin these past few days and feeling quite the swell with the circle he'd been traveling in. Snitches don't usually get such fine carriage rides. Or even meals. And they both paid well. So, he treated himself. Besides, if things turned out as they seemed, he might even be someone in high places himself, and have some of those who always looked down on him thinking differently. Maybe coming to *him* for favors. He wasn't someone to dismiss, after all, he was somebody.

A shadow crossed over him.

"So, Maurice, how are you doing this fine day? I take it things are well."

Looming above was a Musketeer, lording his poncey ways in his poncey uniform with his poncey smile. Maurice usually didn't merit the attention of Musketeers, but maybe this was more proof that he was traveling well. No ordinary *flic* giving him a hard time. He was about to tell the man to leave him in peace when two other Musketeers plopped on either side and wedged him in. And a fourth behind. That was a little less comforting. Surely he'd covered his tracks.

"I know you?" he suddenly wondered, not yet concerned, but curious how the King's Guard would know his name.

"Let's say we have friends in common."

"I got to find some new friends, then," he laughed.

"No, I think you'll want to keep all the friends you can." Maurice twitched at the words, thinking they sounded a bit more ominous than he preferred. The Musketeer's smile had disappeared by this point, but he still spoke in a friendly way. "We hear you've been having dinner with some fancy people these days."

"Oh, and there's a law now against having dinner?"

"I don't think you want to be talking too much about what's legal with us," the burly man seated next to him said, clasping a friendly hand on his shoulder that bit into it. "You could be in the Bastille and behind bars before you had a chance to cough, for all you've done and been left alone."

The snitch laughed back at him, trying to show he knew how to call a bluff, though he didn't laugh with much force because he wasn't sure it was all that much a bluff. The one thing he *was* sure of though was that he could keep a secret, even if it sometimes meant keeping secrets from friends he was snitching for. The more he knew what they didn't, the more all sides needed him. "If I'd done anything," he reflexively spit on the ground, "you wouldn't have left me alone."

"You don't matter enough *not* to leave alone."

The little man clenched his teeth. "You don't think I can have dinner with fine folks?" he snapped back, more defensively than he wanted. "A lots finer than you."

The ponciest Musketeer in front of him stepped closer and kicked Maurice's feet off of a stump they'd been resting on. "I don't think you could have dinner with a rat unless the rat wanted something from you and would be willing to pay for it. So, when we hear that you, of all people, are meeting with a high-toned gentleman – and in a low-life barrelhouse, the kind of dive where no high-toned gentlemen ever want to even bungle the dirt under their fancy shoes – that tells me that he wants to pay for your dingy services but the last thing in the world he wants is for anyone worth anything knowing that he would dare be seen with the likes of you in the light of day. That's what I think."

The little, scraggly snitch sat there, surrounded by these pathetic Musketeers who think they are so special and God Almighty, trying to make him feel small and worthless and nothing, and if they only knew who he was dealing with, far more important people than they would ever meet in their lives, they would treat him a whole lot better, a whole more with respect and honor, the respect he deserved. His whole body tightened. How dare they? What did *they* know? No one important would want to be seen with him? No one important would dare talk with him? No one important?? No one who mattered?

"You don't think the Marquis de Longueville is important?!" he spit out with a laugh. And even if he stretched the truth only a little and had never actually met the Marquis himself, he came close. And he would soon, he felt. He was in the Marquis's circle. Him. So, it was just a little stretch, and what these fool Musketeers didn't know wouldn't hurt them. Take that. I know the Marquis. And you're lucky to be talking to me.

"I think," the Musketeer in front of him said, with an odd smile breaking on his face, "that the Marquis de Longueville is very important. Thank you for the information."

*

A visitor to the headquarters of the Musketeers would have not noticed anything unusual. There was a rash of activity there, yes, but that was true these days. In one corner, there were men doing paperwork, filing reports of their day. The front door was regularly swinging open with guardsmen anxiously arriving and a bit less-briskly leaving back on duty. Duty officers politely did their best to resolve issues of upset citizens, who more often than not left more upset upon learning that the King's Guard had no authority and less interest in mediating disputes with their neighbors, and couldn't be convinced otherwise, no matter how great the pleading.

Yet in the back, if one bothered to walk past a particular enclosure, there was an intensity that didn't exist elsewhere in the small building. One of the men inside pointedly closed the door from prying eyes and ears.

Major Delacroix was seated at a desk in the room, going over a brief report, while his counterpart from the Army sat across, impatiently waiting.

"May I get you anything, sir?" André asked, from his position on call.

The Army officer brusquely turned. "In fact, you can, Captain. You can get your superior here to be more forthcoming and start sharing information with us a little better. The Army and King's Guards are on the same side, you know. You do know that, I assume?" He turned back and focused his attention on Delacroix, with a smiling expression dripping with sarcasm. "It would be oh-so much appreciated."

For the longest while, Major Delacroix didn't respond, but kept reading.

"I'm sorry, Colonel, but your request is above Captain

179

Mersenne's pay grade." The other Musketeers in the room muffled their laughter, as did even one of Col. Benet's two adjutants. Before he could respond, the Major lowered the paper and added, "But then it's not as if the army has been so open with its own reconnaissance."

Diplomacy was not the Colonel's strength, but he had no interest in creating a greater rift at such a critical juncture. "There is no denying that the Army and Musketeers have each been protective of their own standards in the past. But, Major, there is also no denying that the situation all of us here in this room know the severity of, and since the moment His Highness's…crisis occurred, the national Army of France has seen it our patriotic duty to resolve it. The Musketeers have been far more secretive for reasons I cannot understand or accept, and I would ask you, Major, to work with us. Because too much is at stake."

Major Delacroix was stoic. He was under more stress than most anyone could imagine, for more reasons than anyone could imagine, and the last thing he wanted to deal with was a petulant army officer. "I hope what you *can* understand, sir," he finally replied, "is that as the King's Guard, this crisis with the King is something much more personal than the Army ever has to deal with. Your concern is the nation. Ours is the king. And the king *is* France."

He pushed the paper he had been reading across the desk, at last releasing the information. With a sense of relief, Colonel Benet picked up the parchment, but his face twisted in disappointment. "All of us here in this room know this suspicion about the Marquis."

"And now you know what we do."

That was true. Though what Major Delacroix didn't say

was that they don't know everything he did. But that, he thought, could wait for another, more opportune time.

*

"Your Highness, I must advise in no uncertain terms against an attack upon the Marquis de Longueville's estate."

Though Mazarin's words were blunt, they were spoken calmly as he sat relaxed while the Regent paced aggressively through her chambers. Dusk was falling through the windows at this juncture, the two of them having been there alone for several hours, in private conference they admonished others, talking, arguing, questioning one another, going over the possibilities of actions that could be taken.

Major Delacroix had only recently arrived, bringing a report that he felt important to be seen, though it only confirmed what was already suspected, that there was increased activity near the home of the Marquis. But verification in military matters was as vital as the most surprising discovery, he noted. He stayed off in the corner, keeping informed of all discussion, and stood his duty.

"It is our belief now that he holds the king, yes?" the Queen Mother asked, though she knew it to be a fact.

"But not on his property. That would be the greatest risk."

"No, Mazarin, that would be the greatest protection. With an army already in place. Under the Marquis's direct orders. And if turns that the king is not on the property, we still will have succeeded in destroying the Marquis's stronghold."

"This can only end in disaster." The Cardinal had seen it from her so often before. He advised, and if her mind was made up, she did whatever she wanted. He loved her instincts.

181

She was a smart, beautiful, determined woman. And she had a compassionate, yet aggressive streak in her, which greatly appealed to him. He looked forward to their time together. But what she wanted to do here, it could be disastrous. He had to convince her otherwise. The last thing in the world he wanted was an attack on the *Chateau de Longueville*. "There are but two possibilities if we attack, like you suggest. If the king is elsewhere, they will move him deeper in hiding. Yet if he *is* held at the estate, it is worse! To have the king caught in a battle, under direct guard of the enemy, it would be his death. Do you wish that?"

"You ask us to do nothing? Nothing at all? The crown of France does not accept sitting powerless."

Major Delacroix watched the back-and-forth between them, arguing almost like a married couple who knew what the other would say, he thought, oblivious that there was anyone else in the room. He thought it the proper time to step in.

"Whatever she orders, we will protect the Queen Regent."

The Cardinal shot him a look. "Like you protected the king?"

The Major remained stoic. Mazarin, though, finally rose and crossed to the Regent by the bed.

"We are not sitting, doing nothing," the Cardinal insisted. "Each day we draw closer, each day we move the pieces nearer, each day we know more. There is a plan."

It was always the same, Mazarin thought, as he knew all the stares of the others were on him. He had always been distrusted. It made him act even more secretly in his plans because there were few that *he* could trust. He knew the suspicions, he heard them all from the hallways and behind closed doors. Yet here he was, Chief Minister of France. An

182

Italian. What a whimsy the fate of the world can be. Though it was less whimsy, he knew, than the designs of planning.

Giulio, they called him, in his beloved Roma. His mother came from nobility in Umbria, and he always believed nobility was his fate. It had certainly seemed so. He could have been a Jesuit, after all, but wouldn't join the order – no, that wasn't for him, he had higher aims – and instead he served as chamberlain in Spain, and it was there that his dance with gambling first surfaced. A gentleman got him out of serious trouble by paying his debts and then even offered a magnificent dowry to marry his daughter, but – no, that wasn't for him either, he had much higher aims. But it was gambling that stood young Mazarin well, then and much after, and most especially even now. And it propelled him forward.

He had come to the attention of Pope Urban VIII when intervening in a military action against Louis XIII of all people. Fate, always destiny, he thought. And he rose through the ranks after recognizing a personal weakness in the Spanish general, allowing him to negotiate a treaty in the War of Mantua. He had always been good at recognizing weaknesses in those who stood in his way, he believed. And with his ability to play both sides, the great Cardinal Richelieu himself invited Giulio to Paris.

Not just invited, but brought him into his council, and so it was that the young man came to the service of France in 1636. Learning from the master of maneuvers, deception and the willful use of power, he involved himself in the most sensitive missions, acquiring authority, and watching for weaknesses. All the while having mistrusting eyes watch the surprising rise of this outsider. A man who served the crown, yet saw himself as the noblest of the aristocracy.

183

For all the matters and strategies of high power, though, it was not for the first time, nor would it be the last, that it was his gambling that served him so well. During one fateful gambling foray, where all the highborn attended, he had won so many gold coins that even her royal highness, Queen Anne herself, came by to watch. And with her eyes upon him, he gambled all his holdings – and won. It was here that their association began. For crediting her presence alone on his success, he offered the queen 50,000 of the gold écus. It was yet another good, calculated bet. Because days later, he was at last brought to the inner court of the King, and most especially of all, the Queen.

As Mazarin's influence grew, and he became Jules, no longer Guilio, except to his enemies, and only then behind his back, Richelieu himself grew wary of the threat, with the others, seeing this foreigner grow in power. And so it was that his patron blocked promoting his protégé to the rank of cardinal. Instead he made a stunning offer to make Mazarin wealthy beyond most people's dreams, as well as a bishop – but elsewhere, far away from the court. All were stunned further when the young man gambled and turned it down, but he had much higher goals in mind. He always had higher goals. And plans. So it passed that he was sent on the king's mission and successfully united Savoy with France, and thus, in repayment, despite Richelieu's efforts, he was at last made a cardinal, as well, in 1641.

Within two years, his mentor and now rival, Richelieu was dead. Jules succeeded him as Chief Minister of France. As he'd planned. Soon after, Louis XIII himself died. And that left his dear benefactor Anne of Austria as Regent. She gave the man she had grown close to more power. Had him move closer to the palace. And now, five years later, the rumors, suspicions and distrust had only increased. That they were married, that the Dauphin King Louis was their child, that this foreigner had loftier goals. But all Mazarin had, he told himself as he stood before the Queen Mother, were plans. He always had plans.

And so yet again he told her, with others watching his every expression, listening under every word, "We are not sitting, doing nothing. Each day we draw closer, each day we move the pieces nearer, each day we know more. There is a plan."

For a moment, she looked at him as if she was considering his words closely. But instead she was formulating how best to express her own.

"Our enemies approach our borders. While the nation gathers its fragile strength to celebrate its king's reign – they will discover there is no king! As the clock ticks, the Marquis throws a private ball. While the King, my son, remains in mortal danger."

CHAPTER TWENTY-SIX

A dim candlelight glowed in the parlor, as Racine studied the invitation that Charlotte had placed on the table.

"I could only get one," the young girl apologetically told the others in the room. "At least if one of us can get inside, we can perchance find out *some* of what we need. Is that not right?"

Both Gabrielle and Marguerite were seriously less than convinced, most especially the old woman who had seen far too many best intentions go awry in her life. Charlotte put on a positive face, this was so important, she believed, however the more she smiled encouragingly, the more she could tell from the doubting expressions that they had hit a block in the road. Off the in the corner, the old man, Auguste, made sure not to utter a word. But although he sat quietly, and warily, he also sat supportively.

"I'm not sure if you shouldn't perhaps reconsider this course, dear. Going in alone? I don't question your bravery, but…" Marguerite chose her words carefully, "…Safety first, I beg you."

"I agree with Marguerite. And we all three *have* to be inside," Gabrielle added. Though she noticeably didn't have a solution. "There's too much to search. Too much to find out. We need to change our plan. One invitation is not enough."

The room was full of five faces, each lost in thought, covered in reflections of uncertainty.

"Actually," one of those faces began to change into something closer to a knavish grin, and Racine broke the silence, "—this is not a problem."

As the others turned to her in full surprise, she inspected the parchment once more, and then sat down, and calmly picked up a quill. "I'll just forge us two more."

There was a jolt of confidence out of their darkness. Unlikely as it had seemed just moments ago, getting into the high society affair and mixing with that mysterious group of aristocrats now actually seemed possible.

"You are certain you can do this?" Charlotte asked.

"Princess," Racine swaggered, and leaned back, putting her feet up on the table, the boots coming down with an emphatic thud, "I can copy it blindfolded."

"No," the heiress corrected, "I mean, if we get into the ball, can you act civil?"

The next few days were frantic with activity. Finding the exact right parchment to copy the invitations, making the duplicates imperceptible, choosing among Charlotte's gowns for the other two women and fitting them properly, deciding on the jewelry and accessories appropriate for the events, designing hairstyles, and above all, making plans of what to listen for, where to look, how to look, and do so as surreptitiously as possible, and perhaps most importantly, what to do if one of them got in trouble – or worse, caught. And going over these plans time and time and time again until they were as near to pure habit as possible.

Yet after all this was done, one task remained, perhaps the riskiest of all, the one the posed the greatest danger, for if it failed, everything would fall apart. It required the most intense focus and unyielding attention, and that is why it was held for last.

Out in the barn, Racine stood arm-in-arm with Auguste, ready to waltz.

"This is insane."

"No," Charlotte patiently explained to her. "Keep your left arm higher. It is an extension of your femininity."

"I know how to dance."

"We are not talking the polka," she said sweetly, though the former debutante did seem to let it linger in the air for just a moment. "You must glide as if a feather in his arms. A waltz is the dance of pure grace, where two people move seamlessly as one. And…one-two-three, one-two-three…"

Gabrielle and Marguerite stood by a wall, leaving as much room on the floor as possible, and humming to keep time. Candlelight made the expanse look refined, and Racine and the old man awkwardly skidded.

Charlotte grabbed Racine's arm. "Keep your arm up. It is a world of manners, where women offer compliments to men as 'dashing.' And 'debonair.' And 'Oh, how clever!'" Again she grabbed Racine's arm. "Keep your arm up," she commanded. "Where everyone looks for the slightest hint you don't belong amongst them."

"Then I shan't give them a signal," the gypsy snarked back.

"Up. Keep your arms up. Watch your feet. Hold your gaze in his eyes." Charlotte was firm, but unrelenting. "Your feet — you're sliding upon ice, not a rhinoceros charging the African veldt." Again she grabbed Racine's sleeve. "Your arm. Up!"

"I'm about to put my arm up so high," she peered warmly, but sharply at Charlotte, "they'll need a doctor to remove it."

Gabrielle grabbed Marguerite's hand and pulled her onto the floor, and the two of them now gracefully waltzed through the barn, all the while continuing to hum, adding to the aesthesis of this gala ball they had all created, swirling around.

And the unflappable Charlotte remained the unwavering

188

taskmaster. Too much was at stake. And after all, this was something she knew. Something she understood deep in her bones. The one thing, finally, she could do better than anyone here. There would be no let up. And so she kept at it.

"You need to look as if you belong, as if this is of nature to you. Or else we'll all be discovered. Here…"

She quickly cut in, knowing she could demonstrate far better than have her mere words grasped. And she flowed around the room with Auguste.

"Thank God." Racine plopped down in a chair.

"No!!!" Charlotte instantly stopped. "You are not a satchel of potatoes." She rushed over to the chair and hovered determinedly over Racine. "Again. Float down to your seat."

This was all so important. Every movement, every glance, every turn, twist and smile. It had to be right. Racine tried.

"No. Again. Float. Gracefully. *Comme ça.*" Charlotte demonstrated, perfectly, impeccably. Racine made another attempt. It looked akin to an injured swan. "No, again." And then, "Again."

Racine sat in the chair for a moment, hoping to have looked refined, but just flopped there. She caught her breath and looked up at Charlotte. "You're loving this, aren't you?"

"You have no idea." And then she called over, "Gabrielle, Marguerite."

The two women stopped dancing and brought out the tray of pastries and teas that had been prepared, elegantly offering it to Racine, who didn't have even the slightest idea what in the world to do, what was expected of her. Everyone waited. Auguste kept at a distance.

"*Patisserie*, m'lady," Gabrielle asked.

"One lump or two?" Marguerite offered.

189

Racine turned to glare at Charlotte and snarled.

"Oh, two lumps sounds just perfect."

Finally, knowing it couldn't be avoided any longer, she ventured to hold a saucer, and the china cup rattled, as she tried to take a cream puff with her pinky up.

"The finger with the <u>saucer</u> should be up," Charlotte corrected her.

Racine struggled, confused about which finger was which, but finally got it right. She took a dainty bite and a slight sip.

"Yes!! *Magnifique*!!!" Charlotte raised her arms in victory.

Racine defiantly crammed the rest of the cream puff in her mouth.

"We are going to rescue us a king!!" Gabrielle burst out with the excitement of the moment.

The three young women suddenly looked at one another. Gabrielle's words and the exhaustion of the evening and the build-up of the recent days all made them face a reality that they'd been too busy to even pay attention to. But as their faces showed, they now thought they could really, maybe, really pull this off. *Mon Dieu.*

And then, the emotion of the night, of the past days became too much for even Auguste, and seeing everything around him and knowing what lay directly ahead, and understanding what greater good could well-occur from it all, the old man hesitantly, so slowly, but finally spoke up and broke his silence.

"I know I should never have done it." He paused for a moment, as everyone waited. "But it was the best mistake in my life."

CHAPTER TWENTY-SEVEN

The byroad leading up to *Chateau de Longueville* was bathed in light, as torches were planted on both sides of the long approach. It gave the appearance of a wall of fire, and as capriciousness would have it, or perhaps intent, in many ways that's what it was. The glow could be seen cutting through the night all the way into the distant village, so imposing was the effect. Most thought it the height of courtliness, far grander than anything the Marquis had offered before, though some were struck by how menacing it seemed. A bit much, they thought. Overkill. If only they knew.

All along this pathway, elegant carriages arrived, like a caravan it seemed at times. At the lordly portico out front, each invitee was individually greeted by well-dressed groomsmen and servants. It was aristocratic cream in its evening finery.

The grand ballroom overflowed with guests, many of them checking out the others, to find who was fortunate enough to be in their company. And to see, as well, who might have committed a faux pas of poorly-chosen wardrobe, though in this gathering that seemed unlikely. A musical quartet at the far end of the room played gracefully. A few adventurous people chose to dance. And waiters passed amongst these chosen with trays of the finest food and flowing champagne.

The Marquis himself took it all in, from his perch above, a mezzanine that ran the length of the hall. His eyes were ever-vigilant, taking in the swirl below, the jigsaw pieces of his puzzle. He directed an aide, who headed off on some new mission. Then, Eduard motioned over another man, whispered to him, and they went off together.

191

Some of the people on the floor were aware of their host's movements over them, since it was their personal mission to pay attention to all such things Eduard de Longueville did, and they would no more think of not watching the Marquis than they would condescend to speak with the working class. Even if they didn't know what he was doing or saying, they could at least impress others that they knew he was doing or saying something. But most of the people were quite content being a part of something so grand, even if they didn't even know the occasion. A few, however, knew exactly the occasion and the very reason why they were there. And they looked forward with the greatest anticipation to how tonight's gathering unfolded, as well as how did the portentous days ahead.

It was a glorious, glittering and ominous gathering. So much was going on that no one paid the slightest notice when several newcomers arrived in the entranceway. And *had* anybody even bothered to care, it would have only been how three such young and beautiful women were unescorted.

Charlotte, Gabrielle and Racine though were well-noted by the appreciative attendants. Nothing stodgy here, nothing pretentious, not a hint of arrogant superiority. The young women were decked out in gorgeous gowns, beautifully coifed hair, and dazzling necklaces.

As the room opened up before them, Charlotte was at ease in her element. Gabrielle was awed but loved the spectacle. And Racine? Racine felt like a fish wearing a gown.

"How in the world did you wear these things every day??"

"Do you remember what I taught you?" Charlotte asked, like an anxious but proud teacher.

Racine put on her frilliest air and noted the pin Charlotte was wearing. "My dear, I just adore your choisenotte."

"*Cloisonné.*"

The two women looked at one another, each reading the other's thoughts. Charlotte's thoughts could have been read by the illiterate, splashed across her concerned and upset face. "I'm fine," Racine insisted.

Charlotte kept staring into Racine's eyes, to make sure. Satisfied, or at least as satisfied as she expected to be, she admonished them all one last time. "Everyone, please be careful with the dresses. They're special to me."

"Tell me again who I'm pretending to be. Improvisation is not my strength. Look at all these people. When I was a little girl, I dreamed of making an entrance into a room like this, the grace, the grandeur, the…Oh, my God, the waiter there has escarg" – "

"Gabby, <u>please</u>, not now," Racine squeezed her eyes shut. And then grabbed her friend. "Focus."

"We have to find if the king *is* here. And what that other plan of theirs is. And – " Charlotte may have been speaking to the others, but mostly she was convincing herself. She was exhilarated, and terrified. "Please be safe. And good luck."

*

Throughout the ballroom, couples were having the grandest time, being so assertively outgoing while at the same time, as only the upper crust can, skimming across the surface with more ease than a water bug. Every once in a while, though, an aristocrat would surreptitiously grab the attention of another. A few, furtive huddles began to form, as anyone looking for such cabals would have noticed. But it was done with such secretive deftness and almost no one *was* looking, that it all seemed the most natural thing in the world.

Weaving her way, Charlotte was trying her best to nonchalantly search the room as she wandered among the crowd and the dancing. If anyone caught her eye, she offered that knowing nod of "Aha, so fine to see you," she knew so well and had done so often even in her young life, for cotillions were a way of life for debutantes, and they quickly moved past. No one ever wanted to stop you, unless they felt you had something to benefit them – and especially out of concern that the other person might actually want something from *you*. Occasionally, she caught the glance of someone she did indeed know, and they offered happy looks of surprise, to see a kind, familiar face that they hadn't seen in much too long – but almost immediately they remembered *why* it had been much too long, and the tragedy she'd been through and how she'd been exiled off somewhere, and immediately realized they had nothing they wanted to say to her. Their expressions stayed the same, but their eyes showed fear, and so they quickly nodded and even more quickly slid off.

It was just as well to Charlotte, for the last thing she wanted was idle chat. Her scanning eye noticed that several of the Marquis's aides, who she recognized, were furtively whispering to particular guests she thought she might know, though wasn't sure. They were too far away. Moving closer, she off-handedly asked those she passed, "The Marquis…excuse me, have you seen Marquis de Longueville?…I'm looking for th – "

Suddenly, though, looming before her close by was Philippe Gascogne. Almost in her path, in fact, she nearly walked into him but swiftly turned away to avoid being spotted, the worst thing to happen, it had been drilled into her, if you are trying to spy upon someone. Charlotte caught her breath, and when she turned back he was gone, among the throng. But that meant he hadn't seen her.

Far more aggressively, it should come as no surprise, Racine had her eyes peeled, shifting from one person to the next, though without seeming to, a difficult skill the gypsy was adept at, able to make judgments much more quickly than most, as she squeezed her way tightly between couples, so close as to bump against them, though so lightly that fortunately she caused no disturbance or infuriated looks. Which was just as well and turned out to be the very point, because soon she stopped, having just pinched a billfold. It was to a purpose, though, not mere thievery, and she rifled through it, checking for documents of importance, but there was nothing of interest. She tapped the gentleman on the arm.

"I believe you dropped this."

With a look of surprise and mild appreciation, the patrician accepted his property back with a nod. There was a lot of nodding going on that night, Racine noticed. She couldn't tell if it was etiquette or stupidity, rich people unable to think of what to say. She nodded back – it seemed the right thing to do, and he appeared to appreciate it, like it was a secret code to the club. And then, going against all her better instincts, some things came too natural, but she knew she was there for another reason – she grudgingly handed a diamond bracelet back to his wife.

"And you must have dropped this."

Off by an alcove, Gabrielle was the belle of the ball, surrounded by several men, all infatuated with her, each competing for her attention. Some things came so natural to her, as well. But more than just the way of the world since time began, if anyone knew how to play such moment for all it was worth, it was Gabrielle. A sweep of her hair, the light touch of her hand on a lapel, an uncaring laugh, turning her body just so, licking her lips at exactly the right moment, a glance, a smile, a connection. It was an exquisite performance. Though to be fair, some of it wasn't all performance. A girl has to be what a girl has to be. And Gabrielle loved being the life of the party, whatever the reason. And this was certainly the party to be the life of. But most was a performance. Most.

"…Well, if you ask me, the state of the arts in France today are just mere trifles, *ils sont très mauvais*, that's my belief. But let's talk about you a moment – actually, no, let's not…"

They all laughed spritely at her little, witty joke. But of course, these men would have laughed at anything out of her mouth.

*

Though the Marquis himself didn't appear to be anywhere available for socializing, his right-hand man, the Count de Beaufort was on a mission with orders from on high. He found the object of his search, a nobleman who oversaw what the man described to strangers in public as a helpful security force for his grounds, but in truth was the command of a small militia. The Count whispered something brief, and they headed off to talk. A loud trumpet call was blown for attention, cutting through the cacophony of sounds, but de Beaufort ignored it, such was the importance of his charge.

A herald stood at the entranceway, nervous, not sure what he should do, glancing over his shoulder, even though he had been doing it for years. He puffed himself up, used to calling out such things, but not used to this, and at last called out with a big, but quivering voice.

"The Queen Regent, Anne of France!"

If nothing else that night could bring the Count de Beaufort to a halt, it was that!! He spun to look.

It was the Queen Regent herself. Arriving with a retinue of guards and Musketeers, which included the ever-present Major Delacroix, along with Captain Mersenne leading his own outfit, she glided into the hall as if a guest of honor. Which she was most decidedly not.

A belated, hurried fanfare was quickly organized and blasted.

She swirled past the startled faces, and those in her way opened a path, as if the Red Sea was parting. The room was silenced. If these were people uncomfortable at being confronted by someone who might simply dare want something from them, imagine their reaction towards a majestic figure who was, at this moment, the very soul of confrontation. A figure who wanted one thing only from them, nothing more, but it was their utter, total fealty to her son the king and country. Something they not only could not give, but were there specifically to avoid giving. However, shocked as they were to see her regal presence, they were all still well-mannered and better-bred, and as she walked by, they hesitantly bowed and curtsied.

Had they been able to shift their attention and pull their eyes away somehow, they would have been shocked, as well, to see that on the floor now Eduard de Longueville appeared, far off to the side at the foot of the staircase. The Marquis stood stoic, as always. He watched everyone with a piercing eye, thinking intently. What he was thinking would have been impossible to know. And if anyone would discover it, the chances are likely that they would have been very surprised, since most people were by him.

At last, the Regent arrived upon the main floor. The crowd there stepped back, forming a horseshoe around her in the center. Such was their great awe of who she was, no matter their loyalties.

This was a woman, they each understood, with a history. This was a woman who had faced great power. This was a woman not to be trifled with.

The Queen Regent. Anne of Austria. Queen consort of Navarre. Infanta of Spain and Portugal. Archduchess of Austria. And Mother of the King of France.

This was a woman not to be trifled with.

Born into the renowned House of Habsburg that ruled much of Europe and had for 400 years, Anne was the eldest daughter of Philip III King of Spain and Margaret of Austria. Such was the child's heredity that the day her mother died when Anne was only 10, she took on matriarchal responsibilities, and lived that way ever since.

By the age of just 14, she was married to the King of France, Louis XIII, himself the same age. It was a powerful marriage tying two great nations together, yet made all the more powerful when her brother and Louis' sister were married, as well, securing the bond unbreakably between France and Spain.

If she had learned much about survival before (and she had), it was little compared to what she was to face. And she first had to face it as just a child, ascending to the throne of France, whose mother-in-law was not inclined to give up power. A woman, Marie de Medici, whose family – the House of Medici – knew more about power than any in history, having ruled much of Europe for centuries and given the world four popes. And so Marie chose to rule France as Queen, which she saw as her right, not that of a mere 14-year-old from Spain. But that child was not only wise beyond her years, but even more patient, and waited for her opportunity. And when Marie's young son the king eventually saw his influence grow, so then did Anne's – slowly at first, for there was no closeness between Anne and the King. But over time, that changed. And soon, Marie de Medici was succeeded by a patient and determined young woman, Queen Anne.

Yet power remained out of her grasp. When no heir was born, the result of miscarriages, Anne found herself distanced from Louis again and had to fend for herself against even more potent forces. For the King's attention turned to his chief minister, Cardinal Richelieu, one of the most skilled and ruthless in history, who inserted his influence between the King and Queen. Anne continued childless for another 16 years, which only weakened her position and required her to become involved in court intrigues against the great Richelieu. They were battles mostly of lost cause, but the experience she gained in counterplotting, far more than the few tiny victories, was immeasurable.

Her burdens though only grew. In 1635, when she was 34, France – the nation she served as queen – went to war against Spain, the nation of her birth and family. Amidst all the distrust that she had to maneuver through as result, thought a spy at times, she finally gave birth to her son three years later. But even here she had to fight for herself, strengthening her fortitude, because both Louis and the powerful Richelieu tried to prevent her from obtaining the regency of her son. But

Anne, who had grown formidable in her own right, prevailed. And when both men died within months of each other, just five years ago from that day, she was left in power. At last. Regent of France.

And to the shock of the nation, when she was required to bring forth a new first minister, the new Regent turned the power of governing to, of all people, not one of the inner-circle, not to a Frenchman at all, but rather her rival Cardinal Richelieu's protégé, a foreigner of Italian birth, Cardinal Jules Mazarin. But for all of France's surprise, Mazarin was a man who had been so helpful to her previously, and close, and a leader who she trusted. And in that decisive move, the Queen Regent solidified her control on France.

This was a woman not to be trifled with.

And there she stood, surrounded in the center of that horseshoe by a roomful of enemies, and facing them all down. Yet though the room was still, she was all warmth and smiles. No one had the slightest idea what to expect.

"My dear friends," she finally spoke with a gentility on the surface that astonished them all. "How grand to see you all on such a night. So many of whom I know. Baron de Nuviette. M'Lady Arneaux, ahh, dear Henri…"

As she pointedly singled out people, making certain they caught her look, making certain they knew she was well-aware who they were, their faces turned ashen. All the while, her own face kept that same, gracious, far-too-gracious, searing smile.

"I understand well that you are all here on behalf of your king. The sovereign to whom you have each sworn loyalty. You have no idea how I will remember this moment. Remember your dear faces. Remember who is here. Every single one of you. And when the *Gala National* is over tomorrow, and the glory and full power of France continues – as you know it will – I so look forward to seeing you each again. Because, dear friends, you will be remembered. *Merci bien*." She made sure to wait a moment for it all to sink in and stay engraved in their memories. "Please. Enjoy this night!"

With a glowing smile to them all, she coasted off, making her own path through the parting bodies. Some of her retinue stayed closely with her, other of her guards fanned out to canvas the hall. As soon as the Regent was gone, those in her direct presence needed a moment to recover, a moment to know that they were safe and would survive – at least for the night – and then, putting it out of their minds as much as possible, they quickly continued their party.

Having witnessed this show, Eduard now tried to move off, but he was swarmed by nobles full of questions upon concerned questions. "What was that about?" they cried. "Did you know she was coming? Why didn't you warn us? How much does she know? She isn't actually saying she supports us, is she? She didn't mean that, did she? Does this change anything? May I have a moment? May I have a moment? May I have a moment?" Finally, he was able to break away, and signaled for de Beaufort to join him.

*

Charlotte had been having no luck with her part of the plan. The hall was so crowded, and she was so small, it was difficult to make much headway. She looked all the way up to the mezzanine, checking around, and even got a little light-headed, but there was no one there, except several valets. Hearing a commotion nearby, however, she followed the

201

unexpected noise. And there at last, Charlotte spotted her target, the Marquis de Longueville surrounded by a coterie of anxious, questioning men. She carefully headed towards him, winding her way among the couples dancing, socialites maundering, and tightly-knit groups colluding, oblivious of them all, getting close to the Marquis, though not quite yet close enough to hear. But she had her quarry in her sights, and after all this time that's the only thing that mattered. A shiver of excitement ran down her back.

Distracted from those around her, her eyes proudly were intent only on that one man. She didn't notice until too late therefore when a single gentleman took her arm and squired her away, across to the dance floor. Trying desperately but politely without attracting attention to excuse herself while looking back, the young man would hear nothing of it, a decidedly-lovely young girl in his arms trumps everything in life, and she lost sight of Eduard.

Racine had another thought in mind, certain that it was at the outer reaches that people were most likely to speak about the little they knew. After all, it was specifically because they hardly were aware of anything that they were most likely to talk, wanting others to be impressed by how important they were. She carefully slid along, looking for whatever seemed suspect. Bumping into a large man who blocked her way, she fought against every instinct in her body to elbow him in the back, knowing from what Charlotte had drilled into her that it was required of her to stay in this ridiculous dance of manners and (she hated the thought) apologize, so as not to draw attention to herself for rudeness, or assault.

It was then that she noticed that the man she had bumped was that fool of a Musketeer, on duty in his uniform, haphazardly surveying the room.

"Oh. Captain Mersenne," she almost spat out, though in as ladylike a way as possible, given the surroundings. "I wish I could say this was a pleasant surprise."

Why couldn't the oaf have been looking where he was going, she thought. Why couldn't I have been, she admonished herself. Two ships crashing in the night. And him again. France was a big country, just not big enough.

André looked at the exquisitely-dressed woman before him. Her hair drifting slightly down the nape of her neck. His eyes glazed a bit, upset with himself for if there was one thing he knew in his soul as a proud Frenchman, it was that you always remember beautiful women.

"I apologize, m'lady. I hope to do better. And you have me at a disadvantage.

Racine involuntarily snorted. "My guess is that a rock would have you at a disadvantage."

The Musketeer was confused and peered in for a closer look. Then, it hit him. "Miss Tarascon? I'm sorry, I didn't recognize you. You look so different, you look – wonderful."

"You didn't recognize me. Well, that's another impressive example of your skill at investigation. I can see why they made you captain of – " suddenly though she caught herself, the words of his compliment finally filtering in and getting registered at last by her thoughts. "Really? I do?"

"Very much so, I would say."

Racine reacted with a certain unexpected…well, she wasn't sure what it was. But abruptly she recovered, remembering who it was she was talking to. "Well, that's no mind. You are easy with words. It's the protecting France you have a hard time with."

She stood there and crossed her arms. Quickly uncrossing them, remembering her lesson on posture.

Gabrielle, on the other hand, had by now moved off elsewhere from her group of sycophants who'd been of no use at all, but she was having the time of her life and flirting with yet another group of smitten young men. She could get used to this life, she thought. She was made for it. She had already had two offers of marriage this very night. Though she knew it wasn't marriage they really wanted – at least one of them. Three of the men around her now were competing with one another, trying to top their rivals with tales of greater exploits. One truly more impressive than the next, assuming, that is, that they were true. Gabrielle looked to pay the most rapt attention, and even pouted once. Then, she lightly touched one young man on the arm.

"Nooo. Oh, my, you say the most charmingly funny things."

"But not half as charming as you," he smiled and nodded, with grace on his lips and hope in his heart.

"Dear, sir, you will win my heart. And to be surrounded by such handsome men as you all. I shan't sleep. Do you know how excited I will be when I get out of bed tomorrow morning?"

They all laughed. She touched another of the men. "And wouldn't you want to find out?"

They all laughed, again. But of course, he thought, he would absolutely love to find out. So would all the laughing faces. What would it take? What words in her ear would win her? It seemed most any might, and they were each searching silently in their active minds to find the right ones. These other men, each of them thought, glancing at their competition, didn't stand a chance.

"I always do so wonder what the bedrooms in a chateau are like," she said brazenly, the intoxication of the evening filling her. "Such high mattresses, no doubt. A woman's body must surely sink deep into the feathers. And this is such a gorgeous estate. So large. Too large." She tossed off the words almost carelessly, as if her next thought had not even occurred to her until that moment. "I even wonder if any areas of it are blocked off." But of course, the thought had not only occurred to her long before that moment, it had been her very intent all evening. She had learned a few things already, just not anything quite helpful enough, yet. And with that same look of uncaring, added, "Do you know?"

As Gabrielle continued discovering as much information as she could from her newest gentlemen friends about the reason for the ball, and why they were there, and what little they might know about the Marquis and the layout of his home and the guards, Charlotte continued her pursuit of Eduard. She had been able to extricate herself after just one dance, begging off for a promised waltz she said she had made to another, and made her way among the guests, this time being careful to keep from being waylaid by still another would-be suitor. Her eyes darted among the whisperers and revelers, looking for where the Marquis might have gone, all the while doing her best to turn and avert her eyes from any unwelcome invitation.

It was then that, raising her glance once more in her quest, that she saw looming in front of her was Philippe Gascogne. She thought of scurrying away, to disappear unseen, but it was pointless. He was right there.

At first, the Count wasn't certain how to proceed. "Mademoiselle Le Renaud, how interesting to cross paths again."

"A coincidence, I'm sure," she replied politely, but noticeably stiffly.

"You have caught me watching you." He knew all too well there was no point deceptively denying it, it would only turn the situation more awkward. "My apologies. May I help you find something?"

Charlotte didn't know what to say. And the last thing she wanted was to be questioned by this man. Besides, it was she who had questions for him, which she would get to in good time. But not now, not here. Thinking hard, "I've been looking for Gilles St. Chapelle."

The gallant aristocrat appeared to be – Charlotte couldn't quite tell. Displeased? Concerned, perhaps? She laughed quickly to herself, thinking it certainly couldn't be jealousy. Gascogne, she knew, was only in love with himself. Yet he definitely looked out of sorts. But why? Why wouldn't Count Gascogne want her talking with Gilles? What could Gilles possibly tell her that she shouldn't find out? Maybe even funny, dear Gilles – she felt herself redden a bit, she didn't know why – maybe he didn't know himself, something that would be as nothing to him, but if she heard, it might take on new meaning.

"Gilles? Yes, I suppose he would be here. Unfortunately, I haven't seen him since – "

"Since when?" Charlotte couldn't help interrupting, the look of all innocence. "Since the night my father died? My word, I cannot avoid coincidences tonight."

With a quick, but pointed glance, and with something new and most interesting indeed to think about, she turned and walked away.

*

Walking away just as briskly, the Queen Regent swept through the room. She had said her piece and headed now towards the exit, making certain that every single person there was as well-aware of her departure as they'd been of her arrival. She had wanted to send a clear message, and she was quite sure it had been received.

Suddenly, though, Eduard de Longueville approached and impeded her path. She hesitated – she most definitely wanted to speak with the man, she was greatly disappointed that she hadn't seen him before now, for that was as much a reason to come tonight as any, though she wasn't certain that here in full view of a watching multitude of eyes was where she wished it to be – but she chose to stop, as her guards watched warily, ready to leap in at the instant. Eduard bowed.

"I was not expecting you to be attending."

"Sir, you hardly give me enough credit."

"I can only hope it won't intrude on the *Gala National* tomorrow," he said in words of the most-thoughtful concern. Though whose concern it was for, that wasn't clear.

"Nothing done here will intrude on our plans." The Queen Regent held his eyes, wanting to know without question that her point was understood by him. "We have much to talk about."

"The evening is young."

"But important events near." There was much to do, and no room any longer for niceties. "And so, your time is over."

And good to her word, and without another word, she abruptly took her leave.

*

While the ballroom of guests was in a quiet uproar (for they did very little that was loud and improper, except perhaps overthrowing the monarchy in a *fronde*, and even that they were doing in a hush), Racine and André were oblivious to those around them, focused only on other another.

"Certainly I defend my men, but I must be honest, as well, and the truth is, they *have* been known to get…" he thought a moment, trying to be diplomatic, "…how should I put it?"

"Drunk and obnoxious."

"No, well, okay, yes – " he gave a little amused shrug, "but then, you must understand the kind of person it takes to devote his life to being a Musketeer."

There was actually a tiny crack of a smile from her. "So, is that *your* excuse?"

"Me? No. I joined because I like the puffy hats."

"You look dashing."

Racine felt pleased for quickly remembering what Charlotte had taught her to say. She had felt stumped in this kind of conversation, not sure how to respond, and she didn't want him to see her that way. "Oh. And debonair," she added. She wasn't quite sure what "debonair" meant, though she suspected it probably fit. When he smiled with a nod, she figured she had gotten it right, and felt glad.

Charlotte herself had learned some lessons in turn from Racine, about tracking others and being as surreptitious about it as possible. She had a long ways to go, she knew – it's difficult to be clandestine when you feel gawky at the same time – but it helped that few people took her seriously at many things, other than knowing etiquette, so she felt confident she'd be paid her no mind in this room as she searched. And having confidence was a good thing, she was beginning to feel. So, it was with careful, somewhat confident steps that Charlotte took when she at last, once again, was able to spot the elusive Marquis from across the room, at the foot of a stairway. She maneuvered her way closer.

As Charlotte had her eye on Eduard de Longueville, however, she was unaware that Count Gascogne had his own eyes on her. Philippe had been watching her curious movements for a while, not that they were suspicious to him yet or gave him any cause for concern, but they seemed so inexplicable, especially for what little he knew of Charlotte Le Renaud, and as such they certainly made him very interested, for important reasons. So, as the young heiress seemed headed somewhere inexplicable, Philippe stealthily pursued her.

Philippe Gascogne had always prided himself on his skills at tracking. It had served him well on hunts over the years. It had also proved useful when trying to blend in to get information in the halls of *Parlement*, or even at his social clubs, he had to admit. But there usually was an order, a pattern when surveilling someone. With Miss Le Renaud, however, there was little rhyme or reason what she was doing, flitting all over. It was if she was following after somebody, but without the slightest clue how to do so. And being small, that made it all the more difficult to keep her in sight, and eventually Philippe lost the girl in the crowd. He swore angrily to himself.

Gabrielle was now on her own mission. Though the information she had gathered was small, it suggested to her an area of the estate that showed promised. She had reached the top steps of a back flight of stairs, and crept ever-so-carefully along this upstairs hallway, just like she seen them do so successfully in that wonderful little thriller she'd played a maid in, she really should have had the supporting lead, though the story did revolve around the maid, and she darted between shadows for protection.

Up ahead, however, there was an intersection of hallways, and it was patrolled by, of all things, an armed guard. Crouching, and plastered against the wall, she watched him brusquely send a guest away.

Gabrielle was stumped. While she understood the need for security at such a grand manse as this, there were other guards further down the hallway, as well. That seemed a great deal of protection, to a fault. Worse, though, it meant her path was blocked, and she could go no further to find out what in the world it was that they *were* guarding so zealously. How to get past was an answer to which she simply had no idea. It was so unfair.

As Gabrielle pondered the intricacies of a guarded hallway, and as Charlotte pursued the Marquis, Racine and André had by now become pretty much unaware that there was a party, let alone a world around them.

"You see, you see," she snapped at him, "that's what I'm talking about. You are so condescending."

"I was not being condescending, I was complimenting you." He was trying to figure out where the conversation had taken such a wrong turn, and how to get it back. This woman was utterly exasperating, no matter how fascinating she was. "There's a difference."

"Complimenting me. Give me some credit. You've been staring at my breasts."

"I have not been staring…" he caught himself. "Okay, I was, but you have nice breasts. And incredible eyes, great lips and an amazing face."

Racine might well have been indignant, but, honestly, those were still awfully nice compliments, even she knew. She brushed away some strands of hair that had fallen across her forehead. And before she had a chance to say anything, André continued.

"I think you're talented, beautiful, fascinating, annoying, courageous…"

Racine threw her arms around his neck, and kissed him. A surprised André responded back – never mind that he was on assignment, sometimes a man sim – but then she quickly, pulled away, looked at him and – whack! – slapped him.

It wasn't that the Musketeer was offended – he was long past being offended by this woman. He spoke in the most matter-of-fact voice he could muster.

"All right, I'd be lying if I didn't say I think I'm getting mixed signals here."

"I'm sorry, that was wrong."

"You're different from most women."

She didn't know what to say, what to think, she didn't even like that man, all that much at least, she thought, probably. "This is a bad time. You have your duty. And I have my obligation. I have to go."

And so she went. Quickly spinning off and away. The captain was left standing there alone. At last, though, giving a bemused, little laugh, knowing he should have expected no less from this Racine, he returned to his patrol, passing by a dowager staring at him, and offered her a nod.

Racine did indeed have her obligation, which she'd let slide for far too long, and she was back at it, more dogged and absorbed than ever, putting the past out of her head and making up for lost, important time.

*

Upstairs in his private office, Eduard pushed papers aside atop his oak desk and then grabbed them again, as the Count de Beaufort sat off in the corner. An aide waited nervously. He was just there to deliver a message, but when the Marquis was as intense and engrossed as he appeared to be at this moment, no one wanted to dare do anything that would displease him. And coughing at the wrong time could displease him.

"Inform me the moment the courier arrives. And I'm deeply discomforted with security. Make certain vigilance is increased."

The man quickly turned to go, though not from diligence, but he just wanted to be out of harm's way as soon as possible. Out of sight, out of mind didn't always hold true with Eduard, he could ruin a man's life at 50 kilometers, but it put the odds more in your favor.

As private as Eduard's office may have been, it was nonetheless, unsuspected by any of its inhabitants, under surveillance at that very moment. Not by Musketeers, nor trained army soldiers, or any officer of the *gendarmerie*, but rather a nervous, determined young woman who had followed the Marquis up the stairs. Charlotte crept along the hallway, hoping she was doing this properly and certain her pounding heart was giving her away

Up ahead, a door opened, and she saw an aide to the Marquis leave the room. As he headed in her direction,

212

Charlotte flattened herself against the wall, out of view. She held both her breath and the folds of her gown, to make sure neither would make a sound. The man's footsteps tapped off away from her, and she let out a sigh, though one as quietly as possible.

As alone as Charlotte was at that moment, Gabrielle had her eye out for companionship. Affectionate, dashing, willing, and most of all, as highly important as she could find. It had taken some doing, but she had marked her target. A small group of nobles were engaged in conversation near the buffet, among them some man parading himself in military uniform, so these all had to be somebody. That was it, Gabrielle had her idea in mind and at this point was too impatient to troll for small fish any longer. She wanted to move fast. And she wanted just one man, paying close attention to who that would be. Maneuvering her way to join them, Gabrielle pretended to care what they were talking about.

Gabrielle was always very good at appearing interested in what men were saying to her, they seemed to like that, even if she didn't have a clue what they were usually referring to, or if it was posturing blather to impress her. But it was a skill to look deeply fascinated, especially when they were boring her head off. The art of acting is listening, she'd been told, although she was usually just waiting to say her next line. She didn't have any particular line to say here, of course, though she did expect a bit more attention than the few glances and a leer or two she was getting. But they seemed oh-so interested in that man in the uniform, going on and on about God knows what, and so she just had to keep biding her time, patiently. And patience was never Gabrielle's strong suit.

"Your support down in Lyons in important," the officer

intoned. "I know Eduard appreciates it."

"You have our trust, General."

There were expressions of approval all around, and a few calls of "Here, here." Though they were aristocrats, they nonetheless felt special being there in the presence of General Turenne. It certainly didn't hurt their own stature, high as it was, to be seen in conference with the hero of the nation's military.

"My life is dedicated to France," he expressed solemnly, and the others were honored by his honor. There was more to France than the monarchy, they noted. They were all France, as well. Indeed they were the force that allowed France and even the monarchy to run. On and on they all went. Praising one another, and praising above all General Turenne.

Gabrielle continued to look interested, but she had her limits, and she knew she was reaching that limit. The men did seem pleased to have her there among them, it added a flair to being with such a distinguished general, and she got plenty of looks. But no one was trying to impress her, merely impress the general. They just seemed to like to stare at her. Her restlessness was getting the best of her, and she even began tap-tap-tapping her foot. Finally, there was no time left for subtlety and hints and suggestions. Impatiently, Gabrielle turned to the nobleman next to her, fluttered her eyes and made sure her open bodice was in full, glorious view. And whispered –

"I'll bet I'm much easier than you think."

*

No matter how brief was her business, and great its risk,

pomp accompanies majesty. As the Queen Mother was led to her carriage, there was much scurrying around to bring a sense of its importance and completion to the occasion. With a retinue of Musketeers at her side, they passed through a small crowd that had gathered outside the chateau. Some were there because, no matter their politics, royalty was royalty and must have its due, and they loved seeing and being a part of it, even at the edges. Others though were interested in what might be the last view in France of a member of the royal family. The Regent ignored it all as she passed by. Her thoughts were elsewhere. She motioned André closer.

"Was it a wise evening, Captain? Or rash?"

"These days, Ma'am, it's not always easy to know the difference."

"Inform the Major – " she didn't lose her stride, but slowed ever-so-slightly, "Where *is* Major Delacroix??"

André turned to look, but was surprised not to see him anywhere. "I believe he must have lingered."

"Get him, sir. I have plans to discuss."

*

The hallway was deserted, save for the secretive business going in Eduard's private office, and Charlotte had sneaked into a sitting room empty next to it. She was alone inside, with muffled voices leaking through the connecting wall. The only illumination came from moonlight in the window. She pulled her hair back and placed her ear tight against the wood panel, straining to make out what was being said, but it was far too muted and of no avail.

As Charlotte was looking into Eduard's business, so it was

that Philippe Gascogne was himself looking for Charlotte. He had found a high vantage point in the ballroom and peered out, but could spot her nowhere. He had kept an eye on the entranceway, and knew she hadn't left, so a curious frown crossed his face, wondering where she could have possibly gone. It made no sense, and he most decidedly wanted to know, here of all places.

Having more luck was Racine, who was peering through the ballroom, as well, but for a very different purpose. Well-tuned for seeing what didn't belong, from years of others looking at her, she spotted a man far out of place. Amid all the glamour, he was dirty and rough, with a raggedy coat and noticeable bulge in at his hip that she knew instantly was pistol. Further, he wasn't being shepherded out by a butler, but speaking with an aide who the gypsy had seen earlier with that Marquis fellow. As he tramped off alone, Racine followed him, avoiding the watchful eyes of security men she saw everywhere.

Another pair of watchful eyes were carefully, dear God ever-so-carefully making their way slowly, trepidatiously along a second-floor ledge outside the estate. Unable to understand a word that was being said inside the Marquis's office, Charlotte knew – against all her fears and far-better judgment – that the only way for her to hear anything was to follow that ledge agonizingly from one window to the next. With mounting dread, she had to force herself outside. But even more than helping find King Louis, if it meant discovering the truth behind her father's death, then she would do it. "Or die trying" was an expression the girl had heard often, though at this very moment she knew it was not a mere expression. It was reality. Absolutely terrified, refusing to look down, her eyes up against

216

the cool stones of the wall, she took tiny step after tiny step, stopping often to catch her breath and close her eyes to get her bearings, only to take the next tiny step.

*

The *Chateau de Longueville* was a massive estate, a concatenation of so many rooms, halls, hallways, wings, alcoves and levels, twisting into one another, that it was not only easy for a visitor to lose oneself, but easy for anybody there to move around with little notice. That's why security, these days of all days, was so critical. And why it was that the guard, standing on alert at the crossing of hallways, who had been stopping guests all night that had wandered the wrong way, grasped his musket tighter when he heard noises louder than usual. He couldn't quite make it out at first, but as it neared, it was laughter. No, not laughter exactly, but giggling.

Coming his way was a gorgeous blonde woman with flowing hair, nuzzling and snuggling with a bold gentleman, who was happy to have his hands all over her.

"Halt there. State your business."

Gabrielle gave a little laugh, and then kissed her new-found beau she'd only just met by the luckiest chance, he believed, at a small gathering of aristocrats. "Oh, it's…" she rolled her eyes suggestively, "…very personal."

She and her man snickered, and kissed again. Both their hands were searching and probing one another. He pinched her, and Gabrielle let out a high-pitched squeal and threw her arms around him.

The hallway guard certainly understood the ways of love, but he also understood his responsibility. "Guests require orders to be in the halls. You'll have to return to the party."

With her face flushed, and catching hurried breaths as best she could, Gabrielle spoke to him as a confidant.

"Captain – " she panted, knowing that like all privates, he would like being raised in rank, " – how can I say this and remain a lady?" Her hopeful look put her honor in his now high-ranking hands. "Going back to the party will not satisfy the Duke's immediate needs, if you know what I mean – all I ask is to use a room – any one – and we will be done in a very short time — " (She was close to him now, almost breathless, her hand reaching up to steady her breast.) "You are a man, you understand we are all French here, *n'est-ce pas?* – We need a room – Anything for *l'amour.*"

The hall was completely empty. Her eyes directed his and showed it was empty. She just wanted one room. For as quick as it would take. Not a soul was in sight. She stared at the guard. A small bead of sweat crossed her quivering upper lip. She licked it off and grazed his shoulder with her fingertips. "Anything for *l'amour.* There is no one here." It couldn't be denied. There was no one there. He knew it. And then came the magic words, for all men. "I have a friend," she said. "She would like you very much. I will get her after...we are done. And tell her how quite wonderful you are."

And he smiled. And she smiled. And the Duke smiled a great deal.

*

It was wonderful that there were people who could smile that night. For Charlotte, it was simply pure relief that she felt when finally reaching the ledge outside of Eduard de

Longueville's window. She was satisfied just catching her breath and thanking God for getting her there safely. Her heart was still pounding though, and strands of sweat were beading up on her temples and forehead, something most uncommon to her. Oddly, now that she was safe and standing still, she could afford to address her situation, how high up she was, and dizziness began to set in. But by holding on to the wall and leaning into it, she at last comforted herself and settled down. Not that her predicament was over – it had barely begun – but the hellish part was over. Except for returning back.

Concealing herself as much as possible, Charlotte shifted her head and looked in through the gossamer drapes, making out the silhouette of Eduard and that of Count de Beaufort. They had been joined by what appeared to be a courier, though she couldn't be certain, but a satchel was strapped over his shoulder. Between the folds, she was able to see the Marquis place a document inside an envelope and emboss his seal upon it. He admonished the courier with some sort of instructions, but Charlotte could only mark a few words, the rest were too muffled for sense.

The problem was the closed window. Carefully – though, of course, everything Charlotte did at the moment was careful – she reached into her purse hanging around her neck, and patiently took out the invitation. Carefully, she slid it between the panes, carefully trying to carefully maneuver the latch holding them together, carefully. Carefully.

It wasn't working, wasn't working, wasn't…And then, yes!, the latch finally flipped. Slowly – and carefully – the young girl pulled a window pane ever-so-slightly open.

The courier was putting the envelope in his satchel.

"…will leave from here tomorrow at dawn," Charlotte

could now at last hear the messenger clearly say. "I can reach Le Havre in time."

"The Ambassador's ship departs at noon. Do not miss it. You understand my words?" It was not a question. The Marquis rarely asked questions, but most definitely not about something this critical.

Charlotte was overwhelmed. Again, her heart began pumping wildly, but this time it was not from terror, but unbelieving excitement. Her eyes could not have been more wide open, and her ears were burning.

The Count de Beaufort finally spoke up, making sure to reinforce the moment. "Austria must receive this treaty before they will support us with their army."

Only a slight twitch could be seen around the Marquis's eyes, before shooting a glance over and then back to the courier. "The words of Count de Beaufort are ill-chosen. Ignore him. Do only your duty."

The Count shook nervously inside for having spoken out of turn and took his rebuke. Eduard ignored him and continued with the young man.

"Get to Le Havre. Rest assured that between our own resources and help within the palace, your action is well-supported."

Charlotte was beside herself. She had actually discovered something. Her. It might even be important, it sounded important, very, though she couldn't tell what it meant. An army? A treaty. The palace? Perhaps the others would know. She had to find out more, and carefully, so very carefully maneuvered her ear closer to the opening, leaning down, precariously balancing herself upon – when suddenly her foot slipped, and she lost her balance. Charlotte noisily grasped at the sill, being quiet was the least of her concerns right now, but her hands could find no hold and slid.

"Did you hear something?"

Eduard looked up, he had been so intensely absorbed on the grave matters before him, that he was uncertain. He tried to gauge the direction of the noise, if noise there had been, and seeing de Beaufort tense up told him that he had not been mistaken. He spun around. Anything unexpected tonight and in this private enclave was a concern, and a troubled look crossed his face.

The Marquis quickly stood and strode across the room towards the window. He was sure now that the sound had come from outside, but what? He reached the curtains and with a snap, thrust them apart.

Opening the window panels wide, he peered out into the night. But spotted nothing. No intruders on the grounds. Guards all in place. Perhaps it was a bird. Or a broken branch falling.

Underneath his gaze, out of sight in the dark unless he looked where he never suspected, were two hands holding onto the ledge, barely by quivering fingertips. The girl there was terrified, her eyes frozen shut, unmoving. Not because it was the wise thing to do, but because she was unable.

Satisfied that nothing was there, Eduard shut the window, locked it, and pulled the drape tight. Enough with all this, he thought, his concentration now broken. His work here was done, he wanted out of the room, there were guests and other plans to make, and he doused the light.

All was quiet. And still.

And the only thing that perhaps existed at that moment anywhere in the world, at least for her, was a dangling

Charlotte. Through unrelenting palpitations and a focus so narrow that it only permitted her to see a sturdy wall she could support her feet against, the young and panic-stricken girl was able to regain the sense of movement, find some slight purchase, and slowly, inchingly pull herself back upon the ledge. There, her body at last permitted itself to face reality, and she collapsed shaking. After a time, she was able to sit up. She broke into hyperventilating tears, some from the fear, but most the joy of survival.

"Never again," the thought echoed through her head. "Never again, never again, never again."

*

There were, in truth, quite a few things outside, beside a dangling Charlotte that the Marquis might have been interested in knowing. For elsewhere on another part of the grounds, Racine was creeping surreptitiously, following the suspicious man from the ballroom. Avoiding his view when he turned, she hit the ground and crawled after him through the dirt.

Creeping through the back of the estate, the gypsy arrived at a low fenced-in area, which blocked her progress. Her man however had no such impediment and was passed through into a guarded entrance. Racine watched helplessly as her suspect disappeared from view. Thinking hard what could possibly be done, how to get past this obstacle, her mind racing over the limited options with even more limited time, she quickly tossed some stones beyond the young sentry. He spun at the suspicious sound, and with his attention distracted, she scrabbled up and pulled herself over the barrier.

Making her way stealthily towards the stables, she found a

spot to secret herself where she would be able to watch. What she saw though made little sense to her. The scraggly man and others were placing barrels of some sort into the back of a wagon, covering them with tarpaulins.

"You fool," the fellow in charge berated one of the workers. "Put out that cigar. Or d'you wanna blow this entire estate to kingdom come?"

What had been an expression of curiosity quickly changed. For now, a look of great concern washed over Racine's face. Because she didn't understand what in the world was going on. And because she understood enough.

*

As much of a hurry as Racine had been pushing herself, Gabrielle was in no such rush at all. Quite the opposite, in fact, idly biding her time. The same could not be said, however, for the over-anxious Duke, who was expectantly removing his coat and shirt, so full of heated desire that he'd forgotten first to take off his tie. Gabrielle, though, was idly wandering through the elegant bedroom, delaying her moment of undressing, instead seeming to admire all the graceful furniture and appointments about her.

"*C'est marveilleux.* It is incredible. Everything one could hope for and more."

"You will say the same when we finish," the Duke boasted, without a hint of joking. He kissed her full on the mouth, though she managed to turn her head out of shyness, he supposed, leaving him her soft neck to caress. He started to undo her bodice.

"My, you are so frisky. I can't wait," she breathed. But

then she pulled back, as if she'd had a sudden thought. "Oh! But hold that thought. I am going to freshen up first. Then, I am yours. All yours. Only yours. And yours, my handsome, dashing and exciting Duke, alone."

She had been moving away as she spoke, without a care, the most natural thing in the world, as she reached the door and opened it. It was all so seamless that the hapless Duke didn't even know how hapless he was at the moment, just hungering for this beautiful, endowed blonde who would be his, all his. As she stepped into the hallway, she seductively looked back in.

"And if I don't get back soon enough, start without me."

Shutting the door behind her, Gabrielle moved hurriedly back down the hall. As she neared where the guard stood, though, she slowed and began to sashay towards him.

"Oh, *garçon,* please go get some oysters," she haughtily ordered him away. "My friend wishes an aphrodisiac, though why any man would need help when there is…" she displayed every curve of her body, "…me? Crazy. So, off you go. *Vite.*"

Though the hallway guard had appreciated her earlier and done this strumpet a favor out his hot-blooded appreciation of *l'amour* and his hotter-blooded hope for meeting her friend, Gabrielle had gone too far this time and overly-played her hand. It was one thing to offer a young man future dreams of the flesh, it was another to treat a lowly private lower than even he knows he is, giving him an opportunity to assert what very little authority he had.

"*Mademoiselle,* you must ask a valet for yourself. Down the hall, below." To which he added pointedly, "*Vite.*"

"And I thought French men were supposed to be gallant." She gave her best pout, but it was to no avail. His blunt, offended look dismissed her. "You are not ordering me, are you??"

"I am. Go."

She turned her back to him – and the frown on her face suddenly turned into a big smile. This was precisely what she had in mind all along. Whenever Gabrielle was stopped along the way through the halls, she simply told them – truthfully – that she had been given a direct order by the guard himself, and they could check with him if they wish, thank you very much. And she passed on to her intended destination.

Mind you, that didn't mean that what she told them once she arrived downstairs at the valet station was the truth. But the truth got her there, so apparently it had its use in skullduggery, she thought. The more you didn't have to lie, the easier it was. Of course, at some point, the lie is precisely what you have.

So it was when the concerned head valet listened uncertainly to her.

"And this came from the Marquis himself?" he scratched his head.

"Would I be right here if he did not? I can only tell you what dear Eduard asked, in that inimitable way of his." She raised her eyebrows at the man, and his tense reaction made clear he was well-aware. "'Have some imbecile bring milk to *our young guest* immediately.' I trust you know who he is referring to. The 'young guest,' I mean, not the imbecile."

"I am head valet, m'lady," he said defensively, wanting now to prove himself against this impudent woman's challenge to his position. Of course, he knew.

"The…'guest,' Eduard said, was crying, and wanted him quieted so that others wouldn't hear."

"Hear? All the way from the East Wing?"

Gabrielle hid her concern under a passive exterior and thought quickly. "The smaller they are, the bigger they scream." Having thus delivered her instructions, she said, Gabrielle bid him her good night and departed.

Left to his new duties, the head valet went off to the kitchen and wearily made his way back through the hallways carrying a tray and glass. This was much too important an assignment to delegate to anyone of lesser stature. He turned a corner and headed up a staircase.

The East Wing was quite a walk, but that was all the more reason for its valued privacy, so important here. Further along another long corridor, he came to yet one more intersection and headed down it.

"Halt," a security guard ordered.

The head valet snapped at him. "For the King." He had his duty, and this officious little sentry would know what real standing was.

He did indeed have his duty, and he carried it out impeccably. Thinking how that self-important young woman, who might be in favor with his Master now but that would change in a moment, he knew, oh, my, yes, how that girl was unaware what a real place of authority was, like his own.

The only thing he himself was not aware of was that the very same young woman had been following him the whole way. And right now, she was hidden in an alcove close enough to hear every word. And Gabrielle's eyes were like saucers.

CHAPTER TWENTY-EIGHT

A campfire burned dimly off in a small forest clearing, so as to not draw much attention. Blankets were laid out across the ground, and the three women were out of their gowns, readying for bed. Racine had, in fact, stripped hers off long before even reaching the hideaway, so anxious was she to get out of "the damned thing," as she put it, that she walked through much of the woods in her chemise alone.

It had been a consuming evening, beyond anything they allowed themselves to even expect, yet sleep was the farthest thing from their minds, so keyed up were they all. They talked through the night, overlapping one another with what they had learned and were learning still from the others. The news, trying to make sense of it all, was almost too much. They were literally shaking with excitement – though in Charlotte's case it was more because satin, much as she had always dearly adored it in her wardrobe, did not offer near the warmth in a mere undergarment, and she was simply shivering from cold. Mercifully the fire did help, and she sat as close to it as possible.

Gabrielle was the most animated of them all. She was so excited by her news. She was also…well, Gabrielle. Parading around in a skimpy costume, acting out in detail her escapades was, to Gabrielle, the stuff of high drama. Of course, the truth was, it *was* high drama. Her discovery had been monumental, to be sure, but then so had everyone's, each truly significant pieces of a growing puzzle.

But it was a puzzle that had fallen apart. Not only were they all outside now, looking in, but they no longer had a way

227

back inside and, worse, somehow dynamite and a foreign treaty had been thrown into the mix. What in the world?? They had no idea where that left the three of them. There were so many branches to this tree now. So many roads to keep track of. The only choice they had, the only idea they could even conceive of to try was near-unthinkable, since it meant the three of them splitting up.

It was most certainly a distinct risk. Racine was all for it, though; she was sure they were actually far ahead of the goddamned Musketeer bastards on what the three had discovered, and just couldn't stop now. It was too much worth it. But then, she had lived on her own for years. Going off alone wasn't just second nature to her, it was first nature.

Gabrielle, however, was supportive of it, as well. She was a little surprised by that – she knew well the risk, which was much too real, and also dearly loved the company of the others. But she had always had a sense of adventure, of doing what was unexpected, and reveling in its results, and she had grown in recent months to crave it even more. This was indeed a risk, a great risk, but could you imagine… she thought. Could you imagine if we could really do this, what's truly possible, what's in our grasp? Could you imagine? And if there was something Gabrielle could do as well as anyone, it was imagine.

Charlotte put up a good front, but the thought frightened her. She had courage to make all these efforts of the past months, knowing that others were there to catch her. But alone? It frightened her a great deal, but didn't want to show it. The only thing that frightened her more, though, was letting the men who killed her father get away with it. Nothing would keep her from prohibiting that. Absolutely nothing in the entire world. She would do it. She simply had to. Whatever it took.

Quietly, and somewhat absent-mindedly as she tried to occupy her thoughts, Charlotte turned to the pile of ball gowns she had carefully piled and had neatly smoothed earlier, and now smoothed them out once again. With a chagrined expression, she held up Racine's tattered dress and tried to rub out some mud, but it was only out of wistful hope, for it stood no chance. Not only was it covered neckline to hem in stains, but torn, as well.

"I so dearly loved this piece," she sighed and fondly ran her fingers across the detailed beading. "But it put in grand service to its country." Not many of her social set had finery that could say that, she laughed to herself. And it had one more duty left, as Charlotte spread it out to provide insulation upon the cold, hard ground for sleeping.

"He was right there, inches away. Inches. We found him! We found him," Gabrielle couldn't help burst out, excited for what lay ahead, but still with a confounding mixture of unrefined joy and wrenching angst for what had slipped through their fingers, what might have been. "So much for 'Break in, find the king, and we're gone.'" She sat on the edge of sighing. "It was such a hopeful plan."

"And so is this new one," Racine finally spoke up, pointedly. "But too much has changed. We'll be okay. I know everything we've done has been together. But we're <u>three</u> people. So, the truth is we can cover a lot of ground split. We can do things separately that we could never do together. This is good. This is seriously, really, *very* good. It's just…

She caught herself, hesitant about something, but didn't want to say. But the longer she went without saying, the more it was clear what the problem was. Because she kept avoiding looking in that direction.

"I can do it," Charlotte insisted.

"Are you <u>sure</u> you're up to going *alone?*" It had been obvious to Racine from the first where the weakest link in the plan was. Not just a weak link, but almost a non-existent one.

"Yes."

"Because we <u>have</u> to know where that gunpowder is going."

"I know how to trail behind a person." Charlotte was defiant now. Whatever fears she had, and they were profound, took a deep back seat to being challenged, and being left out. "You get the king, and you," she spun to Gabrielle, "you stop the document. You're the ones with the dangerous jobs, not me. You're the ones who really have any risk. You're the ones who may not…"

She stopped, unable to finish the troubling thought. She didn't want to face any of them not returning, and began to withdraw into herself, her lower lip starting to quiver. Racine caught her attention. She made sure the young girl was listening, and closely, before she spoke.

"When the bastards get you down, Princess, just spit in their eye."

Gabrielle kicked down the fire to a few embers, and then began to lay out her bed roll, since she had to awake and leave well before the others.

It caught Charlotte's attention. This was now all too real. "Promise you'll wake me to say goodbye," Charlotte said emphatically to her. And wouldn't look away until she got an answer.

Gabrielle understood her concern, and didn't answer. They all knew what was at stake. None of them really wanted to face it, or put words to it. "Whatever happens," she at last replied, "it is all for France."

"Promise you will wake me and say goodbye," the young girl doggedly repeated. "Promise me."

A crackling fire was the only sound. Gabrielle chose her words carefully.

"I promise I will say goodbye."

*

At dawn the next morning, Charlotte was fast asleep, the blanket tightly pulled around her body, which was curled in a ball to get every possible ounce of warmth. Racine was stretched out, open to the elements. Hair fell across her forehead covering her tightly-closed eyes, her mouth open, emitting occasional quick snorts.

Gabrielle had dressed, however, and was already on her horse, set to go. She looked down at her friends, aware that she may not see them again. She wouldn't wake them, she couldn't bear the words, but she would keep the promise precisely as she had made it.

"Goodbye."

Book Four

CHAPTER TWENTY-NINE

A late, mid-morning haze still covered the countryside, muting what otherwise would have been the lush green of the meadow. The field was dotted with shrubs and an occasional hillock, as crickets frenetically chirped in the grass, and a few birds sang in the distance. It was a quiet, lazy, peaceful day, clear of a soul except for the caravan of gunpowder barrels, guarded by three armed riders, that clopped down a dirt road. Four other men, looking somewhat bored, rode shotgun in the bed of the wagon, their horses tied in back. The procession rolled around a bend and disappeared.

From far back, a young girl on horseback suddenly arrived, slowly and exceedingly carefully tracking them. Trying to keep her distance was wise strategy, but Charlotte had fallen so distant in arrears that she'd long-since lost complete sight of the group and was forced to push her horse to trot a bit faster –

– but when she made it around the bend ahead, she found to her dismay that she had made up far more ground than expected and was now much too close. So close, in fact, that if any of the men bothered to simply turn around they'd have been able to easily see her, coming up on their heels. Worse, the road was now long and straight, and so there was no way to even avoid being seen. Panicked, Charlotte suddenly leaped off her horse and landed in the copse that lined the road.

Safe from discovery herself, unfortunately there was one issue she hadn't factored into her jump. The riderless horse remained standing in the road, in full glory and plain sight. Pawing at the dirt, nonchalant as a horse can be, it was more than happy to wait there and happily rest, snorting in the air.

Charlotte frantically tried to wave the animal over, but alas it was young and not conversant enough yet in human sign language. She didn't want to risk calling its name, that much was for certain, although that would likely have been quieter than the noises it was puffing in the air. The girl did make some hisses at the horse, hoping that might be taken as "Come hither" to the beast, but unfortunately that more had the effect of scaring it into backing away.

At this point, the girl was more mortified than scared – and she was thoroughly scared. She kept glancing up the road to see if any of the men had turned yet, and then back to coaxing the animal. All she could think through her fear was that her friends had given her the easiest job of all, and just two hours out she was unable to track a slow-moving cart. She had been raised a lady and of grace and manners, and so never in her life had been one to offer a curse, however she thought that now might be a good time to have learned. What to do, what to do, what to do…?

Not far ahead at all, the caravan much-too-slowly trudged on, it was frustratingly as like they weren't moving at all. Meanwhile, only a short ways back behind them, a small arm snaked its way across the edge of the road, and its fingers achingly reached for reigns that were lying in the dirt, the leather getting twisted this way and that as the horse attached to it shuffled around, just barely out of reach. At last, blessedly at last, the hand grasped the rope, a moan of relief was heard, and the horse was pulled away out of sight.

As the morning wore on, and Charlotte continued her way, the now-winding road curved through a forest, and Charlotte felt far more comforted with its protection. She'd let the others increase their distance for the sake of safety. Feeling more at ease again, she sang a favorite tune to herself, softly of course, though she was sure the horse seemed to enjoy it. She was caught in the pleasant reverie of the moment and thought this tracking responsibility might work out after all.

It might, indeed, had not the underbrush begun to thin out into a wide clearing. Before she realized what had occurred, the caravan was directly ahead and yet again she was in easy sight. Nearby, however, an access spur forked off to the right, heading deeper into the forest, and Charlotte galloped towards it, her pulse racing in hopes of making it there unseen. It loomed closer before her, but as she implored her horse on, every fallen branch that snapped under-hoof sounded to Charlotte as if a loud, warning crack of thunder. It was like when in a nightmare you ran fast as you could, but seemed to stay in the same place. In time, though, she was able to veer into the side road to refuge.

This path through the backwoods was much more twisting than the main dirt road, curving around trees and around natural mounds and boulders. The going was slower, as well, for there was no maintenance, making the route treacherous. At last, she was able again to hurry along this detour at a gallop, blocked by trees as she was, and determined not to fall too far behind and lose sight of them once more. She saw ahead the access road winding back to the main road and rejoined it.

But once there, she couldn't see anyone. She was very

confused.

"Where are you??" she said out loud. "You couldn't have gotten that far ahead."

And she was right, they hadn't. For all of a sudden, there they were – coming up *from behind*! Charlotte in her haste had gotten too far ahead. Quickly, not giving herself a moment to think, she pressed her horse to speed and flew up the road, her hair whipping across her face and having to push it from her eyes to see, finally finding cover in protected thicket. There, she held herself and her horse silent, and waited, letting the caravan pass.

Waited. Hoping, in the name of heaven, that she would be able this time to follow them. Wherever in the world they were going.

CHAPTER THIRTY

It had been a long night and an exhausting night at the *Chateau de Longueville*. The next morning, the staff throughout the estate was still cleaning up after the ball. The butler oversaw the painstaking effort, making sure everything was as it had been and should be. There was no complaint, it was his job and his honor. But still, such things do always get so out of hand, he thought. The upper class was supposed to know better. Why else have an upper class? A heavy knock at the door brought his thoughts back to the present.

Standing out front, to his great concern, was an attractive, dark-haired woman in a thoroughly tattered and muddy dress.

"Oh, m'lady, are you all right?!"

"Oh, this," Racine tossed off with an air of insouciant dismissal, "just a roll in the hay with some lord, I forget his name, but it probably wasn't his real one. Anyway, I was at the Marquis's party last night, it's like I was telling my friend Suzette, isn't the Queen Mother to die for – oh so clever – " she quickly handed over the invitation as proof to allay any uncertainty " – and realized today I'd lost my necklace. Can you imagine?"

"Please, do come in," the man offered solicitously. "We must find it."

"We must."

As the two of them searched through the parlor, where Racine said she was most-certain she had last seen her necklace, a guard stood watch over every move. There were a great many guards standing watch, Racine noted.

"And what did the choker look like?" the butler inquired.

"Oh, he was about six feet tall, wavy brown hair, a…"

"I mean, the necklace."

Racine barreled past her mistake. "Oh, just lots of jewels, they all look the sa – " suddenly her face brightened excitedly, she actually remembered that damned word, " – *cloisonné*! It was lovely. Oh, my, this dress *is* a mess. I must get soap for it right away."

She started to take off her dress, when she stopped and glared daggers at the men.

"Do you mind??" she snapped haughtily on behalf of her pristine innocence.

They excused themselves, leaving Racine alone. She rushed over to the double-door to the outside and unlocked it, and then drew the curtain to hide that it had been opened.

Returning to the sofa, Racine got on her knees as if searching, and pulled from her dress the necklace she had worn the night before.

"Oh, joy and luck, I found it!" she shouted. "We can go."

It was a beautiful piece, the butler remarked when he saw it. No wonder the young lady was so anxious to get it back without even changing back into more appropriate clothes, he thought. Though he did wonder why she had referred to it as a cloisonné, since it was nothing of the sort. Women, in his experience, were quite meticulous about such things, down to the carat. Ah, well, no doubt she was befuddled from its absence. He gave it no more thought, and after bidding her *adieu*, watching the young lady tromp down the path, a bit less graceful than he'd thought proper, perhaps she had drunk too much the night before, he returned to his responsibilities of overseeing the manor's restoration to its proper state of grace. The clean-up was blessedly finished by noon, and he felt relief knowing that he wouldn't have to face the master's wrath.

By the early afternoon, the bustle of the day was all gone. Everything was stately, refined, exquisite and best of all, quiet. Locked, guarded and secure.

Except for the parlor. For there, an unlocked glass panel slid quietly open, and through the concealing curtain Racine cautiously sneaked back inside, once again in her comfortable clothes, out of that hideous monstrosity she'd had to wear, and carrying a rope. A dagger was tucked in her belt. She peeked into the hallway and saw the two things she was hoping for: that the stairway was unguarded, and not a soul was in sight.

Heading along the second-floor landing, Racine strained to remember the directions that Gabrielle had given her. "'Down the east hallway, 50 meters to…'"

She stopped. Up ahead was a hallway post – and three guards. Worse, further down were two more guards at an intersection. This was not what she expected. So, now what?

Racine swiftly backtracked around the corner to find a nook where she could give herself time to figure this problem out. A diversion perhaps, another way in maybe, possibly a… But the time she was hoping for to make such a decision would have to be later, for suddenly she heard steps close by.

Racine peeked back around the corner. It was worse than she'd presumed. Striding down another hall, a patrolling guard was heading straight towards her.

She spun back out of sight. Racine was trapped – there was no direction she could move, caught between two worst options. This patrol guard almost upon her, and the guard post directly behind. Her mind was whirring. She plastered herself in the nook, literally at a crossroads.

And on the patrol sentry came. One step closer, then

another. They stopped – but not nearly long enough to escape if there had even been anywhere to go, checking rooms most likely, and then once again the clack of boots started up, echoing relentlessly off the marble floor.

The post guards could hear the approach of their mate, but paid it no attention. It was boring duty. None of them thought much of it. Them, the sentries, any of the scouts. There were men training for action, they knew, and here they were, standing inside a mansion. Maybe some of them knew why, but as far as they could tell, they were guarding pottery. But it was for the Marquis de Longueville, and they were proud to be able to tell their friends that. If only it wasn't so boring. Though they left that part out of their stories.

And now, here at last came the patrolling guard, from around the corner. Marching towards them – yet Racine was nowhere to be seen! What in the world had taken him so long, a post guard snarked to himself? If *they* had to be diligent every moment, the least others could do was not slack off and rest whenever they wanted.

The patrol guard saluted them, and headed past. Oh, how officious, the post guard thought, standing there. A salute. There's no one watching you, you don't have to be so pompous. You think saluting us will make up for you stopping to take a break, as if we couldn't tell? And maybe we wouldn't tell on you?

The patrol guard simply marched on, not caring if the others saluted back or not. Because it wasn't the patrol guard at all – it was Racine! Wearing an oversized uniform.

Somehow. And somehow she had eluded the actual patrolling guard himself. And somehow –

It was of no matter how right now, because Racine still

240

had two more guards to deal with, at the intersection of the main hallways ahead. There were so many damned sentries. For God's sake, she thought, they were guarding a 10-year-old child. Usually that only required a single nanny. What did they think, someone was going to break in and try to steal him away?

Racine tried to block out such thoughts and calmly girded herself. Look like you belong there. She halted, stiff at attention. She stared straight ahead. The guards waited for her to speak, but only got silence.

"You're my relief?" the surprised first intersection guard finally broke the long quiet. "Already?"

Racine merely shrugged and then saluted. The man reluctantly saluted back, and headed off. Racine took his place, shoulder to shoulder with her new partner – though her shoulders were a good six inches lower. This second guard looked down at her.

"Didn't have anything in your size, hunh?

He chuckled at her sagging uniform. But Racine just kept her eyes forward. You Neanderthal giant, she thought, the bigger they are, it turns out they really do fall harder. Just like your crony. You'd probably go down in a heap even faster, because you're sort of an idiot. But then, she had to acknowledge that the patrolling guard had gone down plenty fast. Of course, it always helped when they didn't see it coming. And he didn't see a thing coming as he'd marched so obliviously down the hallway. So, now, he was unconscious on the floor of a hall closet, his uniform removed. Knocked out, tied up and his mouth gagged. The holy trinity.

Getting no rise from this new, little sentry beside him, the big guard went back to his business, which was largely staring

241

into space. But Racine stood tense, surrounded by so many armed enemies, and knowing that she still had further to go. Not much further, though, just down that hallway to her right. The room where the king was being held should be just over there. But which one?

She allowed herself to peek off. And to her distress, she saw yet another armed guard in front of a door. But that was good. Because that had to be it. But it meant she was blocked yet again. Oh, hell, people, give me a break already.

What to do?? It wasn't that Racine was running out of thoughts – her mind was always working with plans, thoughts were rushing through her head like a raging river – but she was running out of time. For soon the unconscious guard would be discovered, or the real relief would show up, or people would noticed that she really, really didn't belong there. Or…there was no other option, no more time, any second literally the escapade could be over, she realized that she had to take the risk. The full risk. It was the time for everything or nothing. But always look like you belong there.

And, she thought, that meant do what she knows. And that meant, take the offensive.

Racine whipped off her hat and shook out her hair. The instant that the guard reacted, and before he could say even a word –

"What?" she snapped at him. "You haven't seen a woman before? The Marquis, he likes having the ladies around. Okay? But if you have a problem serving with a woman, hey, I really don't need this, I really don't need this, I have better things to do. Okay? I'll switch. Will you be happy then??! Fine, whatever you want."

The intersection guard didn't know what hit him. Caught

by total surprise, he couldn't say a word as Racine stormed away.

Reaching the sentry at the door, he was caught almost as unawares. He'd heard all the shouting and now saw this pretty woman with eyes burning lightning bolts and barreling at him.

"What is going…"

"Oh, no, not you, too. Look, that man couldn't take standing guard with a woman, and I just don't want to deal with it again, all right? Enough already. So, let's just switch places for right now before there's a fight and the Marquis himself has to come here to straighten things out and get what he wants, which is why he sent me here in the first place. All right??"

The bewildered door guard not only understood, but mainly just wanted to be far away from this crazy person who was wearing what looked like a sack with epaulets and have there be no trouble. Not here, not now. Not with the Marquis's name floating in the air. No, thank you. He happily switched and joined his sane friend. It could all be resolved later.

And so Racine stood guard in front of the door. The men kept looking at her, but when she glared daggers back, they turned away and watched their intersection with their backs to her. The more they could avoid her, the better.

Slowly, a half-step at a time, Racine slid back into the doorway, then just a bit further, now some more, until she was unseen. Out of sight at last, she took a deep breath. And then, she nudged the door open.

And there in the room was an apprehensive 10-year-old boy. Louis XIV.

"You're kind of puny for a king."

She immediately closed the door and removed her uniform jacket. The rope she had brought with her tumbled out in front of the startled child.

"Who are you?!" he creaked.

"Your fairy godmother."

She tossed the rope to him. By this point, he had regained at least a portion of his regal bearing, though inside he was still wobbling.

"I demand you tell me your intentions."

"You're so charming," She had no time for this. "Tie that to the bed."

Without waiting, she rushed over and cracked the window with her dagger, sending shards flying. The boy quickly attached the rope.

CHAPTER THIRTY-ONE

The port city of Le Havre sat overlooking the English Channel. Merchant ships from around the world arrived daily in the harbor to vie for its commerce, but the city took that in with an indifferent eye. Most of the world, after all, considered it a poor step-child to Marseilles. A gloomy, second choice when that southern route wasn't available. But Le Havre always knew better, always knew that because it sat on the mouth of the Seine, it was the heart directly into Paris. And into Paris, then into France. Though Marseilles had been the leading object of nations looking for defense of the Mediterranean, Le Havre knew it was the true route into Europe. And so it meandered on, quietly, secretly surviving. It was Le Havre. *C'est la vie.*

The sun barely reflected off the murky waters, where boats of all intentions and flags filled the harbor. Dockworkers lugged crates, merchants scurried around anxious to make deals before their competitors beat them to it, seamen on shore leave sought out women, virtuous or otherwise.

And down by the quay, the courier sent by Eduard de Longueville was protected by his escorts as he met several official-looking military men. They seemed highly interested in a sealed document he briefly showed before putting it back safely inside his coat.

From an obscured terrace above the pier, Gabrielle spied the exchange intently. She had ridden long and hard to get to this point, and it was all finally coming into place. She moved closer to get a better view, but stopped, with a look of great concern. The courier had left the dock and instead gotten into a dinghy. Along with several of the others, he was being rowed out to a waiting ship.

No one had expected this, and Gabrielle needed time to figure it out. Unfortunately, that was not her strong suit. Sitting alone at an outdoor café, she kept looking out at that ship, hoping it would come in to shore, or that the dinghy would sink, but, no, that wasn't good, because the document would still be on board. Usually these dilemmas were worked out for her and written down in neat acts. She felt like calling out "Line!" for what she was to say and do next, but all that would get her was someone throwing her a rope. She was lost, had not a single idea.

This situation was impossible. She got up and paced around the table, but it didn't help. She was baffled in thought. Anything, she begged, she would try anything. Honestly. Well, within reason and basic decency. She was good at that, trying most anything. But no anything came to her. Where was anything when you really needed it?

Gabrielle began wandering through the patio, around the courtyard and across the dock, looking for any sailor to ask his port of call, any information she could find that might lead to something, anything about that Austrian ship in the harbor. Who was the captain, where was it headed, when would it be leaving, how many men were aboard, what's their motivation? Something to go on. A prompt. Making it all the more frustrating was that the ship was so close, there it was, its tall poles – whatever they called those things, she even could make out some bodies on board. So close, but much too far away.

She met sailors from all over the world, but not Austria. She met *men* from Austria but they had nothing to do with the ship. She even found sailors from Austria, but these were from another ship entirely. They walked off, they all walked off, leaving her standing there alone. Wondering, thinking, and totally lost.

Then, she was slapped on her rear.

"What is it with you men and ladies' butts??" she spun to the man, yet another seafarer, a small fellow who looked to be a step below maintenance crew.

"I heard you talking about Austria, so I come over. I'm from Austria," the man said, proudly pointing to himself. "You like foreign men? We're very exotic."

The only thing Gabrielle found exotic about Austria was Linzer torte, but here finally was a seaman she was looking for. From that very ship. Yet even at this her luck failed, because while the man knew everything about keeping decks swabbed, he knew nothing helpful about anything else. Actually, mostly the man just leered and pawed at her. Time was short, and she had to move on.

"How about we have a shag, missy?" he spit out. "I got an hour before going back to ship."

"That's so tempting, Fritz, but I have to pass. My *one* rule is that a man needs at least half a mouthful of teeth. What can I say? It's my girlish way."

Gabrielle walked away, fast. Anything to get away from there. But suddenly, an idea belted her. And a big smiled crossed her face.

It wasn't long after that a dinghy was heading out to sea with several men including a small seafaring fellow who looked to be a step below maintenance crew, and had a big, anticipatory grin on his face. Under a tarp, two lady's feet stuck out. She pulled them in.

CHAPTER THIRTY-TWO

The caravan had stopped for lunch. The men found shade up a hillside under the trees and ate. The horses grazed. And the barrels of dynamite waited.

"Aye, we're well-paid enough, I'll grant you that," one of the guards replied dismissively, and then nodded to the casks, "I'm just saying I want to be far away after we get there."

Not far away, hiding along the road among a grove of oaks, Charlotte struggled to hear. She crept further around.

"...and how the hell should I know where it's going?" a second man snapped. "Go ask the boss. What do I care?"

"Fine. I will. Big help you are."

This third guard strode off, but Charlotte wasn't able to get close enough to see where he was headed. But what she was more and more understanding about what was at stake told her she must.

A mound bordered the length of the road, next to the wagon. It would offer protection, but to get there meant crossing a short, open span of field. Charlotte made an unhappy decision. Smoothing her clean blouse, with lovely embroidery, she crawled low along the ground, squinting in anticipated discomfort, using the wagon as a shield.

Making it safely to cover, the top of Charlotte's auburn hair peeked up over the ridge of the roadside mound, and the rest of her now-dusty face followed. She was happily protected by the knoll and wagon, but unfortunately had a woeful view of the third guard talking to the boss whose back was to her. She maneuvered across the embankment to hear better.

She could hear just slightly better. If only the man in

charge would move in her direction, Charlotte was most certain she would be able to make his words out. If only, she hoped. Finally, the man did turn around.

And it was Gilles.

Charlotte's body convulsed. She didn't understand. Why was he here, why? She slapped a hand over her mouth to keep from letting out a noise. Losing her grasp, she slid down the mound and had to fight from gagging on the mouthful of dirt.

"All right, break is over," Gilles ordered the men. "Get all the horses and pull out."

Charlotte stayed flattened, as low and still as she could, her eyes shut tight, as much from fear as wanting what she'd seen to disappear. But shutting her eyes didn't keep out the sounds, and as some of the caravan began to depart, she heard one of the men call out.

"Hey, boy, how'd you get loose back here?"

Charlotte's eyes flew open, and she whipped her head around. That was her horse! The man was talking to it. To her shock, he was tying it to the back of the wagon. Worse, to her horror, moments later the caravan was gone. And so was her horse.

*

The head valet stepped imperiously along the long hallway of the Marquis's estate, carrying a tray of lunch. Food fit for a king – literally – he smiled to himself. Not just anyone could have such an important assignment, he knew. If the other *chateaux* only were aware what I was entrusted with. He knocked at the door firmly, knowing that politeness wasn't required here, but etiquette must have its way, this still was the king, after all, but without waiting, entered.

"I have lunch, Your Highness, and if…"

There was a crash of dishes, and the valet came running out.

Far away, very long gone by this point, Racine and the young king were on horses, racing along the countryside, dirt and stones flying everywhere. The hooves pounding the ground, the animals breathing as heavily as the two riders.

*

Gabrielle had made it aboard the ship without discovery and then managed to elude her seaman Fritz, or whatever his name was, which wasn't terribly challenging. It largely consisted of saying she'd be back in just a moment and then rushing off in another direction. What could he do? If he ever called an alarm, he'd have to explain that he'd snuck her on board in the first place.

Gabrielle knew a little about ships, though "little" was the operative word. But she'd done a play that took place at sea, *Ahoy to the Wind*, where she'd been Saucy Wench, a small but important role, and so she knew that anything important on board took place in the Captain's Quarters. And that's where she was headed.

She skulked through the recesses of the main deck, climbed a ladder and crept along, all the while keeping an eye on where most of the traffic was occurring. At one point, though, she ran into a sailor who was taken aback at seeing her. He challenged what she was doing there. She froze and then explained, well, she didn't know what to say, so she said that she was…well, she was – what? –

"I'm the Sauce Wench." What in the world, she thought. Then she realized, "Oh, I help the cook on land. I was told he's in the Captain's Quarters."

It sounded ridiculous to the sailor, but if it was for food, he was all in favor and had better things to do. He pointed in the direction and left her alone. Pleased with herself, though she could still feel her heart, Gabrielle continued on. And at last she found the quarters she was seeking.

Maneuvering to the most hidden location she could find, the young woman peeked through a porthole, And there, just as she expected – there was the courier and an officious-looking gentleman, it must be him, that's the Austrian Ambassador! The representative of the Holy Roman Empire. The diplomat looked pompous and pleased with himself, and picked up a candle from the desk to light his fat cigar and puffed away.

Gabrielle was beside herself with excitement. It was actually going well. It was actually going wonderfully. She'd followed them here, she'd gotten on the ship, she'd made it to the very room where the ambassador was. And there, right there is the document itself! She had tracked it down!

The Captain unlocked the wall safe, as the Ambassador took hold of the papers.

"You can inform your Marquis that when the Emperor has this treaty in his possession, our agreement will be in force. Military operations can commence."

And with that, he placed the parchment inside the safe – and slammed the thick metal door shut. And spun the dial.

Gabrielle watched this with disbelief. All was no longer going wonderfully. This was bad news. Really bad news.

251

CHAPTER THIRTY-THREE

Racine Tarascon and Louis XIV of France sauntered along a quiet, country road on their horses. In a world history of mismatched pairs, they were a mismatched couple to compete with any. The disheveled, rough-hewn gypsy woman, and the child king, regal in his bearing despite wearing a peasant cap, tilted sloppily across his head.

They rode on in silence, far enough out to finally catch their breaths at least for the moment, and traveled at a slower pace. But Racine remained wary of everything around her regardless, every noise, every movement her eyes could spot in the distance. Lessons learned in life don't disappear easily. Yet even she knew their surprise escape that morning provided a cushion of comfort. And so, on they went, heading down the byroad, hidden away from the main thoroughfare

They had ridden for several hours, and it had been an exhausting, parched, difficult journey. King Louis's horse followed the pace of Racine ahead. After a while, the boy looked up.

"Are we there yet?"

Racine didn't answer immediately. Then, however, she spun back to the youngster. "Does it look like we're there??? Oh, wait, look, there's the palace! Oh, I'm sorry, it's a tree."

"I'm hungry. Do you have a good saddle? My seat hurts."

"I can make it hurt a lot more." She turned away and kept her eyes up ahead. "We have a long ride, sport."

"That is not my name."

"I know. I just have a hard time calling someone 'Your Highness' who only comes up to my navel."

With much seriousness, he replied, "You may call me Louis."

"Thank you, little king person." Racine slowed her horse, and let her companion trot up upon her. "Look, I know it's hard for you. I know you've had a bad time. It must have been horrible for you to be prisoner."

Louis made himself look as stoic as a 10-year-old boy can. "When my cousin took me to the courtyard to play, they jumped me right away."

"*La Grande Mademoiselle* is safe." Racine wasn't in the habit of concerning herself much with providing reports on royalty, but she figured he would want to know. And all other things considered, probably deserved to.

"They went after me alone because I am king."

"What is the problem with this Marquis?"

"I hate him. He wants to get rid of my entire family."

Racine's hands tightened on the reins for just a quick moment. "I know how you feel."

Racine rode on, taking the lead again. Yet suddenly, she slowed a bit and became very quiet. And then she pulled up her horse and stopped.

After they'd escaped from the *chateaux*, Racine had acted on pure instinct, racing across the countryside, through rivers to lose the trail, and in forests. But ever since they'd gotten past that, just the two of them simply traveling together, the world had become very different. She was with Louis XIV. He was so small, he just seemed like nothing more than a little boy. But she knew who he was. She knew quite well who he was. But more than that, she knew who she was.

Louis rode up and stopped beside her, uncertain, and curious at her sudden quiet. When Racine finally spoke, the words came thoughtfully, and softly.

"Your Highness. My family are gypsies. They were dispersed from feudal lands by vigilantes and sent out across Europe." Racine didn't quite know how to go forward, how to finish saying what she had begun, what she had long dreamed of saying. At last, she collected herself. "I would like to petition the King of France to help me get them back."

The only sound that either of them heard at that moment was the whinny of their horses. Louis might have just been 10, but he had been raised a king. He knew the import of this. And he knew the sadness of his answer.

"If there was any favor in my power to grant you," the young majesty considered his words with the greatest care, "I would do so without thought. And this, far above all. But, *Mademoiselle* Tarascon – France is at war with the very nations where your people most surely are. It is not in my power. One day perhaps, I can hope, but I fear you will have to find your family without the crown. Please accept the deepest apologies of France."

Racine listened to these thoughts attentively, and then prompted her horse and slowly started again. The king followed after.

As they rode side by side, she continued looking ahead. "You're okay for a little…king person."

"And you are okay for a…well, you."

CHAPTER THIRTY-FOUR

As the early afternoon sunlight streamed through the porthole, Gabrielle was furtively rummaging over the captain's desk, hoping, praying to find something, but of course it was useless. She lifted papers, softly slid open drawers and flipped the pages of a journal, searched everywhere in the quarters wishing that a slip with a combination written on it might drop out.

Nothing dropped out, nothing suggested any assistance for her. She was lost. All she could do was stare at the safe, but hard as she glared at it, it still didn't pop open.

And so, all she could do was think. And only one idea came to mind. It was foolhardy, but when you only have one idea, foolhardy is cousins with brilliant. She peered again at the dial on the safe, and wiggled her fingers – just the same as she remembered Racine dong that first time at the kitchen table, and which she had seen the gypsy do many times since. Gabrielle had listened and watched, and God-willing she had learned something. And with that, in the hush of the room, she turned – and knocked over a lamp and chair.

Out on the Captain's Deck, the Ambassador, Captain and courier were sharing a bottle of spirits when unexpected sounds came crashing their way. At first, the meaning was puzzling, not even certain where it came from, but almost immediately concern flashed across the Ambassador's face.

"The office!"

A frantic Gabrielle was holding a precious document in her shaking hands and trying hastily to burn it in the candle flame on the captain's desk. Before it could all be engulfed in flames, though, the door burst open, and the three men rushed in, along with an armed sailor, his musket held at the ready. Swords and pistols were drawn by the others.

"Stop her!" the Austrian Ambassador cried out in horror.

Before anyone could reach her, Gabrielle – her body shaking ferociously – backed away with the burning document held far from them. "You're too late. Your precious document is gone."

"That's not possible," he snapped. "It's locked up."

A smile was somehow able to come to Gabrielle's face. "Happily, I have a dear gypsy friend who teaches really well about breaking into things." With an almost smirking, self-satisfied laugh, she wiggled her fingers again and chided the Captain, "You really do need a more difficult safe." And with a piercing glare of finality, she returned to hold the eyes of the Ambassador. "You lose. France wins."

The stunned and disbelieving Captain rushed to the safe and madly spun the dials. "It's not possible. Herr Ambassador, I swear to you on my life this safe is…"

He flung the safe's door open – and a look of blessed relief washed over his face. Triumphantly, he pulled the document from the safe and waved it humiliatingly at Gabrielle, with the greatest sneer he could manage.

"Ha! I knew it. You're nothing but a poor thief and worse liar. And now you will pay for it. God knows what paper you destroyed. But here's the document!"

And that is exactly what Gabrielle was hoping for.

"Thank you!!!!" And to quote Racine, "'It's all deception.'"

And in as swift a move as she could, Gabrielle stabbed the envelope with her sword and – before any of the stunned men there could react – turned and dove, crashing through the

256

nearby open portal with it.

The ambassador screamed out. "After her!!!!"

As Gabrielle raced along the side deck, she shredded the document and tossed the scraps into the air, where they floated overboard and were carried out to sea and down into the abyss. She did it! For the briefest instant, all other senses, and especially other concerns vanished totally from her life, and the sole bursting thought that enveloped every cranny of her being was that she couldn't believe she actually did it. Whatever else happened in her life, she – Gabrielle Parnasse – just stopped the Austrian Armada.

Now, all she had to do is save herself. Somehow, she had to get off that ship.

Two men had heard the call for alarm, and rushed at her. She pulled out her sword and fought her best with them, slashing at their advances and keeping the two at bay for at least a moment, though she lost ground. But as she twisted and turned, she was able to position herself to leap on a barrel and grab one of the many hanging lines to swing out of the way.

The port gunwale was ahead, and if she just could get over the side she knew she could regain an advantage, but there was too much ground to cover. However, the mast was ahead – the mast, that's what those poles are called! Focus, Gabrielle, she thought, her mind was exploding all over – and she rushed over to climb the hanging rope toward a safe haven.

As bells rang and more men appeared, three sailors pursued her up the same rope, which swung mightily now from the weight. Gabrielle pulled herself as hard as her arms allowed, they were burning from the strain, but the others kept getting closer, climbing up towards her. Too close, much too close. Halfway up, though, she slowed down to hang on with one hand, almost losing her grip and swinging out, barely able to steady herself with her foot, and she grasped her sword and began sawing at the rope hanging below her. They were almost upon Gabrielle as the hemp started to shred from the blade, one thread at a time, and then in bunches, and on her pursuers climbed, almost near enough to grab her foot, when finally, the halyard was cut through, and those holding on fell and crashed down to the deck.

Gabrielle made it up to the crow's next, and took the deepest breath, gasping for air, struggling for gulps, but she at least felt protected for the moment, and on solid ground, even if that ground was a hundred feet in the sky. But as she tried to collect her thoughts, which seemed a near impossibility, a pellet whizzed past her and then another musket shot. And it only got worse: a seaman was swinging his way toward her on a rope from another mast.

"Oh, please!" Gabrielle shouted out, in exasperation.

Seconds later, he landed right next to her in the crow's nest. But as he reached to grab her, she spun to evade his hands and leaped to grab a sail overhead…and slid the length of it down to the main deck – the wind pelting her body and through her hair, as she held on for dear life – leaping off and hitting the deck with a great thud, but the moment her feet touched wood, she kept her balance and, without pausing a step, continued running towards the edge of the ship where she knew a dinghy to freedom, the very one that had brought her there, was tied.

Her descent down the mainsail had caught the crew off guard, and left them on the other side of the vessel. Alone, Gabrielle hurriedly cut through the ropes holding the small craft to the hull, and it was released and splashed down into the water.

She was close, so close now. But she knew there was still a little more to go. Be careful, get this right. Gabrielle grabbed hold of the ledge and began to climb up. But a flurry of musket balls flew by and she lost balance and dropped to the deck. The exhausted young woman, acting on pure instinct and an abundance of adrenaline at this point, quickly raced across the open space, avoiding all obstacles in her way, and sought out the high ground, which was the ship's bridge. She made it up the ladder and bent over to gasp for at least a breath. But here came four sailors.

"Time out!" Gabrielle shouted at them.

But of course there was no time out option here. And so, as they pounded their way up the steps, she took another deep gulp of air, the last one she thought she might get for a while, grabbed a hanging boom – and swung it across the wide expanse of the deck, landing on the bow.

Gabrielle put her head down and raced once again to where she had already cut loose the dinghy. Where it was still, blessedly waiting for her. Right where she had left it. Her arms pumping, her legs churning. If at first you don't succeed. And looking over the edge, there it was! There in the water, floating, at last waiting for her! Her escape, she made it! She climbed the ledge.

"Halt!" The cry cut through the air. Yet still she pulled her leg over up over. Nothing would stop her this time, though.

But this time, though, two dozen sailors surrounded her. Muskets and cutlasses were drawn. All pointed directly at the young woman.

The commanding officer stepped forward, his voice leaving no room for doubt. "Drop your sword. Stand down."

259

Gabrielle wanted to make one more push. She would be over. She knew she could get there. But to what? A small boat sitting dead in the water? It was a lost cause. She took out her sword and let it fall with a clang off the wooden boards.

For a moment, she just held herself there, laying prostrate on the edge. She looked out across the water to the shore, so close, and then squeezed her eyes shut. Gabrielle Parnasse, greatest warrior in the history of France since Joan of Arc. And lead artiste of the Mont Vert Traveling Theatre Company. And then, the young woman climbed down, sliding slowly to the deck.

She was captured.

CHAPTER THIRTY-FIVE

Poor Charlotte shuffled along the road, covered in dirt, and morose. She'd let herself down, but worse she'd let the others down, who trusted her, who she gave her word to that she could do this, who were risking their lives when all she had to do was just ride a horse and stay behind others. She could ride a horse, she'd been doing it all her life. And she could stay behind others, she'd been doing that her whole life, too. No, worst of all, she'd probably let down France. And it was long gone by now, lost, who in the world knows where? All gone.

And what she had seen, with her own eyes, that was…it – no, she didn't even want to think about it. Refused to think about it. Why did she have to see him? It was so unfair. It was all so unfair. Everything was all so wrong. When did the wrong stop?

She wanted to cry. She wanted just to burst out in tears. Again. She didn't think she would cry, but it just burst out, and her shoulders were shaking in sobs. But it stopped soon enough, and she was all right now. Well, not really all right, she'd lost her horse and lost the caravan. But she wasn't going to cry again. She wanted to. But she was cried out.

She could hear from behind, the slow hoofbeats of a cantering horse. At first, she ignored it, who cares? – but then she realized and excitedly spun.

"*Allo?!!* Assistance! Help, please!"

The rider was far enough off, but she kept waving her arms for attention. At last, he came into view, and as he neared, she stopped waving and her arms and whole body drooped. It was Philippe Gascogne.

Charlotte's heart sank. She was crushingly beyond disappointment, but then also concerned that he of all people would be here, concerned, upset, annoyed, angry, and by the time he rode up, she was indignant.

"*You*. Never mind. Leave me be." She crossed her arms.

"Miss Le Renaud? Charlotte??" He was as surprised as she had been, but soon caught himself with a bemused smile. "How nice to see you again. Out for a bit of nature?"

She stood there, her hair all frizzed, her face dusty, her clothes a disheveled mess, and the streaked remnant of her tears still well-apparent.

"Of course you find this all so amusing. I don't wish your help. If you have any decency – please, go."

"Well – all right."

He snapped at the reins and rode off.

Charlotte just watched, not sure for a moment what to make of this, but if he…and then it hit her.

"Wait!!!"

The young girl went running after. Philippe pulled up, and waited for her to make up some of the lost ground, the slightest waggish expression crossing his face, as he then dismounted and headed back, with a comportment of, in fact, sincere gravity.

Charlotte was piqued at him for riding off, though she did tell him to leave, but a gentleman would have stayed; however a gentleman always listened to a lady. He was most solicitous, she noticed, which she was surprised by and appreciated, and would have appreciated far more if she wasn't so distraught by her failure that kept welling up in her.

"I don't want to talk about it" was all she would say to his repeated inquiries if there was anything he could do to help.

He offered her his horse to ride, but she was too keyed up to do anything but walk it all off. And so they walked on together. Her face was so sad, her body was so sad, the way she held her hands was so sad that Philippe thought she might withdraw into herself before his eyes and implode. She was willing to talk – she was in no mood to listen to anyone, however, least of all Philippe Gascogne, though he did seem a fine listener himself, which she was willing to find admirable, if surprising – but all her thoughts came out in random bursts.

Charlotte stopped walking, unaware that she had stopped, and could only remonstrate, so upset had she become, railing out loud to the world, as much as to Philippe. What was clear to him was that a missing horse was involved, and a cart of some sort, and casks. And also, perhaps, roses. He wasn't quite sure of that latter.

At length, she had talked herself out, for the moment at least, and she stood looking down an endless, very empty road ahead. Philippe waited with her until she was willing to talk again.

"They're gone. The wagon got away. It's my fault. All I was to do was trail it."

They began again walking along the gravel, leading his horse. Charlotte hesitated a moment, like she wanted to say something – something important – she almost stopped, but then continued on.

"What's the matter?"

"I don't want to talk about it."

Philippe nodded and walked on. Then, he said, simply and understandingly, "Gilles St. Chapelle."

Now, Charlotte did stop. She was utterly astonished.

"You know?? How?" She didn't quite know what to say

next, but a question suddenly occurred to her. She had been so intent on her own troubles that she had never paid it any attention. "What are you doing here anyway?"

"I told you. Last night," he replied almost as if he didn't understand her question, though he did. "I've been watching you."

"I thought you meant 'across the room.'"

"Oh. No." Clearly she hadn't known what he meant. He had to clarify everything. "Since I gave my word to your father."

Charlotte could do nothing other than stare. It was unladylike to let your jaw drop, and so hers didn't, at least not so that it was very noticeable. But everything else about her contorting face was abundantly noticeable.

"He was such a great man, a patriot," he went on. "Your father was the one who found out about the plot against the king. He's the one who warned me. To pass on to the Musketeers. Your father gave his life to save the Queen Regent and Cardinal Mazarin."

This was sensory overload for the young girl. Her whole world was being flipped upside-down. She felt a little shaky and had to sit. She curled her knees up and held them for support.

"That's what you two were arguing about in his study?"

"It was so dangerous for him speaking out in *Parlement*." He joined her sitting on the edge of the road. "I kept trying to talk him into letting me help more. Your father always understood his duty to France, its people. But that's why he had so many enemies against the other aristocrats."

"And Gilles was against him."

She understood now. She found it painful to think about,

she didn't want to think about it, wanted to block it all out, but it was important for her to understand. However Philippe realized sadly that she didn't.

"Against him? Gilles St. Chapelle was the one ordered to kill your father."

Words could not describe the ashen shock that swelled up to fill Charlotte's face.

CHAPTER THIRTY-SIX

Although the workday would soon be coming to an end for most Parisian laborers, journeyman builders at the city commons were hammering and sawing as busily as they had been for days, and would work through the night if need be. Though the *Gala National* would officially be beginning that very evening, the reviewing stand for public festivities had a brief reprieve until the morning.

Cardinal Mazarin was on an inspection tour with his aides and festival planners, all of them anxiously assuring him how well everything was going, anything to alleviate the clear concern they saw on his face. They couldn't imagine how the man charged with protecting all of France could possibly have that much stress over the most minor of insignificant details. No one wanted the Cardinal's displeasure to be taken out on them.

Of course, his mind was on matters far weightier than planks and nails, but appearances were of the utmost importance now. The public must have no idea what was going on away from their sight. And so, with the most-seeming interest, Mazarin stopped to take a closer look.

"*Tout pour la Fance*," a worker leaned over to call down to him. "We'll have it ready for Louis. Nothing to worry about."

"Ah, *mon ami*, we can only hope," the Cardinal replied distractedly. "It is all in the details."

Throughout Paris, the city was preparing, each excited citizen in his own way or hers. French flags could be seen hanging outside the windows of residences everywhere, from the ground floors to the top, giving a sense of dignity to even the most run-down neighborhood. Shop owners displayed banners and signs, "*Vive Louis Quatorze*" and sometimes just a simple "XIV," across their storefronts, being sure nonetheless to lock up tight, for as good-feeling as the spirit was growing, they still knew nothing was safe.

No one knew that nothing was safe more than the Musketeers, and last-minute training and instructions or final orders, which infuriatingly kept changing, were being giving to the men assigned to special units throughout the city. Major Delacroix sat in his office, shifting papers and making notes, not knowing how the King's Men would handle the King's Day with no king, apprehensive that nothing had been overlooked, certain that something was, because that was always the case. André Mersenne pulled aside his special unit and relentlessly continued drilling them on what he knew was their most critical assignment.

So, too, was the army on alert. Leaves had long-since been cancelled so that the military would be at full strength to make absolutely certain the festival ran smoothly. To make certain the people filling the city coming in from all over France – many coming in from around Europe even – didn't turn into a mob.

Order. That was the cry of the day to the police, as well. The *gendarrmie* were as pre-occupied with the *Gala National* running without trouble as anyone. For more than anyone, it was they who would have to deal with all the countless smallest of problems in the hidden nooks of the streets which, on occasions like this, are what can build into serious civil disobedience, as they always do.

And so, just as the Marquis had anticipated, the full weight of all the branches of security in France were focused on the one thing only that they believed in need of protection. And the cracks were open for the unexpected and powerful to march through.

For now, though, the streets moved as if nothing was amiss, just perhaps a bit busier than usual, just wanting to get from here to there a little quicker than usual. Yet carriages and horses plodded their way. The people bustled along the roads.

And a wagon with covered barrels innocently jostled down a cobbled street, bouncing slightly, each bounce causing consternation for its guards, and moving slowly. Slowly, not out of leisure, and not even so much to avoid attention, but out of respect, deep and abiding respect for the unpredictability of its contents.

As the city and the shopkeepers, the residents and the army, the Musketeers, *gendarmes*, explosive carts and carriages all went on their business in preparation of the King's Day, unobserved and unexpected by all, Racine and the young king himself rode protectively through the back, narrow streets of Paris.

"Up ahead, turn there," he called, excited to be in charge once more.

As they went past a street corner, ahead rose the *Palais Royale*, the mid-afternoon sun gleaming like gold down on it. Joy covered the boy's face. Home!

All of a sudden, he pulled back his floppy peasant hat to see better, and galloped off, but Racine sped after, to retrain his horse.

"Wait! Wait, I told you. We have to be careful. I don't know yet who the traitor is in the palace."

CHAPTER THIRTY-SEVEN

Though he had every reason to be anxious with the *Gala National* just hours away, Eduard was rarely anxious. Coming to Paris in preparation for the grand night, the Marquis kept up appearances with what he told the overly-curious was nothing more than a courtesy call to *Monsieur* Gaston, even though he found the king's uncle to be a pompous fool, albeit on occasion useful. He strolled through the fancy library, noting pieces of fine artwork and exquisite leather-bound books, though taking little pleasure in them. What others kept in their homes was of little interest to him. Further, even though he wasn't anxious, his mind was still working, thinking and preparing ahead.

A manservant entered. "It will be just a moment." He closed a curtain to block the dimming sunlight.

"You are a new face to me," the Marquis noted warily, not wanting anything new nor surprising today.

"I have only been here five days past. I hope to serve *Monsieur* the Duke well."

"Don't we all." He paid the footman little mind, but caught the servant's attention and held it, "You will serve *Monsieur* best by remembering nothing you see."

The door to the library opened, but rather than the Duke d'Orléans, his daughter, the lovely *Mademoiselle* instead breezed in. She had flourished in health and confidence since the attack on her and her cousin the king months past, and was stronger than others had seen her.

"Ah, Marquis, I regret my father has departed on business. Perhaps there is something I can help you with?" She turned to

269

the manservant. "Please have Maid attend to my wardrobe."

"His note suggested a matter of some urgency," Eduard said brusquely. "I should linger until his return."

The young Duchess waited for the footman to depart and graciously approached her guest.

"How surprising a request. I can't believe my father would have written it."

She tellingly moved closer to the Marquis. And looked at him intently.

"Perhaps then he didn't," Eduard said dryly, yet there was a wryness in his voice that was rarely heard.

"I am shocked."

Mademoiselle walked up to him and stopped close. She held his gaze, something few people would dare do with the Marquis, at any time, and never so near. The beautiful young woman placed her palm upon his chest, holding it there, feeling his heartbeat quicken, before sliding her fingers underneath his jacket. He took her in, watching her eyes tighten, her lips purse, her chin, her cheek, as she ran her nails tenderly, expectantly, with more meaning, firmly. And then they were in each other's arms! The lovers were kissing one another deeply. Eduard grabbed her close, and stroked his hands through her loose hair and down the length of her soft body, cupping her breast and holding his hand there. She moaned and pulled his face tighter to hers.

At last, she kissed his cheek, his neck, the lobe of his ear, and then pulled away. She caught her breath, and gave him one more lingering kiss on the cheek, taking out her handkerchief and rubbing away the deep red of her lipstick.

"I've missed you. I'm glad you came. But why today? Isn't there much risk?"

"The king has escaped."

It was the last thing she expected to hear and brought her to full attention. "How is that possible???"

"There were three women seen in the forest. What was done will have to be discovered later. No doubt they are heading with the little boy to the palace."

"All right. I will go back there. I can handle this." She smiled in a look near jest. "Again. I do have experience at it."

"You'll be careful," Eduard said as they headed to the door.

"No one suspects anything. Even my father." She looked at Eduard for one last, needed assurance. "All else progresses well?"

Eduard brushed his hand across the strands of hair that had fallen on her brow. "No one suspects anything. Between the treaties I have made with foreign nations and alliances with the most powerful estates – it will be as if I am the new king of France. My queen."

CHAPTER THIRTY-EIGHT

The Regent looked up at the painting of her late husband and remembered. It was a time when he had been the king of France. And she the Queen. And now, as mother to the current king of France, all she could do was sit alone in her room, think of former years, and feel helpless.

The Queen Mother did not like feeling helpless. She couldn't recall the last time she had. Even when her husband ruled the nation with Richelieu, she had still known how to maneuver and find a way to hold authority and lead, if only at times in very small ways. But very small ways were often enough when a single word could affect lives. And she had long affected a great many lives.

Now she couldn't even find her son. And she had the whole of the French army at her disposal. The Musketeers, as well – the King's Men.

The King's Men, she laughed bitingly under her breath, even though she was alone. It was as if she didn't want to acknowledge out loud what she had been forced to face for the past months. What a world it was. The king was just a 10-year-old child, and his Men were empty-handed.

What good was power if you were powerless? What good was commanding a mighty nation if it was falling apart? What good was being a mother if you had no child?

She stared at the single candle lighting her room. That's all she wanted. She had drawn the curtains, not wanting even a hint of dusk to enter the room, not wanting anything outside to enter the room, or anyone. One candle would do. She didn't want to sit in the dark, though she had been for the past months, but she felt that sitting amid brightness would be too cruel a joke. No, one candle in the dark was just fine. She liked that quivering flame. Liked its -silence. Like that it tenuously held onto its wick yet commanded attention. A single candle at least showed that darkness could be lit by the simplest thing. And when you feel helpless, the simplest thing can give you hope.

The Queen Mother did not like feeling helpless. She couldn't recall the last time she had.

The people of France did not know the trouble they were about to discover on the morrow, when the national festivities were made public to honor their king, and they found that they had no king. They would be distraught, there would be chaos. They would not care that she had lost her child. They would care only about themselves and their country. And that would be her responsibility, to care about them and their country. When all she wanted to do was care about her child.

She didn't even know if he was alive. Had she done all she could? She had walked into the lion's den and stared down the beast, but what good had it done? She was back here in her palace, in her room, in her chair, alone.

She had tried everything. Over and again she kept telling that to herself, until she had to finally believe it, she had tried everything. She commanded the army, the Musketeers, the police. None of them could help. The great Cardinal Mazarin, the man she had by her side to guide France, the man she had by her side to be her support, even he could do nothing. The very man whom she had chosen, whom she herself wanted there, always wanted there. Nothing. He could do *nothing*. And so she had done nothing.

And the Queen Mother did not like feeling helpless.

273

That's why, still, she would lead. She would keep trying. She was the Queen Regent of France.

But she had tried everything. Everything.

If only there was someone left to help her find her child.

CHAPTER THIRTY-NINE

A Musketeer struggled to keep a smirk off his face, as he leaned on the desk and tried to show even the slightest interest in the indignant girl before him.

"…Oh, yes, actually I do believe you. You can bring 'the king' to us."

Racine was doing her best to control her frustration. And controlling her frustration had never been one of Racine's best attributes.

"The palace is right outside the door," she said, pausing to take a deep breath and counting to…well, four. That was as high as she could go, she would never have made 10, but for Racine, it was good. "I have been waiting here forever. If you'll find Captain Mersenne…"

"Now, when you say 'king,' you *are* talking about King _Louis_ and not a deck of playing cards?"

He looked oh-so serious. A couple of other Musketeers had come by, to join the ridicule, slapping him on the shoulder for his quick-witted riposte. Word had made its way to the palace about the crazy lady at headquarters, and a few men had drifted in. They had all been under such pressure the past days, it was a relief for anything to break the strain.

There was something else Racine would like to break, but this was too important. She understood that. And so, politely, but smoldering, she stepped forward to the front desk and tried yet again. "Is there someone else my brother and I can see?"

Her "brother" sat bundled up by the door, an overlarge high-collared cloak wrapped around his small body, not unlike wearing a tent. A flouncy peasant's cap was pulled low over his forehead, obscuring his face.

Another of the Musketeers had finally had enough with this evening's diversion. "Your brother and you can see the devil. You and your broth – "

Wham! Racine slammed something hard and noisy on the desk in front of all their big, fat, goddamned faces. She removed her hand to reveal the gold, royal medallion of King Louis.

The Musketeers were dumbfound. Men trained to never be caught by surprise were shocked by surprise. The phrase, "Oh, *mon Dieu*," was silently passed between them, as their eyes' caught one another. This is the real thing. This annoying peasant girl knows where the monarch is.

As silence abhors a vacuum, Racine filled it gladly

"<u>Now</u> will you find someone I can take to the king? Who's not an idiot."

A young woman's voice cut through the room. "I may have been an idiot for losing my cousin, but it would be my profoundest joy to deliver him home."

Mademoiselle had stepped into the room.

With grace and kindness, she apologized deeply to the finally-relieved Racine for all such inconveniences, offering that she hoped the dearest, brave woman could at the very least understand the skepticism of the King's Men, foolish and rude and irresponsible though they were and who would, she promised, be reprimanded for that. Racine snatched away the medallion with a jerk, and turned back with a sneer at the guards before she left with her new-found benefactor.

Escorted by three of her valets, *Mademoiselle* led the unsuspecting Racine and her well-bundled brother out the back of Musketeer headquarters, along a stone pathway that led towards the palace. They crossed into a courtyard as a shadow fell across Racine.

"I'm so glad you were here, m'lady, because my brother and I didn't know who to trust. We hear rumors."

"A grateful France offers its thanks."

"My brother and I are so appreciative. We will meet the Queen Mother?" Racine asked excitedly.

Having passed far enough into a secluded part of the courtyard, the young duchess suddenly slowed her pace. And the graceful and kind temperament she had so graciously shown moments earlier suddenly changed.

"Your 'brother.' Do you take *everyone* for idiots? Seize her!"

The valets whipped out pistols, something few attendants come equipped with, and held them on the surrounded, helpless Racine. One of them held back her arm that had instinctively reached for her sword, and he removed it from the sheath.

Mademoiselle's cold eyes stared down the gypsy. "Grateful thanks cannot express the joy at delivering him back to us."

Racine struggled and was able to pull her arm loose, but a pistol was cocked with a loud click. She submitted, with much reluctance, but even more wisdom. The duchess went over to the child and with foreboding bent over him.

"It's been such a long time, cousin. *Bonjour encore*, Your Highness."

And taking hold of his big cap, she ripped it off.

But it wasn't King Louis! It was just an unknown little boy, looking quite bewildered.

Mademoiselle was thunderstruck. Shock filled her body and

then anger soon came to her eyes. This was someone who did not take well being played the fool.

It was with such pleasure that Racine could stare her back, yet respond with a trenchant calm.

"When the King explained what happened to him, when he was kidnapped with you, it just didn't make sense. Because you see, I understand vermin who kidnap families. If the Marquis wants to destroy the royal line, why leave you? Worse, why not have you shot? The King alone was all who mattered. Unless you were involved. And when the King said that it was you who brought him down – no one brings a king anywhere. But I had to be sure."

The duchess controlled her fury, but she showed it clearly in the tightness of her chin. In how her fingers opened and squeezed shut, just once. "Congratulations. Now you've earned the chance of dying. Where is the King??" She intended to wait for an answer, but patience had no place here. "Where is the King?!"

Racine, however, was someone just as determined. She had faced many brutish moments in her life, yet for the first time there was something greater now than herself in consequence. She knew the risk when she had walked in here. Indeed, she almost even expected this outcome. But that was the point. She had to find out. They had to find out. And standing there alone, she wasn't alone here. Though she certainly was in trouble. But mainly, she just hated the bastards. Whoever the bastards were, and wherever. And she stared back, unmoving.

"Get this child out of here. *Vite!*" The duchess snapped at the valets. And then she took one of their pistols and pointed it directly at Racine's head, squarely between the eyes.

"I will ask you one more time." She pulled back the

278

trigger. "Where. Is. The King?"

*

Where the king was, was sitting at the table of a small, but warm and comfortable kitchen table with an old man and woman. He was lapping up pastries and slurping down milk.

"This is a terrible mistake we are making. A terrible mistake." Marguerite Fleury looked at her husband, very concerned. "Cookies before dinner, what was I thinking?"

"Could I have some more?" the boy asked with his mouth full, a few crumbs stuck to his cheek.

Auguste politely corrected the youngster on his manners. "Could I have some more, '*what*'?"

"Could I have some more – *m'lord*?"

The king of all of France just called me, "m'lord," Auguste realized. Well, he just about burst with pride.

CHAPTER FORTY

Gabrielle sat against a dank wall of a prison cell in the Bastille. Water dripped down between several of the cracks, and a patch of moss grew along the hard stone floor.

The floor was getting cold, she thought. Though it could be much worse, they could have shot me on board the ship. But then, they still might. I hope not. There's so much more I'd like to do. Like, have lunch. I would settle for lunch right now. That would mean I made it to tomorrow.

There was a clang, as the cell door swung wide, and a woman was forcibly pushed in, crashing to the wall.

"Racine!" Gabrielle was at first full of joy to see the doorway open and to spot a friend there, her heart leaped, the crown had finally found out and she was being released, rescued, but all that thought occurred in just a snap instant, for immediately she understood quite clearly this was not good.

Mademoiselle stood in the entrance with two guards. She passed her glance between the two woman on the ground. "It must be nice to have a reunion."

Racine belligerently got to her feet and took a step at the duchess, but a guard pointed his musket that held her off. She sneered belittlingly. "You're cocky when you're protected."

"I am cocky all the time," *Mademoiselle* stated, matter-of-factly.

"And yet somehow you don't have the king. Who could figure?"

"It's a shame we'll miss you tonight, even without His Highness. You seem to have such a flair for the dramatic." The royal conspirator was dismissive without any effort. This peasant meant nothing to her. But such a pleasure to taunt. "But how childish to pretend you could stop a revolution. So, we will simply find out afterwards from you where the King is. No matter to me. *You*, however, might find it more painful."

Gabrielle bristled and started to say something. In part, she wanted to defend her friend's honor, but she also didn't want to see this battle of gibes get far out of control to find Racine put even worse off. Though the gypsy had just been threatened with torture, so it wasn't likely that things would get worse.

"Why are you doing this?" Racine asked. It wasn't a plea for mercy. She truly wanted to understand. Cruelty and war she comprehended. But this was another matter. "It's your own family."

Mademoiselle paid her no mind and left. The heavy cell door was slammed and locked. But before leaving she spoke to them through the barred window.

"I am of a birth that does nothing that is not great and noble. My father should have been made king, not a 5-year-old child. But if he doesn't want to take his rightful place and rule, I will."

"I take it you don't have any children." Racine said, quite unexpectedly.

"What??" *Mademoille* peered through the small opening with a look of derision. She smirked. "No."

Racine stepped over to the barred window, and stared back. The two young women caught each other eye-to-eye.

"Well, this is what delivering a baby is like."

Suddenly, she leaped and thrust her arms through the bars, grabbing *Mademoiselle* and pulling her head in. The guards tried to drag them apart. Gabrielle leaped in to help, and it became a tug-of-war. At last, the guards extracted them.

281

The high-bred duchess smoothed her hair. She thought about having the doors opened and making certain that the women was beaten on the spot, and then shot. But no, leave things as they were. For they will get worse. "Rot in hell."

Then, she was gone. And there alone were Racine and Gabrielle. Rotting in hell.

CHAPTER FORTY-ONE

After a long day's journey, Charlotte and Philippe were able to make it to Paris by nightfall. They reached the comforting home of the Fleurys, but no one was feeling particularly comforted. Worried faces surrounded the room.

"It's not good," Auguste said in a shaking voice. "Racine should have been back long before now, you know. That can only mean she was right about..."

He looked at Louis and stopped, realizing how painful it would be for a young boy to discuss the truth about his cousin, let alone someone he once looked up to and cherished. Yet it wasn't a young boy he was sitting next to, but the king. And whether it was well-learned training, or a maturity far beyond his years that comes with *noblesse oblige*, or a child playing magnificently at a game of obligations he was taught to excel at, Louis understood one thing: he knew what was expected of him as King of France. And whatever his age, he was King of France. He touched the old man lightly on the elbow.

"Please, *monsieur*, continue. You have my trust."

Auguste let out a long sigh. "I fear she's in the Bastille."

"We will get her out." Charlotte's voice sharply cut through the pall. She had a determination that hadn't been seen in her weeks before, or perhaps even a day before. Finding out that your life has been torn inside out can have that effect on some people. "I promise. Gabrielle and I will figure something when she gets back from Le Havre."

"I would like to go back home."

It took a moment for the others to realize that when a 10-year-old boy says he wants to go home, that the child in their midst was referring to the majestic, glittering *Palais Royal*, center of French power in Europe, not the flat around the corner. "I am needed," he added.

It was an understandable request. For not only was it the palace, but it was, in fact, for him, the flat around the corner. It had been months since he had seen his own bed, his favorite possessions, familiar hallways, the smells he knew intimately, his governess, valets, instructors, groomsman, his best horses, gilt-edged carriages, army, and above all, far above all, his mother.

Philippe, however, had long been far more involved than the others in matters of royal court intrigue. "I advise against it, Your Highness, not until we know that all is safe. And who to trust."

Something had been bothering the old woman. Something someone had said. Charlotte, she thought. "Pardon, dear, did you say Le Havre? Because word has passed at the market that a young woman was brought to the Bastille from Le Havre. It struck people as so uncommon."

"Oh, *mon dieu*." Charlotte's face went ashen. "Gabby. They're both in prison. Both…God…How am I…"

She just had to think. Think. This was the worst news possible. The others couldn't be arrested. They couldn't. What would she be able to do? It couldn't be left up to her. Please, not after everything she'd been through. Please, couldn't she just have time to rest, to relax, to have someone brush her hair, to tend to her, to offer her some kindnesses, any kindness, a soft bed with an eiderdown quilt, and pillows, covered with pillows, many pillows. She wanted pillows to hold and embrace. The plushest pillows that ever there was.

"Whatever we can do to help. We are here together."

284

Philippe took her hand. And then held the other. "We are all…"

Suddenly, Charlotte leapt up. Excited. Concerned. Excited.

"There is someone I must need see, it's a risk, I have to go, I'm sorry. I'm so…"

Without another word, she grabbed her cloak and rushed out of the house. The others could only sit there bewildered, not quite sure what they had witnessed, looking at one another for confirmation.

Then, however, Charlotte came running back inside. And she kissed Philippe lightly on the lips.

"For luck."

And out she rushed again. The door slamming behind her.

CHAPTER FORTY-TWO

The Queen Regent was attempting to fix the cravat that Cardinal Mazarin was wearing for the *Gala National* that night. Her fingers kept stumbling, and she had to begin yet again.

"This is not necessary, you understand, I do have a valet."

"Quiet, I want no one in here but you." She didn't like the results and pulled it apart. Striping the neckcloth off completely, she strode frustrated to his *chiffonier*, randomly opening its drawers.

"It's the wrong color, it's all wrong for you, all wrong for the night."

"Yes, that is the problem. The color makes it difficult to tie." He took her by the arm and led her back into the dressing room. "My dear Anne, you don't need to do this. You are the Queen Regent, you must prepare for the night."

"No, I must do this. Jules, if I don't I will burst. I cannot sit around her, stand around here, stroll around here, idly think around here, do nothing around here but prepare for something whose pomp I cannot bear. The nothingness will do me in. I swear to God, Jules. I must stay active, do something, even if it's just putting on your damned cravat."

He picked up the silk cloth and handed it back to her, pulling her towards a row of candles. "I think you'll find in this light the color will make it easier to tie." He smiled. She didn't, but not because she didn't appreciate his attempt to relax her. She didn't because she didn't have a smile in her.

"How am I supposed to be oh-so regal tonight? Wave to all, smile as without a care in the world? You're the great Cardinal. Surely you have a battle plan for such a thing."

"I'm sorry. But people don't expect me to smile. So, I've never worked out the intricacies. But you don't need plans. You are royalty. Waving and smiling come as part of the package." He checked her work in the looking glass and gave her his approval. "I am more distressed about all this than I can let others be aware, but I know it is incomparably worse for you. But we will get through tonight, and we will get through tomorrow the way all mankind does. We shall put one foot ahead of the other, and live."

And with that, he offered his arm to the Queen Mother, and they headed out.

"One foot ahead of the other," she said, looking down to check her steps. "And so we live."

*

Eduard de Longueville stood in the center of his boudoir, in full regalia complete with sword, as his dresser finished his preparation and fastened the studs. He listened with distracted interest as the Count de Beaufort read from a dispatch. There were other details, so many others, and far more important that he had to manage that night.

The Count, however, was uncomfortable telling the Marquis the remaining of its news. But he had no choice. "They report that the treaty was destroyed and never went to Austria." He prepared for the worst "It was one of those women. Again."

Eduard paused the dresser – but offered no other reaction. And then, after a moment as if not a word has passed, he simply continued dressing. Meticulous, methodical, focused.

"The folly of these efforts only force our hands in ways I

have always wished to avoid. I merely desired to compel the Royals with reasons to abdicate. Nothing more." He plucked a carnation from the dressing table and put it on. And he provided one, as well, to the Count, who was relieved at not being attacked as the deliverer of such news. "But now, *they* leave me no choice. It is their doing. After tonight, Royal rule will be dead in France."

He headed to the door.

"Very dead."

*

Outside a building, a wagon had been uncovered, and workers carefully – ever so very carefully – carried its cargo inside, hidden by the falling darkness. One barrel of dynamite at a time.

CHAPTER FORTY-THREE

Musketeer headquarters was an unusually subdued place, following their reprimand earlier that afternoon by *Mademoiselle*. The guards milled around, in preparation for the grand event coming so soon, and the intensity was high, but no one had the slightest intention of risking any further censure. They moved about far more quietly than one would suppose for such bold men.

The silence was shattered when the door crashed open, and Charlotte came flying in past everyone. Stunned Musketeers were bewildered by the site of a petite, sweet-looking girl with auburn hair flowing behind her and among the most determined eyes any of them could later recall ever seeing. Only at last was she stopped by a wall of men, guns and swords all pointed at her.

"I must see Captain Mersenne. Please, if he is around, I need speak with him."

Even a man hard of hearing couldn't have helped but notice the commotion, and André made his way from the back, interrupted from his work, to find out what the problem tonight of all nights was. Discovering that it was that the youngest of the three women, he was not happy to see her.

"This is a very bad time," he said sternly. "Very bad. And then with so much else to do, so much else actually serious, actually important, far more than you could know, I'm told that Racine came by here by playing games, causing scenes – and now you. It is a very bad time."

"You have to listen to me," Charlotte implored as firmly as she possibly could. She had no idea what was so important about yet another gala, nor did she care. What she did know was how actually serious, actually important it was what she had to tell him.

"I don't think I have to do anything of the sort." André was through with being polite. This little girl, Colette, he thought her name was, or Carlotta, would have to understand – now, right now – or deal with the consequences. He was finished. If she wanted to push, he was trained how to push back even harder. "You have to listen to *me*."

*

Kneeling on the grimy floor of their prison cell, Racine held a spoon in her hand, working hard to unscrew the floor grating, the slot for the curved edge was too thin. Her fingers kept tightening from the strain, while sweat dripped off them.

"…This is inconceivable, so bad," Gabrielle went on, standing in the center of the room, anxious, concerned, "but I have to believe we can handle it."

Racine kept twisting the metal, it slipped, and then again, but she finally was able to get one screw out. Just nine more to go. It required so much patience, the room for error so small.

"Perhaps I could pretend to be ill, it's a chance, okay, a thin chance maybe, but – "

Racine continued making progress, but what was more difficult was fighting to block out the incessant, yammering noise in the cell. It had been going on for the past half-hour. Her eyes got a little blurry, and she squeezed them closed a moment. Focus, she had to stay focused.

"Nothing in life is perfect, and…" Gabrielle gave a sardonic laugh, "My God, as if being locked in the Bastille you might think that life *was* perfect – "

No, life was not perfect at all, as Racine's spoon broke, snapping off at the base. She snatched at the remnants and, her frustration growing, quickly started in again, but having little success, grinding her teeth.

"I just pray that Charlotte is able to help, I really like Charlotte, she's very sweet, I've always wondered if I grew up with privilege what type of life I might have, I always had this dream, over and over, where I'm a duchess…"

Finally, the dam burst. Racine spun her full attention to Gabrielle.

"Gabby, puh-lease!!! I mean, for God's sake, Gabby. For one moment, just stop being so you. Stop being so…'Gabby.' You've turned talking into an art form. One day people will say, 'Oh, she's being *Gabby*.' 'Look how *Gabby* she is.' Quit 'being so *Gabby*!!!' Gabby!"

Gabrielle listened to this intently. Her mind worked over every word. Then, her face brightened.

"Really?? You think?"

*

A handcuffed Charlotte was led by André at pistol-point through the dark, musty tunnel of the prison. They had been joined by an armed Bastille guard. The girl looked agitated. The sights around her were overwhelming. She had never been inside a prison in her life. Her friends were in profound danger. And she herself was in the gravest risk.

"Captain Mersenne, I beg you. Racine found out about *Mademoiselle*. And Gabrielle…"

"You've no idea the trouble you caused."

This was no time for discussion. They continued down the dank passageway, bleaker with each stop. The young heiress kept trying to look at André, make some sort of connection, but the Bastille guard kept yanking her back.

Finally, they stopped at the cell, met by the sentry stationed there.

"Please, Captain. You must listen." Charlotte was pleading now, clearly on edge, almost ready to burst. The two other men found it most amusing. They'd seen it so often before, all the begging, up to the last minute, but never with a girl so young and refined.

"Put her in," André ordered.

The guard took out his keys and turned to the door. The sentry who was stationed in front smiled a mean-spirited grin at Charlotte, with two of his teeth missing.

"What a nice surprise," he snickered and nodded, referring into the cell. "Three's a crowd, here for a party?"

Charlotte offered nothing more than a blank stare back. Seeming almost in shock, she just looked around her, and at last saw the Bastille guard turn to the door. It was only then that she gave an answer to the sentry. "Yes," she suddenly snapped to his confusion.

"Now!!!" André shouted.

And with that, he leaped at the Bastille guard whose back was to him, unlocking the cell, and Charlotte tossed off the unlocked-handcuffs and slammed herself into the stunned sentry with all the force she could muster. Which, given all her built-up stress and energy, was a great deal.

All four struggled with thrashing vigor. André kept pounding the guard's head into the door, as the man struggled to fight back. The sentry was so much stronger than Charlotte, but caught deeply unprepared.

*

Inside their cell, Racine and Gabrielle came to a halt, bewildered beyond belief by a commotion outside their cell. It sounded like two hurtling carriages were crashing into one another. Yet quieted to nothing almost as suddenly. They were about to head to the door – when it flew open.

To their amazement, Charlotte stuck her head in.

"Hello, girls. Miss me?

The two now-former prisoners didn't have time to miss Charlotte, let alone understand what had just happened, as the young girl hurried them out of the cell. For perhaps the first time in her life, Gabrielle was struck speechless. For the first time, Racine allowed someone else to lead her.

They all stepped over the two fallen guards, which only increased the bewilderment. When Racine saw André Mersenne standing there, waiting for them, a quick brightness at first shot to her eyes, but then instinct took over, and she suspiciously pulled back and became protectively defensive, and then was confused, and bumped into the wall, stumbled, until Charlotte grabbed her hand and pulled her along, with an admonishment to hurry.

A still-shocked Racine and Gabrielle were only finally starting to get their bearings as they followed along behind Charlotte and André through the labyrinth. Charlotte tossed them the guards' swords and then collected hers from the Musketeer.

Gabrielle caught up alongside her young friend, who was struggling to strap on the rapier as they raced along. "I can't even begin to guess how in the world…" she stammered,

293

continuing to have difficulty phrasing words together. "How you managed to…" For that matter, she didn't even quite understand what it was that Charlotte had "managed to."

"I trust you all know what you're doing," André called back to them. "Trust only carries on so far, though. Please tell me you do have a plan."

Charlotte fluttered over. "*Thank* you, captain. Again. Thank you, I know your job is on the line."

"This is France," he replied sardonically. "My head is on the line."

Racine sidled up to André. At first, words failed her, not having the slightest idea what to say. Such things didn't come easily to her, and were even less natural. All she found herself able to do at the moment was walk in silence with this man who actually did put his life, his head on the line. For her. She didn't know what had been said to him, she had no idea what he was aware of, but she knew that André would never have paid attention and then done this if it wasn't *for her*. She knew that. She just didn't understand such a thing occurring. And she felt her palms get very dry. Then, at last, her voice reappeared, and she reached out to lightly touch his wrist. "I am…overwhelmed."

They came to an intersection, where André caught himself and stopped. "I've always said I admire what you do."

"And you. And you, as well."

The two stood there together, and they kept looking at one another.

Gabrielle quickly walked past them. "Get a room."

Up ahead, one of the lamps had blown out, and the tunnel was even darker than elsewhere. Charlotte was anxiously checking her way and listening for footsteps. She thought she had heard someone coming, but it was only a brick crumbling and echoing off the walls. "Hurry, we have to get out of here."

"Does anyone know where we are going, what we are doing?" Gabrielle called out.

By now, Racine had joined the others. Her pent-up energy was exploding, her spirit invigorated, her focus riveted. She stormed ahead. "All I know is that it is up to us to save France. Somehow. Someway. Somewhere." She took out her sword, and held it firm at the ready. "Or die trying."

Book Five

CHAPTER FORTY-FOUR

The *Palais Royale* loomed above the Parisian skyline, dominating everything around with its majesty and importance. Spread across the landscape, it appeared all the more imposing, a sign of national power, impervious to attack. The crescent moon seemed tiny to its grandeur.

An elegantly-designed iron gate opened, and out rolled a cortège of regal coaches rumbling their way into the night. Along the boulevards, crowds had been gathered for the past hour. Nothing was especially orderly, but the presence of gendarmes kept the streets open. Whenever the precession would turn a corner at a distance, the first cries of *"Ici! Ils viennent!"* could be heard, passed along that it was coming, it was coming, and the cries turned to shouts. *"Vive le Roi!"* As the carriages trundled past, the cheering crowds held up candles and waved little flags. A few rocks occasionally came flying from sporadic, hidden nooks within the crush, aimed at the caravan, and though the police did their best to find the miscreants, they had either slithered off or were well-covered by others.

And so, the uppercrust coaches continued on their way, moving through the spirited streets.

*

Far outside the city, in the rural environs of Paris, another sort of movement was taking place. Under the cover of darkness, General Turenne had begun to lead his massed troops.

As they marched down the lanes, villagers took notice, but paid it little attention. These days, there were always reports of military maneuvers. Some even took comfort, thinking how good it was to have protection from outside invaders. Those damn Austrians, this'll show them, they said. Many, in fact, came by just to see General Turenne, the great man himself. "He's smaller than I thought," a woman said, "from what everyone said I thought he'd be tall as a tree." If anyone could keep France safe, it was General Turenne, that was the word being spread. The people waved to him, but he was busy with other thoughts, as he rode by on his horse.

On the militia marched, down the lanes, across the fields, through woods, over bridges and on to Paris.

*

A single carriage headed along a quiet Paris street. Not part of any retinue, the coach was pristine in its ornate elegance. Indeed, being solitary, far away from the demands of any public prying, was its full intention.

Eduard sat calmly, almost bemused at the Count de Beaufort who was unsuccessfully fighting to control his anxiety. "You worry too much. It is your weakness."

"I am pragmatic." Beaufort tried to sit still for the benefit of the most-honored gentleman across for him. But it didn't last long. He soon turned again to look out the window, readjust his cuffs, smooth out his velvet jacket, cough, and check to make sure he had his walking stick, which he had checked but minutes earlier. When a horse rode by in the other direction, he stuck his head outside to make sure it truly had been alone. "When the people hear of the death of the royal

298

family, I fear they could blame us."

The Marquis didn't answer. It wasn't that he didn't care what the masses thought, he didn't tend to care much what anyone else thought. While de Beaufort worried about all the things that could happen, he prepared for what should happen. Please, spare me from the small-mindedness of the world, he thought. Spare me. Spare me.

"Dear Beaufort," he finally spoke with what was almost a laugh, "you will always think like a peasant. While Austria believes itself to be our ally, I have made certain that documents I've kept prove that they alone are responsible for this unspeakable deed. Austria, our greatest enemy. The scourge of Europe. Home of the unquenchable conquering Holy Roman Empire. The fearsome horror of an invading, unstoppable foreign devil. Terror of the masses. Blame us? The people will cry out for us to save them."

CHAPTER FORTY-FIVE

Outside, all France was in motion, even if all France didn't know it. Outside, the city of Paris was a concatenation of disparate intrigues, vibrantly swirling around one another, yet inextricably interwoven. Even if the city of Paris was unaware. It was a world teetering on randomness, but everything was so linked that nothing could really be thought of as random.

For all the machinations of the great world outside, from nations at war crossing down to social classes at civil war, collapsing all the way to the bottom where civil disobedience erupted at the street, inside one ordinary barn on one ordinary alleyway in one ordinary *arrondissement*, a small group of people huddled, trying to make sense of it all and figure out how in the great world they fit into it.

The three women were huddled closely together, though now with Captain Mersenne and Philippe Gascogne in their midst. Whether the latter two had been gratefully admitted into the inner circle, or the circle itself had just naturally (and unexpectedly) expanded without thought had not been determined. Everything, after all, had been spilling together and falling apart so overwhelmingly that one moment blended into the next. It was therefore the most natural thing, as well, to include a 10-year-old child among their coterie, him being the most powerful and at risk of them all.

All they needed to do was understand what they were trying to understand.

One thing above all, though, was certain. "We need to see Cardinal Mazarin." Racine was driven, intense. She'd finally been able to focus as they had raced through the tunnel at the

Bastille, and her mind was still racing. While the others were worried about all the things they were uncertain of that maybe were happening possibly, she was leaping ahead to anticipate how to act when they did happen. "André, you <u>have</u> to get us in tomorrow morning. None of us have any way to see him without you. And we can't put it off. I'm sure of that. It has to be tomorrow, *before* the Gala begins. Can you do that? You must."

"I'll meet you here at daybreak," he nodded. He knew how difficult the next day would be, the day of public festivities, when – as far as the palace still was aware – there was no king. But he knew the necessity of those in the room here relying on him. "We'll gather at…"

"Wait – " Something struck Gabrielle as wrong. They kept talking about tomorrow, tomorrow. She usually didn't follow such details. But she didn't like that duchess, didn't like how harshly they treated Racine, didn't like anything about her, *really* didn't like how she was taking pleasure talking about killing them, which was really so very wrong, and listened to every hateful word. "That duchess, that *Mademoiselle,* said – I remember, she said it with such sneering ruthlessness, like she was so pompous, like she was lording over The Little People, holding the world in her hands, the way you'd expect a scoundrel to stand on the top step of…"

"Gabrielle!!"

"She said they'd 'miss us' tonight. It's *tonight.*"

Charlotte lit up. "The Gala." She understood now what she had been following all along those dusty roads. It all fit together. "That's what the gunpowder must be for. With the entire Royal line inside, they're going to blow the building up."

She was aghast, she couldn't believe a thing so awful, the

moment the words came out of her mouth. But André quickly disabused her of the thought. He was too practiced in such matters, and the logistics simply didn't square. "No, no, it would be a fool's mission. Any attempt would trap the nobles inside, too."

"Where else, then??" Racine asked, at a total loss. But blank faces stared back at her. She ran her hands uneasily through her hair. She hated feeling helpless, hated it more than almost anything. "At the palace? But how? Beneath carriages? Why?! Where could it be? We know there are explosives. I saw them loaded at the Marquis's ball. We know it was headed to Paris. We know this. We know it. So...where else?"

She stormed away and kicked a water trough, hard enough to send it splashing.

"No. It's *there*." Philippe suddenly looked up, as something came very clear to him. It had been right in front of him. How could he have missed it? You fool. "Charlotte was right. It is the Gala. The nobles won't be trapped."

The others stared at him, stunned. What was he talking about?? Eduard de Longueville wouldn't blow up his fellow conspirators and lose all his support. It made no sense. And even if he was that reckless, the aristocrats would certainly have found out of such a mad plan against them, since they were the very ones putting such things in motion.

"It meant nothing to me at the time," he quickly continued before André could correct him. "It seemed so natural. To everyone there. At the Marquis's party, word was passed to go outside at the Gala's intermission. Because we were told there will be a special 'ceremony.'" The room had become silent. "He will indeed empty the theatre of all but the royal family."

Since she had met the others, Charlotte had struggled to

prove herself. This was a time, however, when she had so dearly wanted to be wrong, even among such an imposing group. Her face fell. "Dear God. Such vengeful carnage. And it will accomplish nothing. The next house to the throne will simply rise. It won't end the monarchy. It won't stop..."

But the young king knew better. When he interrupted and finally spoke, he commanded all their attention, which grew riveted with each word.

"No, you don't understand. This will destroy France. Royal lines across all Europe claim the right to rule France. There will be chaos. And no leadership. Because anyone here with a right to the throne will be fighting each other. It opens the door wide for a despot to ride in."

Not a soul in the barn thought for a moment he was wrong. You could see it in the way their bodies tightened and withdrew. All, but one. Louis leaped up from where he had been seated.

"Come. I insist on leading a charge."

"Your Highness," André just as quickly stood and, ever the Dauphin's guard, instinctively moved to block the boy's path to the door, "the danger..."

"It is my danger. My people. My responsibility. *I am the King of France.*"

And so he was. And so, too, was it that everyone realized with an energy shooting through them that they were not witnessing a young, someday pretender to the throne, but were in the presence of majesty which was born and bred and trained to rule. And having a sense of leadership is what galvanized a people. Even when the people are just five of them.

"The gala started an hour ago," Philippe stood, as well.

Racine strapped on her sword. "The three of us can go to the theatre, how long will it take for the full Musketeers and Royal Army to get there?"

The two other women joined her at once, readying themselves excitedly. Gabrielle whipped her rapier in place with a flourish, and Charlotte dropped hers, but caught it before hitting the ground. However, as they prepared themselves, André sensed that something among them was not understood. Something quite important.

"Are you aware that the Marquis has put a price on you all?"

The three women came to a halt. No, it had not occurred to them in the slightest. A price on their heads? Others were actually *trying* expressly to kill them, just to earn a fee? Them? They looked at one another, not believing that their little jaunt to support one another had come to this.

Then, Gabrielle shrugged. "At least now I know I'll be remembered." She turned to the men. "You three do your part. We'll do ours."

CHAPTER FORTY-SIX

The *Grand* Théâtre *de l'Opéra* was a magnificent, ornate Renaissance structure that had been built in 1562 and taken three years to complete. Though it came into being a few years after the great *chateaux* like Chambord and Azay-le-Rideau, they were its inspiration, with elegant lines and many spires around the rooftop edges. And it, in turn, inspired the denizen as home to some of the city's most popular performances.

It stood in the bedecked city square, and was at its glorious best, lit by torches all around. Soldiers bordered the open square. Soaring music that stirred the soul could be heard coming from within.

On stage, the opera was already in progress. A tenor was serenading his leading lady in an aria from *La Finata Pazza* by Francesco Sacrati, that had only made its premiere three years earlier, not with much approval, being Italian. But since it was a favorite of Cardinal Mazarin, who of course was Italian, a few aficionados muttered, it had entered the repertoire, and he had asked for it to be performed in honor of the king.

The seats were packed for the Gala, and heavy woven banners and bunting hung throughout the auditorium. Exquisitely-etched lattice-work paneling decorated the walls.

From the center loge royal box, the Queen Regent, her brother-in-law *Monsieur* Gaston on one side, and Mazarin on the other, appeared to those who would peek a glance at them to be enjoying the performance. So, too, they thought did the young and lovely *Mademoiselle*.

Off to the side, in his own box, Eduard de Longueville tolerated it all, the picture of composure.

*

Along the streets, three women were riding faster than perhaps they ever had. Racine was in the lead, her piercing eyes sharpened to deftly avoid the obstacles on the road, though in her head a raft of thoughts kept pouring in on what real dangers lay ahead to be faced.

Yet Charlotte gave no quarter and was close behind, a skilled horsewoman who was able to direct her large animal around the tightest corners with surprising ease, while Gabrielle held up the rear.

They flew by pedestrians strolling the boulevard, around coaches rolling along, past other riders amazed at being left for dust by the speed, avoiding carts, jumping over frightened dogs scurrying in the street, and pounding on and on. The sight and sound of three beautiful women – was it those three? Yes, I think it might be, a few people wondered – rushing through the night, hair and cloaks whipping around, was something none understood, yet all repeated to friends later.

*

The once-empty square around the theatre was no longer empty. Genereal Turenne and his troops had arrived, in an assemblage that far outnumbered the guards already there. It was an imposing sight to the perplexed officer in charge, but he relaxed when recognizing the French hero coming his way. The officer snapped to attention and saluted.

"Reinforcements," the general reported.

*

Down in the basement of the *Grand Théâtre de l'Opéra*, Gilles St. Chapelle and an aide busied themselves in the storage property room, having locked the door behind them. With great, patient care, since an untoward move could have the worst of consequences, they removed a tarpaulin from heavy oak barrels.

It was manual labor, not something the aristocrat would ever normally deign to have involved himself with, but this was far too critical an activity to leave to plebeians. That it was assigned to him was, in fact, a great honor for the *fronde*, something that would be remembered in tales of the civil war in years to come, he was sure. As the heavyset aide carried one of the casks over and gingerly poured out gunpowder from it, Gilles sat at the table next to a lamp and prepared to lay fuses.

*

The three women cautiously stepped along a narrow lane, leading their horses. Coming to a corner, they quieted the animals and peered around. Just several blocks in the distance, the square was swarming with armed guards. Quickly, they pulled back.

A look of concern crossed Racine's face. It wasn't the size of the battalion – or not just the size – but something else, something more worrying.

"Those aren't the Royal Army."

This was a wrinkle, completely unexpected and even more unwelcome. If it wasn't the army, and it certainly was not the Musketeers, who was that large force surrounding the royals?

And how could the three get past such an unknown barricade?

"We're blocked out," Charlotte moaned. "There are too many. Far too many."

But a smile came to Gabrielle. Her eyes quickly brightened. "No. We'll get in." Charlotte looked at her kindly, but with skepticism. Racine looked at her with distrust. But Gabrielle just filled with pride. "We are on my turf now."

*

At the stage door entrance at the back of the theatre, two experienced armed sentries had stood guard since the building had begun filling up with nobility, actors, stagehands and musicians. And now they had their new orders from the very top, the general himself had come by, and the edicts would be obeyed to the letter. Uncommon orders they were, the men didn't quite understand them, but then it was an uncommon night. The theatre was full of the highest of the mighty in all France, not just the greatest of nobility, but the royal family itself, Cardinal Mazarin, his ministers, the leaders of *Parlement*. Inside, it was a safe haven for all. Guards were stationed throughout the theatre. Outside, if anyone had reason to leave, and no one should, they were told, escorts would be provided. It was the finest security ever, the general had boasted, for the greatest evening ever. Not a detail had been overlooked.

The guards were honored to have been selected. They kept the peace. And continued on their diligent duty.

Suddenly, though, out of the quiet, Gabrielle, Charlotte and Racine blithely marched up as if the sentries didn't even exist, totally unconcerned by anything, chatting mindlessly away.

308

"Halt!"

The women were blissfully uninterested and kept walking, carefree to the world. Unused to being ignored, the seasoned guards appeared fully confused. The women were almost upon them, and the second man brusquely held out his musket.

"Don't move. This door stays closed. No one is to get out."

"We don't want to get out," Charlotte snapped at him. "We are trying to get in."

Racine showed them her sword. "We're spear carriers." The other women followed suit.

"It's for the Andante Rondo Glissande scene," Gabrielle informed them, confidently. "No autographs now. Not until later, of course."

And they glided past the guards. Racine quickly turned to the first man and added, in a voice as if this explained everything, "She's sleeping with the director."

The women pulled open the door and waltzed through, carrying themselves like it was the most natural thing in the world. It closed with a loud clang behind them. They were in!

*

Gunpowder and explosives covered the floor of the property room beneath the stage. Fuses twisted their way along into barrels of dynamite. Gilles pushed a stick into the flame of the lantern, slowly moving it towards what he held carefully in shaking fingers. The aide was anxious to leave. He'd had enough of being around explosives. The ignited tip burst with a hiss. But it was only Gilles's cigar. It wasn't time yet to finish the job. Soon enough. In the meanwhile, he leaned back, and let out a long, satisfying puff of smoke.

*

A bugle blared its call to arms, as the Musketeer Yard was a crush of intense activity. Men were shouting directions, gathering muskets, running to join outfits, leaping on horses. André was in the center of the tempest, a man creating order out of a hurricane.

"Gather arms! Stand ready! *Vite!*" he called out, his voice taking on a command that pushed away any sense of anxiety he felt. "Faster! Go faster!"

*

A regiment of the French Army was already riding with force, pounding its way through the city. At the front, surprisingly, was a civilian, Philippe Gascogne. But it was not as unlikely as it might seem, the aristocrat having been given the imprint of authority. For leading them all was King Louis.

CHAPTER 47

A soprano poured out her heart in a towering duet with her beloved tenor, drawing the attention of the grandiloquent guests, each feeling obligated to pay attention. It was an unlikely blending of two worlds. The one, a make-believe diversion of sumptuous and most-graciously mannered playacting. The other, a deeply consequential *ménage* layered with the false guile and pretenses of *beau monde* society. Where the artifice of one ended, the magnificent performance of the other began, in ways few involved suspected.

Backstage was another world. Performers were rushing around, stagehands frantically carried props, pushed furniture, and somehow managed it all without collision. The three sword-equipped women did their best to keep out of the way, but were surrounded by a baffling array of equipment, scenery, wardrobe, crates, ladders, and a frenetic mass of humanity.

"Incoming," a husky man called out at Charlotte, heading her way with a rolled-up rug on his shoulder. She stepped back, tripping on a rope that hung from the rafters, and then stumbling over a sand bag as she grabbed the heavy cord to keep from falling. An armed guard stared at the disturbance.

"Careful." Gabrielle led the flustered girl to an empty spot out of the way. "Pull that loose, and you'll bring down the house. Literally."

Charlotte snuck a glance up, and could make no sense of the pulleys, counterweights, catwalks and backdrops. It was a foreign world, and she felt lost in the forest of dangling ropes. Racine looked around, as well, but had another purpose in mind always, to get her bearings, check for exits, and spot any guards. But further, what she understood immediately from all she saw among the overly-painted faces, garish costumes, toys and fluttering about was that there was a roomful of people here who made Gabrielle seem rational. Almost.

Gabrielle herself had a beatific smile, and caught the eyes of those rushing around and nodded happily to them, acknowledging being a kindred spirit, though those spirits just wondered, "Who the hell is that?" Or, "Is she here to replace me?"

With the area around them clear at last, the three cautiously crossed over to a side wing, where they peeked out from behind the curtain. The auditorium loomed large ahead and was imposing, high into the balcony.

Up in a side box directly above them, they spotted the Marquis and his guests. Guards lined the main floor in front of the stage. The backstage guard continued to warily eye these three unfamiliar women. They made him very uncomfortable. But he made Racine even more uncomfortable. She had too much bad experience with these things.

"We can't stay here. We have to get to the other side. Away from prying eyes." She took a last glance back at the man staring behind them, and motioned the others toward the curtain and started to wedge her way through.

Charlotte pulled her back. "If we cross, Eduard will see us. Those are his men out front."

"We have to go. We have to get over there. Now."

"We can't."

"Well, then, you tell me what you suggest, Princess."

"I don't know," Charlotte shot back.

"Well, that doesn't help much now, does it? We need to get to the royal box. At the very least, we need to throw off their schedule, and I am telling you, if we stay here, we are dead. Do you understand? We have to get over there."

"And so, what do you suggest?"

As the two argued, Gabrielle stepped between them. "I told you – this is my world."

Before either could say a word, she hurriedly pulled them away through a blind spot and behind a backcloth. It only obstructed the view of the prying guard for a moment, but a moment was all that Gabrielle's world needed.

Oblivious to all this, as they were to so many things, tonight in truth was mostly the world of the aristocratic patrons. For as the opera swirled on and on in front of them in high-toned grace, they understood that not just this special production, but life itself was made for their entertainment. Everything was so elegant. Their clothes were elegant, their lives were elegant, the story playing itself out was elegant. Scene after elegant scene. Before them, the cast on stage stood gloriously in such a fancy boudoir. This *was* their life.

Suddenly, though, in the back of the stage, three…well, "maids" in frilly aprons – and swords, it seemed? – danced through the set, from the left of the stage to the right.

From his perch, a bored Marquis de Longueville had let his eyes wander through the auditorium. His mind was concentrated on the intermission coming soon, but not soon enough, when he noticed an odd reaction from the audience. Murmurings and shifting in seats. And it was all directed towards the stage. Anything different, anything unexpected was of utmost interest to him tonight, and he looked through his opera glasses at the players.

What he saw were maids, bewildering the other singers, completely out of place in the scene, dancing awkwardly across the stage to his right. Three women. With swords. And one of

313

them – he looked closer to be sure and adjusted the focus – one of them was that Le Renaud girl. He was certain of it. That fool Baron's daughter. Charlotte. Acting the fool in her own way. And the other two who had been with her that day. With swords. Three women. Le Renaud.

Eduard was taken aback. He hated more than most anything to be taken aback. He twisted towards the royal box, where *Mademoiselle* was already peering back at him. In their faces they could tell that the other knew, too, that something was very wrong.

Eduard made an instant decision. As adept as he was at planning, he was its equal at instant decisions. He signaled down below to his man by the stage, who rushed backstage.

The three woman at last reached the wing on the other side of the stage, relieved and thrilled at having made it – and survived. Racine couldn't wait to shred her prancey outfit, but already she was planning their next move. Charlotte leaped at Gabrielle and gave her a hug.

But then they saw the curtain was dropping fast. Tumbling down.

"You have to stop that!!" Racine spun to Gabrielle, looking to her in expectation that she would know where that was done.

But Gabrielle's heart fell with the curtain. "It's too late."

"He saw us, the bastard is blocking us out, he's controlling every move, every move, his way, until *he's* ready to act, he's getting away with it." Racine was so incensed, but she had no idea how to change this game.

"This is terrible." Charlotte stared into the heavy drape, which now hung all the way to the ground and blocked any view or fluid access into the auditorium.

It blocked the auditorium, as well. The audience was totally confused, and their murmuring grew louder. Everyone was uncertain what was occurring, or what was expected of them.

Suddenly, though, a pair of hands were seeking their way through the divide of the curtain. A moment later, Gabrielle had pulled the sides apart and broke through onto the front of the stage.

"*Attention, s'il vous plait.* My name is Gabrielle Parnasse. Thank you." Though no one had applauded. "We appreciate you coming tonight, but the show is over, it has ended early. Everyone please go home. <u>Everyone</u>." Without being more clear, knowing it would cause a panic, her eyes move up to the royal box. "Please. Go!"

Seated in her box, the Queen Regent was instantly apprehensive. That there was something uncommon going on, there was no doubt. But it was as if that performer down there was telling her majesty to leave. No, ordering her almost. Was she an agent of the Marquis? Was it a warning? Was she herself imagining things from all the threats they faced?

"I don't like this, Mazarin."

"Guard."

The Queen Regent rose, which filled *Mademoiselle* with grave concern. The royals couldn't leave. That would ruin everything. She hurriedly looked to the Marquis's box.

He peered back at her. Furious. Even at that distance, she could tell the depth of his anger. Plans had now changed, and one did not force a change of plans on the Marquis without consequences. He quickly sent an aggressive twisting signal with his fist back to her. She understood.

The Queen Regent and her party were on the move to depart. They were already nearing the door. *Mademoiselle* knew

315

that she had to improvise fast.

"No, no, please, you – I'm not to say any…" her mind was racing with thoughts. Talk, just talk, say anything, and then make it make sense " – as we arrived, I received a report, and it – there was a report of rebel forces nearing the theatre."

It was what she knew Her Majesty had long feared. What all the crown feared. The Queen Mother rose up.

"*Mademoiselle*, I should have been informed of this the moment…!"

"The army has it full-defended, and Major Delacroix insisted it was safest to be inside, behind guarded walls." The young woman knew what to say now. Her tale had already made enough sense. "Surely you understand. I beg you remain protected. Trust me, dear Aunt. We are safe here."

"I need to speak to the Major."

Before the Queen Mother could take any further action, *Mademoiselle* herself jumped in and took charge. "At once." She spun to the two Musketeers on guard in the box. "Step outside, I must tell you about it."

The three quickly left the room into a small hallway out front. Before the Muskeeteers could take action and go for assistance, she distracted them and commanded their immediate attention.

"Attend me carefully. This is essential. What the Queen Regent wishes – "

But the rest was never heard, for as the two King's Men were listening to *Mademoiselle*, they were set upon by four of the Marquis' henchmen, hiding there in wait, and stabbed to death.

Pushing them out of sight, she removed one of their swords and strapped it on. She directed her men to block the door, and headed off on her own to escape.

CHAPTER FORTY-EIGHT

Amid the tumult backstage, made all the more tumultuous from the mad confusion in the front of the house, Charlotte was frantically searching for the gunpowder. She pulled away drop clothes, looked through crates, pushed aside containers. Nothing. Peering around her, there was nothing she saw that seemed even hopeful. It was just all a carnival to her. But this was making her deeply anxious, and her hands began to shake.

"Excuse me, has anyone mayhaps seen large barrels?! Very big ones." But she was just ignored, nothing but a stranger who others rushed past. "Excuse me, I do beg your pardon, but please…"

It was a lost voice, as people were running in circles, trying to figure out what in the hell was going on. They'd been putting on an opera, and now all the seats in the auditorium had emptied, as the elite patrons were trying to depart, having no more idea what in the hell was going on than did the performers. Something was seriously wrong, someone said they smelled smoke, and they had to get out, too.

No one was rushing out front, though. Dowagers and baronets don't rush, after all. But they do get confused and feel, too, that they each deserve to be first. The clogged aisles moved slowly. Far too slowly for Eduard who at last had made his way down to the main floor.

He needed to get out. Needed to find out what was happening, how Turenne's soldiers were managing the crowd, whether the royals had been maintained inside. This was going too wrong too quickly. He needed to get out and regain control. Needed to get away before what was waiting below made its unwelcome explosive presence known above.

As others pushed forward, he saw an emergency side door and broke away from the worsening queue. At the exit, he looked back at all the sitting ducks and laughed. You have done your duty for France. You have helped create tonight's façade. It couldn't have been otherwise. For frivolous people whose lives had always been mere surface, just pretty diamond-encrusted shells on the outside with nothing but emptiness inside, it was only proper fate that they should continue the charade, whatever happened next. Perhaps they would make it out, only to remain useful pawns for his continuing efforts. And if they ended up giving their lives to France the same way, it was a fitting cost of war. They would be remembered fondly as heroes. By someone, perhaps.

Eduard turned back to the door and freedom, and opened it.

And there in the doorway, this one way out being the best way in, was – Racine! As surprised as he was. But Racine was used to surprises, while the Marquis was not. And she quickly recovered. A wry smile grew across her face.

"*Bonsoir.* Have I found the right door now, M'lord?" Perhaps the Marquis wouldn't remember the damning slight he had given her when they first met, but Racine didn't forget such things as easily. Like, never. "Oh, I am so very glad to see you."

Even if Eduard had no recollection in the least what in hell she was talking about, he did remember her from the stage. And knew her therefore as Charlotte's friend. And these were the women, the three women he kept hearing about. Fighting him. Daring to goddamn fight him. And she had a sword. And she had a challenging look in her eyes that no one looked at

Eduard with. Ever. He had no time for this.

He slammed the door on her and raced off. It was jammed shut, and outside Racine began kicking furiously at it, but it wouldn't budge enough. It gave an inch, but no more. Finally, she threw her body into the wavering wood, and the frame gave way, breaking open. She tore off after the Marquis.

The theatre was nearly empty now. The line of patrons nearly out. The stage had been cleared, as well, the crew and stagehands long gone. All except for Gabrielle, who stood by the apron, searching the auditorium, peering everywhere, looking, looking – trying to make sense of what was going on, who was anywhere, what she could do, and then finally, up in the balcony, she saw a figure moving.

It was that woman. That *Mademoiselle*, quickly making her way up the rows. She was trying to get away, of that there was no question. And if there was one person in the world Gabrielle did not want to see get away, with anything, it was that *Mademoiselle* person. But she was in the balcony, and Gabrielle was on stage. She liked being on stage, but not now. Now, for the first time in years, she wanted to be in the audience. In the balcony. And so, she would. Even if there was only one way.

Gabrielle leaped off the stage and ran over to the wall. She began to climb the lattice-work paneling, higher, holding on until she was able to reach the balcony and pull herself over the rail. And she rushed up the rows.

And as she rushed up, Racine was racing down below, sprinting toward the back doors where she cut off the path of Eduard's exit. Oh, the hell with this, the Marquis thought with growing choler, I really don't have time for this dance, go to the devil and burn in hell, and instead he quickly dashed to his

319

right, but whatever direction he went, Racine kept herself between him and the only way out. He stopped, and with growing fury took the measure of the situation. It was no longer that he had no time for this insane game, but he had no use for this person. This thing. Enough! Yet there she stood, confronting the nobleman face-to-face.

That was a mistake. And with the Marquis de Longueville, you were not permitted a mistake. If the only way out was through her, she would be cut down. An angry, steely glint came to his eye. Racine had seen hatred all her life, but this was a cold fury, unlike any that had crossed her path. A look of such hatred and power that it caused her neck to unwillingly quiver, and Racine knew she never quivered.

Eduard whipped out his sword. The long blade caught the light and glistened, pointed at her throat. He was a master, and his face, his poise, his fiber said you are in my world now. You have outreached yourself. You are foolish. You are alone. And you are going to die. But Racine took no back seat. And one thing she understood about herself, whatever the force against her, it only served to push her to reach that level. She might be out-matched, she would never be out-willed. She had faced death before. But she had never faced it knowing that others would be there to back her. And so, she drew her own sword. They glared at one another. Someone in this theatre *would* be dead tonight. And her lips parted.

"*En garde!*"

Their blades crashed. It was blazing swordplay at its finest, and worse, most deadly. Steel flashed, and the piercing cry of the blades rang loudly. The Marquis threw the strength of his force at Racine with two slashing thrusts, knocking her off-balance, almost tumbling to the floor, but she grabbed a seat for support. And when she fought back with a withering speed, it came so unexpected that Eduard had to quickly make rough defensive blocks. And he never was on the defensive. But that only caused to make him more aggressive. He slashed back, and she returned his heavy strokes. And on they battled, leaping across the seatbacks that blocked their way.

From high in the royal box, the three who remained looked down at the swordplay beneath them and grew increasingly concerned. *Mademoiselle* and the guards had departed for Major Delacroix far too long ago and had yet to return. And now this.

"De Longueville is attacking." The Queen Regent angrily called outside, "*Guard*!! At once! Have the rebels broken in??"

When there was no immediate response – and then no response at all, Cardinal Mazarin stormed past a bewildered *Monsieur* Gaston to the door.

"When your queen calls you, she expec…"

He grasped the door, but to his great consternation it was locked.

"Guards!" he called out. "*Mademoiselle*!"

No matter how loudly he called, no matter how often he hit the door with his fist, there was no answer. He didn't know what to do. *Monsieur* didn't know what to do. The Queen Mother didn't know what to do.

Charlotte didn't know what to do. Standing backstage, scurrying one way, then another, she was alone and lost among her actions. Unaware of the battles out in the theatre, unaware that the patrons had gone, unaware of the royals trapped, unaware of everything except that she didn't know what to do. And that whatever else was happening anywhere in the building, anywhere in the world, what she was trying to do was the most important of all. There were explosives here. They would be set off. But where were they? Where were the explosives?!

The young girl was spinning. This wasn't the sort of place she knew, it wasn't the sort of thing she did. Where was everybody? Where was anybody who could assist her? She heard a noise. Perhaps someone there? She looked and saw a man, the aide to Gilles as it was, though she didn't know that, it was just someone to her, anyone, perhaps he could help, she saw him coming up from the basement and running off. And maybe if she could stop him before he…

The basement! There was a basement! Oh, heavens, of course there would be. And the dynamite must be there. It had to be. She had to stop it.

And Charlotte raced over.

CHAPTER FORTY-NINE

From his encampment in the city, a Royal Army lieutenant looked through his telescope at a location not far off in the distance. Soldiers in the camp had gathered around a map. With a stalwart manner, the officer knelt down with the others.

"Their flank allows a split charge. However, until more civilians clear the area, we must wait. But Your Highness, it is imperative that we must leave you behind for reasons that I'm certain..." He glanced to make sure King Louis understood the gravity of the situation. But there was no king to be found. Troubled, he scanned the grounds. "Your Highness??"

At a site not far off in the distance, the *Grand Théâtre de l'Opéra* was a mass of confusion, as the anxiously exiting crowd mixed with soldiers and was surrounded by a ring of militia. Amid this swirl, Philippe and Louis snaked through the bedlam towards the theatre. The king, still in peasant garb, walked casually, unnoticed, though Philippe held him back a moment, leaving little to risk, and tugged down on the boy's cap.

*

Gilles picked up the candle. It was time. The music and singing had stopped, earlier than he thought it was supposed to, but perhaps he wasn't listening closely. It must be the intermission. He'd sent the aide to make sure, but since the poltroon hadn't returned, he must have taken off. I'll have it out with him later, but Gilles understood. Why come back into a building that was about to be blown to the heavens? I would have kept going, too, he laughed.

Gilles lit the candle with the lantern. This was the moment. At last.

"If you spark that," a girl's voice cut through the silence, "I swear to God you will never leave here alive."

The sound gave him a death of fright to the bones; he almost dropped the lamp, which would not have been a good thing at all. When he spun to the doorway, Gilles was shocked to see her...of all people. But there she was, coming down the stairs. At first, his thoughts made no sense of it. There was no reason for this priss of a girl to be here. Probably she was at the opera, made a wrong turn and got lost. That would be so like her. But she had a sword in her hand, shaking. And the sound of her words. And the look in her eyes. She knew. Gilles understood, she knew.

Recovering, he blew out the candle and set the lamp ever-so-carefully on the table. But this was no acquiescence. For he pulled out his own sword, while effecting a voice of calm and ease. "Charlotte! This is surely..." he searched for the word and gave her his warmest, pointed smile, "unexpected."

She swished her sword at him. It was not a warning swing. She waved it again. "You bastard."

Gilles sidestepped her blade easily, and then knocked it to the side, almost playing with her. He had no intention of causing the girl harm, but intentions can change. When she fought back, he played with her but it was no clowning. He was here on a charge, a critical one, and she was in his way, and getting more so by the moment. He jabbed hard at her, toying with her, and her sword got loose in her hand, but she grasped it with both hands. It looked almost foolish. Gilles was very skilled with a sword, and Charlotte was so very not, yet the overmatched girl at least battled with purpose. But quickly he backed her up through the room.

"Drop your sword, Charlotte. I don't want to kill you."

"Why stop now?? A case of conscience?"

He pinned her against the wall, pressing his sword close to her neck. She struggled, but couldn't move.

"I didn't want to kill you that night either." He moved his face near. His eyes bore into her, as much from anger as from hope of explanation. "Why do you think I sent you off on a rendezvous? To meet?? I wanted to get you away, safe."

"Imagine my gratitude!"

And though not as Racine meant it at the campfire, Charlotte remembered her words – and spit in his eye! His blink was all she needed to escape. She pushed a chair in his way and then did her best to toss another at him, which he barely ducked.

But though the chair missed Gilles, it slid across the room and hit the table, causing a crack in the leg. The lamp upon it was knocked over on its side, and began to roll.

More than anyone, Gilles understood the consequences of this. He wanted out of the basement, out of the theatre at that instant, and raced up the stairs.

Out of the theatre was where everyone should safely be. But there was consternation in the royal box, high above the theatre floor. The three occupants knew now that they were trapped in their box. *Monsieur* tried to break down the door, heaving his shoulder into it, but it made no movement, as if something was blocking its way on the other side, but that couldn't be possible. The more he pounded into the door, the more he grew concerned, not for themselves, he could see their situation, but for his absent daughter.

"My dear??! Are you safe??!!"

Had she gone for assistance? Was she lying there hurt? Or worse? What was going on?

The Cardinal looked out into the cavernous auditorium below. He could hear the sound of swords, he could hear even noises in the balcony above, but there was no one to be seen. It was a helpless feeling for them all, not knowing, yet being surrounded by disturbances. He called out in desperate hope.

"If any guards are present within the sound of my…!"

A crash came from outside the door. There had been no warning, no call of comfort. The Royals and Mazarin stopped in dread. Was this the rebel blow? Was someone coming to take them, or offer assistance, or was mankind crumbling? It was one thing to desire aid, it was another to be defenseless while your sole protection, a single thin doorframe, was about to be breached by the unknown. There was just the sound of thunder cracking. And the noise grew louder, as the wood and their nerves began to shatter.

And then an unknown assailant broke into the room.

"Please! Your Highness, you must go! I am Philippe Gascogne. Quickly! Away!!"

The Royals retreated a step, worried as much by the intruder as his warning.

"I go nowhere with a stranger," the Queen Mother declared forcefully. "Identify your loyalti – "

And it was at that moment, a young boy raced in.

"Please! We must go. Now! *Mother*."

For the briefest, stunned instant, she couldn't react. There before her was her child. Everything else disappeared. For all the horror crumbling around them, she saw only one thing.

"Dear God."

She rushed over and embraced him for the world. Louis

knew the urgency of the moment and momentarily resisted, this was no time for such things, no time, not now, not here, and yet, and yet even he returned her enfolding hug.

His mother held him even tighter. "You are well...? My dearest boy."

Philippe understood well you did not intrude on the crown. He understood something else. "There is gunpowder set to ignite."

It was remarkable how a sentence so simple can grab people's rapt attention. Yet before even the others had a chance to grasp its meaning, and they understood it quickly, the king returned to the moment and acted a king. He broke from the comfort of his mother. "We need to leave. *At once.*"

And so they rushed, as he led them out over the shards of the broken doorway, the Queen Mother pushing aside her sense of joy out of respect for alarm, and Mazarin mixing his alarm with angry thoughts already of revenge, while *Monsieur* – with Philippe anxiously pressing him on – took one last, worried look out into the theatre, wondering where in the world his daughter could be and if she was safe and if, in heaven's name, she knew what was going on.

Mademoiselle had small idea what was going on. All she knew was that plans had changed badly but could still be on pace once she was able to meet up outside with Eduard, but some girl, she looked like that annoying blonde wench from the Bastille but that wasn't possible, was trying to stop her. *Mademoiselle* made her way through the balcony, but wherever she turned, her distant shadow kept following, getting closer and now on her heels. At last she ran into the stairwell and barreled down. Freedom was just a few levels away.

Gabrielle could feel her temples throbbing, and her legs

bursting on fire. It was so hard to keep going, but she wouldn't stop. Couldn't. They gave me this responsibility, and I'll show them, she pounded into herself. They're putting themselves at risk, I can't let them down. She watched *Mademoiselle* hurry down the stairway. Try to kill me, will you? Put a price on our heads, will you? Try to kill that little king and his family and blow up France and destroy the world and all that is good and noble and holy and noble, will you?

Gabrielle had to steady herself on the balustrade at the top of the stairs, and swallowed deeply for air. Not far below, the duchess was getting away. She was close, but there was no way Gabrielle could keep running to catch up. Not possible. Just one way to do this. She'd done it before, well, no she hadn't, Marie got the role, but she'd rehearsed it, just in case. And so, immediately Gabrielle leaped over the bannister and dropped down on a lower level, to block the path of the onrushing *Mademoiselle.*

Oh, what now?! *Mademoiselle* shouted in her head. Stop chasing me already, you churl, this is nothing to do with you. She crushed herself to a stop, spun around and headed back up the stairs higher. There will be another way out.

And Gabrielle took another gasp of air and gave chase. How's this, she thought, for pretending to stop your revolution? That duchess would not get away.

*

Outside the theatre, General Turenne had sent troops around the sides to secure the perimeter. At the exits, wood beams were placed through the door handles, locking them shut. With the rear heavily guarded, the only way out now from the main auditorium was by the heavily-guarded front.

But that front had become the site of even greater conflict. A battalion of the Royal Army had at last arrived and was engaging Turenne's militia. They were caught unawares by the size of the rebel force, which had them outnumbered, and their leading wave had been cut down. Swords were swung, muskets fired, barricades broken. The once-green square was now tinged red with blood. The society patrons who had been milling around after exiting were in near-panic, some caught in the crush, others running if they could for safety. The general was shouting orders and re-directing his men for a second attack. A small skirmish, military minds called it. Hell was what the terrified aristocrats were saying.

And yet it may have been the calm before the storm. For the Musketeers arrived now, and engaged in the battle, joining the Royal Army in reinforcement. Leading the fight, in the middle of the fray, was Captain André Mersenne. The rebel soldiers were forced to regroup.

*

The Marquis would most happily kill this woman. He dearly wanted to kill her. A swift jab, so that she would slowly die. But above all, he wanted out of the theatre – now. Now! And every move he made was countered by her. He was getting nowhere, and stuck inside here. A building that may explode to the heavens while he was there. To hell with killing her. Let her die by explosion, what did he care? He just had to get out. And he had a plan, he always had a plan.

Eduard swung at Racine with a double-pass, forcing her to leap back over a row of seats. Rather than follow the attack, though, he raced instead to a heavy cloth banner that hung from the ceiling. It held firm to the tug, and he began to climb like a rope until he was able to grab the balcony railing, and then swung himself over.

Racine clambered right behind him, and was far more agile, making up lost time. However, Eduard had stayed there, swiping his blade at the banner. It started to rip, threads shredding as he cut through. The closer she got, the more intensely he sawed the thick canvas, leaving Racine swaying high above the precipitous drop. She could almost touch the ledge, but then a loud rip warned her of disaster. There seemed nothing more for him to cut, nothing left to shred, and at last it was true, the banner tore through, tumbling to the ground, just as Racine flipped herself up into the balcony.

As the banner plummeted through the theatre, it rippled briefly, the royal seal of Louis XIV waving majestically, embroidered in gold and surrounded by colorful *fleur de lis*. And then it crashed in a heap below.

Below, the actual Louis was himself racing with the others, trying to keep up with Philippe ahead, leading the Royals and Mazarin through the theatre. They had made it safely into the main auditorium but were unable to leave by the dangerous front, a battle storming outside. They had tried other routes, but all were blocked. There had to be something else, some other exit, some other –

"This way!" The Queen Mother knew the theatre intimately. Most importantly, she knew its ins and outs, having to be able to depart at a moment's notice or sneak away unseen during a performance. She directed them to a hidden exit in the corner of the auditorium. It was little known and less used, intended for emergencies only. This, she noted, most definitely qualified as an emergency.

But when they arrived, it was bolted from the outside, just like all the others had been. They pummeled the door, the noise echoing around them, but it wouldn't budge.

Ominous sounds echoed everywhere in the cavernous auditorium. Pounding feet; flashing steel; doors slamming; the beating on walls; indecipherable, fevered, distorted, mournful voices. From everywhere, all blending into one another. Taking what was already most terrible and making it seem supernatural. From the heights of the structure to its depths.

Coming up from those depths, it wasn't sounds that were of the slightest concern to Gilles, but what was behind him. He maneuvered through an obstacle course backstage of scenery, props, ladders, suspended ropes, and backdrops. There was such a disordered morass that easy access was obstructed, and the only opening was back into the path of the charging Charlotte, her sword drawn and eyes on fire.

This was madness, Gilles thought. There is dynamite below, and Charlotte Le Renaud was impeding his way to safety, waving a sword at him. Charlotte Le Renaud! He could sneeze and it would knock her down. What was she doing? Has she gone the fool?

"You can stand aside," he shouted at her wearily, "or waste time here and die by an explosion."

Charlotte gave her answer. She put all of her force into the effort and pushed a crate to block him.

Gilles thought well of the girl. But if it came to his survival or being the gentleman with her, she would pay the price. "I don't have time for this," he snarled at her.

With a mighty swing of his sword, he lunged at the girl. Charlotte barely avoided it, but went tumbling to the ground.

Hurriedly, Gilles took the moment to climb a nearby ladder up to the suspended catwalk, which led to the other side and safety.

Charlotte gathered herself back up and grabbed hold of the rungs and followed behind. He would not get away.

In the fullest sense, the building had become a theatre of war. Both inside and most decidedly out. But whatever battles were raging on the city square, from which musket roars were now making their way into the auditorium, it was the fighting inside where the personal stakes had been raised to levels so intense that what was occurring elsewhere had almost ceased to exist. It was here inside the theatre that two people, worlds apart, had brought their worlds crashing together.

Racine had barely made it over onto the balcony ledge, her momentum rolling her to safety, but it had left her defenseless. Recognizing an advantage, the Marquis jumped up to gain leverage over her prostrate body. He dove at her to deliver the final blow, but she was able to get to her feet and fend him off.

The enmity between the two had driven them each into what had now become a fury. Frantic, unabated crashing of metal back and forth. He, the trained master of methodical, aggressive brilliance, one of the greatest swordsman in France, yet she keeping up with him with native, unwavering, ingenuity. Unwilling to let this bastard escape long-delayed justice. Infuriating his arrogance with each counter and thrust. Infuriating his desire to get out of the theatre immediately, whatever the cost to herself. Infuriating him to every fiber of his existence – until, at last, exhausted, she could no longer infuriate. Until at last, he wore Racine down and broke through her defenses, slashing her, opening a gash in her right arm.

Racine was hurt. Clearly so, faltering, favoring her side, her blows weak, but trying to hide the pain, as she battled on. But she was in distress. And the Marquis knew it.

"Do me a favor and die."

"No favors."

This was wasting precious moments. "Give up. *Give up.* Why are you doing this? For the sake of God, why in hell have you been doing this??!

He pressed his advantage, pushing in. Racine was forced to backpedal, stumbling, her arm throbbing, her fingers aching, barely able to block his thrusts, and starting, she knew, to lose badly –

– until suddenly she switched hands! She flipped her sword to her left hand, catching the Marquis by so much surprise that he didn't instantly adjust. And in this battle between two such rivals, every instant mattered like it was the world. Now, Racine had the advantage and crashed forward. And as Eduard was pushed in reverse, with no plan how to stop this setback because he never went in reverse, nor was ever without plans, she was ready to answer his question at last. Making sure, first, to hold his apprehensive eyes.

"Because you are screwing around with my family."

*

Down underneath the theatre, in the dank basement, the weakened leg of a table tottered. The lantern that lay on its side began to spin towards the edge – and it fell to the ground, shattering the glass. The lamp's flame continued to burn, and it rolled past gunpowder spread along the floor, towards a pile of costumes stacked in the corner next to wooden casks filled to the brim with dynamite.

CHAPTER FIFTY

The Musketeers and Royal Army had long been at odds, challenging one other for military authority, battling their rival for supremacy. Each thought little of the other, seeing each as mere usurpers to their own right. But differences were put aside by now, fighting to protect the crown and France, and the two forces had been able to coordinate their efforts in the city square. With Major Delacroix heading up the King's Men on the right flank and Capt. Mersenne leading its troops on the left, the militia rebels were forced to spread their defenses thinner than General Turenne had anticipated. The Army's elite Second Division under the direction of Col. Benet were freed to come up the center and force the insurgents back, giving up their important, offensive stronghold and taking far more casualties than the joint forces in the process.

Turenne had retrenched his men in front of the theatre. Though he was weakened, it still left him protection, and all he had to do, what his enemies didn't know, was to hold his ground. Time was his friend. For he knew the explosion that was coming. But where, he wondered, was de Longueville? He should have exited with the other patrons and been here by now, safe and able to help lead. The same with *Mademoiselle*. She was not one to linger, far more the aggressor in fact than Eduard. Perhaps they were lost in the crowd, but that was unlike them. The Marquis especially would have insisted on being in contact. Turenne had concern, but it was fleeting, they could more than handle themselves, he knew. Far more important was that also among those he hadn't yet seen was the king, nor anyone from the royal family. The longer that remained true, the more likely it was that the crown remained trapped inside, and the better for the rebels' ultimate victory. That, after all, was the prize. And he smiled. And ordered a counterattack. Time was his very good friend.

*

Searching for a way out of the theatre, any way out, had taken *Mademoiselle* to the rooftop. Surely there would be an escape ladder down from here. And surely Eduard would have gotten away by now. And most surely that woman chasing her would give up, and she would soon be joining the Marquis, as long-planned.

But nothing was sure when it came to Gabrielle, not ever. She had been unexpected her whole life, so there was no reason to stop yet. She had pounded her way up the stairs, and though starting far behind had been able to make up ground. And when *Mademoiselle* had found her exit and started on her way down, Gabrielle was able to grab her leg and pull her back, tumbling over her.

It had not made the duchess happy, Gabrielle noted.

Not happy at all. *Mademoiselle* pulled out her sword and attacked with ferocity. Gabrielle had only a moment to block the blade with her own. She was quite good at this, she smiled a snarky smile back at her opponent. Not so fine on the attack, she knew, but that had never really been a problem. Of course there had been the other two assisting her. And on stage no one else was *really* trying to kill you. Although she had some questions about Babette St. Clair.

But then, no one had been as skilled as *Mademoiselle*, one of the more talented warriors in the land, though she made sure few people were aware. Surprise had always been her great weapon. Mind you, her sword was an impressive weapon, as well. She had trained all her life, as befitting someone of the crown, she told her instructors, where one day she might be called to defend herself or even lead in protecting her cousin. Or, she always thought, oppose him.

Together, they battled under the moonlight. This was more of a challenge than Gabrielle had thought. This duchess was surprisingly, well, excellent. And she herself had been exhausted from her rush up the stairs. Still, there was something grand about this. Atop a theatre. Fighting for France. A massive crowd below. It was truly *la gloire*. She would defeat this woman attacking her – quite furiously, she noted – or, what was the old saying? Die trying. This was her moment then, at last, and a grateful nation would know.

"You three are all fools," *Mademoiselle* slashed at her.

"And yet here we are. And where did your great plan go?" She deftly blocked an attack, not bad, she thought, and then pushed the duchess back, giving her a moment to catch her breath.

Mademoiselle had seen the fighting below in the square. It was most definitely a worry. But it only served to increase her efforts. "If any of you are lucky enough to survive tonight, you will be hunted down."

"Never anticipate," Gabrielle laughed.

"Always anticipate." And with that, *Madmoiselle* pulled a pistol from her pocket and taking careful aim, fired point-blank at Gabrielle, who just barely dove and somersaulted off.

*

High up on the catwalk backstage, Gilles had his sword against the overmatched, defenseless Charlotte's throat. Ropes looking like nooses hung from the ceiling everywhere, mocking her. She tried to say something to him, but could only get out a cough.

"Your father was a traitor to his class," he said cruelly. "It was my pleasure to volunteer."

The words had the intended effect, as he knew they would, and with pleasure saw the little girl's face and body recoil. But it was not of weakness, as he'd thought. It was the shock of resolve. She took a quick step back and swatted away his sword. And then suddenly rushed him, unexpectedly, with her own blade leading her. He blocked it, though, and with a blow of his own knocked her sword away, sliding along the planks.

She ran for it, she needed the sword, desperately, she was fully vulnerable without it, at his mercy, and so she dove – and skidded across the plank, unable to stop, until her body drooped half over the edge. And she froze. She could only see the great, horrifying distance below. Her head began to spin, and all became unworldly dizzy. She knew she had climbed up here, but that was in the passion of the moment, to not let Gilles escape, that was everything she was thinking of. But here, now, hanging over the ledge of a narrow bridge of wood, suspended by thin ropes over an abyss, it was too much, too much. Panic washed throughout her body and overwhelmed her. She couldn't move.

As she lay there motionless, her other great fear had come to pass, as well. Gilles was escaping. He had slid down a rope to the stage, where he yanked it off its pulley, and it fell to the stage. He then ran to remove the ladder at the other end.

Gilles mocked her with a salute. "Goodbye, Charlotte. We

337

do what we must."

He could see it all in her distant face, as she made it to her knees and forced her way to her feet, holding on to the bannister so tightly until her fingers were ashen. To her horror, there was no way down. She was trapped up here. It pounded at her: the bastard who killed her father was escaping. And that transcended all else. Every other sensibility left her. Her body coiled at the thought, at the anger. The bastard who killed her father was escaping. Everything in her being led to this moment. Everything. And as she imploded, there was only one release for it. Without even thinking, on pure visceral instinct, Charlotte quickly sheathed her sword and began running along the catwalk. Picking up speed, faster. Her legs churning as they never had before in her life.

And she made the leap!

Charlotte soared through the air, her arms flailing, her legs kicking, her heart in her throat, and she headed for one of the ropes hanging down from the ceiling and she reached and reached, and dear God, she grabbed for it, her fingers searching and – she grasped it! And held on for palpitating life, and the rope swung forward and back and forward again and Gilles had no idea what was happening above him and that Charlotte was headed his way. And as she neared him, swinging over, Charlotte let go and jumped and flew down and crashed on top of him!

The two of them crumbled in a pile. Giles was dazed, no idea what in God's name hit him. Charlotte got to her feet first – shaken, but her heart thumping so relentlessly and loudly she could hear it, in part the remaining vestiges of fear, in part the joyous rush of survival, but in part, in the greatest part the intensity of knowing that you have a mission that fills your soul and seeing that it stands before you. And her eyes pierced.

Gilles slowly stood. And he understood in his bones that this was no longer the girl he knew.

*

The battle outside the theatre had grown in intensity, but the Royal Forces had gained critical ground, forcing the rebels to fall back further, their lines breaking apart, and they were on the verge of disarray. General Turenne was spread too thin and needed to be every place at once. He tried to reinforce a failing position on the flank, but that only left his front defenseless.

André saw an opening and immediately shouted orders. "Here! Grab that! Cover them!!" A breach appeared in the enemy line.

That crack was all that was needed. Quickly, his division was able to clear a path, as the rebels retreated, and the barricades were removed from the theatre. At last, he got the doors flung wide – and the very instant after, the Royals, led by King Louis himself, rushed out.

When the crowd that had gathered on rooftops and near enough to watch saw what was happening, a mighty roar was unleashed as the Queen Regent, Cardinal Mazarin and *Monsieur* came running after, followed at the rear by some unknown, incidental nobleman who no one cared about, except the four who had just preceded Philippe out. Shouts of "*Vive le Roi!*" and "*France est Louis!*" could be heard throughout the neighborhoods. Even the aristocratic patrons who still lingered found it safest to blend with the sentiment and join in the cries. "*Vive le Roi!*"

All was going well. All was turning fast. All was joy.

*

Nothing was safe. In the basement of the *Grand* Théâtre, the candle flame leaped to the rags, which burst into fire. All around them were explosives, a room covered in gunpowder, and a mountain of dynamite sitting in barrels, all just waiting to meet.

*

Gabrielle was not safe. Having a good spirit and fighting for glory only went so far. In truth, she had been outmatched from the first against *Mademoiselle*, and was struggling now, her arm too heavy. The pleasure of wielding a wooden sword on stage was nothing to the hard, burdensome steel of a real blade on top of a theatre, having to be kept up, moved there, no, this way, keep it high, block, over here, higher, parry, up, again, don't let your arm drop, against an unrelenting opponent who doesn't give you a moment to breathe, who knows what she's doing, and you, in the end, really don't.

In the end. It had such a finality to the words. But Gabrielle knew all about ends. There was always a reason to them, a higher purpose, whether comedies or even tragedies. The good we learn from the ending, something noble. And as the sounds came up from the street – the cries of *"Vive le Roi!"* *"Vive le Roi!"* and *"Louis!!!"* – Gabrielle knew what was noble here, what the higher purpose was. She could tell. She could tell it in her heart, she could tell it in the sounds, she could tell it in the furious, but defeated face of that unholy duchess. She had done well. She had helped save the King of France. She

340

had helped save France itself! And all on the highest stage she could imagine. It was quite a glorious thing. She would not just be remembered throughout the land, in Mont Vert even, and with pride, for doing something so very real, she would be loved.

"You should never have played out of your depth." *Mademoiselle* pushed forward, another lunge, seeing that girl weaken, ready to fall.

To the end, Gabrielle was dramatic. But oh, it was deeply heartfelt. What are the final words that one would want the world to remember you by, she thought. Ahh, yes. "It was all for France. My glory will always live. And I would do it again."

"Alas, you will never get the chance."

And with a final thrust *Mademoiselle* ran her sword at Gabrielle. She did her best to turn, but fell. And she lay there, unmoving. A hero.

Mademoiselle was exhausted, but outraged. She bent over her fallen opponent and glared into Gabrielle's inert face, making certain that the very last word was not only hers, but emphatic.

"That is what you deserve for ruining everything."

And then suddenly, Gabrielle's eyes popped open! She was very much alive. And furthermore, her rapier was pressed up against a shocked, horrified *Mademoiselle*'s throat.

"Drop your sword and put your hands up." There wasn't an ounce of drama in Gabrielle's voice. "You are going to prison, you heartless, scheming bitch."

With the blood drained from the duchess' face, not believing, not understanding how it had come to this, and with the tip of the sword pressed deeper into her skin, waiting for just the chance to go all the way in, *Mademoiselle* did as she was ordered.

Gabrielle rose to her feet – in charge – and utterly joyous.
"And they said I couldn't play a death scene!!"

*

An actual death scene, however, was playing itself out on the narrow beam that separated the balcony from a great fall to nothingness below. Forced to fight on the rare defensive, Eduard had suddenly turned that to advantage, leaping up on the ledge to gain the high ground. He slashed away now at Racine who was unable to gain leverage. But she fought him off and followed. Almost in a dance along the dangerous ridge, the two adversaries charged back and forth, their blades blurring into one another. They spit out the most bitter of insults, all profoundly meant, but to distract the other, as well. But nothing would distract them. This had long-since become deeply personal, blinding them both to the dangers around. Yet great as his momentary hatred for this piece of dross who challenged him so boldly had become, it couldn't compare to the depth that pushed Racine. Everything she knew about him, everything she learned about him, everything she thought about him, everything he had caused, touched and affected that had torn her life apart. All of it welled up inside her and kept growing. And with an explosive burst of desire, she drove her sword at the Marquis, and the manic, wild fury was so difficult to fend off. He turned to avoid it, and lost his balance, planting his foot to steady himself, but there was nothing there to plant upon, just air.

Eduard plummeted over the edge, falling towards the void below. The floor was far away, but coming up on him fast.

Grasping out of desperation, he was able to grab hold of a banner halfway down, but twisting in it as it furled around him, and getting tangled.

*

Charlotte was no match for Gilles. He had recovered from the shock of her landing on him, and was easily able to fend off her advances. Yet simple as it was, there was something disturbing. For this girl, who once would shrink at a playful pinch or the swoop of a sparrow, kept coming at him, silent, unrelenting. Whatever he chided at her, she ignored, whatever question he asked her, it was as if she didn't hear. "Say something," he prompted. More so, her fury was frightening to him. And as she swung at him yet again, and as he again blocked it with ease, smoke had begun to billow up from the basement.

"I should have killed you, too, when I had the chance." Gilles waited for a response. But again, nothing. "Say something." It wasn't just silence anymore, it had become unnerving. "Say something."

Suddenly, though, Charlotte's expression changed. And that discomfited Gilles even more. A thought came to her eyes. She remembered what Gabrielle had told her that very night, about being in this place, on her – what did she call it? – turf. And she knew it was something Gilles wouldn't know a thing about.

She quickly turned from him and, with a fluid swipe, sliced a rope anchored to the floor. Just like the rope Gabrielle had warned her about. A wry smile crossed to her face. And she looked upwards, directly over Gilles's head, very pleased.

This meant nothing to Gilles – which concerned him. What in the world could cause Charlotte to suddenly stop fighting him, after fighting him with such determination? And just cut a rope that went nowhere in the… And it suddenly occurred to him! With a panicked look, Gilles quickly glanced up at what was falling his way. And what he saw was –

Nothing. Absolutely nothing was falling. Zero. He should have realized. In the end, Charlotte was still dear little Charlotte. The delicate, silly flower, always bungling, no matter how much she glared.

All this thought took but a moment. With a smirk, he turned back to his prey, ready to finally finish her off. Games were over. He'd had enough.

But that intentional distraction, of course she knew there was no way at all she could bring down a house upon Gilles, it was all that Charlotte needed, just his peek upwards – and the moment he faced her again, she stabbed him in the heart.

Gilles crumpled to the ground, only to have enough time for disbelief to register on his face, dead.

All the pent-up emotion hit her. She didn't feel relief, she didn't feel joy, she didn't feel sadness, vindicated, or a sense of revenge. It was everything together washing through her. What it felt was right. She peered down at the lifeless body. And at last she had reason to speak.

"His name was Honoré Le Renaud. Now, *get off his earth.*"

*

With André leading the Royal Forces, they had taken the upper hand. And added with Cardinal Mazarin and even *Monsieur* Gaston, the engagement had now turned into a rout.

344

And suddenly – there, too, was King Louis himself in the battle, inspiring his troops.

Unseen by the young king, however, a rebel stood nearby and spotted the monarch undefended. Though just a private, the history of the world had long been altered by less. And so, for all the great plans and intricate machinations, all of which had failed, it came instead to this. The young soldier sighted a pistol on Louis. He had clear aim, cocked the firing pin, and drew a breath. And with a loud, whack!, the Queen Mother floored him from behind with a broken piece of lumber.

The Royal Forces at last swarmed the enemy and encircled General Turenne's soldiers.

"Lay down your arms!!" Major Delacroix called out, raising a musket and firing it in the air. Though some of the insurgents wanted to continue, most had had enough, and the rest saw the futility of their effort. The battle was over.

A loud roar broke out, as loyalists, soldiers and most of the crowds began cheering. Muskets were placed on the ground and arms raised. Amid the celebration, what few people saw, and those who saw it paid it no attention, nor understood why they should care, plumes of smoke began rising ominously from within the theatre.

Turenne saw it, and understood. But it was a signal of failure now, rather than the grand triumph he had anticipated. But he knew he would fight again, for whoever he believed deserved his leadership. Life and death, it was his destiny. His skills made memories short. The general left his command post and crossed the field of battle with as much pride as he was able. The rules of war, he knew, must be followed.

When the soldiers saw him, from both sides, they parted, leaving an empty path that led to the King of France. The general handed his sword to Louis, who broke it over his knee.

The *fronde* had failed.

But the war was not over.

*

Two people remained who had their own destinies to play out to the end. And destinies being what they are, often arrive intertwined. Some people are simply meant to be remembered together. The eternal two sides of a coin. What one shall sow, another shall reap.

And so it came to pass that the wooden barrels of dynamite in the basement had caught fire. The casks were beginning to glow hot red.

Smoke almost completely filled the room and made its way out the door, through vents, and between cracks in the ceiling, rising into the theatre.

Racine coughed as she struggled to pull up the banner with the Marquis tangled in it, the effort made all the more difficult from some stinging in her eyes, but she couldn't afford to loosen her grip to wipe them. It was all very heavy, too heavy for her she felt, and the weight even ripped the thick woven cloth, causing it to slip from her grasp, before she could regain purchase of it again.

I shouldn't even be doing this, she thought, coughing again and blocking out his shouts, his words meant nothing to her. I should let the bastard drop into hell. But hell would be too good for him. Because then his life would be over. Far better a life of ravaging humiliation, nothing more than a common thug, condemned to the rest of his days in prison, manacled to the lowest dregs, who if luck would have it would beat him every day, subsisting on murky water and hardtack, an object of the most debasing ridicule for the world to see. The frilled shirt would have his soul crushed. He deserved no less.

And so in all the ways they were connected, it had come down to a piece of cloth. Some fates are indeed intertwined. Where thou goest, I shall go.

The dense haze had reached up to the balcony, but Racine's eyes, burning now, were only on the banner. She had to get him, she had to lead him out, trussed up like a pig, had to push him down into the Bastille. It had to be her. She and him. Together. Him in worse than hell, and her taking him there. It had become an obsession to her. Wherever they take you, I'll be there right by your side, making sure you get there. And never get out.

Smoke was getting deeper into her lungs, and her coughing grew more pronounced with the strain. Time had to be growing short, she thought in her frantic mind, as sweat dripped from her forehead. In truth, the fevered Racine had no idea how short the time really was. All she knew was that it was so extremely difficult going, and the Marquis was still so far below, and she was only dragging him up one small pull at a time.

"Hurry! Now!" Eduard shouted stridently, forcefully, far more aware than Racine of the billowing clouds and dynamite below.

If anything could have caused Racine to slow her efforts, the very last thing needed in these final seconds, that was it. "I hardly think that you are in any position to tell – "

"Racine!" Charlotte had run into the theatre from backstage, hearing the noises. "Get out of there! For the love of heaven. The building is set to erupt. We must go! At once!"

The sound of Charlotte's' voice and words broke Racine's agitated attention. She peered down at the prostrate Marquis.

"You can't leave me here."

Charlotte was beside herself with anxiety. "Now, Racine! *Now*! There is no time!"

"You can't leave me," he demanded. He could read her thoughts, the two were near-opposite sides of the same mind, he knew. "Think of me in prison. Rotting. Humiliated."

Racine looked at him, torn. Then she looked down at the imploring Charlotte.

"Come *on*!!"

Back to Eduard. Charlotte. Eduard. He was right there. *Eduard*. She had him in her hands. She had the Goddamned bastard literally in her hands. And then –

"What the hell am I thinking??!" She and the Marquis caught each other's eyes. "Remember us."

And she raced off, pounding up the steps two at a time, headed with all her worth to the stairway exit. And so too ran Charlotte.

The Marquis hung there, suspended upside-down in the air. Alone.

*

As disordered as the massed horde was in the city square, the Musketeers, Royal Army, rebels, public, patrons and Royals themselves, mixed together, pushing, pulling and being directed, nearly all eyes stopped and turned when to the utter shock of everyone, the front doors opened yet again, and out came barreling two harried, disheveled, beautiful and urgent women.

"Get away!! Get away!!" "Go!!" "Now!"

If the panicked, insistent expressions on their faces didn't make an instant, gripping impression on everyone, the smoke they now saw pouring out of the building did. The two occurrences together did their duty. The crowd began to clear, fast. Extremely fast. People raced off, crushing into one another, some getting knocked about, frightened screams. André led the young King off, the Queen Regent and Mazarin made their way with the wave of the others as Philippe opened a path. Within moments, most of the square had been cleared.

The rumble came first, its deep sound immediately followed by a massive explosion. The theatre blew up. Fireballs shot out for blocks around, setting several nearby buildings aflame. Broken wood, plaster and bricks flew everywhere. Rolling swells of smoke billowed unendingly into to the sky. And it began to rain, a thunderstorm of debris pouring down on the square.

When the haze finally cleared, all that remained where once the *Grand* Théâtre *de l'Opéra* theatre had stood was nothing but rubble.

CHAPTER FIFTY-ONE

Smoke remained in the air, soot covered most everyone near, and the acrid smell of burnt remains hung in the air and would linger for a week. Several structures around the square were still on fire, a few of them ruined beyond repair, though volunteer brigades had the danger well-under control. The lingering flames helped light the area that night as much as the bright moon.

The Royal Army had begun to establish a semblance of order, keeping onlookers far away, and rounding up those who needed rounding up.

Mademoiselle was led away in handcuffs, putting on a face of defiant pride, though it was impossible for her to shake the results of her disastrous efforts, and pride had its limits. Count de Beaufort was under armed guard and had become a very little man. Both, within a corner of their own troubles, wondered if Eduard had been able to escape, and perhaps he might be able to help them.

He wouldn't.

Racine watched them carted off, figures so high and mighty being hounded for once, getting not even close to what they deserved but far more than she could ever have imagined. She looked around at the leveled plaza, people cheering, crying, hugging one another, looking dazed, relieved and celebrating, as the Musketeers and Royal Army were actually doing what they were supposed to, how about that, protecting people and keeping the peace. She was taking it all in with a mixture of awe and intense pleasure deep inside her, and feeling a radiant satisfaction she couldn't remember for so long a time, if ever.

And so, she kept strolling around, soaking it all in.

She watched faces, bumped into people, and didn't even think once about picking their pockets, not right now anyway, and wanted to say, "Hey, see all this around you? I did it, me and my friends. You're welcome," but they passed by and she wandered on. A few moments later a path cleared, and she spotted André directing several people. He looked very officious, she thought, it certainly did suit him.

Out of the corner of his eye, he noticed her watching, and excused himself and came over. For a while, the Musketeer just looked at her. She waited, it seemed like he was about to speak, but all he did was stand there, aware of only two things, Racine in front of him and an ethereal swirling of activity circling everywhere that meant France was saved.

"You understand that words can't express…"

He tried to find the words, but as he just said, he couldn't. They simply continued to look at each other, which ultimately spoke much louder than mere words. Looking, understanding and wanting very much. And his fingers cupped her head and ran through her hair, and she threw her hands around his neck, and they kissed. And that swirling of activity circling everywhere around them ceased to exist.

At long last they broke apart, but still held on to the other lightly. Racine stared up at him, and a wry smile crossed her face. "I'm told that I'm different."

In one small public square, the fate of all France had come to a climax. The blast had been that powerful. Yet if it happened again at that moment, if the theatre had once more exploded that demonically, Charlotte and Philippe would not have noticed. Their arms had long been wrapped around each other so tightly that it was difficult to tell where one ended and the other began, their hands seeking out every part of their lover. They had been kissing, and were kissing still, and continued to kiss, and gave great honor to the French name. So, this is what it is supposed to be really like, Charlotte thought, when she allowed herself a moment to think. For someone so sweet and innocent, Philippe thought, and then let his thought just lay there, unfinished, because honestly, he didn't care. The only thing he cared about was how her tongue felt and tasted, and if she would just keep holding on to him, and kissing his neck and any part of him she wanted, and would let him keep doing the same, that was just fine with him. And so the two continued to kiss, and taste, and nip, and stroke one another, which was just fine with her.

At last they stopped, still entwined. She breathed in little bursts, her heart pounding so fast, she didn't believe a heart could beat that quickly. She had something she wanted to say to him, about being with Philippe, dear Philippe, the future and more, it was so very important, and he could see it in her eyes, and he ran his fingertip across her lips, and along her cheek, and tenderly massaged her throat. She looked at Philippe intently, more intently than she had ever looked at anyone. She was about to speak, but then a wiser thought occurred to her –

"We can discuss all this later, right?" she asked, and dove back to kissing him.

Of all people, it was Gabrielle who wandered through the crowd alone. She could see over there the Royals safe, over here the patrons safe, and the nobles gone, and was so pleased with herself, thrilled, in fact. But at this time of all times, no one was holding her in their arms, no one even trying to sneak a kiss, no one simply celebrating the moment with her. That was fine. It was just odd, that's all, a strange feeling. It did take some getting used to. But it was fine, really, she knew what she had done, all three of them. She had helped save France. Her. Gabrielle. Gabrielle Parnasse. Who in the world would have ever thought it, once upon a time? Once upon a time, isn't that how all great stories began? Well, this is how a great story ends. And it was how it should be. It was fine. And funny, life was funny, she loved stories and now she was actually in one. Well, yes, she had been in a lot of stories, but this one was real. It was nice being in a story she didn't have to audition for. Or remember lines. Though there was something to be said for having an intermission. And so she kept walking around alone, passing by the others, thinking all this to herself and more, there was always more, as she moved through the crowd.

"I am told you performed with remarkable courage." A distinguished gentleman had noticed Gabrielle drifting nearby, but then it was always hard not to notice Gabrielle. "From what very little I saw inside, that seems an understatement."

"Oh! Well, thank you," she smiled, as he came over to her. It's always nice when the public appreciates you, she thought, and this was especially nice. "We do what we can."

"I admire courage even more than beauty. And I admire beauty beyond all measure." He elegantly took her hand and lightly, but meaningfully gave it a kiss.

"Well, you have just wonderful standards." She smiled, always knowing what to say to a gentleman. But this good-looking fellow at least had manners. "And what do you do?"

"I am Prime Minister of Spain."

Gabrielle smiled at him blankly for a brief, few seconds, and then held up a finger, as if to say, "Could you wait just one moment." She politely turned around, made an excited fist, thinking, "Yes!!!!," and then turned back, looking as calm as could ever possibly be.

"So, tell me," she asked in her most nonchalant voice, trying hard not to let the quivering she felt give itself away, "have you ever been to the town of Mont Vert?"

"No, I haven't."

Gabrielle's body was one giant smile. She slid his arm in hers, and they walked off under the moonlight.

"We have so much to talk about."

CHAPTER FIFTY-TWO

People had begun to arrive in Paris from throughout France for days. They camped out in parks if necessary, which for most it was, since boarding houses were not only completely occupied, but often put five visitors in rooms meant for two. Private homes found they could charge whatever they chose for strangers glad to have nothing more than a roof over their heads, and these temporary landlords wished the king would have a gala every year. Unlucky stragglers slept on the street, yet considered themselves lucky enough just to be in the capital for the occasion.

On the grand day itself, the most anxious of them already started to show up in the city commons at the crack of dawn. A healthy business was found by vendors selling meat sandwiches, pastries, and cheese, and even fruit, but especially a great deal of wine to keep the bones from getting chilled and ensure the spirit stayed high. By late morning, the plaza overflowed with a joyous, enthusiastic and massive crowd that filled every nook and jammed each cranny. Families hung out from windows, and rooftops seemed at risk of collapsing from the fully-occupied space.

Word had long-since spread through the crowd of events of the night before, truth mixed with rumor, though truth remarkably won out since it was more unbelievable than anything the tallest teller could invent. And it all made the jubilant celebration even more ardent. Not only were they there to celebrate their king, but the saving of France itself! And if there was battle, revolution, intrigue and unforeseen heroes mixed in together, it was all the better.

By the time the festivities had gotten underway with parades, bands, and honor guards, resplendent sunshine washed over an even more resplendent day, as flags, banners and all manner of pageantry covered the grounds.

The expansive reviewing stand had been completed in time and towered over the crowd for all to see. And what all wanted to see, sitting at the dais, was their beloved King Louis, scepter in hand and crown on head, upon a throne beside the Queen Mother, both appearing benevolent and stalwart, as if nothing the slightest untoward had occurred just hours before, let alone the unknown months past. They were surrounded by other lesser royals, civic dignitaries and foreign guests.

Cardinal Mazarin stood out front, his ermine-collared robe flowing in the light breeze, his official medallions of rank and privilege hanging from his neck, as he continued to address the throng.

"…and a day for the glory of France, *toujours la gloire*. *Et toujours le roi*, for the honor of King Louis on this day of festival. This is a day of celebration, a day of remembrance, and it is a day that would be remiss without thanks."

The crowd shouted its cheers. As the sound echoed louder off the nearby buildings, the Cardinal looked imposingly over the ocean of people, yet while he had admonished them all to remember the glory of France, it was the memory of much more recent events that held his thoughts, and made his strong voice and outward calm all the more an effort, but one of the greatest sincerity.

"For it with the profoundest thanks of King Louis," he continued, allowing himself the slightest glance to His Majesty, who offered a concurrent nod, that the Cardinal knew spoke volumes, "that we add our honor today – an honor that cannot be repaid – to three women who are all that France should be. And it is with the profoundest gratitude that we present the *Croix de France* to – Racine Tarascon, Gabrielle Parnasse, and Charlotte Le Renaud."

And to a thunderous roar, escorted out from behind the platform stepped Racine, Gabrielle and Charlotte, their faces beaming with a pride that came close to outshining that resplendent sun.

These were the ones people had heard about. These were the ones who had saved the royal family, saved France. Some in the crowd even recognized them, those were the three who had helped keep the city safe, they shouted to the person next to them, struggling to be heard over the din, I actually spoke to them once, I did too, hurray for them all, over here, look over here, three cheers, look at them, they did it??, yes, it's them, they're *incroyable*, those are the ones?, there they are, they're wonderful, they're so beautiful, God bless them, amazing, I think the blonde one waved to me, three cheers.

One by one, Mazarin placed a jeweled French cross around the neck of each woman, along with a kiss to each cheek. And if his hug was a little stronger than most honorees would get, it was more meaningful. If most people in the crowd didn't see it, the three women all understood.

Amid the cheering throng, all roaring as one, a lone Musketeer, André Mersenne, stood with the honor guard, beaming.

Among all the commoners, some were surprised to see an aristocrat, Count Philippe Gascogne, in the front of the cheering crowd, cheering the loudest.

But the proudest of all, in that massive and wildly celebratory gathering that overflowed into the streets of Paris, were an elderly couple, Auguste and Marguerite Fleury, bursting with emotion in a special box of honor. No one in the crowd paid them much attention, and the few who did were bewildered, not knowing why such a pair were standing where they were, being congratulated by those around them. But there they stood, both in a place of high cachet, both wearing small medals pinned to their lapels. No one knew why. But they knew why. And soon enough, they knew, others would, as well. Perhaps they'd even invite their little friend over for cookies again, when he had the time.

And, yes, lest he be overlooked among all the other dignitaries on the dais, peering out at all the acclamation, the Prime Minister of Spain was feeling good about his fine taste in women, and heroes.

But most of all, feeling the best of everyone, albeit in a sense of shock though they knew this moment was coming, stood Racine, Gabrielle and Charlotte, soaking it all in. Letting the waves of support wash over them, not that they had any choice in the matter. There was nothing one could do to stop it. The roars, the adulation They waved to everyone, which only brought loader cheers.

And, yes, it all understandably got the better of Gabrielle, who stepped forward and began taking her bows. The other two grabbed her and dragged her back.

"*Mesdames et messieurs,*" the Cardinal did his best to quiet the crowd. It took some doing, but when at last he could be heard again, he spoke out loudly. "It is with equal pride and anticipation that we hold one further declaration."

The three women looked at each other. They had been told of the ceremony, and the protocol, and what all to expect, so that everything would go smoothly. But this? Not a word.

They'd had enough, more than enough for a lifetime. What now??

King Louis himself now came off his throne and down to the front. There were great cheers, and cries of surprise, but he raised his hands for silence. The three women were silent, as well, but then they wouldn't have been able to speak had they wanted to.

In his small voice, but loud enough to display his majesty, the king spoke out.

"It is with the greatest admiration of the Crown that we have created and request for the honor of France that our three heroes accept admission into the proud service of the Royal Musketeers."

The women were in shock. If ever a moment deserved a reaction of "*Oh, mon Dieu,*" it was this to them. The crowd exploded once again.

And then, as the occasion and import and meaning of the declaration hit them at the same time, and they both understand what it meant most of all to one of them in being accepted at the highest level of France, an outcast no more, Charlotte and Gabrielle looked at one another – and took a step back, leaving Racine alone to glory in the moment.

The gypsy stood there, overcome with joy. But when she finally was able to regain her composure and noticed what her friends, her family had done, that she was standing there alone, in front of the others, she dragged them back up with her. This wasn't her moment, it was all of theirs.

And then, as one, they raised their swords high in the air.

Epilogue

Across the expansive countryside, three figures far at a distance, rode across the bright land, thundering hoofbeats churning up the earth.

As they neared, splendid in pantaloons, red neckerchiefs, sashes around their waists...and blouses each with a single, embroidered wild rose – and with their hair flowing in the wind were Racine, Gabrielle and Charlotte.

Riding as the Wild Roses.

Their faces were full of joy and pride and hope. But they were full, period. Remembering the past hurdles they had overcome, appreciating deep into their souls the present that surrounded them, yet more than anything looking forward to whatever was to be, together, or even if necessary, alone, knowing that it was all part of a greater whole. Knowing now that they, too, were part of a greater whole. And so they neared, getting closer, closer, looming ever larger – as they rode to the glory of France.

And kept riding on.

About the Author

Robert J. Elisberg has been a commentator and contributor to such publications as the *Los Angeles Times*, *Los Angeles Daily News*, *Los Angeles* magazine, C/NET and E! Online, and served on the editorial board for the Writers Guild of America. He is a regular columnist for the Huffington Post, and has contributed political writing to the anthology *Clued in on Politics*, 3rd edition (CQ Press).

Born in Chicago, he attended Northwestern University and received his MFA from UCLA, where he was twice awarded the Lucille Ball Award for comedy screenwriting. Not long afterwards, Elisberg sold his screenplay, *Harry Warren of the Mounties*. He was on staff of the animated series *Flute Master*, for which he co-write three of the *Skateboy* movies based on the series. He also co-wrote the independent film *Yard Sale*. Most recently, he wrote an upcoming comedy-adventure screenplay for Callahan Filmworks.

Among his other writing, Elisberg wrote the comic novel,

A Christmas Carol 2: The Return of Scrooge, which reached #2 on Amazon's Hot New Releases in Humor Parody. He also co-wrote a book on world travel. Currently, he writes a tech column for the Writers Guild of America, West. He also co-wrote the song "Just One of the Girls" for the Showtime movie *Wharf Rat*, and wrote the book for the stage musical, *Rapunzel*.

His other daily writings can also be found online at www.ElisbergIndustries.com.

Made in the USA
Lexington, KY
18 July 2013